TIME ENOUGH

LISE MAYNE

Praise for *Time Enough:*

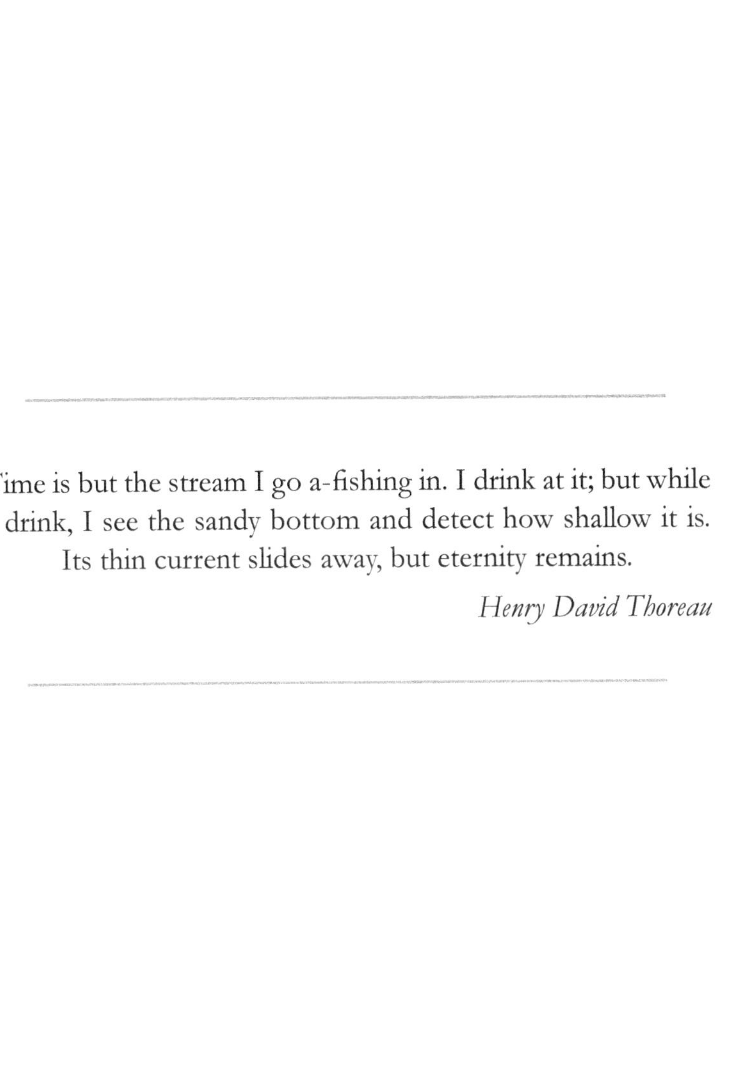

Time is but the stream I go a-fishing in. I drink at it; but while I drink, I see the sandy bottom and detect how shallow it is. Its thin current slides away, but eternity remains.

Henry David Thoreau

Dedication

Time Enough is dedicated to my grandparents who worked hard in an unfamiliar land to build the best life possible for their family. They made my life possible. To anyone forced to migrate, no matter the reason, may you find home.

PART ONE
ELLAN VANNIN

When the summer day is over
And its busy cares have flown,
I sit beneath the starlight
With a weary heart, alone,
Then rises like a vision,
Sparkling bright in nature's glee,
My own dear *Ellan Vannin*
With its green hills by the sea.

Manx National Anthem
Eliza Craven Green, 1854

CHAPTER ONE

Goll sheese ny liargagh:
A bad omen.

Port Erin, Isle of Man
May, 1904

NAN said, "Come, *my chree*. You must visit *Themselves* with me tonight." So Euphemia went, though she'd so much to do after supper, before the evening singsong 'round the hearth. And Baby Hugh might fuss in her absence, wanting to nurse. Besides, she was bone weary, as usual at the end of the day, having cooked three meals for nine people and tended to the baby since before dawn. The boys needed supervising to do the dishes properly, the floor wanted sweeping… she sighed, inhaling the comforting scent of the chicken they'd had for supper. The carcass needed stripping for tomorrow's sandwiches. No matter. Nobody could deny Nan. She ran the household with a gentle but firm hand; although Euphemia was her daughter-in-law with six children to raise in the tiny cottage, Nan was in charge. Love and respect bound the two women together, and routine kept the days running along smoothly. Euphemia's curiosity was piqued by Nan's invitation, too. Her eldest son, Henry, always accompanied his grandmother to Faery Hill of an evening, for the ritual offering to the *Little Ones*. Henry's eyes posed a question. Euphemia returned his gaze with a shrug of her shoulders as she closed the red cottage door. Blackie, the sheepdog, tagged along.

Gripping Nan's elbow, she carried the wicker basket in the crook of her left arm, clutching her skirt as they climbed Cronk Howe Mooar. A cool breeze, fragrant with gorse and blackthorn flowers, swept them along. She heard little blue tits chirping in the thorns. Robins, too, chatted softly amongst themselves, preparing for nightfall. Euphemia allowed all the sights and smells to distract her, knowing that Nan was listening for the faeries on the wind. *Do they have words for me tonight? Is that why I'm here? But Manx faeries don't speak English, so I won't understand.* A giggle bubbled up, but she suppressed it. She wouldn't make light of Nan's beliefs.

As the path ascended, the wind teased their hair and swished their skirts. Sheep browsed on the purple and yellow hills. Clouds roamed the sky, basking in the last rays of summer sun. Waves crashed at the foot of the cliffs edging the landscape. In the distance, cattle were lowing, waiting to be driven in for the night. *Just like in the song about Little Lord Jesus*, came the sudden thought, and Euphemia wondered if her baby had awakened. The image of Hugh tossing in his cradle tugged milk from her breasts.

"Hang on a mo, please, Nan." She handed over the basket and untucked her blouse, wet on the front with milk and round the waist with sweat. *Never mind, the wind will dry it. Ah, it feels good to stop, catch my breath. Nan's not out of puff, though. She's used to it, I reckon. It is so beautiful here, looking out to sea. It's like all mankind sprung from the tiny Isle of Man. Like the Garden of Eden. For me, life began here.* Nan gave her a nudge, interrupting her thoughts. *There she goes again, urging me on, as though we've an appointment to keep. What's the hurry?*

Skylarks reeled overhead and, above them, seagulls threw lonely cries across the water. A few more steps and they reached the summit of Faery Hill. *Our courting place. We haven't climbed this hill in years. Why not? We should come up, have a picnic with the little ones. Our little ones, not the "Little Ones," though they'd be welcome too. I wish I could see a faery, just once. Or hear them, like Nan. Henry says he can, too. They've the gift.*

The drowning sun spilled curdled milk across the Irish Sea. She hadn't been on the water since William had rowed their boat along the coast to Kitterland, the islet near the Calf of Man. She smiled at the memory of making love on those wild shores on her honeymoon. They'd been free to go naked as Adam and Eve; not a soul lived there. For a lark, they flashed their bare backsides to tease the fisherman in the boats offshore. The memory made her glow. *Our one and only holiday. We ought to go back, take a picnic, just the two of us. William never even goes out to fish anymore. Always too tired now.*

Crests of waves sparkled, pierced by gannets expertly diving into the depths. Blackie raced ahead to a green mound and sat, patiently waiting, obviously following Nan's routine. *So pleasant. Peaceful. Little wonder Nan visits, morning and evening, and she had five boys and all. I ought to have come along before now. Doesn't take a belief in faeries to feel the magic.*

She recalled performing the ritual with William long ago when Nan was ill and once more felt her wonderment at the notion of faeries living under the hill.

"Lovely, isn't it?" Nan echoed her thoughts. *She always seems to know what I'm thinking, bless her.* Affection washed over Euphemia as she nodded in response. Nan dropped to her knees on the grass; Euphemia followed suit.

Nan reached into the basket she'd packed, and, from under a tea cloth, extracted two cups no bigger than thimbles. Setting them in a depression on the mound, she drew out the handkerchief tucked in her sleeve and then smoothed the square of white linen on the grass with her wrinkled, knobbly fingers. After carefully rearranging the cups, she filled them from a battered flask in her pocket, before sprinkling crumbs from a small loaf, reserving a good-sized piece for Blackie, who wagged her tail but didn't beg. Whispering in Manx, Nan bowed her head and placed both hands on the ground. After a few moments of silence, Nan tapped Euphemia's arm. Her eyes had been closed as well, observing Nan's rituals.

"Help me up, would you, lass? It's not the getting down, but the getting back up that's hard." She moaned slightly. "My dress made that noise, not me." She laughed.

"Of course, of course, Nan. Why don't we just sit awhile? May we?"

"Aye, *Themselves* won't mind if we tarry a while," she said, relaxing. "They know we're here but will stay put 'til we leave. The rascals will listen in on our conversation and gossip about it later."

"Thank you for bringing me tonight. I'd almost forgotten how fine it is, the place, and the ritual, both. I used to do it with William, remember?"

Nan nodded. "Those were troubled times. All things must pass. It comes 'round right in the end. Remember that, *my chree*."

"Can you hear the faeries, Nan?"

"I do betimes. Always have."

"But you go to church. How do you reconcile both beliefs? The Sisters in the orphanage said—"

"No harm in holding to the old ways, lass. God is everywhere. With *Themselves*, too, ye ken. Everyone needs a belief in a higher power, otherwise we sink into a bog of despair. So many troubles… What do you believe in, *ban my chree*?"

"Hmm, good question, Nan. I once followed the Catholic faith at St. Hilda's. But then, when I left and some things went wrong, I lost my beliefs. I go to church now for the sake of the children, and you. As to the faeries, well, they don't speak to a Yorkshire lass like me, any road. Hmmm… hmm." She started to hum. That's it. "Music. I know! I believe in music. It lifts me up; gives me hope. Yes, music. I just realized that." Her head buzzed with the revelation. She thought she could hear a tune, soughing on the wind.

"That's God, too; *Themselves* agree. Can't you hear their flutes? Listen." She cocked her head like a robin, then clicked her tongue. "Ah, the English. I'm sorry to say that they don't understand Manx traditions, any more than they ken our language. I should have taught you more about the meaning behind our ways. It'll be up to you now, as the mother, to pass them on to your children." Her voice seemed to come from far away and a forlorn look clouded her blue eyes. Euphemia shuddered with apprehension. Someone had walked on her grave, Nan would say.

"Whatever do you mean, Nan?" Her fear harkened back fifteen years. *Is she sinking into depression again, after all this time?* "You're here, Nan. We're all here. Our Henry's learning from you; the others will too. There's no rush. Don't you always say there's time enough: *traa dy liooar*, is it? I've learned that phrase, you all say it so often." She attempted a laugh. *Please, please let me bring her out of it, like I did before.*

Nan patted her hand. "Well done, *my chree*. You've an ear for Manx and music. One and the same, really." Then she looked out to sea. "I'm sorry but there is no more time." Her muffled voice dropped the words into her lap. She pounded her fist against her thigh, then raised her head to meet Euphemia's eyes. Suddenly it seemed the birds fell silent. The wind dropped to earth. *Whatever can she mean? She seems angry and sad, both.*

Nan inhaled as if preparing to push a boat into the water. "The *Little Ones* had something important to say, t'other night. Terrible news, I'm afraid, *my chree*. *Themselves* said someone in the house will pass over. Soon. '*Goll sheese ny liargagh*: he's going down the slope, fast.' Didn't need them to tell me that. I know it. As do you."

"Know what?" A roar, like crashing waves on the sea, blocked her ears against Nan's shaky voice.

"Please, we must be honest and face facts, dear. I've suspected since New Year's morn. Saw it plain as day in the ashes from the *chiollagh*, which I spread on the floor to foretell the year ahead, ye ken, according to the old ways. The faery footprints led out the door, not in. Luck has left our house." Nan paused and looked past the cliffs, breathing harder than she had after mounting the hill.

The ominous tone tempted Euphemia to laugh. Nan seemed to sense her doubt. "I didn't want to believe it, either; I've watched for the signs, and I'm sure. William's been poisoned by the lead mine. We call it "the milk reek," *my chree.* The sweats, the shakes, and especially the ill temper—so unlike my boy. He's getting worse every day. *Goll sheese ny liargagh.*"

Euphemia's lips parted, but the protest caught in her throat as if clogged with ashes from the hearth. She collapsed backward, nearly overturning the little cups. Nan lifted her head and held the cool flask to her lips.

"Drink a bit, lass."

Euphemia jerked upright, grabbed the flask, and gulped. She coughed and wiped her mouth with the back of her hand.

"It can't be," she said, sputtering. As she tipped the flask back again, whispers whirled around her. "Yes, yes, it is. Yes, it is. Yes, it is." The hair rose on her arms. Her head swam. Tears stung behind her eyes. The whiskey burned in her throat.

"Aye, doesn't bear thinking about, *my chree,* I know. I tried to pretend, too. I've seen you do the same, seen the worry at you when William coughs or shouts at the boys. It's not him; 'tis the sickness, *my chree.* Oh, God, the loss of another son to those damned mines." She hit her thighs, as if hurting herself could ease her pain. Euphemia recognized that impulse. "So many families torn apart. So many wid—" A sob completed the awful word.

True. Eva, Mary, Amy, others whose names she didn't know, gone away, forced to find work in English factories after their husbands' passing, their children left with kinfolk, or orphaned. *If anything happens to William, could I leave my six youngsters, least of all my newborn babe? To be raised by their grandparents, who mightn't live long enough to see them grown?* Now tears and milk spilled freely. *My milk will be spoiled tonight, curdled. Hugh will get the colic and scream like a Banshee—*

"Shh. There, there, I've a solution." Nan's voice brightened as she expelled one word: "Thomas." Euphemia thought she detected a note of excitement, where usually Nan sounded disappointed, even angry, when mentioning her youngest surviving son.

"Thomas? What? You think he might come back? From America? No." She reached for Nan's hand, which trembled in hers. "Please, there's got to be another way, Nan. What about the farm? Henry loves helping Grandad with the sheep. He's nearly thirteen. He could quit school, I could help—"

"We've not enough land to support the family, lass." She hunched her shoulders and sighed, picking at the grass. "That's why our boys were forced down the mine in the first place. Only our Arthur avoided that fate. His bones lie here, looked after by the *Little Ones*. My sweet lamb. Took by the diphtheria. The mines got the rest of them, one way or t'other. First, the twins; buried alive. Inseparable in death as in life, lying under Snaefell." Her voice trembled. "Only good from that was Thomas bringing you to help out. Heartbreak laid me low. I fairly had to climb Snaefell meself to get out from under it. I loved you like a daughter from the start," Nan said. Blood rushed to Euphemia's cheeks. Nan had never expressed love for her in words.

"Ah, but then the mines won again, didn't they? For Thomas left to escape working underground. Leastways, that's what he claimed. I suspect there was more to it, though." Her inflection seemed to pose a question. Euphemia lowered her gaze, cursing the blush she felt in her cheeks. A long pause. Then, Nan continued.

"And now, why, the mine's killing my William. Well, not if *Themselves* and I can help it." Her voice retrieved its headstrong tone. "Thomas brought me a daughter, and you've given us grandchildren. He'll do his duty again, you'll see. I'm awaiting his answer. It's the one way out."

"No, no, please, Nan—" The last thing she wanted was Thomas' return. Well, there could be one worse thing. She fell back on the ground, damp seeping into her clothes. She yanked at the grass with clenched fists.

"Come, lass, the dew's falling. You'll catch your death. We'd best get back or they'll think we've been fetched away. Not a word to William, mind. I'm prepared for a battle with him. Quick, there's the first star. Help me up," she said, patting Euphemia's knees.

"We mustn't be caught here after sunset or the *Red Caps* will take us, sure. The way down is much easier. I can almost run like a girl. Ah, was, was," Nan expressed her customary wistfulness for times past. "Here's the basket, *my chree*. Who'll get home first?" She threw the challenge backward as she trotted down the hill with Blackie trundling along behind.

Euphemia stumbled and tripped down the rugged path, the empty basket banging against her side. Thomas' parting words stabbed her ears, like the sharp stones beneath her feet: "You'll rue the day you turned me down, Pheme. Wait and see." Or was it a voice in the bushes? Her heart pounded. *What did Nan say would happen, should a Red Cap appear—I'd be carried off to another world?* She quickened her pace, following the smell of peat smoke rising from the whitewashed cottage up ahead. In the twilight, the footpath almost disappeared. She knew the way, but when was the last time she'd run anywhere? Arriving at the red door, she leaned on the frame to ease the stitch in her side; she waited for her heart to slow before pushing down on the metal thumb latch. Warmth and light from the peat fire spilled across the threshold. Blackie greeted her with a tail wag and a "Woof." She dropped to her knees to pet the dog.

Lifting the teapot in salute, Nan said, "Here she is, young'uns. I told youse she'd not let the *Red Caps* get her. Hand me your mother's cup, Henry. She's white as a sheet."

Chapter Two

"Ogh-cha-nee: Woe is me. *Ta graigh-ayn:* I love him."

The Phynodderree: A Tale of Fairy Love
Edward Callow, 1882

GRANDAD rosined up his bow, preparing for the evening singsong. "What would youse like to hear tonight, young'uns?"

"*Phynodderree*, please, Grandad," Edward begged. "*Phynodderree! Phynodderree!* I love saying that word!"

"Shh, mind you don't keep repeating it or you'll conjure up that hairy elf, foolish boy," said Nan, snapping a tea towel in the air. "You mustn't tempt fate." She stood at the kitchen dresser, replacing her precious crockery on the shelves, arranging it "just so." Then she sat in her bent willow chair and set it to rocking.

Euphemia shook her head, amazed. *She acts as if everything were normal. When I can hardly stop my tears. My throat burns. Grandad obviously doesn't suspect; he's cheery, as always, when he's entertaining.*

"That old chestnut? I know it's your favourite since my fiddle can practically play it without me. Sing then, boys."

The Phynodderree went down at dawn to the round field
and lifted the dew from the meadow.
The maiden's hair and cow's herb,
he trod them both beneath his feet.
He stretched out his width across the ground
and threw the grass towards the left.

"Tell us again how the hairy elf flattens the crops into patterns, Grandad," John asked when the song ended. "You've seen the circles in the fields, yes?" His wide brown eyes gleamed like burnished pennies in the firelight. Euphemia smiled. *Sweet, sweet boy. My eyes, my hair. Maybe I am softer on him than the other boys, but he's so sensitive. He'll grow out of it, as have I. Too soon.*

"Look, can you see the elf in the flames, John? Bending the wheat in all manner of patterns and designs, making mischief? He's like you, Edward, in that way," Henry said, punching his brother's shoulder. Henry sat cross-legged on the rug like his younger brothers, Edward, John, and Tom. *Except his knees jut out a lot further. Henry's a scarecrow. Head and shoulders above the rest, too. Tall like his father.* Edward nudged back hard and then scooted off to sit beside John. *Henry's an awful tease. Our Edward, on the other hand, likes to dish it out but can't take it. Just like his father.* Her fingers were as cold as the steel knitting needles in her hands. *A Phynodderree just appeared, indeed. I've summoned it.* She shuddered. *All of us gathered 'round the hearth, we're like a quaint old painting. It might just as well be a hundred years ago; nothing ever changes here.* A surge of pride warmed her through like hearty soup, from the inside, out. *My sons: five strong and healthy lads, each one different and special in his own way, from the eldest, so eager to become a man, to the youngest, still at the breast. And my sweet Ann, my own small faery girl, quick as a fox, bright as a penny. How she loves to rock on Nan's knee of an evening. However am I going to break her of thumb-sucking? A family. All I wanted. Why I chose William and stayed, to live in this crowded little cottage on the edge of the sea. On the edge of poverty, too. The only home I've ever had.*

Her mind turned to how the scene would change if William became too sick to work, or even… passed away. No. She couldn't help sighing aloud. Nan shot her a look. *You said I must face facts, Nan. Henry, he'd go down the mine, though not yet thirteen. The other three boys would be relegated out of doors to the cold, filthy washing floor below the water wheel, separating ore from slag, like so many village boys. Poor women too, come to that. Only Ann and the baby would be spared, for a while. Whilst I, what on earth would I do? Stay here, take in washing? Or go back to Douglas? God forbid.* Anger suddenly boiled up and she tasted metal. *Why is William lingering outside? He ought to be here with us, damn him. Oh, don't. God, don't damn him.*

"*Themselves* can do anything, can't they, Grandad? Good and bad?" John persisted. Grandad set the fiddle and bow aside to stuff his pipe with fresh tobacco. A gust of cold air blew in as William opened and closed the door behind him. Everyone turned. Euphemia suppressed a gasp as her heart dropped. *Hark at his pallor and the circles under his eyes.* She noticed Grandad's bushy black brows gather in a frown. *Does he know William is ill? Nan could never keep it from him. They're like one person after so many years together. That's what I dreamt of for us someday. We'd be a couple of old fools teasing each other, singing the same songs, playing with grandchildren…*

"Grandad? They do magic, yes?" John kept at it. *Ach, that boy's like a dog with a bone. Now, where was I?* The knitting needles lay askew in her lap. She'd dropped the last stitch.

"Where was I?" Grandad stared blankly at John. He tucked his pipe between his teeth and picked up his fiddle. "Ah yes, you asked about the *Phynodderree*. Half man, half goat. You never know if *Himself's* inclined to grant a wish, but no harm in asking. Just remember, *Lhiat myr hoilloo*: to thee as thou deservest. You might well get what you deserve. *Themselves* are neither good enough for heaven, nor bad enough for hell, and they delight in tricking us mortals." His blue eyes sparkled as he deliberately squeaked his bow and lowered his grey head in the children's direction with a menacing look. They instinctively moved back.

Grandad sputtered a laugh.

"And what *do* we deserve, Da?" William's voice scraped across the room like his chair on the slate floor. "To slave in a mine threatening to close every day, for starvation wages? Potatoes and proverbs, that's what we live on. Don't these bairns deserve better?"

Silence, but for the popping fire and the knitting needles clicking out of time. Euphemia's shoulders tensed. *It's no use; the wool keeps slipping. I'll have to unravel all tonight's work. Start again.* Her eyes blurred.

"Mum, don't knit," Henry said. Euphemia pursed her lips. *Cheeky.* "Please," he added, with a look that reminded her of Blackie, begging forgiveness. His father's harsh tone toward Grandad had obviously upset him. And the other boys, too, sat frozen, hunched over, staring at the fire. Euphemia wound the skein around the knitting and placed it in the bag next to her chair. Edward's head shot up as though he'd been struck by lightning.

"Sing us an English tune, Mum. Tom, you next, in Manx," he said.

"My goodness, you're a proper choir director tonight, Edward. What shall it be, then?" Her heart wasn't in it, but she hoped to lighten the mood. "Early one morning, just as the sun was rising…" Somehow, she made it through. *Flat on the high C's, dammit. Should've chosen a lower key.* Henry fetched her a glass of water.

"Ah, beautiful, *my chree*," Grandad said, repeating the refrain on his fiddle. "Tom, you're learning to sing from the best. Did your wife's voice soothe you, Son?"

William dropped his head on the table, covering his face in his crossed arms. Euphemia cringed. *Oh, that song was a poor choice, dammit. Too sad. He's overcome. Dare I go to him?*

Grandad resumed playing. Nan rose to her feet, leaving the chair to rock, cradling Ann, fast asleep in her arms. She motioned with her chin to the boys. Euphemia lifted Hugh from the cradle and hastened after Nan to settle the youngsters into their trundle beds. Edward and Henry scrambled up the ladder to the loft quicker than usual. *All that talk of the Phynodderree. Maybe he's after them and all.*

Grandad spoke to William, his warm tenor carrying easily to the back rooms. "We Carines are one of the oldest families on *Ellan Vannin*, ye ken, probably here since the time of Olaf the Black. You're no doubt related to the bugger, given that crop of dark hair on your hard head. Mine's grey now, more's the pity, but still just as thick. The Manx are a handsome lot. I turned many a lassie's head in my day, now I tell ye—"

Nan cleared her throat to draw Euphemia's attention to her eye roll at Grandad's boasting. "That man," she said, her voice warm with a smile, as she lowered Ann into the trundle bed below John and Tom. Euphemia stood rooted in place, clutching the baby.

"Put him down and light the lamp, *my chree*. It's too dark to see these scallawags."

It took two matches, her hand shook so. Nan lifted the boys' covers.

"You can't sleep in your clothes, lads. Go get into your nightshirts." She tapped their backsides, then made her way to the washstand. Their wan faces matched the white sheets. Nan wet a cloth while the boys quickly donned the nightshirts waiting on a chair. After a perfunctory wipe-down, she tucked them in, planting a kiss on each forehead.

"Don't fash yourselves, boys. Your Da's just tired and not feeling well. Sleep tight. God bless you, my loves. Nan will always be with you, no matter what." She added words in Manx, put her finger to her lips, and tipped her head to call Euphemia out of the room. Grandad's voice penetrated the wall, sterner now.

"Stop being so cantankerous and set an example, William.

We've survived invasions, plagues, famines. Manannan's mist hid us from the Romans, kept us safe. *Ellan Vannin* is our home, best place in all the world."

He accompanied his assertions with notes on his fiddle. *Why does he play while he talks?* Euphemia wondered. *It's annoying. Ah, but his words are a song. I could almost sing it myself, so often have I heard the refrain.* William's next statement echoed her thoughts. *We're connected, like Nan and Grandad.*

"Ach, I've heard it a thousand times, Da." William growled his exasperation. His next breath caught in his throat. He coughed and coughed. The flat of a hand struck wood. "Fine words, they are. But they don't put food on this table, do they? Goddamn mists haven't prevented the English stealing our wealth, have they? Next, they'll be taxing the very air we breathe. It never ends."

The music stopped with a painful sound like the pull of a rusty nail. *The two of them are just sitting there now, staring at the fire.* Euphemia pictured their faces in profile; jaws set, bushy eyebrows furrowed, high cheekbones catching the light. Two sides of the same coin.

Gathering Hugh to her hip, she followed Nan next door to her own room and laid the baby down on the bed. Her hands trembled as she fought with his diaper pins.

"Here, lass." Nan gently moved her aside. After removing Hugh's wet nappy, Nan left him to kick his chubby legs. "He loves to be naked," she said, shaking her head. "Just like a man."

"I hope the cold air doesn't make him wee; I've no more clean sheets." Euphemia let herself fall sideways, next to him. "What does it matter, any road?" She moaned into the pillow.

"Hush, hush now, darling girl. *Foddym gra gyn danjeyr dy bee dy chooilley nhee dy mie,*" Nan whispered. She petted Euphemia's head, twirled a strand of her hair that had fallen from her coif, rubbed her index finger along her chin.

"What's that you say, Nan? Oh, I'm that worried. I can

hardly breathe."

"Don't take on so, darling. All will be well, the saying goes. Get yourself to bed and rest easy. I'll settle his little lordship, *smoor* the *chiollagh*, with prayers to *Themselves* and blessings. William can bring the cradle in later. Up with you, wee man. Oh, you're getting heavy," she groaned, as she lifted him and headed for the door. She opened it and Grandad's voice entered.

"We've come through worse, my son. A Manxman's always a leg to stand on. Our three-legged man rolls along. Don't give in to despair. For all our sakes."

As if he hadn't heard, William spoke in a voice that sounded as far off as the waves below Faery Hill. "There's rumours they'll close Bradda Mine, Da. They claim it's no longer profitable. Damn English. Money's all they care about. Never mind a man's livelihood."

"*Oie vie. Immee dy chadley.* You'll need your strength for tomorrow. Go on, get some rest now. Things'll look better come morning."

Grandad's tone with William is like Nan's with me. Poor old folks, doing their best not to panic. To keep our spirits up. Then she registered William's words. *What's that he said—the mine might close? Christ, what next?* Shivering, she put her feet on the cold floor and hastened into her nightgown, then burrowed under the damp sheets. She swam her legs back and forth to create heat. *Dammit, my feet are freezing. Ought to have left my stockings on. William, come to bed,* she silently summoned him. *Let me hold you while you weep in my arms. We'll cry together.* She squeezed her hands into fists. *I've closed my eyes to his pain, and he's suffered all alone. What's wrong with me? I always go on pretending, no matter what, I guess. Learned that at the orphanage. Pretending my mother would come for me, that she hadn't meant to abandon me, she'd rescue me, and we'd be together again, safe, rich… Castles in the air.*

Suddenly Nan's words came back to her: *Goll sheese ny liargagh? Something like that, about a slippery slope. Bad, at any rate. The faeries told her, she said. Wish I'd made an effort to learn Manx, for my children's sake if nothing else, though it's a beautiful language. I've had plenty of time. Why do the faeries only speak Manx? Did they teach the people, or t'other way around? Oh, for God's sake, I'm in such a dither, I'll never sleep. I'll say my prayers. Pray hard. Not that it ever amounted to anything.*

That's not true; you're here, safe, with a family, aren't you? She longed to cry. Like she did in the orphanage, weeping into her pillow with promises to be good if only God would bring her a mother to love and protect her. She didn't hear William come in. But when the baby cried to be fed before dawn, she wriggled out from under her husband's arm, heavy across her waist. Same as always.

CHAPTER THREE

Shaghyn dagh olk: Avoid all evil.

St. Hilda's Home for Girls
Bradford, Yorkshire, England
1886

S T. HILDA'S was the only home Euphemia had ever known. Now, at fourteen, she'd have to make her way in the world with the few skills she'd been taught and no one to help her. She'd tossed and turned, night after night, terrified of what she might become. The other girls had whispered about it. Had her own mother been a streetwalker, of necessity? Euphemia had thought of another way. She'd talk to her favourite teacher; convince her she'd heard "the call." Lie through her teeth.

Euphemia pleaded with the woman sitting across from her on a narrow bed. "It's what I want, Sister. To become a nun, like you." Sister Michael looked at her with pity in her soft brown eyes and a kind smile then shook her head.

"No. You don't. You think you do because you don't know any better, pet. It's no life. Nothing's your own, not even your time."

"You seem happy enough, Sister."

"Do I now? Do I indeed?" Sister Michael said, standing up and crossing to the tiny window in her cell. "Well, my calm demeanour's thanks to a lifetime of practice. It'll surprise you to know I ran away once."

"Really?" Euphemia couldn't believe her ears. Sister Michael, the most devoted nun and teacher of them all? "Why? Where'd you go? How'd you get there? What happened? How'd you end up back here?"

"Slow down, lass, it's not that exciting, I assure you." Sister Michael laughed. "I was only eleven. I tried to board the barge on Bradford Canal and was sent packing. Then I was rounded up in short order by the constable. I often wonder what might've become of me if I'd made it. Heading for home I was, though my parents had given me up. Too many mouths to feed. Unlike you, I remember family life." Her voice sounded as sad as the cooing of the mourning doves outside. She opened the window and scattered birdseed from a bowl she kept on the small table next to her Bible. "Come on, babies. Time for supper." A flurry of wings made her laugh with delight.

"Oh, so you remember your parents. I wish I knew mine, at least my mother." A familiar sting burned her eyes. No, she mustn't. Sentimentality was frowned upon. A sin, like vanity.

"Well, I'm not sure which is worse, Euphemia." She dusted her hands. "I struggle with resentment. All we can do is pray to forgive, pet. The hardest part of the Lord's Prayer, I reckon. Your desperate mother left you at our doorstep so's you'd be safe. That proves her love. She didn't throw you in a rubbish heap or in the canal, as happens. I took it upon myself to name you. A good Scottish name. My mother's, in fact. After the only girl amongst the saints, set free in the Colosseum—"

"When the lions refused to eat her but licked her wounds instead." Euphemia smiled and finished the oft-repeated tale. "I know, Sister. Her Saint's Day, September 16th, I think of as my birthday. Say, I've no last name. Never needed one, but I will if I leave. I know! 'Michaels.' After you."

"That is sweet, though, of course, my real name isn't Michael. It does have a ring to it: 'Euphemia Michaels.' Good. I'll mark it in the register." She crinkled her eyes in a smile. "My advice is to set out, find your own purpose in life, hopefully have a family of your own. Staying here will break your spirit. I'd hate to see that. Besides, the Lord has given you many gifts, not to be wasted."

"Such as? I don't feel special." Euphemia blew out her cheeks and rolled her eyes, though anxious to hear Sister Michael's opinion.

"Your good heart, for one, always helping the younger girls and the new arrivals to adapt. I've watched you. You'll make a fine mother someday. You're a natural. Not to mention your pretty face and beautiful singing voice. Father Matthew will miss you in the choir."

"I love the choir, too. Don't make me go, Sister. What shall I do? I can't sleep for the night terrors."

Sister Michael took her by the shoulders and sat her down, advising her to don all her clothing in layers rather than carry a bag, and put personal items like her comb and toothbrush in the pockets. She gave her a bit of money she'd squirrelled away under her mattress, along with the address of a rooming house in Liverpool run by a former orphan girl who'd stayed in touch. With many a warning about the world, especially men (of whom the poor dear knew nothing, Euphemia later realized), Sister Michael opened the gates a few days later and sent her off, briefly returning her hug.

"Mind how you go, Euphemia. I shall pray for you every day. Write to me once you're settled."

Euphemia never did. She found the rooming house and hired on, thanks to the reference, as a maid of "all work." All work: scrubbing, polishing, dusting, sweeping, climbing stairs to change bed linens and collect chamber pots. Was life here so much better than the orphanage, compensated by room and board and not much else? At least at St. Hilda's, she'd had the other girls for company and the joy of singing in the choir. She'd lived by routine, guarded from men, as the nuns reminded them. Better food, too, prepared just for them, not leftovers from paying guests. She slept in a cold, open room with four other girls, each with their own bunk, a bedside table, and a cupboard for their clothes. Her habit of curling up on her side and rocking herself to sleep had been noticed by one of the older maids, a stocky, red-haired Irish girl, who mocked her by sticking her thumb in her mouth, whining. That curtailed any further attempts at friendship. From then on, she spoke only when spoken to, and at night she lay still as hot tears dampened one side of the pillow, then the other.

To relieve the tedium of sixteen-hour days, she practiced her repertoire of hymns while cleaning. She went to church on Sundays with the other servants and the landlady, Mrs. Dawkins, who dissuaded her from joining their choir, though praising her enthusiasm. "My goodness, I think the angel Gabriel himself couldn't outdo you, my dear. Sadly, there isn't time for you to attend practice."

She daren't complain. The girls told of a poor lass who'd become too ill with consumption to work. Mrs. Dawkins had turned her out. The body had been found floating in the River Mersey; by murder or suicide, nobody knew. Had that been her mother's fate? Euphemia shuddered. *I mustn't get sick or let on I'm tired. I'm lucky to be alive, as Sister Michael said. Lucky me.*

One day, a boarder named Mr. Leeman happened upon her as she set the dining room table, singing her heart out. He praised her voice, insisting she'd fit right in with the chorus at the Gaiety Theatre in Douglas, just across the sea on the Isle of Man. A salesman for soap, he regularly took the ferry across to supply the tourist hotels. He'd gladly arrange an audition, and even pay her fare since the company covered his. Mrs. Dawkins crossed her arms, frowning when Euphemia told her.

"I promised Sister Michael I'd keep an eye on you. I don't trust this oily bugger. Are his motives above board? A young, innocent like you, all of fifteen; why, he's old enough to be your father—"

"Exactly, ma'am." Euphemia nodded. "He says the manager of the Gaiety is his friend. He showed me his card, said they're always on the lookout for new talent. He says my face is so lovely it would be perfect for company advertisements, like Miss Lillie Langtry. The shade of my hair is called chestnut, and my eyes are nut brown, like the ale, he says, though I've never seen it, so I wouldn't know. Just what they're looking for in a model, he says. He'll get my photograph sent to the company. Wouldn't that be something? Fancy! My face on the soap box! Nobody's ever told me I'm pretty before—"

"Hmm." Mrs. Dawkins' pressed lips made an upside-down line. "He's turned your head, my girl. Mind how the Sisters warned us against vanity. There's something shifty about him. It's not safe for you to go off with a stranger."

"Why? What's the worst that could happen? If I don't get on at the Gaiety, I can always work in Douglas, same as here, any road. Mr. Leeman says there's lots of hotels. The Isle of Man's climate's so mild, he says, that factories in London send their workers there for holidays, all expenses paid. I wonder what they do on holiday—"

"Well, I'll provide you a reference, just in case things go awry. You're a hard worker and no mistake. A credit to St. Hilda's, just like me. Be sure to write so's I can let Sister Michael know you're safe."

Mr. Leeman registered them in separate rooms in the bright pink Sugarland Hotel as promised. *A hotel painted pink; fancy!* Euphemia oohed and awed over the sights of Douglas, with its multicoloured hotels lined up along the promenade where ladies and gentlemen strolled arm in arm, enjoying the fresh salty breeze off the Irish Sea. Mr. Leeman hustled her to the shopping district in search of "presentable" clothes. He insisted she also choose a lacy peignoir, more suitable than her plain cotton nightdress "for a lady staying in an 'otel." Gallantly carrying the packages upstairs to her room, he stepped in behind her, closed the door, and suggested she model her outfits, including the peignoir. The back of her neck tingled when he mentioned the nightdress, but then she chided herself. *What harm could it do? It's not revealing, and he did buy it for me. The lace is so dainty. I love it.*

Emerging from behind the dressing screen having wrestled with all the ribbons and buttons, a sudden heat flamed across her bare chest. "It's a bit too big."

Mr. Leeman laughed. "Don't worry. You'll grow into it." He handed her a glass of whiskey.

"Oh no, thank you. I don't drink."

"Oh yes, you do. How d'you expect to make it in the theatre trade unless you know the ropes? They'll think you're a ninny. Bottoms up!" He clinked her glass with his own and watched as she struggled to down the fiery beverage, coughing and spluttering, then bending to catch her breath.

His fingers tipped her onto the settee. "Never mind, never mind, dear, it's always like that, the first time. Here, let me loosen those tight ribbons—"

Suddenly his mouth smothered hers; his hands tugged at her buttons until some popped off and bounced on the wooden floor. A seam ripped, a row of lace dangled from her wrist, the stench of his tobacco breath filled her nostrils. Something hard pushed against her groin as he struggled to wrench her nightdress above her knees while still atop her. She screamed. His hand covered her mouth. She couldn't breathe. Squeezing her stomach muscles, she twisted and bit him, hard. He threw off her hand, and she hit the tumbler sitting on the table. It rolled to the floor and shattered next to the sofa. Her fingers wriggled under one of the legs, found a shard of glass, and raked it across his cheek. Blood spurted into her eyes. She screamed again. Then came a sudden banging on the door. A man burst in and yanked Mr. Leeman off her, allowing him to roll onto the floor before wrenching him to his feet and punching him in the face. She sat shivering and sobbing, as the stranger dragged Mr. Leeman down the hall. She heard his feet thump on the steps.

When the manager heard how she'd been so ill-used, he offered her work as a scullery maid. Downcast eyes, face aflame, she accepted. Despite his assurances that no one thought the incident had been her fault, shame twisted like a snake in her belly. She admonished herself, pinching her forearms black and blue in self-torture. *Mrs. Dawkins was wise to him. What a ninny I've been.* The other maids later told her that the doorman had thrown her assailant into the street with a warning never to return.

Weeks later, she summoned the courage to knock at the Gaiety's back door, still hopeful that she might have a chance in the chorus line. The doorman sighed. "Not another one. I'm sorry you've been misled, lassie." Taking pity on her, he offered a tour of the theatre. She declined, hearing Sister Michael: "Once bitten, twice shy." She burned the peignoir in the stove, smashing the fabric against the logs with the poker, picturing Mr. Leeman's lecherous face. She kept the dress and the fancy smalls, determined to save for a ticket to see a show at the Gaiety someday. At least she'd have something to wear.

She worked hard, kept herself to herself, and within the year, became a kitchen maid and began to learn cookery. The kind, helpful staff gently mocked her Yorkshire accent and quaint expressions. She might've done the same, for her part, as she struggled to understand their Manx. She chose not to ruffle feathers. She spent her one day off a week strolling the promenade or sitting at the seaside. In her tiny room at the very top of the hotel, she imagined herself the Lady of Shallot in her tower, recalling the poem they'd memorized in school.

That horrible Mr. Leeman had been honest about one thing: the Isle of Man was beautiful. The town gleamed like a necklace on Douglas Bay. From her perch, the sandy beach washed by the silver sea constantly beckoned. The incessant cries of the seagulls, so annoying at first, had faded into the background, becoming part of the natural landscape. Green hillsides framed her view of the river of tourists constantly strolling the wide promenade. The hotels along Douglas Bay strained and elbowed each other against the prom. She never tired of looking left and right at the painted facades. Each hotel was dressed in its finery: gleaming staircases, sparkling bay windows, hanging baskets of flowers, all vying for the attention of holidaymakers with money to spend. The pink Sugarland reigned supreme, smack-dab in the middle of the crescent. On her day off, Euphemia collected seashells and pretty stones from the beach to decorate her window ledge. For the first time ever, she had treasures to call her own.

Chapter Four

To Douglas Head how many thousands stray
To taste the healthful freshness from the sea;
To stroll about and pass the hours away,
A sweeter spot, methinks, could scarcely be;

"Douglas"
James Middleton Sutherland, 1883

SHE'D bumped into Thomas on Douglas Pier while strolling along, gazing at the bathers down below. He excused himself, though she had jostled him. Tipping his hat, he began a light conversation about the folly of the bathers jumping into the freezing water. Euphemia laughed in agreement, saying she'd be afraid to catch her death. He offered her his arm to stroll along; somewhat worriedly, she accepted. *What harm could it do, out here in the crowd?* He remarked on her height which allowed them to walk shoulder to shoulder.

"Unlike most girls," he added.

"Oh, so you pick up a lot of girls on the prom, do you?" She stopped short to cast an exaggerated frown.

"A few, yes. But none as pretty as you." His grey eyes glistened like rain on stones.

"Goodness, I'm sure you've never said that before." She enjoyed their teasing banter.

They entered a tea shop, and he insisted on treating her. She expressed shock at the expense, all the while stuffing herself with clotted cream, scones, and fresh strawberries.

"Never mind, Euphemia. It's the price of visiting Douglas," he said. "Euphemia," he repeated. "An unusual name. Quite the mouthful. I'd call you 'Pheme' instead. More elegant, don't you think?"

Bold as brass, he is. But he can call me what he likes, so long's I get more of these cream teas. She smiled and helped herself to another scone.

They arranged to meet on her next day off, once she'd admitted she wasn't a tourist but a hotel kitchen maid. He expressed relief; they could meet again. Thomas would take the train from Port Erin, fetch her at the Sugarland, and then they'd tour the city in the horse-drawn tram, enjoy hake and chips on the pier, perhaps take in a show at the Gaiety. He had plenty of ideas for ways to spend her time and his money. Euphemia's heart skipped a beat as she suddenly realized how bored and lonely she'd been. This big, blustery, fun-loving man, with eyes the colour of pussy willows and a shock of raven hair, excited her a lot and frightened her a little.

Things progressed quickly over the next few weeks: a hand alighting from the tram became an arm around the waist, became a brush of lips on the cheek, became a passionate kiss in the stairwell off Sugarland's staff entrance. Euphemia revelled in the attention, the flattery, the tender words whispered in her ear, the luxury of eating out with the taste sensations of ice cream and ginger ale. Thomas introduced her to lager, but she hated it, and she refused strong spirits outright. She revelled in the security of his broad shoulders next to hers on the crowded prom. Whenever they visited the shopping district, he'd steer her into alleyways, to steal kisses and breathe warm air on her neck all the way up to the lobes of her ears. His caresses sent shivers down her spine and warmth flooding between her legs. But late one afternoon, as they were parting in the hotel's empty stairwell, he kissed her with an open mouth, leaning in to insert his tongue. A hard bulge pressed against her thigh. Her breath caught in her throat. Her body shook and her knees buckled. She pushed him. He fell against the wall, then whirled around, stuttering an apology.

"Oh, I'm so sorry, Pheme. I didn't mean… I went too far. It's just that, you are so beautiful, so wonderful really. Oh, please don't be angry."

Euphemia stumbled to the first step of the staircase and flopped down, dropping her head between her knees. Thomas rushed over and knelt to offer his handkerchief. His ruddy face had turned ashen. She dabbed her eyes and sobbed for a few moments before wrapping his ice-cold hands in her own.

"No, it's not you, Thomas. You see, I've had a bad experience—" She proceeded to describe what she'd vowed never to tell a living soul. By the time she'd finished, sputtering out a sob, Thomas was pacing the floor, clenching his fists and swearing under his breath. His reaction startled her. *Will he ever want to see me again? Does he think of me as spoiled goods?*

"What? Don't be silly, Pheme. You mustn't blame yourself. Why, if I'd been there, he'd not have lived, the blackguard! Taking advantage of your innocence—"

"I still fear running into him, as he comes back and forth to Douglas. I've imagined catching a glimpse of him around corners, stalking me," she said. Cold sweat had broken out on her forehead. "I feel such a fool. My landlady in Liverpool warned me, but would I listen? No, I knew better. I've never had a mother to guide me, you see. Growing up in an orphanage doesn't prepare you for the world." She stood up, teetered a bit, then smoothed the front of her dress. "That's why I love hearing about your family, Thomas. They sound so caring and kind.

When can I meet them?"

"I'm surprised and relieved, you still want to… after… well, hmm, hmm." Thomas cleared his throat. "It's not the best time, unfortunately. The tragedy I told you about… Mother's not coping well. She spends most days in bed. It's been a job for us men to keep the house up, and that's a fact. It's such a great relief to get away, especially with you—"

"P'rhaps I could help. If I take the train next Monday, you could meet me at the station and I'd spend the day tidying up, make a good meal… it would be my pleasure."

"On your day off? You're pulling my leg. You'd do that?"

"Course I would. I want to see your home. The tiny cottage sounds like something out of a faery tale."

"It's a faery tale, all right. Both good and bad. Mum might introduce you to the faery folk and all."

"Really? Now I must go! I've heard that faeries are a special part of this island, but that's all I know. I don't think there's any in Douglas, any road. But it's said they live just out of town across Faery Bridge. I'm longing to see the countryside. Please tell your mother I look forward to meeting her. She might think me low-born, being an orphan, though—"

"Never." He shook his head. "We Manx aren't above ourselves. We judge people by their deeds, not their birth. She'll think you're an angel, which you are." He took her hands in his and brought them to his lips. "You're cold. Take a hot bath tonight, if you can. I'll see you Monday then. The ten o'clock train?"

Euphemia nodded. "Yes. Just for the day, mind. I mustn't jeopardize my situation by missing work. I'm so enjoying learning to cook." She patted his arm and leaned in to softly kiss his lips. "It's only an hour's journey to Port Erin, correct? Good, then I shall be back well before lock-up at eight o'clock." She smiled and patted his arm. *He's a good man. I think he's fond of me.*

* * *

A few days later, the bellboy called out Euphemia's name in the kitchen. She jumped and sliced her finger with the butcher knife. *Dammit! What's that idiot on about? Someone dropped off a note. For me? Nobody knows I'm here but Thomas… and perhaps… him? Oh, Oh.* Her hands froze on the knife. She nodded to the boy to put the envelope, indeed marked with a scrawled 'Euphemia Michaels,' on a shelf; her hands were covered in gore. She'd have to wait until teatime. The letter smouldered there while she stumbled about the kitchen, banging her hip against the counter, boiling over the milk, spilling soup as she shakily tried to fill a tureen. Finally Cook lost patience, handing her the envelope with a wave toward the office.

"I can see the worry's at you, lass. Read it in privacy. Perhaps 'tis family news."

Euphemia bit her lip and scurried off, clutching the paper in slippery fingers. She tore it open. No date, no greeting. Just a blur of inky venom.

> *What a nasty bit of goods you turned out to be, you little bitch. Here's me thinking you'd be grateful to me, helping a little nobody like yourself get a leg up in the world, but you had to act the chaste maiden. You've been with lots of men. I've seen you waltzing down the prom with that big, dumb-looking brute you've latched onto. The two of you are very cozy. Buying your favours, eh? Found his way between your legs right quick, I bet. Meanwhile, your manager is telling all and sundry to steer clear of me, so I'm losing the soap trade in the Douglas hotels. Thanks to you, you little slut. You'd best watch your back, Missy. I'll teach you a lesson you won't soon forget. See enclosed.*

No signature. *Bastard!* He had been following her; she hadn't imagined it, after all. She unfolded a torn bit of cardboard inside the envelope. The front of a soap box decorated with Lillie Langtry's beautiful face. Only the image was disfigured, blotchy with bumps, bubbled, perhaps sprinkled with… acid? Maybe. *Oh, God, Oh, God, Oh, God…*

That night, she clutched her most precious seashell beneath her pillow and rocked herself to sleep.

CHAPTER FIVE

Eddyr daa stoyl ta toyn er laare:
Between two stools is a fall.

WHEN he found her waiting at the Port Erin station, carpetbag in hand, Thomas readily agreed that she should leave Douglas.

"Leeman. He's been watching me. Us." Her voice shook. He took her by the shoulders and said he'd simply tell his parents that he'd brought Euphemia to help Mum recover. He'd kip in the cowshed, and she'd have his room. He smiled into her eyes and surrounded her in his massive arms. Relief washed over her as she melted into his embrace.

After meeting Mr. Carine, Thomas' father, a tall, smiling man with thick, silver hair and heavy black eyebrows, she surveyed the cottage: dirty clothes heaped by the back door, dishes in the basin, floor unswept… *what a tip!* Mr. Carine read her thoughts. "Most welcome, you are, lass. As you can see, we men-folk fail at housework, what with the two boys down the mine and me in the fields."

Two boys? Thomas never mentioned a brother. At that moment, the door flew open, and a lanky man strode in, saying something in Manx. His blue eyes stood out like marbles in his dirty face, and his bright teeth enhanced his smile. Thomas responded gruffly, then took Euphemia's hand to present her to William, his elder and only remaining brother, the other three having passed away. Euphemia smiled inwardly at William's sudden flush, visible beneath the grime. He stuttered and offered his hand, looked at it, and instead merely nodded. He removed his filthy cap, and his dirty face crinkled in a smile.

"Hello, Miss. Euphemia, is it? Pleased to meet you. You've come to help us out for the day, I understand." *That voice. Smooth as glass. I'll bet he's a fine singer.* His eyes met hers with friendly, open curiosity. Her heart skipped a beat. *My goodness, but he's handsome.* Her chest tightened and her breath quickened. *He looks nothing like Thomas. I'd never guess they were brothers. That crooked front tooth stands out a bit when he smiles. Endearing.*

"Actually, she's staying. I'm putting her up in my room." Thomas' tone cut between them. He whirled her away before she could respond. "Come, Pheme. Mum's waiting." She glanced back as Thomas dragged her toward his parents' bedroom and saw William's scowl.

Euphemia experienced the sting of sibling rivalry as a bystander. Thomas surveyed her every move, interrupting conversations at mealtimes to focus attention on himself or to heap compliments on Euphemia's cooking. He became agitated, anxious, even aggressive in William's company. Where was the cheerful, boisterous fellow she'd met in Douglas?

In contrast, William exuded calm and confidence. When she joined the talk at suppertime, he would lean forward, his eyes so intently focused on her that they sparkled like the sea at sunset. *He doesn't flatter me. He seems really interested in what I have to say. Nobody's ever given a toss about my opinion before. Not even Thomas, who nods and then continues talking on his own railroad track. Like most people.*

Every day after washing up, William greeted her in the

kitchen, then checked on his mother, bringing her a pot of tea and sitting with her to chat. He told Euphemia of his obligation to visit Faery Hill with the family offering and report back; Mum feared bad luck would descend if the faeries were neglected. He eased her mind with soothing words and a teaspoon of whiskey in her tea.

Euphemia admired his caring nature, both in words and actions. His sharply defined features, big hands, and ready laugh attracted her. She revelled in the timbre of his singing voice as they harmonized 'round the hearth, or *chiollagh* in Manx. At last, she sang again, accompanied by Mr. Carine's fiddle. Thomas talked or found some other way to make noise. He didn't, wouldn't, or couldn't sing.

She coped with the stormy weather in the house by dedicating her efforts to cleaning, washing, and tending to Mrs. Carine morning, noon, and night. She barely left the cottage except to use the privy and slop the pigs. By the time she'd stoked the evening fire, she fell into bed exhausted. But wanting.

Thomas would sneak in to join her. Things progressed quickly, from kisses to soft whispers while fingers stroked the length of her body. Then one night, he touched and tickled the damp softness between her legs, and something happened. She dared not make a sound, though she wanted to cry out. She'd never experienced the like. In the Home, the girls had been told to keep their hands clasped in prayer under their pillow at night, and a matron patrolled the rooms at odd hours to ward off bed-hopping. Sometimes she'd heard girls moaning but she'd put it down to loneliness. Now she knew. A key opened a secret door to a room glowing with light. And pleasure.

From then on, Thomas encouraged her breathless response, tickling her until she became wet, hot, dizzy, barely able to breathe. He spoke words she'd never heard but knew were forbidden, and his murmurings shifted her mind into another realm. Afterward, it became a dream she could barely remember. A warm tingle raced up her spine, and she floated above her body, weightless yet safe, supported by strong arms on either side. She'd learned to put a towel beneath her, for she spurted hot liquid. Initially, she tried to hide it, ashamed. Thomas laughed, saying it wasn't piss, but "love juice." Then he'd take his turn, supporting himself by his elbows, igniting the flames between her legs with his erection. Hot fluid spilled onto her naked, sweat-soaked belly, making her come again. Collapsing for a moment, he'd whisper into her hair, praising her as a wonderful, amazing treasure. She couldn't formulate words in response. He'd roll off the narrow bed onto the floor, where she'd join him, yanking down a blanket. He insisted she thoroughly wash first, adding vinegar to the water, sluicing between her legs over the bowl. He assured her this would protect her. *From pregnancy? How'd he know this?* She followed his instructions and then brought him the wet cloth and towel. Then, her body so heavy she could barely move, she'd lie next to him and cover them both. His hairy chest became her boat, carrying her to a quiet shore. They'd lay together until first light disturbed their dreamless sleep.

She remained a virgin—just. Thomas continually surprised her, using his tongue, or tickling her with a feather, or teasing her with a smooth, wet stone rubbed against her nipples, across her flat stomach, and then down, down, to become a shard of burning sun inserted in, out, in, out, until she bit her own hand to stop the scream. He left her mouth watering, craving more. Memories of stolen pleasures returned during the day, warming her cheeks with embarrassment and desire. She and Thomas restrained their passion in front of the others. *Had Mr. and Mrs. Carine ever…? No. Impossible. They were too good. This is the "sin" the Sisters warned of, leading girls astray. What would Sister Michael say?* One day, she resolved to stop. She'd tell him so that night. Then came the click of the latch. That night, and the next, and the next. At cockcrow, she'd awake with a start and kick Thomas, sending him scurrying out. *What would Mrs. Carine think of me if we're discovered? Not to mention… William.* She imagined his face, stark with shock and disappointment. It almost made her stop. Yet she couldn't. *Stop. Don't stop.*

One night, Thomas said he'd something important to share. He removed her cautionary finger from his lips, though he kept his voice low. "Listen, Pheme, Mum's getting better thanks to you. You two get on like a house afire. It's time I made my move. I hate working underground, me. I've been of a mind to leave for ages. Off to America. Then I met you." His words came out thick, like treacle from a jar.

"But how? Where will you get the money?" Euphemia said, furrowing her brow. She'd become aware of the family's poverty, how they lived hand to mouth.

"I've been saving a long time, selling peat." He rolled on his side, seeking her eyes in the dark. He placed his hands on her face. "Come with me. To America."

"Peat? From where?" Euphemia knew Mr. Carine had a peat bog on his land, their own supply as he'd so often bragged. William and his father would cut the turves, dry and haul them to the cottage for heat and fuel. They never sold any. It was meant to last years.

"Does your father know? And William? It's precious. When it's gone, there won't be any more, your father says." Euphemia frowned. *Something's amiss.*

"Of course not. There's plenty. They haven't caught on. We're fewer in the family now, at any rate. It'll do, betimes."

"Fewer?" She bolted upright. "Lucky your brothers died… saves on peat, eh? Leaving a goodly supply for you to sell off under their noses?" Euphemia wrenched away. "I don't believe you," she said through her teeth. Her stomach churned. Her hands became ice. *Stealing from his own family. And them so loving, so unsuspecting. Oh. How could he?*

"Shh, Mum and Dad'll hear."

"Serve you right. Get out. Go back to the barn. I can't abide you." She got up and crawled into bed, turning her back. When he touched her shoulder, she flinched as though she'd been burnt. "Go. Or I'll scream. I hate you."

* * *

From then on, she distanced herself from Thomas, ignoring him at the table and barring her door at night. He tried to catch her alone, saying it wasn't wrong; he'd pay them back, once he came to riches in America. She avoided his entreaties, shooting him looks filled with as much venom as she could muster. She observed his attacks on William with clear eyes: the petty arguments, unfounded criticisms, snide remarks.

Mrs. Carine became well enough to join them for dinner. She soon put a stop to Thomas' carping, but the undercurrent of antagonism remained. But he wouldn't leave off trying to cajole her, standing too close at the stove, smelling her hair, rubbing her shoulders, whispering in her ear to come away, to let him back in her bed. She'd stiffen her back and hiss, "Why don't you just go? Before you bleed your family dry?" He'd retaliate, traipsing across her clean floor in his muddy boots instead of going around back as William and his father did, or spoiling the soup she'd left on the stove, adding salt when she wasn't looking. Childish pranks. *He was a bully at school. I see that now.*

Under the strain, Euphemia considered returning to the Sugarland. She'd easily get her job back. Mrs. Carine had improved. Her passion for Thomas had burnt to ashes. Her mind reeled. *But what if Leeman finds me? How can I leave Port Erin, so pretty, so peaceful? Here, I'm appreciated, even loved, maybe.*

Besides, she'd made a friend down the village: Jill. Her first genuine friend. A girl to chat with, laugh with, share stories and recipes with when she visited the cottage with its red door overlooking the sea.

I've found a home. Not THE Home for unwanted, abandoned babies. A place to grow, plant a garden in the spring, tend the new lambs...

With William. William's here. And he's nothing like Thomas. "Not by a long chalk," as Father John used to say. I love him. Does he love me?

Chapter Six

Sooree ghiare, yn tooree share:
A short courtship, the best courtship.

May, 1889

WILLIAM made no attempt at seduction. Instead, he took her hand and led her up the purple hillsides and down to the sea, up Faery Hill for the view, and down to Glen Rushen to wade in the brook and chat on the banks. She longed to see faeries, but William warned her of the Manx belief that the *Little Ones* were dangerous if caught unawares.

"Fancy!" she said. "I thought faeries were sweet."

William laughed. "No different than people, that way, Euphemia. Sweet and sour, both."

Anxious to experience his world, she accompanied him as he tended the Manx sheep, intrigued by their dark wool and four twisted horns.

"Gosh, they're so different to the white flocks of Yorkshire."

"I love their beautiful, soft brown coat. The colour of your hair."

"Not you, too! It's been compared to brown ale, to chestnuts, to cinnamon! Men!"

She laughed at his blush and went on to ask why the Carines raised the Loaghtan breed; she'd seen white sheep on the hillsides nearby.

"We've not much land, is why. Loaghtans survive on almost nothing. Most sheep have a will to die, we say, for their stupidity, but your Loaghtan has a strong will to live. Like a Manxman, Dad says." His voice dropped. "Truer words were never spoken."

They headed up Cronk Howe Mooar to take in the unbroken view across the Irish Sea. As they walked, they talked. Actually, she talked: of the Home for Girls, the drudgery of the laundry, but also the joys of learning to read, recite poetry, and sing in the choir, then leaving Mrs. Dawkins' rooming house in Liverpool for the prospect of a better position in a Douglas hotel and the Sugarland, where she'd trained as a cook. She never mentioned Leeman, hoping Thomas would keep her secret. She merely said she'd come to Port Erin to help his mother and decided to stay.

"If that's alright with you folks, of course. I've never known such happiness. I simply adore the cottage: the red door, bountiful garden, and cozy fire. Oh, and the bright kitchen with its lovely crockery. And your parents are the most wonderful people—" She hesitated to add her feelings for him. He might think her forward. Perhaps he even suspected that she and Thomas had been lovers.

William nodded and smiled at each item on the list, guiding her up the steep, rocky path. Once they were seated side by side on the carpet of purple heather, she drew him out.

"Do you like it here, William?" Maybe he also planned to move, escape the mines and the poverty. It seemed ages before he answered.

"Well, since the twins died, I've been forced to change my

plans."

"Oh, I'm sure. I can't imagine what you've suffered. I'm so sorry." The salt sea air stung her eyes, and the wind swirled in her loose hair. She hastily pulled it back into a knot at the nape of her neck. *What had he planned? America, like Thomas?*

"Yes, it's a shame you never met them. Two peas in a pod, they were. And funny! Kept us laughing morning and night. The three of us slept in the loft where I am now on me own. I used to curse their snoring; it raised the rafters. Now I'd give anything—" His voice, thick with sorrow, faltered. She rubbed his shoulders and brought his hand to her lips. Men could cry, she realized. *He's so sensitive, thoughtful, and kind. I never want to be without him.*

"Sorry, sorry, Euphemia," William said, wiping his face with the back of his sleeve. *Poor man needs some handkerchiefs. I'll make him some.* "Sometimes it comes over me, like. Up here, I can be alone, tell my troubles to the *Little Ones*. It's even better now with you." He took a deep breath and squeezed her hand. "I hope they aren't offended that you've taken their place," he said, casting a glance toward the faery knoll. He seemed serious. A tingle ran down her spine. He cupped her chin and gazed into her eyes.

"By heck, in the sunlight, your eyes are so beautiful, Euphemia. All colours: green, brown, even specks of blue. I've never seen any to compare." His voice rang true.

"Thanks. I grew them myself," she said, then joined him in laughing at her cheeky response. *Where did that come from, I wonder?*

"Well, you did a good job," William said. "Any road, as you say (here's me picking up your Yorkshire expressions), Ralph, Mel, and me, we planned to pool our savings, buy more land, more sheep, and run a farm together. Thomas wasn't involved. I've no idea what he wants, always flitting off to Douglas, chasing wo—Oh," he halted. "I didn't mean… Forgive me." He stumbled over his words, turning to take both her hands and search her face, "Please don't take offence. I'm glad he found you."

Euphemia laughed. "Don't fash yourself, William. There, one of your Manx expressions for you. I've no illusions where Thomas is concerned." *Should I confess? How close we'd been?* Heat burned her cheeks. *No, best not.* "So, have you thought about what you'll do now?"

After nearly a year, the scars obviously hadn't healed. She'd never experienced grief herself. Not for a real person. Only for the mother she'd never known. People seemed to handle pain in different ways: some ran away, others buried it, some fell apart. Despite his tears, William seemed strong.

"I still want to buy land, but it'll take much longer now, working in the mine and saving, after expenses. It's the taxes, ye ken. It's hard for a man to get ahead on *Ellan Vannin*. Dad's not getting any younger. I'd like me own cottage, and a family someday. I shall care for my parents, 'til they pass—" His voice wavered, and he looked at the sea. "Not very exciting, I reckon."

"It's lovely, William, your love and concern for them," Euphemia said, squeezing his hands. "Your Mum and Dad are such fine people. So real. As real as the faeries are unreal."

"What? Don't let them hear that!" William said, putting a finger to her lips. "They're listening, as we speak. Let's give them something to talk about, eh?"

His hand rested on her shoulders, and he laid her down onto the heather. Now she could admire his eyes, grey-blue, the irises outlined in deep navy, almost as dark as his unruly black hair. His body was thin but wiry with muscle. He was tall like herself; they fit together like a pair of spoons where they lay on the hill. He kissed her lips, her eyelids, her neck, her shoulders. He began slowly, watching her face, awaiting her reaction. Caressing her through her clothing, he took no liberties. Still, their hearts were racing, and their breath came in gasps when they drew apart.

Euphemia appreciated William's restraint, though he obviously wanted more. Much better this way. They were friends, first and foremost. He respected her as his equal, making her feel competent, worthy of love. After many long walks, longer talks, and sweet kisses, she gladly accepted his marriage proposal on Faery Hill. They gave a special offering to the faeries to bless their union before announcing their engagement at suppertime.

William's parents expressed delight, welcoming Euphemia as the daughter they'd never had. Thomas stormed out and fairly spat in her face when she followed him to the cowshed later. He swore and threatened, but she knew he'd keep silent about their intimacy, lest she tell William and his father about the stolen peat.

"Thomas, you know we'd never last as a couple. Besides, I've no wish to go to America. I love it here. I love William."

"Oh, and I suppose my feelings don't enter into it, eh? So long as you've got what you want."

His dark tone and crossed arms conveyed his bitterness. Was he angered by her rejection or simply jealous? She studied his face. *Perhaps I've really hurt him. No, he just wants what he can't have. Like the dog in the manger.*

"Well, one of us has to be sensible, any road. You don't want a home and a family. I do. And listen, you must stop selling the peat. It belongs to the family, which I'll soon be part of."

He grumbled, saying it meant working longer in Bradda mine; passage to America by steamship cost five years' wages. She crossed her arms. "Better than thieving from your kin," she said. "You'll just have to work harder and spend less. No more trips to Douglas. You can stay home and be more help around here."

"My God, you sound like my mother. Perhaps I've made a narrow escape," Thomas said, slapping his leg. "But you will rue the day you rejected me, Pheme. We're more alike than you know."

Euphemia wanted to slap his face. Instead, she turned on her heel, swallowing the bile in her throat. She didn't trust him to keep quiet if provoked.

Every evening for the two months of wedding preparations, Thomas retreated to the pub. He then refused to attend the ceremony, going off to Douglas. He returned a week later to face his parents' fury. Euphemia had never seen Mr. or Mrs. Carine angry. They both spoke at once, hardly pausing for breath, one taking over where the other left off. She relished his tongue-lashing; he deserved every bit of it. William stormed out back the minute Thomas stepped through the red door. The smell of his cigarette smoke drifted through the open window. He'd obviously overheard everything.

"You shun your brother on the most important day of his life? The whole village is talking. You've shamed the Carines. The minister is appalled. William had to get Joseph to stand up for him. After all we've been through, all we've done. We raised you better. Out of respect, you—"

"I'm moving out," Thomas interrupted, like an axe chopping wood. "Youse are looking at the Isle of Man's newest representative for the soap company."

Euphemia's knees gave way. She grabbed the counter for support, tipping over the dishpan. *Leeman? Oh, God. He's never gone into league with that devil...*

"Yes, I ran into an old acquaintance of Pheme's in a pub in Douglas. I recognized him right off by the scar on his cheek. The drunken sot gave me his contacts in Liverpool. Then I made short work of him for you, Pheme. He got what he deserved, as we say, eh, Dad?"

Euphemia couldn't hear; a rushing shockwave knocked her to the floor. Arms lifted her under the shoulders, water dampened her lips, a cloth cooled her forehead. Thomas carried her to her new double bed. As he bent over her, she recovered enough to reach up and slap him.

"What on earth? What's the matter with you, Pheme? I thought you'd be pleased."

"Pleased? Speaking about that horrible man in front of your parents? Christ! What if William heard? You purposely humiliated me." Her mouth filled with sand and sweat rolled down her sides. He pushed her backward, squeezing her arms.

"And what if I did? It's nothing, compared to what you've done to me—broken my heart, left me for William… you were my girl—" he sputtered, collapsing to his knees beside the bed. Tears burst from his eyes and rolled down his round cheeks. His shoulders shook as he lowered his head, reaching for her hand. He turned the ring on her finger.

"I still can't believe it," he said, letting her hand drop. He slumped backward, breathing a heavy, ragged sigh as he landed on his seat.

Euphemia's anger curdled to fear. His hurt ran deeper than she'd recognized. He'd pounded Leeman to a pulp; what else might he do? Hurt William? She struggled to her feet, poured a glass of water from the dresser jug, and resolved to gain control.

"Listen, Thomas. You're off to the wilds of America. That doesn't suit me; I'm after stability. We'd soon be fighting like two cats in a bag." She stopped for a sip of water and time to think. "Travelling 'round, you're sure to meet some comely lass willing to follow you to the moon and back." She laughed lightly, hoping to cajole him. "Being a salesman will suit you to a T; you're very persuasive. And you're free of the mine now." She patted his back and handed him the glass. "It's for the best. I'm happy for you," she said, and meant it. He'd leave the cottage, and no doubt quickly earn enough for his passage and be off. For good. "Let's each go our own way, then, eh? Part as friends?"

Thomas struggled up from the floor by pushing against the wooden bed frame. He looked at her. His glare pierced her eyes like a sharp knife. "Friends, eh?" He frowned. "Well, now we're family. I hope you're satisfied."

* * *

Euphemia and William were married in October. Within ten months, Euphemia gave birth to her first child, Henry. Amazingly for a first birth, she laboured but three hours. The pain was worth it for the joy of having a babe in her arms.

"You're built to be a mother: broad hips, big feet. Tiny women like me suffer terribly, delivering bairns," Nan said. Outspoken, was Nan, as Euphemia called her now. Mr. Carine had become 'Grandad,' to his joy. They were her parents in all but name. William delighted in fatherhood, cuddling the babe like a newborn lamb, even changing nappies. Euphemia often became overwhelmed and distraught when the baby fussed for no apparent reason, fearing it would die. Thankfully, Nan hovered nearby, reassuring her with soft words, ready to step in.

The four adults fell into a harmonious daily routine, followed by evening chats and singsongs. Grandad made her repeat *"Traa dy liooar,"* whenever she became flustered, laughing at her with his sparkling sea-blue eyes. "Don't fash yerself, darlin', for there's time enough. What doesn't get done today'll be there, tomorrow. Washing, ironing, cooking… chores are never finished. Be satisfied with what you accomplish each day. Instead of listing what you didn't do, take count of all you did."

Nan taught her to knit, and she soon created sweaters and scarves from the Loaghtan's soft, brown wool. Preparing meals for the family didn't seem like work as she developed new skills under Nan's tutelage. She'd anxiously take the first bite of a dish, then smile at the praise.

Thomas, the only thorn in her side, showed up once a month on his rounds outside Douglas. He'd boast about his travels and how easily he earned money now compared to working in the mine, deliberately goading William who scorned the bait. Her husband's forbearance impressed her, but still, she wished he'd retaliate with a good kick to his brother's arse, just once. Nan shut Thomas down with talk of the new lambs or gossip from the village, whilst readily accepting his gifts of soap, far superior to homemade. Thomas never failed to give his salesman's pitch at full volume, honing his skills. They couldn't help but be impressed. *He ought to've been on the stage.* Perhaps Leeman could've got him a job at the Gaiety, Euphemia wished she could say. *That'd shut him up.*

"Your gift of the gab will make you rich betimes, Thomas," Grandad said.

"Too right, Da," Thomas answered, but he didn't smile.

Anytime they were alone, Thomas persisted in making advances: a squeeze of the forearm, a slight lean forward to nose her hair, a finger grazing her neck under her coif. Euphemia resisted, but gently, lest she rouse his anger or his lust. She fought her own demons, as well. If he brushed her leg under the table or whispered as he helped her carry dishes, she flashed back to their passionate moments. Her heart pounded, and a thousand bees buzzed in her head. Liquid as warm as honey trickled down her thighs. The chaffing of damp, rough fabric between her legs made her groin and nipples throb. Heat raced from the crown of her head to the tip of her spine. She imagined the scent of desire emanating from her body, like smoke from burning embers. *Can others tell? Can he?* His penetrating eyes said, "You can't fool me, Pheme." Struggling to control her ragged breath and shaking hands, she'd brusquely turn away to some chore requiring immediate attention, usually baby Henry, to jolt her back to reality.

I'm a respectable wife and mother now. How wonderful. She glowed with love and pride. Her husband had given her everything she'd ever dreamed of: a home, a family, security. He made love tenderly, if a bit… quick. William obviously lacked sexual experience. She wasn't about to educate him. Better this way; she feared the craving, the unbridled desire she'd known with Thomas. She was satisfied indeed. Encircling William's waist with her thighs, feeling him shudder with release, warmed her through. She revelled in his contented sighs, his warm, tobacco breath in her mouth. With a final kiss, he'd wrap her in his arms and drift off to sleep, puffing like a Manx steam engine.

She rolled over and looked at William's sharp features, stark in the moonlight. *The man sleeps like a baby. Well, not like our baby. But still, he looks so relaxed, free of his daily cares and exhaustion from mining.* She smiled.

Thomas will soon leave for America. I'll be out of harm's way. His presence in the loft, where he now slept when at home, loomed overhead. She prayed not to dream of him sneaking into the double bed. He'd caress her so lightly between her legs, maybe with a feather, insert his tongue in, out, in, out, then rise to kiss her with breath tasting of ripe apples. He'd blanket her with his heavy, hairy body, rub her until she fairly screamed with something like pain but so good—so good, not of this earth. She rubbed herself until her body glowed with pleasure. And shame. Was this betrayal?

She curled away from William like a hedgehog so he wouldn't feel the pounding of her heart. God forbid he should awaken to find her in this state. She inhaled. She breathed. She thought and she breathed.

"I plight thee my troth," she'd said to William. And meant it. His bright, crooked smile melted her heart and kept her feet on the ground. Caring for him, making his lunch, even doing his laundry was rewarding. His laugh, jokes, songs, and concern for her and their wee babe, Henry, filled her cup. *Thomas, the dreamer, the schemer, the liar, is not for you. Thank God.*

Thereafter, each time Thomas blustered through the red door, never bothering to remove his shoes, she steeled herself. She held fast. For three years. Three solid years.

Chapter Seven

Cha boght as lugh killagh:
As poor as a church mouse.

June, 1904

"DON'T worry, Henry," Euphemia said, laughing at the look on her son's face as he opened the red door. "I've kept a bit o' supper from these hungry gannets otherwise known as your brothers."

Henry hurried to the table before Nan caught up with him, out of breath from trotting down Cronk Howe Mooar. *Nan can't beat Henry by any stretch, but she's got no trouble besting me. I don't get much exercise, working indoors most of the day. Still haven't made it for another evening walk. Always too busy. Our Henry never misses, rain or shine. Faithful as Blackie. Good as gold. I hope the faeries had positive words for a change.*

The slanted evening light outlined Nan's small, hunched form where she leaned against the doorframe. Euphemia watched her white head bob, checking off family members one by one: Henry, Edward, Tom, John, and Grandad, all seated at the table, Ann in her highchair. Her eyes registered concern at

51

one empty seat.

"Just outside, he is, Nan. Washing up," Euphemia assured her. *God, she's so worried about him.* Ah, good, Nan's eyes responded. The boys seemed startled, their glances curious. Euphemia smiled at them and returned to the stove. *Have the children picked up on my fears? Hugh's more fussy than ever, not latching properly and screaming with the colic. Maybe he's cutting a tooth, or perhaps worry's tainted my milk.* She shooed the cat out from underfoot as she started dishing out. *I'm not waiting. Supper's getting cold.*

William's ablutions after his day's labour seemed interminable of late. He moved at a glacial pace, stripping to his underwear in the back garden to wash in the tepid water Euphemia always made ready. It started out hot but was barely warm by the time he got to it. He'd leave his work clothes on the bench and don the indoor clothes hung on the line. When the back door opened, Euphemia's shoulders dropped with relief. Home, safe and sound, one more day; walking seven miles to Bradda mine with his mates, singing all the way, gobbling a second breakfast of ham and eggs at the canteen before plunging into the depths for ten hours of toil with pick and shovel, and then making the weary journey back.

Euphemia sighed. *That never used to matter; he'd rush in the back door with a cheery hello after his wash, sometimes forgetting dirt behind his ears.*

"Here's our William," Grandad said. "Good to see you, Son. *Kys ta shui?*" Blackie waggled over to the door, and William bent to pet her. Everyone but Ann in her highchair and Hugh in his cradle turned to smile.

"Good to be seen, Da. Fair to middlin', me." In three of his long strides, he crossed the room in his stocking feet to wrap his arms around Euphemia's waist. Her impatience evaporated with his kiss on her cheek and the touch of his callused forefinger tracing the edge of her chin. She let out her breath, relieved as if she'd removed her corset. She rested her head on his shoulder for a moment. *Home. He's my home.*

"How's his lordship been for you, my love? A little gentle-man, I hope," he murmured, glancing at the cradle in front of the hearth.

"Yes, though I think he's teething. My goodness, that razor of yours wants sharpening," she said, running her hand across his bony cheek.

He pecked her lips, then faced the children seated around the table. Crossing his arms, he feigned a stern tone. "And the rest of youse? Proper little terrors, I'll warrant." He ruffled Tom's hair and leaned down to kiss Ann's blonde head before taking his seat.

Grandad held his knife and fork in the air, then proceeded to bang the ends of the handles on the table.

"Nan, are you going to sit down so's we can eat? We're starving, aren't we, lads?"

His sparkling blue eyes sought agreement, and the boys nodded eagerly as if they hadn't been through this a million times. Euphemia laughed, delighted at her father-in-law's love for his role as head of the family. *William and I brought life back into this house after so much loss.*

Nan came up behind and swatted him lightly on the shoul-der. "That's a good show of manners for the youngsters, Hus-band. And it isn't right to say we're starving. We're blessed."

This teasing banter initiated the evening show. After for-ty-odd years of marriage, their bond exuded warmth and secu-rity. Euphemia hoped she and William's life would follow their example.

"We'll say our prayers before we eat, as usual, whether your stomach is stuck to your backbone or no, you silly old man," Nan said. She took her seat and clasped hands with him and Henry on her left, bowing her head.

"Grandad gave the blessing, keeping it short. "Tuck in, everyone! What would the toffs in Douglas think of us eating kippers and mash with our fingers, eh?" He pinched a bit of fish and mashed potatoes from his plate and stuffed his mouth. His dark, bushy eyebrows danced in time to his exaggerated masticating, making the boys laugh.

"Well, I doubt they'd eat kippers, anyway," William said, his voice colourless. "Nothing but roast beef and gravy's good enough for the English."

"What's a 'rosbif'?" Edward spoke around a mouthful of bread.

Euphemia inhaled deeply, anger rising. *With those two words, William's gone and spoiled everything. Dammit, I wish he'd stop inviting "The English" to supper. Like a curse word, never minding I'm English. I know what he means, but still—*

"See, me own bairns don't know quality food, Da. Never et beef in their life; never will, most likely." William spoke into the cup of tea he gripped with both hands. Euphemia noticed his eyes watering. She blamed the steam rising from the cup.

"Whist now, Son, consider Euphemia's feelings. It's a lovely dinner, lass, as good as any in the hotels in Douglas." Nan flashed her crinkly smile. Euphemia played along.

"Well, as everyone knows, my culinary skills come from the famous Sugarland Hotel." She almost sang, to lift the mood. "There's many a fine gentleman's savoured my cooking, albeit with a knife and fork, all fancy-like." She mimicked the action, pinky fingers outstretched. Tom burst into laughter; his mouthful of milk proceeded to dribble from his nose. Edward snorted and Henry joined in. *Good, I've cheered everyone up. Keep going.*

"I can cook roast beef with the best of them. It's the haunch of a steer, Edward, like roast mutton, only more tender. Supposedly King Edward's favourite meal, so it became the Sunday special for the tourists. A hell—oops, a heck of a lot of work, now I tell you. But this is better to my mind. More flavourful. Especially when eaten with the fingers, the Manx way. Eh, Grandad?" She made a show of licking her fingers. "Yum!

Fit for King Edward himself."

Grandad smiled and cocked his head. "Our Tom seems to agree. Leave some pattern on the plate, lad," he said, chuckling.

Euphemia leaned toward William. "There's berry bonnag for dessert, dear, with fresh blackberries and cream. Your favourite." William grunted. She tried to keep the mood jovial. "I'm lucky I learned to cook at Sugarland, eh, Nan? Otherwise, I'd've been no good to you!" She laughed and Nan joined in. "And I love cooking for my family. It gladdens my heart to see everyone enjoying my dinner."

Tom sucked his fingers and smacked his lips until she tapped his shoulder lightly with her spoon. "Quiet, you." She turned her head to the end of the table, seeking William's eyes. "Hard day down the mine, love?"

"No more'n usual." He shrugged. "'Every day's a good day above ground,' we miners say. The opposite's true also." He pulled back his shoulders and ran his big hand through his raven hair, shot through with strands of grey. "Just tired is all, darling. Forgive me, everyone. You're right, Da, this is a treat. You're the best cook in the world, my love."

Too late. His temper had sprinkled ashes over the table, though kippers and mash usually made for a jolly meal. The boys continued to eat quietly, while Nan did her best to compensate by asking Ann how she and Jenny Kronchent had spent their day. Ann held up her doll, withdrew her thumb from her mouth with a pop, and started to talk about the new litter of baby pigs in the barn.

"Goodness, I hope you're not taking Jenny into the pig shed," Euphemia said. "She's delicate."

"I know she's *decilat*, Mama." Ann smoothed the doll's sateen gown and wound her little fingers in the black woollen curls. She bounced the doll's tiny leather-clad feet across the tray of her highchair.

She adores being the centre of attention, reigning over the table like a princess. Our missy must soon give over that chair to the next one like they all have since Henry. I wonder how she'll feel about that, then. We've spoiled her, I'm afraid, as the only girl. I'll have to watch carefully so's there's no rivalry between her and Hugh. That, I won't abide.

"Me and Jenny Kronchent watches them play in the mud from the fence. Jenny says piggies stink. But they're funny. Oink, oink." Ann giggled, then her voice took on its whiny tone. "There's no one to play with but Jinxy, and he's off chasing mice. Why can't me and Jenny go to school, Mama?"

Edward piped up. "You're too little, and you can't bring a doll to school, anyway, Silly. Especially not one with a dumb name like that. Everyone will tease you."

Tears filled her blue eyes. She stuck out her lip. "The faeries named Jenny, didn't they, Nan? You said so. They told me her name. We don't know anyone with that name, do we, Nan? If Jenny can't go to school, I'm not going neither!" She kicked the footrest of the highchair. Her bowl tumbled to the floor. Henry knelt to collect the pieces.

"Why don't you give her a wooden bowl, Mum?" Henry said. "I'm tired of this, aren't you?"

"Edward, you leave your sister be. Next time, you'll go to bed without supper."

The commotion woke the baby. Euphemia stood to see to him. Nan motioned to the boys to begin clearing the table. William headed for the front door.

"I'll bring in more turves for the night after me smoke," William said.

Euphemia sought Nan's eyes. *Go on then, Nan. What're you waiting for? I thought you were going to tell him.* Nan avoided her gaze, brushing crumbs from the table. Euphemia's throat tightened. *Well, maybe I'll tell him myself.* She flopped down in her rocker, nuzzling the baby against her breast. She hummed the 'Gartan Mother's Lullaby,' her favourite. *No. Don't think about it, don't think about it, don't think...* She found herself burping the baby harder than necessary. *Sorry, my little dove.* She kissed his head, inhaling his clean, warm scent, and switched sides, watching the children tidy the kitchen.

Henry poured hot water from the copper kettle into a deep basin. He always washed the dishes. Edward dried. A shoving match would ensue as Edward tossed plates back into the water, claiming they were dirty. "Your bickering gets on my last nerve," Euphemia often complained to no avail. Tom swept the floor, while John took the slops to the pigs. Ann fed Blackie. Everyone pitched in as Grandad tuned his fiddle and rosined his bow for the evening songs at the *chiollagh*. Before long, they gathered near for stories and tunes. Except William. Euphemia resented his absence. *We used to sound so nice, singing in harmony. He never sings now. I ought to have noticed that.*

Cigarette smoke drifted in through the open window as Grandad's initial soft notes took flight. Euphemia blew out her cheeks at William's self-imposed distance. She got up and removed Hugh's wet diaper before setting him down naked to air his bottom. *Diaper rash again, dammit.* The other boys laughed and tumbled about with their chubby little brother on the rug. Edward blew raspberries into Hugh's tummy, blubbering *"The Phynodderree! The Phynodderree!* He's gonna get you!" Nan snapped a tea towel in his direction before taking up her rocking chair. Ann climbed on her lap.

"Here, Euphemia," Grandad said, playing the first strains of the lullaby. "Sing your favourite song to soothe the savage beast, lass. Such a pretty tune. And get lanolin on Hugh's bum. It's red as a strawberry."

She nodded and did her best to sing, though her throat ached, and the tears were close. She grabbed her shawl from the back of her rocker and picked Hugh up to rock him. "Sleep my child, for the red bee hums, the silent twilight falls…"

Tears dropped on Hugh's head as she choked on the ending. *William's staring up at the stars again tonight. Sipping from that damn flask tucked in his vest. He thinks I don't see it. We don't even get a chance to talk anymore, just the two of us; he stays out half the night. When will I find the right time to tell him Nan's plan? I reckon a man deserves some time alone after burrowing underground all day like a mole. But what do I deserve? The only time I get to myself is in the privy. Even when I take a bath, Nan's there to fill the copper. Sometimes I wish...*

The door flew open, disturbing the fire.

"*Raad Mooar Ree Gorree* is bright, eh, Son, since there's no clouds? King Orry's Road shines like silver when it's clear," Grandad said, gently easing his bow across the strings, not looking up. "Good to get some fresh air."

"Yes, there's not much of that down the mine." William's voice was bitter as cold tea.

"I want to go with you, Da," Henry said, leaning forward on his haunches, eyes pleading. "I'm done with school. Lots of lads my age are working. I'm almost thirteen and a man, so."

Nan leapt from her rocker. Ann slipped down and started to whimper.

"You'll never go down that mine, at all, at all." She shook her finger and raised her voice in a rare show of temper. Edward and Tom shied like startled horses. John's huge brown eyes widened, and his little mouth formed an O. "Over my dead body. It killed our twins, is the cause of—" Her voice broke.

William started as if she'd thrown a bucket of cold water over him. He turned to lean against the door, hands braced as though something was trying to enter. The latch caught with a soft click. Euphemia held her breath, wondering if she should comfort him. He might be ashamed. He seemed to be gathering all his strength. *He's realized Nan knows... Oh, God.*

Grandad scowled and tapped the back of his bow on the arm of his chair, telling Nan to sit. She did after gathering Ann back in her arms, soothing her in Manx. Restarting her rocker, she said, "No, you'll stay in school, Henry. Become a schoolteacher, a politician, just as you like. You're a clever lad. Mining's not you."

"But, Nan—"

"That's my wish, too, Henry," William said, his voice a hoarse whisper. His hands trembled as he leaned down to catch Jinx. With the cat in his arms, he looked at the boys as if seeing them for the first time. "For all of youse, though I'm not sure how. Damned if we do, damned if we don't."

Euphemia hoisted Hugh to her shoulder and buried her face in his blanket. *No, I won't tell him. It's her job, as his mother. If it were my son, I'd want… Poor Henry looks so dejected. In such a hurry to be a man. He's no idea—*

"I know, William, I do, I do," said Nan, planting her feet to halt the rocking chair. "I ken your struggle. Don't fash yourself. Come, have a cuppa with us. We need you here of an evening, not away with the faeries. Euphemia, dear, put the baby down. Sing, you two. A happy tune. No more tears."

Nan. She can be bossy when she wants to be. And mostly, she wants to be. Bless her.

Chapter Eight

Ta broilt chaa boggagh arryn croie:
Hot broth softens hard bread.

THREE days later, William stormed in well past suppertime. He'd walked to the village after work for the mail. And a few pints of bitter, no doubt, Euphemia suspected.

"How could you, Mother? What's the bloody idea? By Christ, you've got a nerve." He tossed a piece of paper on the table. It just missed landing in a bowl of stew. The children had been too hungry to wait. Euphemia lost her grip on the milk jug at his shout.

"Dammit, William. You scared the bejesus out of me, shrieking like a banshee. Look what you've gone and made me do. Ah, Nan," she moaned. "Your best jug." Her hand shook as she dropped to the floor.

William scowled. He hadn't washed or changed his clothes, and his sapphire eyes blazed in his grimy face. *He's a ghost, in reverse.* Euphemia shuddered. *Christ, what's Nan done? Is Thomas coming home? God's truth, I've never seen him so furious. I wish now I'd warned him. I mustn't let on I knew anything—*

"William Harold Carine," Grandad said between his teeth.

"Ta shen foddey dy liooar. You'll not speak to your mother in that tone. Nor any of us, come to that. Apologize this minute, or, grown man or no, I'll thrash you." Grandad's chair crashed backward. At his menacing glare, Edward and Henry cowered in their seats. John covered his ears. Tom's spoon clattered in his empty bowl. Grandad's long legs crossed the room in two strides. He raised his hand to strike William. No one had ever seen this side of him before.

Nan reached out for Grandad's arm as she said, "Leave it, *my chree.* The milk will polish the slate." Her voice remained calm.

Euphemia slumped back on her heels and put her finger in her mouth. She tasted the blood that had stained a shard of porcelain. "Ouch, Mama, an owie," Ann said, peering over the side of her chair. *Dammit, the blue jug that took pride of place on Nan's dresser. Now it's like pieces of sky. How ever will we replace it? William's so upset. I ought to have prepared him, I reckon...* Tears flowed down her cheeks. She started to sob, and Ann wailed. Blackie barked.

"I take it you've received a letter, William." Nan acted as if nothing were amiss.

"Course I have, and you know damn well what about. I can't believe you went behind my back—"

"*Janoo leshtal,* William," Grandad interrupted, arms crossed, face aflame.

William stopped. He removed his cap and yanked his damp hair straight up from his head. He lowered his head and took a step back.

"Oh, Da. Sorry, Mum. Please forgive me. By heck, I shouldn't have even stepped foot inside in me work clothes. Seems I do naught but apologize these days."

Ann pointed at his hair. "Funny Daddy," she said. William's crooked smile flashed for an instant.

"Yes, Daddy is silly, darling girl. Go on with supper, youse. Mum, speak with me outside, would you, please?"

Euphemia made to follow them. Nan wagged a finger.

"No, I must talk with William alone, *my chree*. Not in front of the children."

"That's not right, Nan. I'm entitled to know…"

"Doesn't enter into it. He's my son."

"Oh, leave off your arguing, the both of youse." William's tone hurt her ears. "Euphemia, I must speak with Mother alone." He strode through the kitchen and threw open the back door. It hit the wall.

Ann jumped and shrieked. Euphemia trembled with fear and rage. *How dare Nan shut me out? She told me her plan to contact Thomas, but what's she really cooked up? And William, not taking my part. That's not like him. He'd best apologize to me later or he'll get a piece of my mind.*

The boys took up their spoons and slurped while Ann sputtered. Fat tears rolled down her cheeks, and she incessantly banged her heels on the footrest. Grandad slammed the heavy door as he went out. Euphemia's head ached and her cut finger throbbed. She made to lift Ann and bumped against the tray.

"Ouch! Dammit, why is it that when you've hurt a finger, you always bang it? I need a plaster."

Ann reached for her hand and kissed it. "All better, Mama?"

"Oh, that helps, my darling. You're such a big girl. Mama must set you down here again. Eat your stew now, please, darling."

Euphemia wrapped her hand in a tea towel and collapsed into her chair. Henry fetched a plaster. Grandad came in, scowled over his bowl, pushed it away, and lit his pipe. When the back door swung open, everyone turned toward Nan, who crossed the threshold first.

"So, and how's my stew, then, eh? The butcher said he'd given me the best cut of lamb," Nan said, waving away the curiosity clouding the air along with Grandad's pipe tobacco smoke. Edward and Tom spoke at once and Tom raised his bowl.

"Delicious, Nan."

"Yummy. May I have another helping?"

William had done his ablutions, changed clothes, and brushed his hair. Euphemia swallowed her anger. *God, but he's pale. His eyes put me in mind of Blackie when she's been scolded. Nan's sorted him out and no mistake.*

She ladled stew for them both. The dregs went into Tom's bowl. She set the empty pot down and pointed to the bread.

"Sup on the gravy, Tom, for there isn't any more." Ever hungry, Tom reached for Ann's half-full bowl. She smacked his arm.

"Leave it be, greedy guts. She'll need it when she wakes up, poor baby." Ann slumped in her chair, thumb in her mouth. Henry lifted her out and kissed her head.

"I'll put her down, Mum." Euphemia thanked him with her eyes. *Good as gold is Henry.*

That evening, Grandad declared himself too tired to fiddle. Edward groaned. Nan just rocked and hummed on her own, while Euphemia unravelled her half-finished sweater; her nerves were as twisted as the wool. She made Henry hold out his hands to rewind the skein. She'd be more careful when she started over. Keep the tension relaxed and count the stitches. *I'll have to start knitting in the cowshed. I just might and all.*

After a brief smoke in the yard, William joined the boys on the braided rug. They all stared into the fire except for John, who lay on the floor drawing faeries in his exercise book as usual.

The strained silence soon made everyone dozy. The old folks turned in. William saw to the nighttime chores, stoking the fire, putting Jinxy out, and lowering the lamps. Euphemia hurried to the bedroom and wriggled between the icy sheets; even in spring, the night air chilled her to the bone. *I must find out if Nan has convinced Thomas to return.* She tasted sweet bile in her mouth. As if she were pregnant again. She prayed to calm her pounding heart: "Now I lay me down to sleep…" She prayed for everyone in the household, for her friend Jill, even for Blackie and Jinx. But not Thomas. *Don't you come back, you bastard.* She prayed that hardest of all.

William finally joined her after tucking Hugh in his cradle next to them and laying the iron tongs across to prevent the faeries from stealing the babe. Euphemia sighed. *Nan and her superstitions. How would faeries manage our chubby Hugh?* She almost giggled at the image of tiny wings beating nine times to the dozen, unable to lift off with the heavy bundle. *No harm in it, I reckon.*

William lay still, arms folded on his chest. *Puts me in mind of the statues on the tombs in York Minster.* Euphemia shuddered. Her teeth chattered. She rubbed her frozen feet against his bony ankles. *We need to talk. Seriously.*

He turned his head on the pillow and cleared his throat. "Well, Mum's performed a miracle of sorts. Thomas will sponsor us to come to America. He'll pay the steamship fare besides."

Euphemia jolted upright. *What? What's he on about?*

"He's always bragged, saying a man earns thrice the wages, provisions are thrice as cheap, and the climate in Michigan heals all ills. He exaggerates, I know, but maybe it's the answer to our situation, my love. Mum went behind my back knowing I'd balk, so she arranged it herself. Maybe it's good." He leaned up on an elbow, his blue eyes seeking her reaction under his heavy eyebrows. "Say something, please. Throw me a lifeline here."

Her throat constricted. Her tongue stuck to the roof of her parched mouth. *So, that's her plan. I figured she'd ask Thomas for money or to come back to help. Maybe both. But for us to move? She's gone daft. It's no good, no good at all.* She opened her mouth. William responded before she could speak.

"We'd live and work on his farm, just until we saved for a place of our own, ye ken. What's that look? You disagree?

Listen, what choice've we got? I don't want our boys down the mine. Do you?"

She shook her head, twisting the bedsheet in her icy fingers.

"Course you don't. Snaefell. It wears heavy on us. I sometimes wish Mum would let us forget. That's what drove Thomas away, partly. But I worked the mine all these years for my family's sake. Now, to top it off—" He struggled to sit up and took her hand, frozen like hers, but clammy. "I've suspected for some time, sweetheart. I've got the milk reek. Tremors. Sweats. Headaches. I vomit in the privy where you can't see. The weight of an anvil's on my chest."

He held her shoulders as she broke down. *Nan had said true. The faeries too, come to that. Now, with his admission, there's no more denying or pretending. Face facts. Face...* She pressed her lips together to stop from bawling.

"I daren't see the doctor, lest the manager find out and send me packing. But soon, soon, they'll catch on. Already, I can't work as fast so my wages are suffering. You've seen my pay packet. I can't earn enough for my family. Some of my mates are trying to help—" He pounded his fist under the blanket. "Now there's talk of Bradda closing, so the whole village will be out of work. Where'll that leave us, eh?" He brushed the outside of his index finger along her chin, smiling, though his eyes betrayed his suffering. She bit her lip hard. She mustn't scream.

"Mum reckons I will improve once I'm out the mine; Michigan's climate's supposedly so healthy that even American people with consumption move there. According to Thomas," he said, with a raspy laugh. "God, sounds like I'm quoting the Bible: 'The Word, according to Thomas.' That's a laugh. Hardly." He coughed, fighting to breathe. Euphemia poured a glass of water from the jug on the dresser. She needed time.

"Ach, but it'll break Mum's heart when we leave," William said, at last. "Mine too, I imagine. We're crammed into this cottage like sardines in a tin, but it's my home. The children are happy. Not to mention we must leave the village, all our friends… well, the school could be better, and everyone's always in each other's business—" She placed her hand on his lips. *I have to make him see sense.*

"But to emigrate, William? I did it once. You haven't a clue how hard it is. A new country, foreign ways, struggling to fit in… And I only crossed the Irish Sea, not the Atlantic, for pity's sake." She exhaled loudly and tugged her hair off her damp neck to twist it into a coif. She almost relished the pain of pulling her hair. She squeezed her nails into her palms.

"Yes, but you made a better life. At least, I hope you still think so." He gently took her face in his hands. His eyes shone grey in the moonlight, the lashes as long as a fawn's. His features reflected his character: high forehead, broad cheekbones, square chin, full lips. After all these years, his handsome face still took her breath away. Tears spilled from her eyes as she nodded.

"Aye. Well, that's a relief." He puffed out his cheeks. "I'm sorry for all this mess. Da worked the mine, too, and he never got sick. I'm just unlucky, I guess." His voice caught, and his Adam's apple bounced as he swallowed.

"It's not your fault, William. I could get my old job back in Douglas. Return on my days off. Nan could look after Hugh and Ann; Henry could work at the mine. He hates school, any road—"

"Are you listening to yourself?" William drew back. "Leave your children for Mum to raise? You wouldn't last a week. I've been wracking my brains too, but that's no solution. Thomas has made a generous offer—"

"Generous, to be sure. It's just that Thomas… Thomas and I—" Sweat trickled down her sides. *We can't go and live with Thomas. It's impossible… He'll find out, they'll both find out, and our lives will be ruined.* Tears burst from her eyes, draining her strength to fight.

"I know. You started as friends, parted as enemies. Go ahead. Cry, my love." He surrounded her shoulders and spoke into her hair. "He envied us, is all. Especially since he thought you belonged to him at the start. But I never got on with him, even before you came along." He coughed slightly again. "Yet I bless the day he brought you here. You coaxed Mum out of the darkness, after the twins… you know I love you for that. And for so much more besides." He began to kiss her neck and shoulders. She wriggled away. Making love might soothe him, but she couldn't. In a strange way, she denied his pleasure to punish him: for his weakness, his sickness, his inability to stand up to Nan. They were ruined already, though he didn't suspect.

Hugh stirred and whimpered in his cradle. *He wants feeding. Changing too, I shouldn't wonder. Good, that'll give me a chance to think of more arguments.* William patted her backside when she crawled across him. He kept talking as she lifted Hugh. He was soaking wet, as she'd thought.

"Shit!" she shrieked, pricking her sore finger with the diaper pin. "Goddamn it! Should've lit the lamp." *Maybe I should run away.* She sucked her stinging finger. *This is a nightmare. Please, please let me wake up.*

"Aye, he's a rare one. Hard work never suited him. Couldn't stand the mine; said it gave him nightmares. Lame excuse. That silver tongue of his made him a great salesman. He earned the means to leave Man right quick, didn't he? Mum exploded, remember? It irked her to turn to him now, I reckon. Proving him right, after all. I hope he isn't gloating." He paused, dragging in a ragged breath. "I do believe he means well." Hope lifted his voice.

"Means well? Ha!" Euphemia blew out her cheeks and rolled her eyes as she snuggled the baby against her breast. "You're sure? Seems mighty odd to me—"

"That's enough talk for tonight, love. Let's settle wee man and then sleep on it, shall we? We're both done up, and tomorrow's another day."

You can't fool me, William. We're going. I've no say in the matter.

Chapter Nine

Cha nee shen ny to shin seose, agh shen ny ta
shin cur seose ta jannoo shin berçhagh:
It is not what we take up, but what we give up,
that makes us rich.

RUBBING his cock between her legs until she could stand no more, Euphemia slid from underneath, shoved him down, and mounted his hips. Riding hard and fast, she cried out.

"Mama? Mama? There's a noise." Henry's small, pinched face appeared at the open door.

"Oh my God." Euphemia's whole body flushed, and liquid poured down her thighs. She leapt up, then hunched over to hide her nakedness. "It's alright, darling. Don't be afraid. Mama and Uncle were just… playing."

Thomas rolled over, swung his heavy legs across the bed, and stood up. "Here, I'll take him, Pheme." Henry's blue eyes widened.

"Listen, young man, when you're put to bed, you stay there," Thomas growled. He grabbed the three-year-old's tiny arm and steered him toward the door.

Henry's lower lip trembled. Euphemia shoved Thomas

aside.

"Leave him be. Get off with you." She crouched down and touched Henry's cheek. "Mama'll get you a biscuit, ducky. Wait right here; I'll just be a tick."

Thomas came up behind her and encircled her breasts. "Come to bed, Pheme. Go put him down and hurry back. There isn't much time. They'll be home soon."

Pushing against him, she threw him off balance. He landed on the floor.

"Damn it, Pheme. What's gotten into you? One minute, you're fucking me, and the next—"

"It's over, Thomas. For good. Don't ever touch me again. I've made a terrible mistake."

"Mistake? That's all I am to you?"

At his raised voice, Henry started to cry. Rushing toward him, she knocked over the bowl of vinegar beside the bed. *Wash, wash, you must wash.* Thomas shouted; Henry bawled… she slipped on the wet floor.

She jolted awake. A nightmare. A memory. She lay trembling and drenched in sweat next to William, snoring blissfully as a child. She heard the oven door bang. Nan was putting the kettle on and baking scones. *Reliable as that crowing rooster, she is. And just as annoying, with her meddling. She's no idea what trouble she's caused. I've half a mind to tell her so. But then she'd know the truth. I wonder if she knows. Those sideways looks, odd remarks… Maybe the faeries told her; wouldn't put it past the buggers. She'll bloody well know I'm angry, any road.* She sat up and combed her damp hair with icy fingers. *I'll never forgive her. Never. I'm ruined.*

After mulling it over for several days, enduring Nan's sheepish looks across the brooding silence, Euphemia made a decision: she'd write Thomas and set him straight. She begged off attending church on Sunday, faking a headache. Setting her jaw, she put pen to paper.

June 24, 1904

Dear Thomas,

I trust you are well. William received your letter offering us passage and sponsoring all eight of us. I must say, this is most unexpected. I understand your mother proposed the idea—

A pool of ink soiled the page when she set the pen down. *Dammit.* Resting her elbows on the table, she pinched the bridge of her nose. What could she say? "No, Thomas, I shan't take up your offer for the sake of my children, who may end up orphaned, or my husband, who'll surely die if nothing changes. We'll stay here, thank you very much, and cross that bridge when we come to it."

Really? Despair strangled her. Tears splashed into the dark lake, leaving splotches of white on the page. Crumpling the paper, she let her head fall on her crossed arms. She howled. Blackie joined in. *Poor girl, I've frightened her.* She hadn't been able to cry, really cry, on her own. Baby Hugh slept blissfully in his cradle while she paced and cursed and sobbed until she collapsed in the rocker, wiping snot on her sleeve. She reached for Jinx, who struggled to free himself, then finally settled. She'd become so attached to the little beast with his white mittens, round, comical face, and stub of a tail. Jinx purred and she rocked. She rocked and he purred, kneading her thighs like bread. The tingly sensation reminded her… She stood up, setting him down, and returned to her chair. Reaching for a clean sheet of paper, she admonished herself for the mess and the waste of paper. *Set the ink on your left side this time, idiot, as Sister Michael taught, so's there'll be no smudges, smears, or spills. Clear. Clear as mud.*

We are grateful for your offer, Thomas. I am certain we can be of help on your farm until we get a place of our own, that is. Our boys are strong, well-behaved, and obedient. I know you wouldn't want us to end up destitute. It's a miracle that you can afford us this opportunity…

Two neat pages were soon filled with descriptions of each of the children and her hopes for their future in America. She signed off, *Yours truly, Pheme.*

Pheme. Thomas' goddamn nickname. *William always says Euphemia. After almost fifteen years and only one slip, have I lived up to my namesake's virtue and goodness as Sister Michael hoped? The lions took pity on Saint Euphemia, merely licking her wounds. Wish someone would lick mine.* She twisted her lips. *You're no saint, Pheme. Thomas proved that ten years ago. You're guilty as sin.*

Chapter Ten

Carrey liorts ny share na braar foddey jeh:
A friend by you is better than a brother far off.

WILLIAM murmured, stirred, and rolled over. His brow creased as he sat up. "You look as if you've not slept a wink, my love. Whereas I'm sleeping better than I have in months. I see a way ahead, a future for us." He stretched his arms. "Is your headache still troubling you? Stay abed. I'll give Hugh to Nan. I'd best be off—"

Euphemia shook her head and grabbed his arm, determined to make him listen. "Ask yourself, William, why would Thomas take us in? There's no love lost between youse. As to me, how ever will I manage the journey, let alone, once we get there? I've never been on me own with the children—" Her voice broke. *What kind of mother am I without Nan? I can't picture myself looking after them all on me own.*

Her thoughts whirled like a spinning wheel. *Nan's right, there's no choice; I'll send the letter. There's got to be another way. I'll tear it up. We'll move, all of us, to Douglas. I'll work; Henry and William will get jobs...*

William reached for her flailing arms and fixed her with his blue eyes. She could barely focus, through her tears. "It's a huge commitment on his part, I agree. He's posted a bond. Didn't say what it cost. I'll find a way to pay him back. He swears Michigan's climate will cure me. Mum recognized the milk reek before I did. She told him. We're lucky—"

"Yes, how lucky we are." The word "lucky" stuck to the roof of her mouth. William brought her head to his chest.

"We must think of the lads, first and foremost, Euphemia," he said into her hair. "They'll never go down the mine; that's why Mum's so insistent, ye ken. I'd never have asked Thomas for help and she knows it, but now it's done, well, personal feelings aside, it's a chance I have to take. For the children's sake, and yours. I could—"

She reached up and touched her fingers to his lips. On impulse, she sat up and straddled him. William sat up, shaking his head. She shucked up her nightdress and rested her knees against his sides. *God, he's thin. How could I have been so blind?* She grasped his shoulder with one hand and led him in with the other. Aching with anxiety, she sought release for them both.

"But it's morning, my love. Time to—"

"Hush. You'll wake the baby."

* * *

During the morning routine, Euphemia sang brightly, going so far as to wrap her arms around William's neck and plant a deep kiss on his lips before he set off. She laughed at his blush. Grandad winked in their direction. Edward made the naughty sign, rubbing his two index fingers together.

"Euphemia! The children," William said, swaying when she let him loose.

"Oh, fiddlesticks!" She tapped his arm, handing over his lunch bucket. Nan agreed, saying the youngsters ought to see their parents in love. *Yes, in love. As ever.* She could taste William in her mouth. She still breathed his scent, smiling at the sudden notion that they'd conceived a child. A burst of joy preceded a finger of fear tracing her spine. *God forbid. That's all we'd need. Best take a bucket of vinegar to the privy, though that's no sure method, dammit.*

All day, she distracted herself with housework, dreading suppertime. William planned to announce their move. *How will the children react? Does Grandad already know? Course he does. He's so quiet today; I miss his whistling. Henry'll take it the hardest. Stop, just stop. There's nothing you can do about it.* Her head whirled so, she thought she'd be sick. *William's made up his mind, and he's your husband. "Love, honour, and obey." I wish I'd known what those vows meant when I made them.* She held the baby close against her breast. *Does any bride really understand? I sure didn't. To leave Nan, Grandad, Jill, go traipsing off to America and God knows what. No, that's a lie; I know what. Thomas.*

That afternoon, for the first time ever, she walked out with Ann to greet the boys on their way home from school. The atmosphere in the cottage was stifling. Grandad sat playing sad tunes on his violin instead of working. She and Nan barely exchanged two words all day. When Ann went for her nap after lunch, Nan had a lie-down. *Worrisome. Like after the twins died. She's going back into herself. How ever will she and Grandad cope?* Then Ann distracted her, pointing down the lane.

"Yes, here they come, sweetie," Euphemia said. "No wonder it takes them so long to get home, lallygagging about, the rascals." Ann opened her mouth, but Euphemia swept her up, touching their foreheads together, putting a finger to her lips. "Shh, let's surprise them, eh?"

Ann nodded and giggled. They scurried behind a bush next to the stone fence. *There's our John collecting wildflowers. Away among the faeries, as Nan says, off in his own dream world. Hark at Edward and Tom, sparring as usual.* The two were trading punches as they walked side by side, which soon turned into rough-and-tumble on the gravel. Though a year older, Edward was no match for Tom who outweighed him. Caps askew, the boys wrestled until Henry shouted.

"C'mon lads, best get our chores done before Da gets home or there'll be hell to pay. Move your arses! John, let's go." *He rounds them up like Blackie herding sheep. Ah, here comes Henry's best friend. Don't give us away, Blackie, there's a good dog.*

"Ahem. Too right," Euphemia shouted as she leapt into the path. Ann chortled with delight. Henry jumped, exhaling the word "Mum." She laughed at their surprised expressions. *What fun!*

"Ha, ha, fooled you." Ann slid from Euphemia's grasp to skip around the boys.

Henry whirled her in his arms. John rushed over, tugged at Euphemia's skirt, and held out his flowers. "For you, Mother," he said, his brown eyes shining.

"Ta, my sweetheart. But you oughtn't pull them out by the roots. The whole plant will die." His generous expression became solemn. She patted his cheek. "Not to worry. You didn't know, duckie. Let's get them into water, eh?"

She couldn't shatter the moment. *They'll know, soon enough.* "Off youse go, lads. Nanny'll have the bonnag ready."

The three youngsters flew off, Ann toddling behind. Blackie shadowed Henry, and she took Henry's arm, cheerily asking about school. He shrugged and sent her a curious glance as if to say, "Why are you here? What's wrong?"

"Ah, 'tis nice to come along and meet youse. I should do it more often," she said. "What a pretty lane. I love the stone fences, don't you? They're like the frame on a picture." She ran a hand along the rough ledge. "All covered in moss and lichen, they must be ancient. I wonder who stacked them so carefully, eh? Hard graft, and no mistake."

She kept chattering all the way to the red door, pretending. Edward and Tom were seated at the table, wearing their milk moustaches, stuffing their faces with warm soda bread. Nan leaned down to put a shepherd's pie in the oven. John presented his flowers.

"You are the sweetest, John," Nan said. "What have we here, so early in the season? Tiny yellow ones, celandine: *lus-ny-pileyn*, and lookee here, some blue faery thimbles: *mairanyu ferisk*. The bees collect their nectar for honey. We all love that, don't we?" She fetched a jug from the dresser and turned to Henry.

"Cut some gorse on your way back, *my chree*. I'm afraid you're on your own tonight to visit the *Little Ones*. I'm making bread. I need gorse to heat the oven; mind your fingers on the thorns." She handed him the basket and a pair of secateurs. "Oh, and fetch turves for the fire before you go. Grandad's stacked the peat today. He's done up."

"I'll go along, Nan." Euphemia jumped at the chance. "Just let me feed Hugh, please Henry." She'd made up her mind. As the oldest, Henry deserved to know, ahead of time. Otherwise, he'd be so hurt, he might never forgive them.

Henry's long legs ate up the path; he awaited Euphemia at the top of the hill. Breathless at the exertion, she leaned down to pet Blackie. She straightened, putting a hand to the small of her back, and admired the view. A Viking horde glittered golden on the choppy waves. Sweet gorse painted the hillsides bright yellow. Henry bent to cut some thorny branches, gingerly placing them in the basket. Skylarks whirled and dipped high above while gulls shrieked like banshees across the inlet. Euphemia inhaled deeply, taking it all in. *How will we leave here? It's home.* She shut her eyes and teetered, losing her balance. Henry's hand steadied her.

"I'm not much for heights, me. Never should've closed my eyes."

"You all right now, Mum? We'd best hurry. *Themselves* know if we're late. Besides, my stomach's growling. My mouth's watering for warm bread and shepherd's pie. Come."

She inhaled and leaned forward, her leg muscles screaming at every step. *My, for a woman of thirty-three, I'm not very fit. You'd think with all the housework I do... but I reckon there's no substitute for walking, especially uphill.*

"Whew, I'm tuckered," she said.

"*Moghrey Mie, Mooinjer Veggey,*" Henry intoned when they reached the small knoll which Nan said marked the entrance to the faeries' dwelling. The green smell of damp grass met their nostrils as they knelt to make the offering. Henry removed his cap, and the brisk wind ruffled his thick hair. *His hair's as black as Jinxy's fur coat. No wonder I fell in love with that kitten, the runt of the litter. Henry's Manx is very good, at least to my ears. Thanks to Nan and Grandad. I hope he doesn't lose it. Does anyone speak Manx in America?*

"What do you say to them, Henry? D'you reckon they hear? Nan and Grandad believe, but I—"

"Oh yes, Mum." Henry leaned on his haunches. "Can't you feel the rumblings below our feet? We're rousing the wee ones for their evening romp on the hillsides."

He gestured with both arms, and she realized the sleeves of his jacket were too short for him. *Oh dear, hark at his bare legs sticking out of his trousers. He needs new clothes. Are the other boys in the same state? How could I have missed that? They grow too fast. Trust Henry not to complain.*

"Here, take my faery bracelet. For luck. I can easily make another. I gather the thread on the hedgerows. Nan says it's a gift when you find it. Rare." He extended his arm for her to untie the twisted white thread. His eyes smiled into hers, and he winked. "You might think it's wool, Mum, but no, t'isn't. Feel. Different texture." He tied it on her wrist and patted her arm. "I love to think of the *Red Caps*, weaving tiny garments in the moonlight—"

"Henry, I've something to tell you." Henry frowned and cocked his head. Euphemia cleared her throat. "Please, don't say a word 'til I've finished."

He didn't say a word. Hands clasped around his knees, tears spurted from his eyes, and he began to sob as the news sank in. He dropped his head, sputtering. When she tried to encircle his shoulders, he twisted away.

"I'm not going," he said. "I'll stay behind. How will Grandad and Nan fare without us? Grandad plans on teaching me to farm, become a champion shearer, butcher the pigs. Soon's I'm outta school. I'll quit. I've had enough of book learning, me. I want to work for wages." He took a deep breath, and the tone of his voice deepened. "Besides, to live with Thomas. I don't like him."

Oh, God. Never. He can't possibly…

"Wh—what? You must barely remember him. You were three—" Euphemia's words caught in her throat. She craved the whiskey Henry had given the faeries. *Maybe I should steal from them, for a change.*

"I don't know, Mum, but the very mention of his name gives me chills. I never listen when Nan reads his letters aloud. I leave the room. He's so full of himself, bragging about America and all." He tucked the cloth in the basket and winced, pulling his hand back. A gorse thorn pricked his finger. "Ouch, dammit! Oops, sorry, Mum," he said. He smeared blood on the grass and pushed himself up. "I'm not going. That's that."

"Alright, alright, calm yourself. We'll talk it over with your father. I didn't want you taken unawares," she said, forcing a smile. "Let's leave the faeries to their doings, and we'll get on with ours, eh?" Her bright tone rang false, she knew. She had to speak above the roar of waves in her head. "I'll take the basket. You run along, stop outside, and wash your face. Don't let on, please. Da will be furious."

She stumbled along as Henry and Blackie disappeared around the bend. The sun tossed its copper cloak on the hills behind her back. Clouds of evening mist and peat smoke drifted above the horizon as the white cottage came into view. She could hear birds fussing in the hedges, tucking their babies in with bedtime stories and evening snacks. Baby Hugh would be anxious for his nighttime feed. Still, she could hardly force her feet to move toward the inevitable. *If only a Red Cap would appear. I'd ask for a wish. Maybe three. If only.*

Chapter Eleven

Ta fuill: Blood.

HENRY'S eyes fixed on Da, unblinking. *I'll not let on that I know, as Mum wished. Good of her to warn me. Treated me like a man, she did.*

"What's 'emigrate' mean, Da?" Edward frowned. The boys sat cross-legged on the rug, leaning in. Da claimed Grandad's usual chair by the hearth, whilst Nan, Mum, and Grandad gathered round. The boys exchanged quizzical looks. Henry held his breath as Da said they were going to live with Uncle Thomas in America. Edward, Tom, and John sat open-mouthed. Their faces drained of colour, and their eyes stood out like marbles on the sand.

Henry waited for Da to finish, then raised his hand like at school. "Nan and Grandad, they'll come too, yes?"

Nan's pained expression answered. She lowered her trembling chin and kissed the top of Ann's blonde head. Ann sucked her thumb, brows knit, eyes roving from one person to the next. *She has no idea what's going on. Then again, neither do I.*

"No, Son, they can't right now. Maybe in the future." Da looked down at his hands. His eyes flickered in the firelight.

"Besides, who would look after Blackie and the sheep?" Grandad said. He struck a match and lifted his pipe, but his hand shook too much to light it. Everyone stared until the match burned down, and Grandad blew it out, lowering the pipe to his lap.

"The piggies need feeding, right, Grandad?" Ann pronounced, before popping her thumb back in her mouth.

Nan's slight laugh became a sob, smothered in Ann's hair. Henry uncrossed his legs and stood, keeping his eyes lowered as if to find his way across the room. He scrambled up the ladder to the loft and threw himself on the bed. The clatter of dishes and a soft fiddle tune eventually made him drift off. It seemed only moments later that a warm hand on his cheek brought him back to awareness of his pounding head on the soggy pillow. Darkness swallowed the light of the full moon shining in the window. Despite the quilt draped over him, Henry shivered.

"Henry, *ban my chree*, you mustn't take on so." Nan smoothed his hair and rubbed his shoulders. He stayed still, where once he'd have reached for her embrace. "There's naught for it. Your father's ill, you see, and growing weaker. He didn't say, but soon he mightn't be able to work and the mine's likely to close—" Henry opened his eyes and took Nan's wrinkled hands, squeezing them against his chest.

"I won't go," he said. "I'll stay right here with you and Grandad. You'll never manage without me."

Nan shook her head. "No, Henry. You must go. Never mind, love, the faeries will see us right. You and I, we'll ask the *Little Ones* to bless your journey." She paused. "Just think; a trip across the ocean aboard a steamship, then adventures of all sorts with Uncle Thomas in America. A whole new world." Henry opened his mouth to argue, but she moved her hands to cup his cheeks, then placed a finger gently on his lips. Reaching for the covers, she tucked him in like old times. "*Foddym gra gyn danjeyr dy bee dy chooilley nhee dy mie, my chree.* Now, go to sleep for real. Things will work out."

Not for you and Grandad, they won't. Not unless I stay behind. Henry ground his teeth until his jaw ached. When Edward joined him, anxious to talk about the news, he feigned sleep. What was there to say?

* * *

Following the announcement, Henry took refuge in the hills and cowshed whenever he could. As winter dragged on, he came to hate crossing the threshold of the red door. Peace in the house had shattered like Nan's jug. Henry could almost hear the porcelain crashing on the slate as he was about to lift the iron latch one afternoon. *Everything broke that day.* He turned to sit on the bench, pet Blackie, look at the hills, breathe in the sea air, enjoy the warmth of the sun… Anything to avoid going inside.

"Time enough," Nan and Grandad always said when anyone fussed: "*Traa dy liooar:* 'Tis not the time, but the work that counts. Each task is its own reward. Everything will get done in good time. All is well." No one depended on the clock, which Grandad usually forgot to wind; their bodies were synchronized to daily routines, from morning 'til night. Henry sighed. *Now Mum drifts around like a ghost, not humming, just muttering. And Da's temper—Jesus. At suppertime, he pounces like Jinx on a mouse at the slightest thing: Tom slurped, Edward laughed, Ann whined, or I didn't see to the fire. Christ.*

He spares John, at least. But what about the rest of us? It pains to see Ann squirming in her highchair, whispering to her dolly—she's not used to raised voices. We must walk on eggshells around Da, Nan says. It isn't fair. Then again, she gets on my nerves too, with her fussing: touching the boys' hair, pinching their cheeks, speaking only in Manx. I can't even tell her how I feel. She shushes me on our walks up Faery Hill, and I can't hear the flutes on the wind anymore. It's so lonely.

"Run away, hole up until they've gone. Find a place to hide." *Hey, who was speaking?* He tipped his head back against the whitewashed wall and pressed his palms into his temples to silence the voice in his head.

The evenings around the *chiollagh* offered little comfort. Grandad constantly interrupted himself to blow his nose, unable to finish the songs he'd known all his life. Sometimes Nan would fill in, but mostly she just hummed, rocked, and cuddled Ann, while Mum's knitting needles shot sparks. The adults declared earlier and earlier bedtimes as winter set in. Henry had plenty of rest, but not much sleep.

One February night during a coughing fit, Da halted Grandad's fiddle. "Please. No more. I can't stand it. It's bad enough—"

"Sorry, sorry, my son." Grandad jumped at his words, and the bow screeched on the strings. "Yes, off to bed with youse now, lads," he said, setting the violin beside his chair.

How ever will we get to sleep now, without music? Everything's ruined. For once, he rushed to follow Edward up to the loft. After hastening into their nightshirts, they leapt into bed. Cold, damp sheets were clammy hands grasping at their limbs. Nan hadn't yet slipped the warm flatirons into the beds. They shuffled their legs to generate heat until Edward deliberately kicked close to Henry's groin. Snarling, Henry turned his back and yanked at the covers. After a tugging match, they silently called a truce, and Edward fell instantly asleep. Edward seemed oblivious to their situation. All he could do was talk about the adventure of travelling on a ship. *But then, he is only nine. And he's an idiot.*

Henry sank into the feather tick, pressing his hands between his knees. "America." He puffed the word out loud. It hung in the air like mist.

He tried to imagine living in a forest. Grandad said *Ellan Vannin's* hillsides were once covered in giant oaks before the Vikings razed the forests to build longboats, long ago. The occasional survivor now stood alone, venerated as a faery tree, never to be felled on pain of bad fortune. In his letters, Uncle

Thomas described deep snow blanketing the trees all winter. Henry shuddered. *It's cold enough here in winter, and we've no ice or snow. And they fish from a lake, not the sea, in winter and summer both, he says. Do you stand on the shore or go out in a boat, I wonder? I hate boats. I'd rather be a miner than a fisherman, any day. Are the fish sweet like ours though?*

Uncle Thomas said no one went hungry in Michigan; there was plenty to eat year-round. This appealed to the boys' incessant craving for food; there was never more than one helping at any meal. Henry's stomach banged like a hollow drum by bedtime. Hunger pangs were worse than his growing pains. The only cure was sleep, which eluded him these days.

Maybe life is better there. Could it be? Henry flipped over and tucked his hands under his pillow. He flopped like a fish on a line, unable to get comfortable. *But it's not home. An ocean will separate us from Nan and Grandad. They'll die here, alone.* He thought of all the days he'd spent roaming the fields, tending his dear little Loughtans and their sweet lambs with Grandad and Blackie, the island's best sheepdog, proven by her awards. How could he leave the white cottage with its cheery door and warm *chiollagh*? He'd even miss his mates at school, though he preferred being on his own on the hillsides. Gathering faery thread. Feeling the magic all around him, hearing songs on the wind. His eyes tingled and his stomach rumbled. A sweetness in his mouth forced him to sit up and swallow. He longed for a glass of milk or water; it was too cold to go downstairs.

What if Dad dies on the journey? Or before? He's so grey with dark rings around his eyes, and his constant coughing—he's more tired and cantankerous than ever. He fell back, turned his face into the feather pillow, stifling a sob. Edward stirred and flung out his arm. Henry tucked the blankets over them both. Curling into a ball, he decided to imagine the faeries cavorting on Cronk Howe Mooar, not a care in the world. He'd beg them to arrange for him to stay behind. *An extra drop of whiskey or a bigger piece of cake, that should do the trick.* Suddenly, he saw himself in the cottage with only Grandad and Nan for company, seated at a table with five empty plates, a silent highchair, no crib. *If there were only us three, would we ever laugh or sing again? The other side of the coin. What would the future hold, then?*

* * *

One rainy April afternoon, the cottage door flew open, and Da pushed his way in with an armload of fabric bags. Gasping for breath, he leaned over and dropped them on the floor, then slapped an envelope on the table where the boys sat practicing sums. Mum insisted they keep up their studies when lambing made them miss school. Da's arrival gave them an excuse to set their pencils down.

"Here we go, Carine Family: passage for seven to Boston aboard *S.S. Ivernia*, the newest, fastest ship in the Cunard fleet. Departs Liverpool, July 19th. Cost me a day's wages to collect the tickets in Douglas, but we're sorted. We leave just shy of three months." He shook his whole body like a wet dog. "Ach, I'm soaked to the skin, me. A cup of tea would do nicely, ladies, if you please."

Edward and Tom shouted and danced around the kitchen as Nan put the kettle on; John excused himself and joined Blackie on the rug by the hearth. Henry swallowed hard and stayed put, arms crossed over his chest.

Mum's face fell. "Seven, you say? But we're eight! There must be some mistake," she said, bouncing Hugh vigorously against her hip. He hiccupped, burped, and spurted milk on her shoulder and in her loose hair. "Oh, dammit." Nan handed her a tea towel and continued taking cups from the dresser.

"No, all is well, darling. *Foddym gra gyn danjeyr dy bee dy choo-illey nhee dy mie.* Wee man is free. Makes sense. Not so for the rest." Turning to hang his dripping hat and coat on the stand, he mumbled, "Those tickets cost many a pound. I'd never have done it on me own."

Mum nodded but her look remained puzzled. "Oh, right then, but what do you mean by three months? I count four."

"Aye, but we must be in Liverpool ten days ahead, according to the ticket master, for inspections and to buy supplies. Glad I went into the office, or I mightn't have known." He planted a kiss on her cheek and tickled Hugh's chin. Then he pointed at the bags. "Lookee here, aren't they fine? From the best luggage shop in Douglas; a brand-new carpet bag each, even for Hughie. Packing begins in earnest, now, my love."

"What d'you think I've been doing these past months, you silly bugger?" Mum said. "But you never expect me to fit everything in a carpet bag, for heaven's sake! I want my crockery, my wedding dress—it's not as if I can come back to fetch them!" She burst into tears. Grandad reached for the baby, who'd begun to howl. Da shook his head.

"Only the essentials, Euphemia, and we're hard-pressed at that," he said. "They charge for luggage by the pound, I learned. Please, don't make it worse." He closed his eyes and pinched the bridge of his nose. The wedding dress landed at his feet. He looked at it and coughed, leaning on the table for support.

At the sight of Mum's face, Henry snatched up a bag. "It'll fit in mine, Mum." Then, squeezing his hands at his sides to steady his voice, he said, "Seven tickets is right. I'm not going."

Da's eyes widened, and his face flamed. Henry held his breath. His heart pounded and his mouth was parched. *What can he say? He can't make me go. I'm a man now. I'll work in the mine by day and help Grandad keep the farm going.*

Nan crossed the room to retrieve the mounds of white fabric on the floor. "We'll store it in the trunk, *my chree*, wrapped in tissue and dried vervain to keep the faery lasses away. Wouldn't they just love to steal it?" Folding the dress in her arms, she smoothed it. "Just so. You're thinking of our Ann, someday?"

Mum bit her lip and knelt beside the trunk. She reached in and fished out a ball, heavily wrapped in newspaper. Cradling it in her arms, she headed for the bedroom, shoulders trembling.

Da signalled the boys to help him. Henry arranged the tissue paper atop the dress before latching the trunk full of household goods: china cups, cooking implements, the rooster and hen salt and pepper shakers Mum treasured, a wedding gift from the Sugarland. Things she couldn't be without, she'd said. Henry recalled her smile and light, happy tone as she'd lovingly packed each item. She'd almost sounded excited. The boys shoved the wooden case across the floor to the threshold, then together they hefted it onto a cart for storage in the cowshed. As they walked back, Da yanked Henry by the arm.

"We are not breaking up this family, Henry." He fairly growled. "You are coming with us. No arguments."

I won't, Da. Argue, that is, Henry answered silently.

Supper consisted of cold bully beef and biscuits. Mum kept to her room, so Nan took Hugh to her for nursing, then returned to sip her tea and feed Ann from her own plate.

"You crying, Nanny? No. Don't. Don't cry," Ann said. Nan shook her head, but the tears spilled on her apron front.

Later, walking up Faery Hill, Nan spoke against herself. "Stupid, stupid woman. I must be strong. It's my doing, after all. And for the best."

Other matters pressed on Henry's mind. "Please, please let me stay, Nan. Don't make me go. I'm almost a man, so."

"Cry for the moon, Henry; it canna be. Your mother needs you more than we do." Nan's tight grip on his arm contradicted her words.

She wants me to stay, as much as I do. I'll speak to Grandad. Yes, that's the rock I have to shift. He'll tell Da what's what.

"Be brave and help her as best you can until your father recovers," said Nan. "You're the oldest; it's up to you to set an example and guide the youngsters. Uncle Thomas, well, he's not used to children, at all, at all. Still, he's promised to set all of youse on a fresh path in America. I'll hold him to it. *Ta fuill ny s'chee na ushtey:* blood is thicker than water."

Blood? Who said anything about blood?

"Funny, I see family resemblances in each of youse, now you're growing up," Nan said. "Blood really does will out. Our Tom's named for Uncle Thomas, but he's nothing like him. Instead, he's like my father: strong as an ox, built like a bull, and just as hard-headed. Edward, why, he takes after Thomas, with his quick mind and mischief, whilst John's the spitting image of his father, but for his lovely eyes and hair from his mother. He's William, through and through—quiet, sensitive, kind. Ah, was, was. That he..." Her words drifted away like dandelion seeds floating on the breeze.

The notion that people took after others intrigued Henry. "Really, Nan? This is the first I've heard of it. Even the baby? Can you tell me who he's like? Our Ann, too?"

"Ann? Why, she's a clever, bright spark like me," she said, laughing. Henry tried to imagine Nan as a three-year-old. Impossible. "I ken that look, Master Carine." Nan raised her eyebrows. "Yes, believe it or not, I was a pretty lass, once. Our Hugh? Too young to tell. Let's hope he becomes a musician like Grandad, his namesake, eh? He already seems to love music. He looks so comical, bless him, rocking on his knees in his diaper."

"And me, Nan? Who am I like?"

Will it be Da, Grandad, or someone else, already passed on? How does it happen? In the blood? Nan continued walking. They reached the base of Faery Hill before she answered.

"Truth be told, I can't rightly say. You put me in mind of the twins, Mel and Ralph, betimes. Like them, you see what needs doing and you work with a heart and a half. They shared a heart between them like they shared everything else. You've their love of animals, too." Her tone warmed whenever she spoke of her twin sons. "In looks, why, you're the spitting image of William at this age. You'll break some girl's heart one day, I reckon." She squeezed his hand. "Ha, made you blush."

"Ach, you're a tease, Nan, worse than Edward. Go on with you."

"I'm serious. I wish I'd said it before." Setting the basket down, she gathered her skirts and lowered herself to the ground. Her clear blue eyes looked at Henry under her dark lashes. *Ah, yes, I see how lovely she was. Now she's just… Nan.*

"I see some of my Grandad in you, too. Your great-grandfather, Henry Bell. He possessed deep knowledge of the old ways and the *Little People*. I'd need time to teach you—" Her voice thickened with unshed tears.

"The Bells, the Carines, we go back generations by the many headstones at Kirk Christ Rushen. I certainly don't ken them all." She yanked a tuft of grass and tossed it in the air, then brushed her hands together. Henry began unpacking the basket, setting out the cups, dispensing the whiskey.

"Then again, you've traces of your mother, our dear Euphemia: practical, strong, short-tempered betimes, eh?" She patted his arm. Her eyes sparkled. "Perhaps you're just yourself, *my chree*. A good lad. Good as gold, as your dear mother says. Almost a man, so."

Chapter Twelve

*Ny cappanyn sharroo va shin streeu dy scughey ersooyl
voin ta, cummal yn medshin smoo to shin feme jeh:*
The bitter cup we strive to remove
holds the medicine we need most.

A few weeks after the trunk incident, Henry learned more about Nan's real feelings about their move. Stacking dried peat in the lean-to by the open kitchen window, he overheard her chatting with Mum's best friend, Jill, who'd come for a farewell tea. The other boys were at school; Henry had quit. Released from the musty funk of the schoolroom, he revelled in the fresh, salty air and dove into farm chores full-time. Having turned thirteen, he considered his freedom long overdue. Most village lads stopped school at eleven and headed for the mine. Although thankful his mother had prevented that, he remained anxious to start at Bradda once the family left. *No matter what Nan says, mining's in my blood.*

Henry stood on tiptoes and peeked in to gaze at Jill: blonde hair, deep blue eyes, shapely figure… Henry got a tingly feeling at the mere sight of her. He never managed more than a raspy hello, embarrassed now that he'd lost control of his voice.

Perhaps it's wrong to spy. I hope they haven't eaten all the scones. He hoped they wouldn't hear his stomach growling as he leaned on the windowsill. Jill was clearing the table, her hair a cascade of curls bouncing on her shoulders, loose as she wasn't married. He pursed his lips, imagining kissing her. He'd have to practise first… With effort, he tuned in to Nan's words.

"I never imagined us alone in our old age, you see. With five sons, why would I? But first Arthur caught the diphtheria at five; he's on Cronk Howe Mooar with the faeries. Then our Ralph and Mel. Twins. A strapping pair, ready with a laugh and a helping hand, always working together. Died together, too, they did, in the Snaefell fire, buried under the mountain—" Mum rubbed Nan's shoulders and murmured softly. Jill poured water for the dishes.

"Ach, my heart broke in twain. Couldn't get out of bed. The thought of them burned alive… the men could hear them screaming but the smoke blocked their passage—" Nan paused. This oft-repeated story never failed to move Henry to tears.

"'Twas before youse came, Jill, though I'm sure you've heard tell of it. The only blessing from that: Thomas brought Euphemia in to help me," she said, smiling at Mum.

Mum nodded as she whipped a tea towel from the rack. "I shook with fear, Nan, thinking you'd never accept an English girl, let alone an orphan, even as a housemaid. You've always been so kind, the mother I never had. How would I have known how to rear a child without you, let alone manage a household?"

A rush of sadness knocked Henry backward. *Poor Mum. What it would be like, never knowing your parents? No Mum, no Da, no brothers or sisters. Well, I could do without one brother, me, but still—*

Jill handed Mum a plate to dry. "Nan taught me how to knit, sew, even thread a needle—"

"Thread a needle?" Jill seemed shocked. "You didn't even know how to thread a needle?"

"Not the way Nan does it. You must pinch the thread between your thumb and forefinger; you'll never miss the eye. Right, Nan?"

"I'll try it. Makes me cross-eyed," she said, mimicking the gesture. Nan and Mum laughed. Henry wished he could join in. *Jill's such fun to be around. So much more relaxed than Mum.*

"What astounds me is how you two work together so well," Jill said. "My mother and I are like two cats in a bag in the kitchen."

"We've each our separate duties. I contribute my laundering skills from St. Hilda's. We earned our keep, learned to mind our manners and respect our elders. I know my place."

Nan's eyes widened. Mum's face reddened. "Oh Nan, I only meant, I didn't mean—it's your kitchen, always has been, always will be," she said. "You and me, we're a well-oiled machine after so many years. Wouldn't have it any other way…" She lowered her head and began stacking the clean dishes.

"Don't fash yerself, *my chree*. Can't have been easy for you, stuck here with me bossing." She laughed. "My mother and I fought too, Jill. A struggle for independence is natural." Now Nan turned to rub Mum's shoulder. "You'll soon have your own kitchen, Euphemia, and you'll manage just fine."

Mum's head shot up. "Oh, but I'm that worried, Nan. At St. Hilda's, the rooming house, the Sugarland, here, there's always been women to guide me—"

Nan talked right over her. "Your wedding day's one of my brightest. A daughter, at last. Weren't you just the loveliest of brides in the dress we made, and William, so handsome in his suit? Ah, was, was," she said, exhaling a deep sigh.

"Shame we don't see him dressed up more often, instead of covered in filth from the mine or in his work clothes." She frowned. "He's still handsome, though nearly forty. He might come to Kirk Christ Rushen once in a while, too. It's so peaceful there, it'd do him a power of good. Heal his troubled mind."

She went to sit at the table and smoothed the scratches in

the polished wood. "I love sitting in the churchyard, surrounded by the ancestors' gravestones, so weather-worn they can hardly be read. Our people. Time stands still—"

Mum cleared her throat. "He needs his rest, Nan. Sunday's his day to lie in."

Henry nodded in silent agreement. *Poor Da. So tired.*

"I know, lass. Well, he soon won't have his mother nagging him about it." She shook her head as if coming awake. "What was I telling you, Jill? Oh yes. Well, we thought William and Thomas would keep things going. Then out of nowhere, Thomas takes a notion to leave. For America. Mighty risky, says I. No worse than the mine, says he. He couldn't bear working underground, he claimed. Truth be told, the cottage seemed too small, what with him and William at each other's throats after your marriage, eh, Euphemia? A rose between two thorns."

Henry almost gasped as a plate slipped from Mum's hand. She just nabbed it. *Nicely done, Mum. My stomach drops just like that at the name "Thomas."*

"You never said, Euphemia, how you came to Man, so far from Yorkshire…" Jill's query blew lightly into the air, a soap bubble rising from the basin. *Would Mum answer? I'm dying to know.*

"I've tried to forget the past, is all, Jill. Growing up in an orphanage is no picnic, you can imagine, though the Sisters were mostly kind. In fact, at one time I thought I'd become a nun." She paused, setting the plate carefully on the dresser. Then she laughed. "Silly, I know." Jill and Nan joined in.

"I, for one, am glad you didn't," said Nan as she straightened the vase of wildflowers on the table.

"Me too, now. But I couldn't imagine life outside the Home. My favourite teacher, Sister Michael, questioned my calling. Rightly so. She counselled and helped me. I took a barge from Bradford Canal all the way to Liverpool for a job—"

"Goodness, how old were you?" Jill kept her eyes on Mum while wringing the dishcloth.

"Fourteen."

Like it's nothing; a lass on her own. Fourteen? Henry frowned. *Yet I'm too young to leave school? Unbelievable. Mum having adventures.* He strained to catch every word.

"My gosh, you were brave, lass. You must've been terrified," Nan said.

"Not really. I kept my wits about me. I didn't feel brave. My choices were to leave the orphanage or become a nun; they would no longer support me."

"So, you're in Liverpool. Now what?" Jill said.

"I became a maid of all work in a house run by a former orphan from St. Hilda's. No improvement over the laundry, but at least my life was my own. I did my best to be cheerful. I'd been in St. Hilda's choir, so I polished my voice along with the silver."

"That's you all over, *my chree*," Nan said.

"One day, after I'd worked there about a year, a man heard me singing and said my voice could summon the angel Gabriel—"

"True," said Nan.

Quit interrupting, Nan. I want to hear. Henry cocked his head like a robin listening for worms underground.

"Well, praise wasn't allowed; the nuns cautioned us against vanity. This fellow promised to arrange an audition with the chorus at the Gaiety Theatre in Douglas, Isle of Man. I'd never heard of it, but it sounded exciting. He'd pay my fare, put me up in a hotel… needless to say, there was more to it—"

"Oh dear," Jill broke in, and Nan said, "He was pestering you for favours. Scoundrel!"

What, what? Henry didn't understand.

"Yes. I was a ninny. Fortunately, my lungs stood me in good stead. I screamed blue murder and the manager came running. They threw the man out, took me in, gave me a job. That's how I ended up at the Sugarland." Mum's voice always warmed when she described the hotel. "Lovely. Everyone treated me kindly. I worked my way up and learned to cook. That's when I met Thomas." Her voice lowered.

Nan interrupted. She began replacing the dishes on their customary shelves.

Dammit. Henry almost swore, before clapping his hand over his mouth. *She's ruined everything. Now I'll never know—*

"Yes, our Thomas is in a position to help his brother's family, and that's all to the good. I trust he's settled down, finally. Doing well, by his account, though I wonder—you see, there's something I haven't told you."

About Uncle Thomas? Henry perched on the stool with bated breath.

"Ye ken how we *smoor* the hearth of an evening to keep the fire going all night and bless the house? You must do this, you girls. Never brush the dust on the floor to the outside, but always into the *chiollagh*, or the family's luck will leave the house."

Everyone knows that. What's she on about?

"Well, on New Year's Eve, we do the opposite; spread the ashes from the fire all across the floor and leave a gift of money and oatcakes for the *Little People*. In the morning, there'll be footprints, clear as day." She paused, pointing to the hearth then turning to Jill. "Ye ken, lass? Your mother's Manx; she knows." She paused. "Good. Well, I never said, *my chree*, as I didn't want you to worry, but this year, the footprints led out the door, not in. Very bad."

"You did tell me, Nan. T'other day, remember?"

"I did? Oh. Well, the *Little Ones* have told me more than once that William's health is failing. That's why I wrote Thomas, though it pained me. Youse must go to Michigan so's William can heal."

She took the dishcloth from Jill to wipe the dresser. "It's the climate, Thomas says. But to miss seeing our grandbabies grow up—" Her voice cracked, and she moaned, leaning on the dresser for support.

Jill encircled Nan's shoulders and led her to the rocking chair. Nan rocked and wiped at her eyes with her apron. Henry wanted to leap through the window, dry her tears, and say, "Don't fret, Nan. I'm here."

Then Jill posed the question he'd wondered about. "D'ya think there are faeries in America, Mrs. Carine? Likely it's very different."

Nan pulled Jinx onto her lap and hummed. Mum busied herself rinsing the teapot. *So that's what she took from the trunk. She prizes that.*

"What worries me is, how will I make a decent cuppa without my Brown Betty?" She creased her forehead and patted the teapot. Nan and Jill burst out laughing.

What's so funny? Well, Nan is smiling now, at least. Maybe I should go in, have my scone. Jill will pour my tea. The blackberry jam will be so sweet. Henry uncrossed his stiff arms and shook out the pins and needles in his hands. Jill's voice carried through the window.

"That's your biggest fear, Euphemia? Not crossing an ocean? Not starting over in America? You are a funny duck!" Jill snorted with laughter.

"The tea leaves swirl and make the best cuppa, you see. William's gift, our first anniversary." Suddenly she stopped and handed it to Jill. "Yes. Please. I'll be happy to know Betty's cared for."

* * *

That evening, on the trek to Faery Hill, Henry thought of Mum placing her precious teapot in Jill's hands. The hugs, the tears. So much left behind that couldn't be bought again, at any price. Gifts, mementos, things passed down through the generations. There'd been talk of an auction, but Nan balked, saying she wouldn't have the neighbours picking through their belongings like crows on a carcass. She'd carry out the dispersals herself and send the money on.

Even Ann suffered the awful task of choosing what to take and what to leave. *Of course, she's spoiled as the only girl. Us boys don't have much. Still, it's harsh to make her choose one doll. Good thing she picked Jenny. It made Nan so proud.*

He saw Nan's face when she'd presented the doll to Ann last Christmas. Studying the embroidered blue eyes, Ann announced the doll's name was Jenny Kronchent. Unheard of names. Stranger still were incidents Ann blamed on Jenny: broken dishes, things moved or misplaced. One morning they found scribbled markings on the wall. While Mum washed away the charcoal, Ann punished Jenny, sitting her in a corner, shaking a finger at her. "Bad Jenny. Naughty Jenny." Nan blamed the faeries, wondering aloud if *Themselves* had left a message. But Henry noticed Edward's hands leaving black marks on the towel by the water pump.

"He's mean, Nan," Henry said, after reminding her of Edward's cruel trick. "I can't stand him; always trying to get someone in trouble or teasing Ann. Is Uncle Thomas like that? Is that how he 'takes after' him? No wonder I've a bad feeling—"

"Yes, somewhat like Thomas. No real harm done, though. Just another of Edward's silly pranks, *my chree.*"

"He's that—"

"Let it go, Henry. You two may need one another, someday. Remember what I said about blood."

"Yes, 'thicker than water.' What does it *mean*, Nan?"

"Mind your kinship ties, lest you become enemies. Remember Cain and Abel."

"Ach, he's bloody selfish and annoying. He never helps me. Gets in my way, more like." Henry almost spat.

"Patience is a virtue, *my chree*. Mayhap he's meant to teach you that. Everyone we meet, we learn from if we pay attention. Even sorrow teaches us. Hard lessons."

She exhaled a deep breath. "Quick march, Henry. The *Little Ones* are impatient, and not virtuous by any means."

He pointed with his chin. "I'd rather spend some time on the shore tonight, Nan. Can you make it uphill?" Her soft blue eyes met his in an understanding smile.

"Meet you back here. Careful on the rocks, *my chree*. Tide's coming in."

Chapter Thirteen

Slane lhiat: Goodbye

July, 1905

HENRY scudded down the steep trail, then balanced awkwardly on huge, slippery rocks and gazed out to sea. Waves rushed to lick his boots. Gannets drew circles in the pink and yellow clouds, suddenly becoming arrows that pierced the waves, emerging with a fish every time. The victors squabbled on rocky outposts, protecting their catch. Ravens patrolled the shore in pairs. *Nasty pickpockets, acting as if they own the place, like schoolyard bullies. I hate bullies, me.* He inhaled the pungent smell of kelp drying on shore. Vivid sea stars and anemones decorated the walls of tidal pools teeming with miniature fish. He wiggled a finger in the water, awakening the anemones. A delightful childhood game.

He turned over the afternoon's revelations in the same way he lifted rocks to watch hermit crabs scramble away. His heart clenched as he came to grips with the fact that Nan had lost all but one of her children. He'd never tallied her losses before. *No wonder she wants to save Da. She was only "Nan." I didn't know her at all. Mum neither, come to that. They were just there. For us. Not for themselves.* He reached down for a shell and smoothed the hollow inside. *Whatever lived here is gone. The house is empty.* He cupped it over his ear. *Only the pounding surf remains.*

He decided to search for a stone for Nan as a gift. Too soon, the sun set the rim of the world alight, flaring like crumpled paper in the *chiollagh. Ah, here's one; speckled with silver, heart-shaped, just right. Ah, and here's one for me, shaped like an island.* He slipped one in each pocket.

He straightened his back and sheltered his eyes from the glittering waves. So many happy times here, fishing with Dad and Grandad near shore, rowing around in their skiff. His vision blurred. A word chimed in his head—orphan. *Mum's an orphan. I'll be an orphan when Nan and Grandad pass if I stay. The last Carine in Port Erin. Never see Mum and Dad, my brothers, or Ann. Would I join them then, or stay?*

He let his tears flow. His toes squelched inside his boots and the rising breeze set his teeth chattering. *Yes, that's why I'm shivering; ought to've worn my sweater.* Almost at the top, he let out the breath he'd been holding. *Nan's right; I must go. If Da doesn't make it, Mum'll be orphaned again, but with five children this time. No help. The others are still young. What kind of man is Thomas? Will he like us?*

He yanked his rock from his pocket and flung it over the cliff. The moment it left his hand, he wanted to reel it back in like a fish. *Oh well. Slane lhiat.* The desire to stay by the sea tugged at him like the moon drawing the tide. Nan was calling. *Time's up. Goodbye, Man and your Calf.*

* * *

On their final night, Grandad gathered the boys at his feet after supper. "Manannan's mist hid us from the Romans, young'uns, and thus we've our own ways, unique in all the world, going back time out of mind. A rare language, too. Keep it, use it, lads," he said, his voice quaking. "Your birthright, so. When you face hardship, remember: *Quocunque Jerceris Stabit.* Our motto. The three-legged man means we can't be trounced, no matter how the fates toss us." Grandad drew on his pipe and puffed out a cloud. Henry inhaled the sweet smell of tobacco smoke mixed with the peat fire. His eyes were dry. He could barely swallow. *The last time I'll hear Grandad's familiar words. I wish I could hold onto his pant leg like I used to.*

Da pushed away from the table. "Well, the mists didn't prevent the goddamn English from stealing our wealth, did they, Da? Nor from taxing us down to the very wedding dress Euphemia must leave behind." He gestured with his mug of beer, sloshing some on the slate floor. "Nor provide miners a living wage on this rock. A working man can't even afford his own house, for Christ's sake." His voice fell almost to a whisper, and he coughed. "As to speaking the Manx language, what for? No one knows it in America, or anywhere else, come to that."

Henry and the others stared at the fire. The ticking clock kept time with Nan's rocking.

"I only want the lads to ken their home. Our *Ellan Vannin,*" Grandad said, his voice muted and sad. "So's they'll find their feet, like our *ny tree cassyn.* And your native tongue matters, my son. It's alive and can die, too, just like a person. Be proud—"

"What's the saying about pride, Da? *Yiow moyrn lhieggy.* Before a fall, indeed. Aye, we've fallen far when we must leave—" He interrupted himself by draining his mug, slamming it down, and making for the door. Soon cigarette smoke and the sound of coughing streamed through the open window. Henry caught the pain in Grandad's eyes under his furrowed brow.

"Whist, never mind," Nan said, clucking her tongue. Mum sobbed. Hugh started to wail. Nan placed Ann in Henry's lap.

"He's worn out, *my chree.* Can't help himself. We're at the end of our tether, truth be told. Nanny'll make a warm toddy to help us sleep. Tomorrow's a big day."

Henry and John served the steaming drink while Tom and

Edward set the table for morning. Mum packed their lunch. Henry smoored the hearth with Nan. Together they knelt and said the blessing, holding hands and fervently asking the faeries to support the journey ahead. As they finished, they stared into the embers until Henry turned to hug Nan. They held each other until their aching knees forced them to collapse on the rug. Nan rubbed his back with soothing Manx. When he climbed up the ladder, even his fingers and toes ached. He feared he might lose his grip.

Edward pulled the covers over their heads and whispered, "Da's horrible making Mum cry, swatting me like a fly when I'm just trying to make everyone laugh. He's no fun anymore. Mean to Grandad, too. I can't wait for morning, can you? Fancy, we're crossing the ocean on a ship!"

"Oh, shut up, Edward," Henry said, through clenched teeth. He rolled over to face the wall. The rock he'd tossed away splashed in the pit of his stomach. He wrapped his arms around himself, tucked in his knees, and begged the faeries to help him sleep. He needed rest for the day ahead, but the full moon held his gaze. Just as he drifted off, the cock crowed.

He dressed, tiptoed through the cottage, and carefully lifted the latch. In the half-light, Blackie followed him to the shed. He milked the two cows, leaning his forehead against their warm flanks, speaking in Manx. Ding, hiss, ding; his rhythmic double-time soon filled both tin pails, with a squirt for Jinxy. *Poor Ann can't bring her kitty. I wish we could explain to our four-legged friends.* He toted the pails to the kitchen and retrieved a cloth bag from the bench. Whistling to Blackie, he grabbed his stick for driving the cows.

"I'll miss you girls," he told them as he guided them through the gate. He'd shared Grandad's delight in purchasing the expensive Ayrshires; the rich cream brought in extra money. *Grandad managed our livestock well. With my help. Whatever will he do now?*

Walking on, he purposely avoided the sheepfold. Leaving them pained him almost as much as parting from his grandparents. In the past, he'd practically lived in the fields, learning husbandry of the *lugh dhoan*: "The Loughtans are special, Henry; only ones left in all the world. When you're bigger, I'll teach you shearing. You'll become a champion, like me." *No chance, now. Besides, Uncle Thomas said farmers despised sheep in America.*

"How could anyone hate sheep, Grandad? Don't they need scarves and sweaters, meat, lanolin—?" Grandad didn't know.

Would the old folks survive? Determined to leave them in good stead, Mum had cleaned the cottage spic and span. "Shipshape and Bristol fashion for a while, Nan. Won't get as untidy, any road, without—" She'd halted at Nan's stricken expression.

Henry had helped Da stack peat turves for winter fires. Henry's stomach flipped as he remembered how Da had cursed each time the turfing iron slipped from his grasp. Instead of their usual easy pace and camaraderie, they'd cut into the hill ferociously, Henry flipping his fork at speed to keep up, then trundling his barrow across the bumpy field to offload the wet turves before racing back. He'd only made two trips when suddenly his father doubled over.

"I'm done up, Son," he wheezed. "I'll hire some men. It's more'n I can manage." His weak smile eased Henry's anxiety somewhat until he saw his trembling hand reach into his vest. After tipping his flask, he sprinkled the last few drops on the ground, then bent to pinch some peat. He forced it into the flask's throat and corked the metal bottle, avoiding Henry's eyes. *Does he mean to give up whiskey, then? Or has he gone mad?*

Only this last ritual remained. Henry pressed his fist against his empty hand as he headed toward the pink curtains rising over the hills. He collected faery thread from broom bushes all the way up Cronk Howe Mooar. He knelt and opened his bag. After sprinkling bits of cake, he poured whiskey into a cup, saying, "*Mooinjer veggeywere*, bless our journey, *Little Ones*. Uncle Arthur, please send some *Little Ones* to help us. Don't let Da die. Please, please, let him live. *Gura mie ayd. Slane lhiat.*" His voice cracked. "I'll not visit youse again. Keep Nan and Grandad safe."

He brushed his face with the back of his sleeve and raced down the hill, Blackie loping alongside. White sheep dotted the violet, green, and yellow hillsides. Gulls squawked below the cliff, arguing over their morning catch, while a falcon shrieked above. *Lucky devil, free to come and go as he pleases.* Wind ruffled his hair and tickled his nose with the smell of burning peat. A king's ransom in gold shimmered on the waves. "King Orry's treasure," Grandad would say. Henry squeezed his eyes shut to engrave the image in his mind. When he opened them, the picture stayed for a moment. "You needn't fret, Grandad. I'll never forget you, *Ellan Vannin*. My home. *Cooinaghtyn ta.*"

Smoke curled from the chimney. The thatched roof drew a line on the pale blue sky. A heavy horse drew a wagon to the red door. The wagon, the cottage, a few chickens scratching in the hazy morning light; what could be a better picture? If only he could keep it. Halting to catch his breath, Henry closed his eyes. Shapes stood out, black and gold. Then…

JOURNEY TO THE NEW WORLD

"The Migration or Importation of such Persons as any of the States now existing shall think proper to admit, shall not be prohibited by the Congress prior to the Year one thousand eight hundred and eight, but a Tax or duty may be imposed on such Importation, not exceeding ten dollars for each Person."

Section 9, Constitution of the United States, 1789

Chapter Fourteen

Cair Vie! Fair Winds!

Douglas to Liverpool
July 9, 1905

EUPHEMIA heard voices in front of the cottage. William's friend James, who'd lent the wagon, shouted that they must get loaded and be off. Euphemia's temper flared. *Men! Always in a hurry to be on the road, with nary a thought for preparations.* Henry opened the door. *He'd been off somewhere instead of here, helping.*

"Where in heaven's name were you? For God's sake, get cracking, there's still much to do." She brushed her forehead with the back of her hand, twisted her loose hair into a knot, and expelled an exasperated sigh as she fastened the straps on the lunch basket. Nan scuttled about like a crab, rushing the children's breakfast. When Jill arrived to lend a hand, as promised, Euphemia dug deep to find a smile. She could hardly bear to look at her. Silent words stood between them as she lifted a basket from the crook of her friend's arm.

"How thoughtful: you knew Nan wouldn't feel like cooking tonight. I'm worn out, and we haven't set foot out the door."

"I know, it's been so hard," Jill said, patting her shoulder. "Don't get het up; you'll spoil your blouse. I'll see to the baby."

William got up slowly, lifting his hands from the table like they'd been glued there. "Well, this is it, I s'pose," he said. "Best say our farewells to everyone. Nice of them to give us a proper send-off."

Grandad nodded and followed him out, leaving the red door ajar. The men stood laughing and joking in the yard. *What's there to laugh about, I ask youse?* Euphemia wanted to shout and slam down the bowl of devilled eggs she was fixing for sandwiches. *Best save Nan a bit of crockery.*

With luggage and lunch loaded, the boys gathered around the wagon, turning their shoes in the dirt. Jill held Ann, who wriggled to be free. Euphemia donned her woollen jacket, then leaned down to gather Hugh from the cradle and crossed the threshold. She didn't allow herself a last look. Balancing Hugh on her hip, she joined Nan at the gate. The neighbours patted her arm and shoulders with sad smiles.

Hugs and handshakes, backslaps and sobs. John's face got scratched when Nan tried to pry Jinx from his arms. Off the cat strode, as though he'd more important places to be. Ann made to follow; Edward held her back. When Henry wrapped his arms around Nan's waist, she gently withdrew. Euphemia, too, wanted one final hug, but Nan stepped back and held her by the forearms, tapping their foreheads together, holding her in her blue gaze.

"Parting's best done quick, *my chree*. We've cried all our tears, said our goodbyes. Mustn't break down in front of the neighbours. Hop up in the wagon, lass," she said, her voice bright and firm. "Henry, take Ann on your lap, there's a good lad. Remember, I'm counting on you to help your mother in my place. Move along now, James, please," she called. "Mind how you go. *Ta graih aym ort.* Youse are my heart."

Standing apart, shooing the other ladies away, Nan held

her weak right arm with her left hand, waving and smiling, as the neighbours shouted, *"Cair Vie! Cair Vie!* Safe journey! *Slane lhiat.* Be sure to write!"* Children chased after the cart until James turned into the crossroads. Euphemia caught a last glimpse of Blackie straining at the leash in Grandad's hand as the cottage disappeared behind the stone fences. Nan knew best, as always; Euphemia's eyes itched as if dust had blown in her face. She stole a look at William, afraid he'd lost his composure. He stared past her, glassy-eyed, twisting the pinky ring she'd seen Grandad place on his hand. *He's pale as that ghost of a moon in the sky. We're both the same, I shouldn't wonder. Looking like we've been sent for.* She shuddered and clasped Hugh against her breast and rocked him, though he didn't fuss, his eyes open wide, reflecting the sky.

"Nanny, I want my Nanny," Ann sobbed, leaning out from her perch on Henry's lap, hands extended, dropping her doll. "Hush, hush, now," Henry repeated softly. Edward's excited voice floated back from the seat next to James. Chattering like a magpie, he'd scrambled up front to the best seat whilst Tom and John were squeezed next to William. John slipped down to the wagon floor, jostled by every bump in the road. He handed Ann her doll and then sat twirling a bit of straw.

Euphemia shut her eyes against the slashes of white on the hills but couldn't avoid inhaling the scent of the cottages' peat fires, nor hearing the cries of skylarks wheeling overhead. Suddenly she remembered a picnic with William, long ago. *Henry was likely conceived next to the tumbling waterfalls of Glen Rushen nearby, with the water rushing—oh, God, I forgot to visit the privy. Dammit. Too late.* She shifted Hugh so he wouldn't rest against her swollen bladder and crossed her legs. At the next bump, she begged James to stop. Her face was afire as she hid behind a gorse bush.

In Douglas, her spirits brightened at the sight of the cheerily painted hotels lined up like cardboard cut-outs along the promenade. She longed to visit the Sugarland one last time, meet some old connections, enjoy a cup of tea, perhaps stroll along the sea wall, or take one of the jolly red and yellow horse-drawn trams to the shops. When she suggested it, the boys shouted with glee. William frowned.

"Straight to Victoria Pier, James, please." His eyes begged acceptance. "Sorry, love. We'd have to stay overnight, and ye ken what a room costs in Douglas—an arm and a leg. Three legs, for a Manxman, eh?" He snorted at his lame joke. "We mustn't miss the ferry."

Ann popped her thumb out of her mouth. "Faeries wait," she said in all seriousness. Euphemia leaned across Henry to pinch her daughter's rosy cheek.

"I'm afraid they don't, sweetheart. You're right, of course, William. Let's hurry, please. Hugh wants a change." And she needed the privy again. Her innards turned to water. She swallowed her disappointment. *Stupid me. I should've arranged for us to come a day earlier. Why didn't I think? But there was so much to do. Ah well, perhaps it's for the best. You can't go back.*

The traffic was chaotic. James expertly guided the horse through the people and carriages coming and going higgledy-piggledy everywhere. She felt like she'd travelled backward, once again amongst the tourists who came in their thousands from the factories in London and Liverpool for their yearly paid summer holiday on Man. The narrow beach on Douglas Bay teemed with holidaymakers in swimming costumes. They'd tiptoe or plunge in. "Bracing," they'd proclaim the icy water with forced laughter. Then they'd shiver behind a cloth screen, sipping hot tea from a thermos, pretending to enjoy themselves until they'd rush to their hotel for a hearty meal and perhaps a show at the Gaiety. The factories provided seven days per year of freedom, and the hotels profited nicely. Everything was just the same.

The further down the promenade they drove, the more Euphemia fumed. *My children never enjoyed a donkey ride on the beach, nor played at the penny carnival. We ought to have brought them, at least once, stayed at a hotel, gone to the theatre, visited the shops… Work, work,*

work. Not a holiday in fifteen years. The factory girls beat me in that respect. William's such a homebody.

The past seemed to shrink down to a single pin that pierced the top of her hand. *One thing about Thomas; he never stinted on earthly delights.* Her cheeks flushed, and her palms began to sweat. Distracting herself, she assessed the outfits of the women strolling with gentlemen on the pier. *Like I did once—oh, God, stop it.*

"We aren't properly dressed, any road," she said, pretending to address Ann. With her free hand, she brushed the dust off her woollen skirt.

Henry jerked upright with a stricken look. His cry sounded an alarm.

"Road! Oh no, Mum! Castletown Road. We've crossed Faery Bridge. We never said hello to *Themselves.*" He moaned. "We're in for it now, Nan said."

Euphemia shrugged her shoulders, but the distress in his voice alerted James. "Don't fash yourself, lad. I offered our good wishes. Mustn't risk bad luck, eh?" He pulled up near the terminal. "Here we are, folks. I'll be glad to get back home out of this morass. I'll never understand the appeal of Douglas, meself."

'Course you don't. Euphemia stopped herself from rolling her eyes. *Like someone else I could mention.*

"Hop down and lend a hand with the bags, lads," William said. "I must get tickets for the next sailing."

William returned brandishing the tickets, seemingly pleased they were on *The King Orry.*

Edward said, "Grandad would be proud, eh, Da? The first Manx king. We're Vikings!"

"To be sure, Edward. A good omen, he'd say." William caught Euphemia's eye as he gestured toward the ferry. "All aboard. Our journey begins, Carine family."

Euphemia sensed his trepidation. His gaze said, "It's here, love, the moment we discussed, many a night." She smiled at him ever so slightly and nodded. *No use bemoaning the past; we're in this together, for better or worse. Like always.*

"Where's the faeries?" Ann piped up as they boarded. "Mama, you promised me and Jenny we'd see faeries. All's I see is boats."

Everyone laughed, nearby passengers included. Once the ferry pulled away from the dock, William rubbed his hands together and clapped.

"Come on, let's scare us up a cuppa. It's four hours to Liverpool."

William left Euphemia in the ladies' lounge with the children while he searched out the smoking compartment. Seated beside her, Henry looked around and remarked, "This is nice, isn't it, Mum? It's not rough at all."

"Yes, I remember the ferry as pleasant when I came across. Don't expect the same on the ship. Thomas says the conditions are atrocious. I'm bracing myself. Especially with a baby," she said, discreetly nursing Hugh under a blanket. A lady sitting nearby asked the baby's age, and they began chatting while the boys gobbled egg sandwiches.

Soon the horn announced their arrival. The Liverpool docks swarmed with people, carts, carriages, and horses. Overwhelmed by the bustle, noise, and unfamiliar smells, they manoeuvred through the crowds to find Water Street, the main thoroughfare. Their lodgings, arranged through Cunard, were standard third-class.

Oh, God, Euphemia groaned inwardly. *Ten days crammed in one room. How ever will we manage?* "A poor excuse for a hotel," she observed. She wanted to spare William's feelings but couldn't. *The place is a tip.*

"The best we could afford, love. I'm sorry. The agent said it would be adequate to our needs." William placed Ann gently on one of the beds and landed beside her.

"Well, he's a man, ain't he?" Euphemia pressed her lips tight, surveying the room. Four single beds for seven; no crib.

Adequate. She expelled a sigh.

"Here, Da. Let me help," Tom said, untying and removing William's shoes.

"Thanks kindly, Tom. I'm that knackered," he said. "I'll just have a cat nap. Tuck in with me, Ann." He closed his eyes and was snoring in seconds. Ann sucked her thumb, wide awake.

"Dead to the world. We should all be so lucky," Euphemia said. She portioned out the last of the sandwiches and ginger beer, then organized sleeping arrangements, all while running over the shopping list in her head. She told Henry he'd help get supplies while Dad minded the children and rested. Edward sat up, protesting that he should go, too. She pulled his ear. "Hush up. You'll do as you're told. If anything, Tom would be more likely, for he's stouter and less of a flibbertigibbet. But I don't want any of youse out amongst the crowds."

She shrank a bit at Edward's hurt expression. *Perhaps my tone is harsh, but, Jesus, I must be stern. They must mind me to the letter, otherwise how will I keep them safe?*

The room smelled as fusty as moldy hay, and the mattresses were as lumpy as stale oatmeal. Euphemia turned down the beds and looked askance at the grey sheets. They collapsed in bed after a quick wash-down in cold water. Ann woke them all at sunrise, whining and scratching her legs. Euphemia examined the red bites covering the child's calves and back.

"Bedbugs! God, that's all we need. I must wash this place down when I get back or we'll all suffer, and our luggage will be infested. Henry, add turps and calamine lotion to our list. Get up, lads. Bread and cheese for breakfast. I'll find milk while out. It's water for now."

She prepared to set off, list in hand. "Back in a tick, William, with fruit and veg from the market. Given the state of this room, imagine the food they serve downstairs. We'll fix our own meals. Don't smoke, for heaven's sake. I can't open the windows."

When they reached the street, Euphemia couldn't help unburdening to Henry. "Dad's already tired. Pray he passes inspection, or he'll be refused passage." As she spoke, her wary eyes scanned the sidewalk, and her fingers clutched the basket.

Henry looked at her, uncomprehending. "Ex—examination, Mum? Like at school? Do they switch you for mistakes?"

"No switches, pet." Euphemia shook her head, forcing a smile. "No. A physical, it's called. The doctor listens to your heart and lungs, sticks a tongue depressor in your mouth, checks your eyes and teeth. You've never been sick, so you don't know. I'm not worried about the rest of us. We're hale and healthy, but if they discover Dad's ill, he won't be allowed aboard. I'll not leave him."

Henry bounced on his feet. "We'll go home, then." He almost sang the words.

Euphemia covered her mouth with her free hand and shook her head. "No, love. We'd have to stay and find work." She hated his crest-fallen look, but he might as well face facts. They'd no money to turn back.

A man bumped her, offering a brief "Pardon, ma'am." She rubbed her arm, wincing, and touched the clasp on her leather handbag. Secure. Henry started to shout, but she signalled stop. Mustn't draw attention. Somehow, they negotiated the chaos, whirling in and out of doors to the tinkling of bells, Euphemia struggling as the basket became weighted down with tins and bottles, and Henry balancing packages. Fortunately, well-stocked shops were within walking distance of the hotel. Liverpool catered to ships efficiently, though with little regard for cleanliness.

They returned to find broken glass scattered on the floor, John drawing on a newspaper, his shirt blackened by printers' ink, and Baby Hugh crying with hunger and a wet nappy. Henry crunched glass under his boots. Edward and Tom admitted to breaking the kerosene lamp. Cuddled next to William on the bed, Ann plucked her thumb from her mouth to ask for sweet-ies.

Euphemia slowly removed her coat, then lifted Hugh from the dresser drawer that served as a crib. "Mama's back, duckie," she said, loudly enough to be heard through the paper-thin walls.

William sputtered, and sat up, bleary-eyed. "Sorry, sorry, love. Must've dozed off. It's so hot." He stumbled to the rickety table, rolled a cigarette which he didn't light, and asked Henry for the receipts. Making notes in a tiny book, his brow creased as he questioned the purchase of soap.

"Stop fussing over trifles, William. I'm going by Thomas' list. He should know," Euphemia said around the diaper pin in her mouth. Removing it, she struggled to fasten the nappy, accidentally scraping Hugh's tummy. He howled. "Dammit! Sorry, sweetheart." She picked him up and spun around. "William, by God, if you pinch every penny, I'll go mad."

"It's ten years since Thomas travelled, and he wasn't on Cunard. Surely a first-rate ship provides soap. We'll need an extra bag at this rate. That'll cost."

"What's penny-pinching, Mum?" John asked. "Does it hurt?"

"It certainly does." She shot daggers at William's back as she moved toward their bed. "I'm sick of it."

William wouldn't meet her eyes. Tom knelt to unpack the basket of food while John collected Euphemia's coat from the floor. Edward scowled.

"I want to come next time. There's nothing to do." He bounced the rubber ball he'd brought along to play knuckle-bones. Henry caught it with one hand and said, "Clean up this mess. Stop larking about."

"There's too many people and vehicles for me to keep an eye on you as well as manage the shopping. A shopkeeper told us there's seventy thousand people in this one square mile. We were jostled by every single one, I swear," Euphemia said, rolling the soiled diaper into a ball, but there was nowhere to clean it. *I'll need a soaking bucket. How'm I supposed to wash out diapers and hang them up in here? Maybe there's a laundry service. That costs, I shouldn't wonder. Everything costs.*

She yanked at the hair clinging to the back of her neck. "Edward, you can bloody well change a nappy. Babe'll get diaper rash unless he's kept dry. You're the oldest, after Henry. Mind Hugh and keep Ann occupied instead of roughhousing. Now, we've a lamp chimney to replace and all."

"Pee-uw! It stinks." Edward plugged his nose. "I am not changing that."

"You are, so. Belt up. You're getting on my last nerve." Euphemia raised her hand as if to swat him. He grabbed the broom.

"I smell food," Tom said, rubbing his stomach. "I'm so hungry, Mama."

Euphemia put her hand on his cheek and kissed his head. "I know, pet. You're used to regular meals. Look, we've meat pies and jacket potatoes for lunch, but first, Hugh must be fed. Edward, run down and fetch two buckets of hot water from the landlady. John, you collect the papers and toys. Henry, get everyone washed when Edward brings the water, whilst I lay down for a bit. I'm shattered, like that lamp."

William coughed. "I'm going out. For me smoke. Back shortly," he said, closing the door on Euphemia's plea to stay close. *What if he gets hurt, robbed, falls down… anything at all? I'll be alone here. Why can't he just stay put?*

She fed Hugh. That passed for rest. Then she directed the children to sit on the floor. "A picnic every meal since we've only the two chairs. We'll make the best of it, eh?"

"What's town like, Mum?" John slurped as he spooned gravy from the pie. "This is good."

"You should just see it, John. People, carts, horses, all moving hither and yon, mounds of garbage and horseshit… the stench is overpowering!" She unfolded her legs and held up her hem. "My skirt. However will I get it clean?"

"Don't worry, Mum. I'll brush it for you," said Tom.

"Aw, you're a dear, Tom. Any road, you're constantly pushed and shoved, and so many street urchins, you must keep your wits about you. I s'pose it's no different than when I was here… I don't recall—funny how you forget…" She suddenly realized her mind had erased that voyage. She searched her memory and couldn't find it. *Probably best.*

"The rats are well-fed. They run in the streets like alley cats." She shuddered. "Lord, I need a bath. No wonder all the ladies wear gloves." She stood up to fetch a damp cloth for dirty hands. Her legs tingled with pins and needles. "Henry, remind me to get some, please." She handed him the cloth to wipe Ann's face. "You think that diaper reeks, Edward? It's nothing to the stench of this city."

"Not only that," said Henry. "I can't make out what they're saying, half the time. Is it English? I can't understand so I don't answer. They must think me daft."

"Well, I'm sure the Liverpudlians find your Manx accent and my Yorkshire difficult, too. How do foreigners make themselves understood?"

"I've no accent, me," Henry said, creasing his brow. "It's them."

"Liverpudlian!" Edward repeated. "Such a funny word. Liverpudlian, liver—"

"Puddle." Ann giggled, pointing to the floor. Hugh rocked back and forth on hands and knees, having crawled away from his blanket. Euphemia had allowed his flaming bottom to air.

"Puddle, puddle." Tom snorted. John laughed until he gasped for breath. His giggles infected everyone.

"Well, you're a Liverpudlian now, I reckon," Euphemia said, holding him in the air. He chortled, smiled, and continued to pee. "Just like a man."

The boys blushed and busied themselves clearing up. William opened the door, removed his hat, and went to lie down.

"There's pie, dear," Euphemia said. No answer.

CHAPTER FIFTEEN

Ta cooinaghtyn yn chree ny share na cooinaghtyn yn chione:
The remembrance of the heart is better than
the remembrance of the head.

July, 1905

IT took two days to purchase and organize supplies, requiring the addition of one carpet bag and William's continual grumbling. Being cooped up had frayed everyone's nerves; Euphemia decided it was time to venture out. Nan and Grandad's parting gift of money provided new clothing for every member of the family, a dress set, and two working outfits. The landlady lent them a pram and recommended a department store, Bunny's.

They'd never bought ready-made clothes for the children or themselves all at once. The cost would be astronomical. Fortunately, Nan had entrusted Euphemia with the funds; William couldn't balk. After four hours of shopping, Euphemia with Ann, William with the boys, they met out front. Everyone wore their new clothes; they'd brought carpet bags for the exchange.

"Oh no, the faeries have stolen my girls!" William pretended to be desperate.

"It's me, Papa, it's me," Ann sputtered, her eyes filling with tears. She wore a long-waisted cotton dress, wool stockings, and white gloves. Euphemia had braided blue ribbons into her blonde hair, sapphire blue to set off her eyes. *She's an angel. Well, in looks at least.*

William lifted Ann and touched their noses together. "Ah, my bonnie, just teasing; I'd know you anywhere."

Euphemia turned her attention to the boys. *Henry looks the part of the man he considers himself, in his tweed jacket, vest, and long pants.* He lifted the cuffs to display new boots. The younger boys looked smart in their Glengarry caps and knickerbockers held by suspenders, which Edward and Tom couldn't refrain from snapping. William seemed to stand even taller in his grey, pin-striped suit, white shirt, and tie.

"That bowler makes you look dashing, William," Euphemia said. "Wouldn't Nan be pleased?"

He tipped his hat, bent over, and lifted her gloved hand to his lips. "Doesn't your mother look beautiful, lads? Pretty as a picture, like the day we were married. I'd do it all over again."

There's my sweet William. Please, please, let him stay.

"You're like a queen and king in a faery story," John said, his copper eyes glowing. He reached out to feel the fabric of Euphemia's skirt; she gently brushed him away. She sought her reflection in the shop window to admire her new straw hat, trimmed with a dotted ribbon. The matching tie around her thick white collar completed the natty look. "I love my boater, don't you?" She turned her head from side to side. "Fancy, eh? And my full skirt." She twirled. "The fashion for gores on the skirt is twelve, the clerk said, but I think seven will suffice. Don't you agree, William?"

He nodded. She gently swatted his arm with her new umbrella. "You haven't the foggiest, have you?"

William laughed, then ran his hands across his chest. "My white shirt's a fancy bit of goods too, and no mistake. Just for special occasions, mind; the clerk called it a 'coat shirt' because—"

"Coats! Oh no, William, we need new overcoats and slickers, as well!"

The boys groaned. Henry furiously pumped the pram up and down to calm Hugh. *Poor babe's been confined to the pram all morning.* Euphemia lifted him and he nuzzled her breast.

"The little ones are past it, love. Me too, come to that," William said.

"Where's the bunnies, Mama?" Ann tossed her braids side to side. "You said we'd visit bunnies."

"Look up, silly." Edward huffed and rolled his eyes. "The name of the store—Bunny's. There's no bunnies in a shop." He clicked his tongue.

"She can't read, silly," Henry said, mimicking Edward, then added. "Keep a civil tongue in your head for once."

Euphemia started like someone had walked on her grave. *He sounded just like Grandad then. He fancies he's a man. A mite big for his new britches.*

"Behave yourselves, boys." Euphemia employed her umbrella on Edward's shoulder.

"Can too read. Can too." Ann stuck out her lower lip, hiccupped, and began to sob. John took her hand and pointed out a horseless carriage to distract her.

"Come on, let's have us a treat, Carine family. We shall have tea in a shop like the toffs," William said.

He led them down the street and stopped at the entrance to a teashop. Leaving the pram outside, Henry carried Hugh, while Edward reached for Ann's hand. She stuck her nose in the air and grabbed John's hand. The waitress brought a highchair "for the sweet little girl," and the boys sat straight as pins, munching cucumber sandwiches. Euphemia glowed with pride at her children's behaviour. *A credit to us. Even Edward and Tom are quiet for once. Gives me confidence for the journey, it does.* She sent a smile to William. His eyes gleamed back at her.

When tiny, decorated cakes appeared for dessert, he surprised Euphemia with a gift: lace handkerchiefs and a bottle of scent. The boys gasped; gifts were for Christmas only. Euphemia held the bottle to the light.

"Such a pretty shape. A keepsake. You bought violet, my favourite." She removed the tiny cork and touched the lip of the bottle to the inside of her wrists. "This will remind me of home," she said, extending her bare arm for William to smell. He kissed it. A frisson of pleasure raced to her shoulders, down her spine, and landed in her lap. William grinned.

Placing both hands on the table, he said, "I've decided; we shall have a portrait. There's photography studios along here."

"William, we mustn't," Euphemia shook her head. "I've hardly any money left from Nan. We need—"

"With us all lookin' so smart? Please. The old folks'll treasure it. It'll be worth the cost, you'll see."

* * *

When they entered the studio with its thick carpet, velvet-covered settees, and dark furniture, Henry couldn't stop staring at the gallery of people in ornate frames lining the walls. He was curious about the process used to capture images on paper. He wanted to ask but dared not interrupt the man organizing various poses, muttering as he arranged the adults and moved chairs, then scurried to the camera to tuck his head under a black hood. He spoke to himself: "Should the parents both be seated? Or the father stand with his hand on his wife's shoulder, holding the little girl? Whatever shall I *do* with all these *boys?*"

"My goodness, I ask myself that same question every day, sir." Mum tossed her head back and laughed. "How can we help?"

While the photographer consulted the parents, Tom lifted Ann to view a parrot squawking in its cage. She stuck her finger through the bars and suddenly, whoosh! The huge grey bird was flapping free. Edward raised his hands. Mum ducked. Da shouted.

Everyone watched open-mouthed as the man calmly coaxed the parrot to his shoulder. Transferring the bird to its perch, he closed the cage with a click and a look at Tom, before turning to the parrot, "Who's my lovely Jim?" The parrot bobbed up and down at every word.

"Oh, he is lovely," John said, gazing into the bird's shiny black pupils encircled with yellow. "Wherever did he come from? They don't live here, do they?"

"You came all the way from Africa, didn't you, Jim?" the man said in his "Jim" voice. Then he added, "But I bought him in a shop down the road."

Jim squawked, "Good Jim. Clever Jim," mimicking the man's voice. Ann clapped her hands. Edward whistled. The photographer smiled.

"Now the excitement's over, would the young people kindly join us over here?" He waved away Mum's blushes and apologies. "Don't worry, Madam, all part of the service."

The photography session had been interminable, hot, and boring, but nothing compared to the trials of the next day. They waited in line for inspection, sweltering in their best clothes. Henry shook in fear as the doctor approached. They'd never been examined by a doctor; Hugh and Ann kicked and screamed. Mum was furious when informed they must return to have their bags fumigated. Somehow, they got through it. That night, they all collapsed, too exhausted to talk, barely able to eat supper.

When a boy delivered the message that the photographs were ready, Euphemia entrusted Henry with fetching them.

"You're sure you know how to get there? They're all paid for, one for Nan and one for us. Mind how you go. Come straight back, mind."

Henry wandered down the streets, perusing shop windows,

dreaming of having money for candy. Despite the bustling crowd, his spirits soared as if he'd been released from a cage, too. *Mum's fussing is getting on my last nerve. Ach, I'm anxious to be on the ship. Maybe then I'll get some time to meself. We're crammed in that hole like sardines in a can.*

The tinkle of the bell and Jim's squawky "hello" from his perch on the photographer's shoulder made him feel welcome.

"Good to see you again, Jim," Henry said. "And you too, sir. I'm here for the Carine portraits."

The man seemed surprised. "You have to sign for them, young man. One of your parents ought—well, if they trust you, so do we, eh, Jim?" Jim bobbed his grey head. "They turned out fine if I say so myself. You're a handsome family, and your mother's a right beauty. Photogenic, as we say in the trade." He slipped on white gloves before placing the photographs on the huge desk. "Two copies, boudoir size, as ordered. Touch only with your eyes, please. Now, we've some nice frames, not too expensive—"

Henry stared at the black-and-white images. *I hardly recognize us, in our new clothes. We look like "somebodies." English, even. Ann's blonde hair looks white. Nan will love how she's holding Jenny. Why she's an angel; all that's missing is wings.* The man smiled as if reading his thoughts. He'd suggested the individual pose, offering a free print on condition he might keep one for display.

"She could be a model, that child. I've given you an extra set of your sister, for the grandparents, free of charge. May I use the family's portrait also, for advertising? A picture's worth a thousand words, as they say." He rested his gloved fingertips on the desk and smiled. Henry nodded.

Won't Mum be pleased? Shame you can't see the colour of Mum's suit; it matches her hair, though you'd never see it under that hat she fancies. How fair she is. Ann takes after her, I can see now. She sat in an ornate chair, Hugh swaddled in her arms, Ann alongside. Standing behind, Da towered over them. Dark rings shadowed his deep-set eyes. *He looks as solemn as the vicar. We weren't supposed to smile but look, John did.* Henry smiled at his sweet expression, then frowned as his gaze fell on Edward. *A right show-off with his hand on his hip, chest thrust out like a puffed-up robin, eyes half-closed, he almost spoils the picture. Then there's Tom, with those doorstop ears.* He chuckled, remembering Jim flapping around, Tom in pursuit. Jim croaked, remembering too.

He leaned in to study his face. The man handed him a magnifying glass. He resembled Da: nearly his height, same wide forehead, thick, dark hair. *Though Da wore that silly bowler. Boy, my head is shaped funny, almost a triangle. Luckily my ears have flattened out. Maybe Tom's will, someday. I've a pointy nose, like Da, and both of us have fuzzy eyebrows, like caterpillars. Nan will be sorry she can't see our eyes, blue as faery bells, she'd say. I hope she'll remember them.*

Lastly, he looked at the baby. *In that frilly dress, could anyone tell he's a boy? Hugh will never know Grandad, or Nan, who gave him Grandad's name. He'll always be a baby. None of us will ever change from this photograph. I wish we'd bought a frame.*

Henry knew Nan and Grandad's sacrifice. One day, he'd overheard them chatting on the bench outside the kitchen window. Dust faeries danced about in the silent cottage. Mum and Ann were feeding the pigs, Baby Hugh dozed in his cradle, the boys were at school. Da was down the mine, earning last-minute wages. Worn out from stacking turves, Henry was having a snack at the table. He ran his hands over the nicks, cracks, and dents. *Grandad and Nan won't need this board, now.* Their voices floated in upon the lace curtains billowing in the breeze. He perked his ears to listen.

"*Kys ta shiu?* D'ye think we'll ever get used to the quiet?" Grandad said.

"No. Are you angry with me?" Nan seemed a bit tetchy.

"Course not. Don't be droppin' your chin on my account, woman. I ken what it's costing you. A shame our Henry can't take over the farm one day, though. He's a natural."

Oh Grandad, you never said. I wanted that. Henry laid his forehead on his arms, stifling a sob.

"Ah, can't be helped, so. It's ourselves I'm worried about. Maybe we should sell up? Move to the village?" Henry strained to catch Nan's answer.

"See how we get on, *my chree.* What would you do without your sheep, eh? A woman can always occupy her time, but a man—" She clicked her tongue. "Drink your tea before it's cold."

"The worry's at you, Beth. For more than their leaving, it seems."

"We're married too long for me to hide anything. Aye, I'm not sure of our Thomas. A leaky vessel, him. Always was."

"But he's bettered himself. He isn't a fool."

"No, he isn't that. But a leopard doesn't change its spots, Hugh. He's found a way around hard work, make no mistake. I ken his faults."

"This can't be occurring to you just now. Why'd you devise this plan, Beth?"

Henry nodded in silent agreement. *A leaky boat? I've never liked him—*

"He won't disappoint me. His pride won't let him." Her voice became thick, as though stuck in her throat. "Oh, Hugh, who'll walk me to the *Little Ones?* I can't make it without our Henry."

Henry drenched his shirt sleeves while Nan drenched her apron.

"I'll take you, *my chree.* Like old times. Drink your tea. It's cold, the way you like it."

Henry sighed, staring at the photograph with blurry eyes. *They'll be there, at Cronk Howe Mooar, about now. Say hello to Themselves for me, Nan. Moghrey Mie Mooinjer Veggey.*

He cleared his throat and brushed his sleeve across his face. The photographer's dark eyes shone, and he went to pat

Henry's arm. Henry stood up, almost tipping over the chair.

"Yes, these'll do. Thank you very much, sir. Wrap them separately, please."

While the man readied the packages, Henry talked to Jim in the cozy foyer. Since there were no customers, Henry ventured to ask a favour. "I wonder if you'd show me—" The photographer agreed. Henry spent an hour examining the camera, visiting the dark room, learning about plates and emulsions and developer.

"I'm going day and night, around the clock. People want a photograph before leaving. Can't say I blame them, but I need an assistant; Jim's too busy showing off to be of much help." He looked Henry up and down, bobbing his head and rocking on his heels.

Is he offering me a job? Maybe I could stay here, work, make enough money to go back home…

Suddenly he became aware of the time. He raced out with thanks and a wave to Jim and hurried down the crowded street. Mum met him on the landing. She slapped his arm hard, nearly making him drop the envelopes.

"What time do you call this, then, eh? You've given me a fright. Straight back, I said. I was about to set off after you."

"Sorry, Mum. The man showed me—"

"Never mind." She calmed her voice and pulled him inside. "Hurry, we're anxious to see."

Everyone gathered around as Mum unwrapped one of the packages. Ann pointed at the baby, saying he looked like a dolly. Mum agreed. "Hark at our little Liverpudlian. Adorable, isn't he? We look—ah, poor Nan. She'll be happy and heartbroken, both." She dabbed her eyes with her handkerchief.

"You're right, John, we look like royalty. We spiff up real nice, eh? You're glad now we did the photograph, aren't you, Euphemia?"

"Yes. For the first time, I'm also glad I'm an orphan.

There'll be no one to miss me."

"Go on with you," Da said, sounding angry. "Mother and Da think of you as their own, ye ken. They'll pine for you, every day."

"I just meant… ah well, no point dwelling on such thoughts, any road," Mum said, opening a bottle of ink, setting it on her left. She dipped her pen, flipped the photograph over, and dictated aloud: "Henry William, 13; Edward George, 10; Thomas Percy, 8; John Michael, 6; Ann Francis, 4; Hugh Steven, 15 months. With love, William and Euphemia, July 18, 1905." Then she held Ann's portrait aloft. "Ann Francis and Jenny Kronchent. How'd you spell her name?"

"I know, Mama, I know! Q, T, X—" Ann called out letters, tapping a finger on her chin.

"Nan and Grandad know our names, Mum," Tom said, furrowing his brow. "Why write them? They're not likely to forget us, are they?"

"You lot? You must be joking," she said with a slight laugh, ruffling his curly hair. "It's good to record your ages. I'll do the same on ours when I get time."

"You should put me down as fourteen, Mum. It's my birthday soon," Henry said, but she seemed oblivious. She blew on the ink, then flipped the photograph again.

"Don't touch, Mum. You'll leave finger marks," Henry said when she began counting with her fingertip.

"Six children. Nearly fifteen years. Not to mention—ah, where has the time gone?" she whispered. "Soon I'll be saying 'was, was,' like Nan. It used to annoy me. Now I understand."

Slipping the photographs back between the sheets of heavy card, she re-wrapped the brown paper, ironed it with her hand, and wrote the address. Then she stood and straightened her skirt.

"There, that's sorted. Henry, you remember where the post office is? Not far. Nip 'round and post this, will you? Edward, go with him. Best travel in pairs." Edward raced to tie his boots. "No shilly-shallying this time, mind, but you may each buy a stick of candy with the change from the stamps." She counted coins into Henry's palm.

"Are you pinching the pennies, Mum?" John said.

She stopped and made eye contact with Henry, then shook her head as though waking from a dream. "Never mind, bring some sweeties back for the young ones. Good as gold they were through that horrid inspection, poked and prodded like cattle. What a trial. I'm glad it's over and done with."

"We all passed," Henry said, smiling at her. "Nan's words to the *Little Ones* surely helped. Especially for Da—"

"The rest has helped him, to be sure. We're off tomorrow." She blew out her cheeks. "I hardly believe it. We passed muster, as they say. We've our inspection cards. We're golden."

"I do believe the faeries were with us, Mum," Henry said, buttoning his coat. "Da hardly coughed during the examination."

"Could be. Now if only he wouldn't hack all night, we'd all rest. P'rhaps out in the fresh sea air, he'll breathe more easily. I know I will." She glanced over at Da, snoring on their bed. "Journey hasn't even started and I'm fair worn out. I never realized how much I relied on Nan," she said, as if to herself.

Then she patted Henry's shoulder and held out the package. "I hope Nan and Grandad… It's so hard. Ah, well, best look ahead, not behind, the Bible says. Mustn't end up like Lot's wife and turn to salt."

Henry didn't understand the reference but noticed her tears. He hastened to take the package, fearing she'd smudge the ink.

"Off you go, pet. Mind the horses. Get that Mackintosh toffee Ann likes. It's lovely to share." She winked and pinched his cheek.

I'm too old to have my cheek pinched. Sometimes she forgets. But his insides glowed. Edward called out "slowpoke" and tore down the hall. Henry clattered behind.

"Wait, Edward. You've no idea—"

A bar of sunlight met him at the door.

Chapter Sixteen

"The Phynodderree Arose At Dawn"
Manx song, Traditional

Departure
July 19, 1905

EUPHEMIA insisted they take a hackney carriage to the dock to ensure they'd arrive clean and fresh. After the driver helped her alight, she removed her boater and stared up at the blue sky, drinking in the moment with Hugh against her chest.

"It's really going to happen. Feels like a dream." *Or a nightmare,* a voice rang in her head. *Ah well, maybe it's best, setting off to make a new life.* She'd argued with herself back and forth, day in, day out, for months. *William does seem better now he's not underground and has time to rest. Last night's silent lovemaking was our send-off. Quiet, but sweet. He took his time, and we both were satisfied. Maybe it'll be good for us to be on our own. Well, not exactly on our own…*

She felt the urge to grab his hand, tell him she loved him. He was busy paying the cabbie.

"Look Da, the wall says King's Dock and we were on *The King Orry.* Lucky again," Edward said.

"You're sure good at reading signs, Edward." Henry smirked and elbowed him. Edward stuck out his tongue.

"English king this time, Son. Not so lucky for Manxmen."

"We hate him, don't we, Da?" Tom said.

"Hush, someone might hear, take offence," Euphemia whispered. She eyed the people milling about. "Mind your tongue."

The cabbie directed them to the tender for the ship while passing their bags down to Henry.

"Have a lovely voyage. Best of luck," the young man said, patting Henry's back. "I'd give me right arm to be in your place, Chuck."

"Would you now? Well, I'd give mine to stop at home. And my name's not Chuck." William scowled at his rudeness, tipped his hat as the driver set off, then distributed the carpet bags amongst the boys. Euphemia considered reprimanding Henry until she looked at his face and thought better of it. She handed Hugh to William, dabbed her eyes, then bent to Ann.

Ann squirmed. "We're not dirty, Mama. Me and Jenny washed."

"We need to look extra nice to board the ship, don't we? Are you boys respectable? I was too preoccupied to check." She made a quick survey and stopped at Tom. She spat on her hankie and attempted to polish his cheeks. He ducked.

"Pee-uw! Something stinks, Mum," Edward said, pinching his nose.

"I just changed Hugh. Can't be him." Euphemia patted the baby's bottom, hoping it was true.

"No," Edward said. "it's the river that smells high: dead fish, rubbish and horseshit."

"It's the River Mersey. So much traffic here, you can't expect it to be a spring like home," William said. "Come along now."

Euphemia gathered everyone together and followed William down the quay. The boys gaped at the SS *Ivernia's* red funnel. A plume of smoke soiled the brilliant white clouds.

"How tall is that chimney, Da?" Edward pointed skyward.

"I've no earthly notion, Son. At least a hundred feet, I reckon. St. Peter's coughing at the foot of the Pearly Gates today." He smiled, then added a cough of his own.

Oh, God, please don't let that start again. I've prayed so hard. He mustn't show weakness.

"What pretty flags, look," said John, pointing to the masts, where the Union Jack and the ship's colours fluttered in the breeze.

"How does she float? Isn't she too big and heavy?" Edward said.

"Where will we sleep, Mum?" John asked.

"When do we eat? I'm starving," Tom said.

Their questions dropped into the sea of passengers on the gangplank. Boot heels clanged on the metal ridges of the walkway. First of the family to advance, Euphemia glanced down at the filthy River Mersey, an open sewer far below. Her stomach churned. She imagined a child slipping through the rails. She clutched Ann's cold, tiny hand while gripping the rail with the other. They herded the boys like goslings, William taking up the rear, Hugh in his arms. Everyone shuffled like cattle in a chute. From decks high above, hundreds of passengers tossed streamers to well-wishers on the dock. That crowd had boarded earlier. *Upper crust, indeed.* Euphemia envied those travelling "First Class." *Why are there classes at all? We're just as good, I bet.*

Within moments of setting foot aboard ship, they found themselves surrounded by a group of boys dressed alike, shepherded by three young women in black. Orphans. She'd seen wan faces like these on Liverpool's streets. She searched out William's eyes, pleading, worried she might faint. He pushed his way ahead, shouting at the boys to stick together. Henry lifted Ann to keep her from being trampled. She kicked out. Her doll fell.

"Jenny! My Jenny!"

Henry couldn't bend over. John dropped to all fours and found the doll under someone's foot.

"I'll keep care of her, Ann," he said. Euphemia nodded her thanks, then searched for William. The soles of Hugh's booties wriggled up ahead. Crushed against a large woman, she stumbled down a narrow, winding staircase. Their harsh reception made her wonder why Thomas had insisted on the Cunard Line: "When I crossed in '86, we were packed in like sardines. Bloody foreign vessels. I'll not have that for Pheme."

William had tossed the letter on the fire. "Why doesn't he just pay for seven first-class tickets, then? Leave me in steerage."

It seemed third class meant third class, no matter what the ship. At the bottom of the iron steps, a steward hastily directed them to their berth in the English-speaking, married, sleeping quarters. Euphemia's anxiety choked her as they proceeded down the hot narrow passage. Another steward waited to show them into the cabin. Their own cabin near the prow of the ship. She and William exchanged shocked looks. Their bags were already stacked against a wall.

"You're all sorted, sir. This is one of our largest family rooms, so you've eight bunks, but I'd advise you sleep with the little ones, ma'am," The steward shook the iron railings on one of the metal bunks. "You'll be glad of these rails. Keep you secure in your beds."

Secure in our beds? What does he mean exactly?

"By God, Thomas spoke true for once," William nearly shouted, his voice bouncing off the metal walls. He pointed to the sink between the beds. "Look, soap, after all, love."

She nodded, unable to speak, astounded they had their own room, let alone beds made up with gleaming white cotton sheets, wool blankets, and feather pillows. John and Tom immediately scrambled over the bars and began bouncing on the spring mattresses, delighted at the bunks. There were hooks for coats and a shelf that served as a seat and baggage compartment. William stowed the bags while Euphemia saw to their coats.

"Hang on, dear," William said, retrieving his wallet. He tapped his finger against his nose and winked at Henry. "Can't be too careful."

"Maybe I ought to keep some of our money," Euphemia said. "There's a load of street urchins aboard with only three young lasses supervising. I wonder where they're off to?" She blinked and suddenly seemed to notice the lights flashing. "Leave off, Tom. You'll break it." Then she altered her tone. "Electric lights, imagine. On a ship. No glass chimneys, eh?"

"There's a funny smell, Mum," Edward said. He sniffed loudly, then let out an almighty sneeze.

"Cover your mouth for pity's sake, Edward." She handed over her handkerchief. "It's just disinfectant," she said, recognizing the pungent scent. "We used it in the Sugarland. I'm glad it's so clean. There'll be no bedbugs; it's very strong. Not like that Liverpudlian tip. I was that worried, going by Thomas' letters. Things've changed in ten years, I reckon."

"Our own cabin," William said. "Not in my wildest dreams—" he paused to inhale, then coughed into his clenched hand. "You're right, Edward. That stench gets up your nose. We'll get used to it." He tugged his handkerchief from his breast pocket and wiped his eyes. "I'm forced to admit, I appreciate Thomas' pushiness. We mightn't need the supplies."

Euphemia moaned. "Oh, that would be disappointing. So much time and expense—" The brutal excursions to the shops, the haggling, the penny pinching, all wasted.

Edward opened a door. "Look, an indoor toilet, Da, like a fancy hotel. I thought we'd go in a chamber pot and dump it out the port hole!" He snorted with laughter.

"We'd have to be stacked up like acrobats to reach and it

might spill back on us." Tom giggled. John made a face.

"Don't be crude," Euphemia said. "Settle down."

"The lads are just excited, my love. We're as well off as First Class toffs, boys, eh? It'll be a lovely holiday for your mother: no cooking, meals served three times a day, no laundry to do. We'll never get her back working once she's lolled about the ship for more than a week." William took her hands and tried to twirl her around in the narrow space between the bunks. He pulled her in close and nuzzled her neck. "You smell nice. Violets, mmm."

Before the ship could depart, they were summoned to muster on the third-class open promenade. Euphemia stared, disbelieving her ears, as the steward announced a final doctor's inspection. She crumpled against William. He dared mumble that this hardly seemed necessary.

"We were in Liverpool a full ten days ahead, sir. Inspected, see? We've the papers to prove it." His hands were shaking. Euphemia shared his inner struggle against a show of temper.

The officer explained that Cunard would be charged a hundred American dollars for each passenger failing inspection in Boston. Those passengers would be shipped back and set ashore in Liverpool; no refund. Euphemia clapped her hands over her mouth, but her shriek escaped.

"Not to worry, Madam. It's a formality. Won't take long." The man gave her a stiff nod before proceeding down the line.

Doesn't matter how long it takes, we could end up turned back, right this minute. Euphemia's shoulders began to shudder. Henry offered to relieve her of the baby. She shook her head. She needed someone to hold. Edward, John, and Tom huddled together, faces white, lips pressed together, hands in pockets. *Poor lambs. I wish I could spare them. Mustn't cry. Mustn't.*

For three hours they stood in line as the July sun pounded the deck and gulls shrieked overhead, dropping the occasional gift on new hats and coats, adding to the general mess and distress. The two doctors, seemingly as exhausted as the passengers, performed a once-over on each person, making notes as they proceeded down the queue. A few people were taken aside, including one of the orphans. A steward carried him off, kicking and screaming. Their chaperones cried and begged for mercy, to no avail. Euphemia shivered. *That could be us.*

Fortunately, the hasty physical didn't reveal William's illness. When they were dismissed, Henry whispered in Euphemia's ear, "The faeries, Mum. They've come aboard to see us right."

"Let's hope so," she answered, struggling to breathe. She stumbled to the railing, wishing she could rip off her corset and throw it overboard. She took a ragged breath and said thanks to God, or the faeries, either one. Someone had saved them.

When at last the tugboats yanked *Ivernia* from her moorings, a cheer rose like a balloon from well-wishers quayside, though none of the steerage passengers reacted like the first and second class passengers waving and tossing streamers over the high railings. Exhausted, frightened, or numb with grief, the men stood, hats off, silent; a few women keened and wept. Babies cried; children shouted. The hundreds gathered together let out a collective sigh when the lines fell away, and the ship headed into open water.

Euphemia's tears stung her eyes in the raw, salt-laced wind. Balancing Hugh on her hip, she joined the crowds headed to the after-hatch. She motioned with her head for Henry to gather the others, but he stayed beside William who was lighting a cigarette. She shrugged, too tired to argue, and put Edward in charge of getting everyone below deck. *I hope they've something hot for us to eat. I can't even nurse 'til I've had a cuppa. My new blouse is likely ruined from sweat or leakage. We needn't have bothered; our fine clothes mean naught—we're third-class.*

Chapter Seventeen

Boayl nagh vel aggle, cha vel grays:
Where there is no fear, there is no grace.

Aboard SS *Ivernia*
July 20, 1905

A steward approached at a smart clip. "Extinguish your cigarette, if you please, sir. Proceed to the smoking room. Fire regulations prohibit smoking on deck." His tone brooked no argument.

Da's face flamed as he pinched the end of his cigarette and enclosed it in his palm. The man in the impeccable uniform strode off, polished shoes tapping the iron deck.

"Ach, I'm dying for a smoke, but I can't stand the thought of a roomful of men smoking. My lungs aren't what they were." He withdrew his handkerchief.

Henry caught a flash on Da's right pinkie. "Grandad's ring?"

"Yes. A bit loose. Da was a bigger man…" He revolved it to show the flat front. "It's called a signet; see his initials engraved there? You can just make them out: HWC. 'Hugh William Carine.' I'm named for him, your second name's after me, and baby Hugh, after him. Tradition, ye ken. Da gave it to me—" he covered his face with the white cloth.

He can't hide his feelings. I won't say a word; it'll embarrass him. He hates his weakness. I don't fault him. Henry shoved his hands in his pockets to avoid grabbing Da's hand. He braced himself against the stiff wind. Concerns swirled in his head like the litter floating in the Mersey. *A miracle we passed muster once more. The Phynodderree did us a good turn. Will it hold as we cross the ocean?* His throat burned as though he'd swallowed seawater. *The ocean. What if there's a storm? Could we run out of coal halfway? What if we sink? We can't swim.* Clenching his fists against his sides, he fought himself. *Stop it. Stop it now.* He stamped his foot, which Da took as a signal.

"You're right, Son. Mum'll be wondering what's keeping us." Da rubbed his hands together. "I'm starving, aren't you?" He clapped his hand over his mouth and winked. "But don't tell Nan I said that. She'd say we're blessed. We are, in truth. I can't believe we're aboard."

That's better, Henry sighed. *He'll be alright.* They stumbled down the steep iron staircase to join the others. Mum's packed lunch had disappeared even before the on-board inspection. When the steward rang the bell summoning third-class passengers to dinner, the boys raced to the wooden benches.

The dining area, in the middle of the hall between the rows of cabins, held four tables. Everyone chose a seat, pressed for elbow room. Da introduced himself to a family of twelve but they didn't speak English. Mum smiled and nodded at the wife, also holding a baby on her lap.

Waiters served mutton stew with one thick slice of buttered bread, a mug of tea or coffee for the adults, a glass of milk for the children. After the tumultuous day, Henry's ravenous hunger demanded more than one helping. He considered Mum a good cook but had never tasted such rich, delicious broth. He wondered if he dared ask for seconds. John's eyes said the same. Edward and Tom didn't hesitate to lift their bowls. Da shook his head.

"Be glad of what you get, youse," he said, under his breath. "Uncle had to bring his own food, cook it, and eat standing up. They've hundreds of people to feed, not just you gannets." He tapped Edward lightly on the arm with his spoon and fixed him with a sharp look. "Don't be a greedy guts, Edward. Show an example."

Mum fussed over the baby, hiding her blush. The head waiter, wearing a white jacket and gloves, nodded at Da. Henry lowered his head, glad he hadn't asked.

"I hope you enjoyed your meals," the man said. "You may now wish to observe the sunset from the open promenade. There's a smoking room for the gentlemen and a ladies' lounge. Have a pleasant evening." He bowed and snapped his fingers for the tables to be cleared. Mum signalled to the other lady who seemed to understand as she gathered her children together.

"Poor dear," Mum said to Henry without moving her lips. "Ten children. How ever will she manage?" His eyes searched out the tallest girl. *I can guess.* The girl didn't return his gaze. She sat with her thin arms wrapped about her waist, her watery blue eyes in her wan face looked as tired as her mother's.

They'd just secured a space near the rail when the sun slipped into the water, tossing golden streamers in its wake. A crewman indicated Tuskar Rock Lighthouse in the distance. "That rock's sunk more ships than any other along this coast. There's a lighthouse now, thank God."

Henry shuddered, imagining their ship smashing against the giant black outcropping. The sea drew a line below the rocks, topped by a gleaming pillar. The man elbowed Henry.

"Three hundred feet tall, she is, three years to build. Ten men lost their lives, but probably saved thousands. She blows the horn every half-minute when there's fog. None tonight, praise be."

Henry nodded. The fellow turned, and their eyes connected. "Here, I'll show you something, look." He prodded his fingers under his collar and extracted a gold chain. Leaning forward, he displayed a pendant bearing the figure of a hunched man supported by a staff, ankle-deep in water, carrying a child on his shoulder. "Saint Christopher. Protects travellers. You want to get you one. Kept me safe all these years." He winked and moved on to another group of passengers. Henry could hear the same speech, word for word. *He's said it a hundred times. He doesn't know I've got me own protection. Not to worry, Nan would say.* He twisted his faery bracelet under his sleeve.

He saw again the Douglas Head Lighthouse off Man disappearing in the distance, as he whispered goodbye to Grandad, Nan, and Blackie. Now, as he overheard the steward say that the lighthouse signalled proximity to Queenstown, he tried to murmur a final farewell to *Ellan Vannin*, their island home. A sob escaped. He brushed his rough sleeve across his cheeks. Standing next to him, Mum held Hugh against her chest and touched his arm.

"I know, darling. The old ones are thinking of us too, I shouldn't wonder. We must be strong, eh?" She pointed across the water. "Hark at the tugboats coming to fetch us. They're so jolly, like little toys. I love them."

Edward and Tom pushed to see. Da lifted John to watch *Ivernia* make harbour. Silhouettes of passengers darkened the dock. People started to mount the gangplank. By their clothes and hand-held baggage, they were third-class. Henry was incredulous. *There's room? The promenade's already as crowded as the streets of Liverpool.*

"This tops off the load, mate. Make ready," one crewman shouted to another.

"Like we're cattle." Da blew out his cheeks.

Mum handed Henry the baby and rubbed Da's shoulders.

Beside her, Ann tugged at her skirt.

"Da, Ann wants to see," John said, jumping down. "I'll hold your Jenny, Ann. She mustn't fall in the ocean, eh? I'll never find her, then."

The electric lights softly illuminating the promenade and the peaceful harbour created a relaxed mood, different than the departure from Liverpool. Some passengers sang songs, played tunes on the fiddle or penny whistle, others even danced a jig. Henry searched out a spot away from Edward but within view of his parents. He wanted to be on his own. Inhaling deeply, he removed his cap to fan his face.

"It's so hot and muggy," he said aloud. A red-haired boy next to him answered.

"Aye, 'tis that. Can't wait to get out on the ocean, me."

Henry stuck out his hand, giving his age as fourteen and his place of birth as Port Erin, *Ellan Vannin*.

"Where might that be, pray tell? Born in Dublin town, me, but we hail from Liverpool, most recently. Name's Connor."

Grandad would've disapproved of the boy's limp handshake. He always said it signalled the person was untrustworthy. But in no time, they began sharing stories. Henry surprised himself, describing Uncle Thomas as a wealthy farmer pouring riches on the heads of his Manx relations. Connor's sparkling green eyes and contagious laugh spurred him on. He seemed interested to listen but said little about himself.

I hope he won't think me a braggart, Henry worried later. He regretted talking so much. *Seems a lively sort.* Tucked comfortably in his bunk, sleeping alone for the first time in his memory, he drifted on smooth waves.

Next morning at breakfast, the head waiter suggested everyone go topside to observe Mizen Head. "Your last view of the British Isles, ladies and gentlemen. We've a bit of fog—" The boys raced upstairs.

"Stay near the stairs, mind, so's we can find you!" Mum

called.

The open promenade teemed like an anthill. Henry struggled to breathe. *I'd rather be surrounded by sheep. This better be worth it.*

In the heavy mist, the rocky outcropping of Mizen Head became a blur. *No wonder the mists hid our island; it's like floating inside a cloud. You can't see for looking.*

"They need a lighthouse here. It's as dangerous as Tuskar, if not worse." The steward with the medal stood nearby, signing a cross over his head and chest. Henry introduced himself.

"Pleased to meet you, Master Henry Carine. Ralph Gallagher's my name; Seaman, First Class. Sorry if I worried you there. It's my Catholic upbringing, is all. *Ivernia,* why she's the safest, fastest ship on the Atlantic. We'll be in Boston eight days hence. Meantime, enjoy your trip. It's the adventure of a lifetime and you'll never forget—"

The ship's horn blasted. Everyone jumped, then laughed. Suddenly a beautiful voice dropped down from the upper deck.

> *A pure heart full of goodness*
> *Is fairer than the pretty lily,*
> *None but a pure heart can sing,*

"Ah, there's a Welsh angel in the clouds," someone said. "It's *Calon Lân,* if I'm not mistaken."

> *Calon l yn llawn daioni,*
> *Tecach yw na'r lili dlos:*
> *Dim ond calon lân all ganu*
> *Canu'r dydd a chanu'r nos.*

The mist gathered the listeners under a damp blanket. No one clapped when the song ended. Sobs broke the silence.

"I'll do ours, Da, as we learned at school," Tom said.

> *Then I hear the wavelets murmur*

As they kiss the faerie shore,
My own dear Ellan Vannin
With its green hills by the sea.

"You missed a bit, lad, but it's made a special send-off. You've a voice for singing, like your mother," Da said, his voice filled with tears.

Snippets of songs in different languages filled the spaces between the ship's foghorn blasts. A piper played a mournful tune. Then a choir of boys' voices swelled like a wave across the deck, singing "God Save The King." Henry made out a pair of arms in black sleeves in the air, directing. The men removed their caps, and many voices joined, even on the upper decks and the crew as well. The foghorn intoned the final note.

"How lovely," Mum said. "The young ladies seem to know what they're doing with those little blighters. You boys steer clear, mind." She bounced Hugh on her hip and took Ann by the hand. "Come on, pet. You too, John. We're drowned rats. Still, I'm glad we didn't miss it. Let's get out of these wet things. I need a cuppa."

By afternoon, with *Ivernia* on the open water, the promenade decks and lounges fell quiet. All but the hardiest passengers were confined to their bunks. Da had said they were fortunate to be in the ship's prow. Now they discovered that's where the waves smashed first. The eerie banging and creaking of the iron walls terrified John and Ann, who huddled together in one bunk. In the hallways, stewards raced to clamp portholes, secure upper hatchways and mop up. Henry knew he'd never forget the smell.

"That stink makes my head hurt," Edward said. "I want to go on deck."

"Well, you can't, flibbertigibbet," Mum said, before turning on her side to be sick in a bucket next to her bunk. "The sea's rough. Sleep, for pity's sake. My last nerve is—" She threw up again.

Henry didn't feel ill, strangely. He kept his balance, tending to the baby, comforting the younger ones. Ann covered her ears at the creaking of the hull.

"What's that? Is it the bad elf?" Her lip trembled.

"No, sweetheart. It's the waves. We're safe in our beds, snug as bugs in a rug. Tom, sing us a lullaby, please."

No one got much sleep that first night. They learned the value of the iron rails.

Next morning, seeking respite from the dank, sour odours in their enclosed space, Henry sought out Ralph at his station near the stairs. He said keeping his eyes on the horizon would do the trick. "You'd make an excellent seaman; you so quickly gained your sea legs."

"I wish my mother could come aloft, but she can't move," Henry said. "I must help, but I'll come up as much as I can. Thanks for the tip."

Silently, he vowed never to set foot aboard ship again. He hated being surrounded by the heaving grey-green sea. His dreams were filled with the sensation of falling, gasping for breath, drowning amidst writhing sea snakes in the skeletons of sunken ships. He'd jolt awake with a weight on his chest, drenched in sweat. *Now I know how Da feels when he can't breathe. No wonder he gets cross.*

On the third day, he came topside for air and found himself in the midst of a sea burial. Standing with other passengers in the fog and rain, he spotted Ralph, clutching his medal.

"Sea burial is an honour for seamen, Henry. Poor sod died in the line of duty, struck in the head by a falling pipe in the engine room."

"Why can't they wait for a proper service on land? Doesn't seem right. What about his kinfolk? He'll have no headstone."

Henry imagined the hot, dark engine room throbbing beneath his feet, heard the clank of a pipe hitting the floor, saw the man lying still, his head covered in blood. All at once, the deck came up to meet him. His knees buckled. Ralph just caught his arm.

"Don't go losing your legs, Henry. Or your lunch. As they say, 'We've four meals a day aboard ship: two down, two up.'" With a slight laugh, he tapped Henry's shoulder. "Cap off, lad."

The body lay wrapped in sailcloth on a board held aloft by two sailors. One of the orphans' chaperones directed the choir, singing "All Things Bright and Beautiful." When the droning engines ceased, the captain read from the Bible. At the words "Earth to Earth," the men tipped the board over the rail. No splash. The passengers recited the Lord's Prayer, sang another hymn, and when the ship got underway again, returned silently to their compartments, heads bowed. Henry remained fixed to the spot, wondering why the captain used the traditional words; the corpse would be food for fishes, not worms. His teeth chattered. *If Da died, would they throw him in?* He imagined him in his suit and bowler, lying on the ocean floor. *Dead. Dead to the world.* He wouldn't tell the others about the service.

Still, his appetite was good. Mum said stews and soups were efficient preparations for large crowds, like in the hotel. He wondered what the rich folks in the upper decks were having.

The next day, he ran into Connor. They ventured onto the saloon deck to spy on the cookery. On tiptoe, they peered through the windows at trays of roasted chickens and grouse alongside heaping baskets of vegetables and fruit.

"Food for the toffs, not us, Henry. Ach, can you just imagine biting into that crispy chicken breast?" Connor dramatically placed his hand on his chest as he slid down the wall.

Suddenly Ralph emerged from the storehouse with a basketful of fruit. The boys clambered to their feet, expecting a reprimand. He tossed them each an apple and a wink.

"Meet me here in an hour, lads. I'll take you to the engine room when I deliver tea to the stokers. You'd like to see how the ship works, would youse?"

"Yes, sir!" Connor saluted.

Henry envisioned the body slipping from the plank. *That man had been struck by a loose pipe… I'll make an excuse. Mum wouldn't like it.* A bit of apple caught in his throat. He swallowed hard. "Mm, delicious. *Moghrey Mie Monninjer Veggey.*"

Connor's eyes widened. "Whaddya mean by that, now? Are you declaring this to be a vegetable, when I knows damn well, 'tis a fruit!"

Henry loved Connor's lilting Irish accent, wondering if he heard a Manx accent from him, and what it sounded like. "No," he said. "I just thanked the faeries for my good fortune."

With a sideways glance from his green eyes, Connor fished a small knife out of his pocket. Connor sliced the apple, stabbing each piece with the tip of the blade. *He's like a pixie: sharp, pointed features, freckles, mischievous grin.* When Henry admired the silver and pearlescent knife handle, Connor shrugged his narrow shoulders.

"Twas a gif' from me Da. He said as 'ow a man 'ud need a blade of his own in the New World. Meself, I can't see this bein' much help in a knife fight, can you?" He laughed and popped another slice into his mouth, flashing small, white teeth. "Mm, can't remember the last time I et an apple. Not since I pinched one at the market in Liverpool."

"I wish my father gave me a knife—well, he couldn't, for he'd have to gift each of us, and there being six—"

"Yes, with Da and meself, why it makes it easier in the present department. Ma died years ago; I don't remember her, so I don't miss her." He paused, then sliced a piece and handed it to Henry on the tip of the blade. "The ones I feel sorry for is them orphans. Headed to Canada, it is, to be foisted off on farmers. Horrible," he said, shuddering.

"How d'you know that?"

"Made the acquaintance of one. Michael. Rounded up off the streets of Liverpool, he was, just last week. Said as how he was doing fine picking pockets for a living. What right've they got, carrying him off? He'd no choice in the matter at all. Now he must sing for his supper." Connor began paring his nails.

"May I see?" Henry's thumb itched to test the blade.

"Nah, best not. Might cut yerself, you being unfamiliar with a blade and all." His crooked smile seemed friendly, but he clicked the knife, snapped it shut, and pocketed it. Ralph appeared around the corner to fetch them. Henry said his Mum needed help, below.

Must be nice to have no one to worry about. Though it does make it easier in the excuse department. Seeing the engine room doesn't appeal to me, any road. I'd rather not know the workings of this beast.

154

CHAPTER EIGHTEEN

Craue beg 'sy chleeau: A little bone in the breast.

July 23, 1905

HENRY longed to spend time on the open promenade with Connor in games of tag, leapfrog, knucklebones, and dice. Connor's skills impressed him, not only his dexterity at onesies and twosies with knucklebones, but also his ability to spin the wooden top he carried. He'd wind a length of cord into grooves carved on the sides of a tiny boxwood top, then grip one end of the string as he tossed it to the deck with a brisk jerk, sending it reeling upright on its metal tip. The challenge between them was to see who'd make it spin the longest, no small feat on the heaving deck. Henry could not master the art. In fact, one time the top thudded against the galley wall, summoning a steward who shooed them off. Connor's green eyes twinkled as he pocketed the top and strolled away, tipping his tiny nose in the air. Henry groaned at his ineptitude.

After the steward had disappeared, Edward turned up. He caught the knack of top-spinning "lickety-split" as Connor observed, patting his back. Henry grabbed Edward's arm and pulled him aside while Connor went to retrieve it.

"Be off with you, Edward. Go play with the orphan boys. Connor's my mate, not yours."

Grey eyes narrowed at him. "I'll play with who I like. Let me be, or I'll tell Mum."

Henry dropped his shoulders. Mum said their quarrels got on her last nerve. Da would give him hell if he troubled her. She'd enough on her plate.

Connor led them to the galley. They peeked in the window. "There's nobody about. That chicken is calling to us. What say I guard the door, while you, Edward, pretend to be spinning the top and then you, Henry, run in and grab it."

"What? Why me? It's your idea," Henry said. He didn't like the thought of stealing. Still, he didn't want to appear cowardly.

"You're bigger. Your long legs'll cross lickety-split. Quick, before someone comes."

Connor pushed the door and Henry stepped inside. His heart pounded. His knees trembled, and his hands were sweating, but the smell of roasted poultry tempted him. His mouth watered, anticipating warm, fresh meat. *Like Connor said, they'll never miss it.* He reached the table in two strides, grabbed a plump, brown chicken from a full tray, jammed it under his jacket, and turned. He heard Connor speaking with someone. The door flew open.

"What the devil are you doing in here?"

Ralph. Oh no.

"Uh, um, I just—"

"I know "just" what you're up to, you. Thievery. What's that? No, don't put it back!" He slapped Henry's arm. "Your filthy hands've been on it. Lucky I was the one who caught you, Henry. Scarper! Don't let me find you or your mates here again, or I'll turn you in."

"Yes, sir. I mean, no sir. Thank you, Ralph." Henry's voice quaked as he stumbled past him, his knees almost giving way.

Ralph's disappointed look stabbed his heart. *I should never have done it. I'm so ashamed.*

Hidden around a corner, Connor motioned to him. Passing over the greasy chicken, Henry slid down the wall. He feared he might faint, or throw up, or both. Laughing, Connor employed his knife, distributing slices of juicy white meat. Henry shook his head, pushing hard against the wall, breathless as if he'd run up Faery Hill. His stomach lurched though the ocean was quiet today. When he stood up, he nearly fell, as if he'd been pushed. *The faeries. They know.*

"Jesus, Mary, and Joseph, but that chicken tasted fine, boys. Pinched food tastes twice as good, as a rule. See youse." Connor strolled off, tossing a coin in the air. *Likely stolen. Seems used to thieving. I'm not. Never again, I swear, Monninjer Veggey.*

"Whew, that was a close call, Henry," Edward said as they headed back down the iron steps.

"If Mum finds out, I'm dead." Henry wheezed, as if a chicken bone were caught in his throat.

"Don't fash yourself. I'll never tell," Edward said. He patted his shoulder.

Can he be trusted? He's a secret to hold over my head. I'll be more careful from now on.

That night there came a knock at the cabin door. Da struggled out of his twisted sheets and threw his long, skinny legs over the bed rails. He tottered and banged his hip against the rails.

"Ouch, dammit. Who on earth could that be?" he said, wobbling across the room like a drunkard.

Peeking over the sheets, Henry spied a pair of black shoes and heard a voice he recognized. *How did Ralph find my room? Must've followed me.* He held his breath. Da closed the door behind him and remained in the hall with Ralph. When he returned, his jaw was set, and he fixed his deep blue eyes on Henry while answering Mum.

"It's nothing, dear. Just a steward I met in the smoking lounge. Name of Ralph. Nice chap. Checking in to see how the boys are getting on. Good of him, really." Henry got the message.

"How odd. Service with a smile." She turned over in bed. "Well, we must get rest. Tomorrow's the dreaded day. Doubt I'll shut my eyes."

Henry listened to Mum's whistling snores and Da's ragged breathing all night. He tossed and turned and at one point, gagged on bile. Leaning over the bed, he tried to vomit. Nothing came out. *Ralph. Da. They know.* He slapped his forehead. *Why, oh why did I listen to Connor? Stupid, stupid. To prove myself. To a thief?* He twisted his sheet into a knot. On top of it all, tomorrow, today by now—the vaccination muster. That was sure to hurt.

Many adults had started grumbling on Day One. Henry'd heard that some men had scarred their upper left arm with the tip of a knife, to avoid the shot. Henry had asked Da, "Should we try? I don't want a needle."

"No," he said, rolling his eyes. "They think they're clever, but they won't get away with it. They fear the shot contains mercury and is poisonous. Like lead," he said, with a wary glance at Mum. "I'm sure it's fine, love, otherwise they wouldn't give it. Besides, what choice've we got? We can't enter the country without the smallpox vaccination. It's to the good for everybody."

Morning arrived with a sharp whistle sounding in the hallways. Henry helped dress the children. Even Edward pitched in, tying John's shoelaces and attempting to comb Ann's hair; she squealed like a banshee. As they closed the cabin door, Mum distributed pieces of MacIntosh toffee. "Calm our nerves." They fell in with the crowd mounting the iron staircase.

Da pulled Henry aside on the promenade deck. "Mum's got the worry at her, Henry. She doesn't need more to cope with. No more tomfoolery, eh? I expect taking the chicken wasn't your idea; not like you. Here's one of Grandad's sayings to remember: '*Eshyn lhieys marish moddee, irrys eh marish jarganyn:* Lie down with the dogs, rise up with the fleas.' Grandad had a saying for every occasion, didn't he? Used to annoy me." He laughed, then tapped Henry lightly on the cheek. Their eyes met. "Lesson learned, eh?"

When his turn for the inoculation came, Henry didn't flinch, thinking the pain just desserts for his crime. His brothers and sister, especially the baby, howled and screamed like everyone else, even adults. That night, Hugh came down with a fever and cried incessantly. At her wits' end, Mum begged a steward to fetch the doctor, despite the risk posed by any whiff of illness. When the man finally appeared, he performed a quick examination, then suggested a cold bath.

"Well, that's what I have been doing, of course; any mother knows that, Doctor, let alone one with six children." She stamped her foot.

"I'm not saying you're a bad mother, Mrs.," the doctor said, touching her hand.

She flapped her hands, sobbing. "I fear the injection's harmed him, Doctor. There's talk of poison—"

"Quackery," the doctor said. "Perfectly safe; meant to prevent illness, not cause it, for heaven's sake. These bloody superstitions—"

Mum interrupted, pushing stray hair off her damp forehead. She twisted her hair into a ragged bun. "He won't nurse, and my arm's so sore, I can't bear to lift him. I keep vomiting. The smell down here would kill a mule."

The doctor began to pack his bag. "Must get back upstairs, Mrs. I'll send something to help you relax and get some rest."

Mum grabbed the doctor's arm. "Upstairs, is it? Oh, I see—the toffs are more important. Like that fancy woman who walks her dog on our deck with her nose in her handkerchief like we're filth." Her voice became a wail.

Henry covered his mouth with both hands. *She's shouting.*

At a doctor. Please, please calm down, Mum.

"Euphemia, dearest. This isn't like you," Da interjected, reaching for her hand. She slapped him.

"Don't shush me, William. I'll have my say! Who does that bitch think she is? Let her use her own promenade deck to walk her ugly dog. I suppose the upper crust don't want the mess on their shoes. We're not allowed on their deck, by God." She threw her arms in the air, stamped her feet, and lost her balance, slamming against the iron bunk. "God damn it!" She rubbed her side and scowled at the doctor.

"That old bag should have to sleep below decks with her smelly dog," Mum went on. "Oh, no. They get fresh air in their cabins while we suffocate here, hatches battened down. That's what's making us feverish, Doctor." She reached for the handle of his bag.

Da put his arms around her, motioning with his chin for the doctor to leave. He didn't hesitate.

Da rocked Mum, humming softly. Seated next to her, Henry soothed the baby. He and Da exchanged weak smiles. Shortly afterward, a cabin boy delivered medicine for "A Mrs. William Cor-rine!"

"Quiet, please," Da said, taking the bottle and hustling him out. They'd only just managed to get the baby and Mum settled together in their bunk. The other children lay wide-eyed in their bunks in shock. Mum had never made such a fuss. Ann hugged Jenny and cried herself to sleep.

"So much for Mum's wonderful sea-going holiday, Da," Henry whispered. "She's been in the ladies' lounge twice if that."

"She fears some of us may be turned back. Besides, she's never been good when any of youse got sick, remember? Knowing what happened to Arthur—" He faltered and brushed his hands through his hair. He coughed and swallowed hard, his Adam's apple bobbing up and down. Henry fetched water.

"Ta. Thank God, it's almost over. Three more days, and we'll reach dry land. I'll kiss the ground. I used to think that was just an expression." His crinkled smile didn't touch his eyes. Henry fought the urge to hug him. He wished they could weep in each other's arms.

Chapter Nineteen

Lurg fliaghey hig çhirrymid, lurg sterrym hig kiuney:
After rain will come drought,
after storm will come calm.

Boston, Massachusetts
July 26, 1905

AFRAID for Hugh's life, Euphemia prayed on her knees, insisting the children join her. He wailed and screamed, then became listless, too weak to nurse. After two days of constant vigilance, his fever broke. Henry never left, except to rush topside for fresh air whenever she slept. William groaned and sweated in his bunk. He seemed to be reacting to the inoculation, exacerbating his weakness. Euphemia dosed him with the laudanum, terrified and ashamed to call the doctor. In close, stifling quarters, the children amused themselves with clapping games or tickling and kicking each other on their bunks. Henry supervised them in the dining room at mealtimes and brought food back. The boys shared uneaten portions.

Euphemia's anxiety prevented her from swallowing more than tea and broth. Meat turned her stomach. *Oh, God, Oh,*

God, Oh, God. Her mind revolved like the giant water wheel at Snaefell. *If I'm sent back with Hugh, and William dies, my children will be orphans. Left with Thomas. He couldn't raise a cat.* She'd never prayed so fervently in her life, with different words: "If Hugh should die before I wake, I pray the Lord his soul to take. If William should die…" *Oh please, please, God, let them live.*

After the vaccination, she had recruited Henry to brush her hair; she couldn't lift her arm. Unfortunately, Henry did not excel at hairdressing.

"Ouch! Henry, you're meant to be brushing my hair, not tearing it out by the roots, for pity's sake." Euphemia put her hand to her scalp. *If only Nan was here. Henry's willing, but he's still a boy, though he thinks otherwise.*

"Sorry, Mum. I was just thinking about Edward and Connor and the games we played—"

"Oh, those two scallawags. Getting up to all sorts," she said, glancing across the room to ensure everyone was asleep. "I shouldn't have laughed at their silly prank; only encourages them." She giggled. "I feel guilty. Ever so slightly." She suppressed another laugh. "Rascals. But she deserved it, I reckon."

They'd spied on the woman with her dog and followed her to the steerage deck. Edward had collected the dog's deposit on a newspaper. Connor chased after her, discovering the location of her cabin. They'd placed the open newspaper outside her door. As Edward told the tale from his bunk, the children leaned forward, bouncing on their seats. "Then what happened? And then?" Luckily for Edward, William was asleep.

"You should've seen her face, Mum. She ran around like a chicken with its head cut off, stamping her fancy shoes, lifting her skirts, blaming the stewards." Edward imitated the lady's cries and expression. John and Tom nearly fell out of their upper bunks, howling. Ann chortled at the general hilarity. Euphemia noticed Henry remained quiet.

"Serves her right, Connor says." Edward passed Henry an

odd look. *What's going on between those two?*

Euphemia had tried to look cross but couldn't help laughing. "You are very naughty, Edward. That boy's a bad influence." She waved the handkerchief she'd used to wipe her eyes. "I should make you apologize. Next journey."

Now, as she recounted it again, Henry seemed bitter. "Boy, if I'd done that, Da would've tanned my hide." He tugged at a knot. She flinched. "Edward gets away with everything."

"Gently now, Henry. Please. You hold the knots away from the scalp, like so," Euphemia took the brush and demonstrated. "Oh, I wish I could cut this damn mop. Just one more thing to manage. I'm so tired." She tugged a handful of hair from the brush. "I'll be glad when this journey ends; it's been a nightmare. I'd no idea what we were in for, though Thomas said *Ivernia's* the best."

She leaned in, examining her face in the mirror. "Will he even recognize me, an old woman of thirty-four, with six children?"

"Remember what the photographer said, Mum? That we were the handsomest family and you the prettiest lady? 'Photogranic' or some such. The fuss he made over Ann—"

Euphemia barely registered Henry's words. "Yes, Thomas is a lot of things, but he isn't a penny pincher. The presents he bought me: this vanity set, for one, mirror, brush and comb. French ivory. Beautiful and practical, both."

Henry halted the brush mid-air. "He bought this? For you?"

I ought not to have said that. Oh dear. She breathed into the oval glass and rubbed it on her skirt. The movement made her flinch. "Dammit, my arm. The strength's been drained out of it." She held up the mirror as Henry resumed brushing. *Who's that, reflected there? Crows' feet at the corners of the eyes, dark circles beneath, a line between the brows. You look right done up, girl. Vanity, vanity, all is vanity, the nuns' refrain.* She misted the glass again. The glass and her eyes both clouded over.

From William's bunk, a moan. Henry stopped and placed a hand on her shoulder. "Uncle Thomas says Da'll improve working out of doors, doesn't he, Mum? Do you think he's right?"

"Well, he believes so, or he'd never have sponsored us," she said.

"Why didn't he just sponsor Da on his own? We could've joined him later—"

"Da wouldn't leave us, now, would he?" She clicked her tongue as she turned and looked directly at Henry. "All will be well, as long as he passes inspection. I know how you feel about Uncle Thomas but mind you show him proper respect. Make him glad we came. It won't be easy. Your father and Thomas—" she paused. "Let's just say, we'll have adjustments to make, any road."

Henry frowned. "What do you mean, Mum? Are you worried he won't like us? Me?"

Oh dear, I've gone too far. She shuddered. My fears mustn't put him off. He needs to accept what comes. Face facts.

"What'm I saying? You'll be good as gold, like always." She turned her smiling eyes on him and reached up to cover his hand on the brush. "It's been dire straits, eh? Hope we've seen the worst."

She shook out her hair and re-wrapped her precious comb, brush, and mirror in their flannel bag. "Thank you for your help, love. I looked a fright. Mustn't scare the inspectors."

She placed her icy hand on his warm cheek. "You've done so much to help, Henry. Nan and Grandad would be proud. There's more than one way to be a man. Remember that." She touched his arm "Fetch Hugh for me now, please, so's I can nurse. Poor lamb, this sickness has weakened him. I can't wait 'til we're settled."

* * *

Guided by a pilot boat through a forest of masts, *Ivernia*

finally approached the Cunard Wharf at East Boston. Thousands of steerage passengers pushed and shoved their way topside, cheering wildly at their safe arrival. On the dock, a band played, though the music couldn't be heard above the roaring crowd. Henry held Ann so she'd see them make harbour. Edward watched enthralled, but Tom and John jumped up and down, and William whistled. Euphemia's heart soared with the gulls swooping overhead. John again pointed out the colourful snapping flags decorating the ships. Stout brick buildings with three to four rows of narrow windows shone blood-red against the blue sky. It reminded her of the Merseyside dock.

Seems like a year since I stood there worrying about the journey. Eight days have passed and it's over. She shook her head. Horrible. I'll put it behind me, like I did on my first trip from Liverpool. I never want to be aboard ship again, as long as I live.

She hated being pressed against the people pushing and shoving on the deck, especially holding Hugh on her hip. She feared her corset might burst as she struggled for breath. Her throat was parched, and her head pounded with questions. *The whole world is here. I wonder what these people are expecting; why'd they leave home? Did they choose to come, or were they forced, like us? How does William feel? He didn't want to come either. No more than Henry. And I least of all, though they don't know it.*

"You alright, dear?" she said, leaning on his shoulder. Her voice caught. "Saints preserve us, we made it. Just one more hurdle. We must be brave."

He looked into her eyes but didn't answer. Her heart dropped. *He's overcome. I must be strong for both of us.*

Ann squirmed in Henry's arms. "Jenny and me wants off. There's a monster. I hate the noise it makes. I'm hot, Mama."

"It's the *Buggane*, Annie. Grandad told us about him, remember? A hairy elf with—"

"That'll do, Edward," Euphemia reached over and tugged his ear. Ann put out her arms for William to take her. He didn't move.

"Not long now, sweetheart. Just set her down, Henry. Take Hugh. I'm hot, and it's ruining my blouse."

She noticed William scanning the teeming crowd. *He's looking for Thomas. How's he expect to find him amongst that lot?*

"Where's Uncle Thomas? Will he know us?" Tom shouted.

"There, there, look. A man is waving his hat looking straight at us. Is that him, Da?" John pointed to a large man, head and shoulders above most of the rest.

"Where? By God, I think you're right. How on earth— you've never met him! You've a keen eye, John, and no mistake," William said.

"I just knew it. He reminded me of Grandad somehow," John said. "It will be nice to meet him. I'm tired of the ship, too. Can I take my coat off?"

Searching amongst the people mingling like bees on a honeycomb, Euphemia wanted to see Thomas, and yet, she didn't. Her stomach flipped, and an aching surged in her groin. As if her monthlies were starting. *Oh, God, not now.* Her breasts ached. She realized she'd been holding her breath. Milk started to flow as she grabbed Hugh from Henry. She'd have to nurse him standing up.

The passengers surged forward, but the rails for third class remained fixed in place. Only those with citizens' papers and doctor's approval were permitted to disembark. Meaning only first and second-class. Two thousand people moaned as one. William's knees went out from under him. He collapsed against Euphemia's sore arm.

Connor and his father stood nearby. His father's face flamed red as his hair as he shouted, "Call this a free country, do ye? Jesus, Mary, and Joseph! What with yer inspections, examinations, vaccinations, numbers, tickets, stamps, and the divil knows what? What I'd like to know is, where's the freedom of it?" He spat, hitting another man's shoes, provoking a shoving match.

Euphemia shook her head in disgust. *Damn fool, making an uproar with the last inspection pending. They can turn us back for any reason.* She noticed that Henry had caught Connor's eye. The pinch-faced lad shrugged. "What good does it do?" he seemed to say. *He's right. His father's show of temper could risk everything. Some men just can't control themselves.* She swirled her skirts and directed the boys to follow William back downstairs.

"*The Buggane, the Buggane!* Please, Mama, no!" Ann's cries echoed in the stairwell.

CHAPTER TWENTY

Cum nynekenghey, bwoie:
Curb your tongue, boy.

Immigration Station, Long Wharf, Boston
July 27, 1905

THEY endured an uncomfortable night in the stagnant heat below. At dawn, they re-packed their bags and dressed in their best once more. At least their stomachs were happy; left-over first and second-class fare had provided a buffet supper. Now the whole family knew what they'd been missing. When Edward complained about the unfairness, Euphemia thought of Connor's father and his ineffectual protest. *Whoever said 'Money can't buy happiness' has never been poor.* "It's the way things are," she wanted to say but didn't.

Henry helped Ann and John dress while Edward and Tom sat on their bunks watching their father's straight razor sliding up and down the strop in preparation for the ritual of shaving. The tinkling of the brush against the shaving cup, the lathering of soap, the rasping of the blade on stubble... the whole proce-dure enraptured the boys.

"I can't wait to shave," Edward said, eyes riveted on William as he stretched his neck, pinched his nose, and whirled the blade along his bony chin with nary a scratch. "That looks tricky around that bump on your throat, Da."

Euphemia looked at their fresh, eager faces and felt a wave of nostalgia. *They grow up too fast. In such a hurry to become men, poor lambs. They've no idea what awaits.* "Did you?" A voice in her head set her straight. *Where does it come from? Who is speaking?*

"That's better. Feel this, lad." William reached for the nearest spectator's hand. "Soft as a baby's bum."

"Language, Mr. Carine," Euphemia said with a smile.

"Only speaking the truth. Come, do the back of me neck, love. Save the cost of a barber. See how I trust your mother, lads? Don't give your razor to just any woman," William assumed a solemn expression, then leaned over to rub his cheek against hers. "Smooth, eh?"

"Hold still, you bugger, or I'll have your guts for garters. Boys, enough gawping at this silly old man's performance. Get yourselves washed and dressed." She gestured with the razor. "Edward, brush Ann's hair. Don't make that face. Ann, hold still. John, tie your laces. We don't want to trip on the stairs, now, do we? Oh, never mind. Henry, you do it. Tom, you—well you just try and stay clean at breakfast. Quickly now."

The instructions rolled off her tongue as she cleaned up William's neck and sideburns.

She wiped down the razor. "And where's my fee for barbering?"

"How's this?" William planted a firm kiss on her lips.

She gave him a light tap, then ran her hand along his chin. "You'll do, I guess," she said, turning around. "Now, you boys collect our soap, toothbrushes, all our bits and bobs. Waste not, want not. Shove the stuff anywhere in your carpet bags."

"Do we get to keep the towels, Mother?" John asked.

"Certainly not. We're not thieves."

Euphemia caught a look pass between Edward and Henry. *What're those two scallywags up to?* She brushed curiosity away in the flurry of packing up.

After a meal of runny porridge, all third-class passengers were briskly evacuated from the ship to the quayside next to the Cunard immigration centre. In the pouring rain, they awaited entry into a huge warehouse. Henry remarked that the other passengers were nowhere to be seen.

"It's always the same, Son," William said, clicking his tongue. "The toffs are somehow immune to disease, unlike us common folk. Why wouldn't they be, with their fine food and fresh air throughout the passage?" He extracted his handkerchief from his pocket and wiped his face, glistening with sweat despite the chill. "You can be sure their money's from the sweat off another man's brow."

"Just like the goddamn English, right, Da?" Edward said, looking up at him.

"Too right, Edward."

"Ssh," Euphemia said, banging her heel on the ground. "No more of that talk, lest we attract attention." Euphemia shivered. Her boater smelled of wet straw and offered little protection from the rain. The boys' Glengarry caps drooped, Ann's braided blue ribbons flopped on her damp dress, and the baby's cotton bonnet clung to his head. William brushed water from his shoulders.

"We're luckier than most, but not as well off as some, Da used to say." William sighed and stifled a cough.

"Go on with you, William. We've plenty to be thankful for. Our Hugh's better, Thomas is waiting. Our ordeal will soon be a memory."

Euphemia lifted her chin and smoothed her skirt with the flat of her hand. *I must keep his spirits up, though my heart's fluttering like the sparrow we once found in the chimney flue.* She extracted the bottle of laudanum from her handbag. The last drop. *He mustn't cough in front of the doctors.*

"Hold hands, children. We could lose each other. Henry, keep hold of Ann. Ann, don't let go of Jenny. And everyone, keep a grip on your carpetbag."

Inside the airless wooden building, the cries of babies, shouts of officials, and suffocating heat accosted their senses. A river of steerage passengers flowed through the doors, braided into streams by iron bars and wooden partitions. Endless queues were supervised by men in uniform who seemed officiously polite. The fetid stench of bodies sweating with heat and fear caused people to retch, and some to actually vomit. The smell of disinfectant pervaded the space, as it had on the ship. An hour went by. Euphemia saw that William's face was drained of colour, and his body was trembling. *Cold? Fear? The milk reek? What is it? Oh, God.*

"What is it, dear? Here, lean on Henry. You mustn't fall down."

"God, I need a smoke." His hand shook as he pinched the bridge of his nose.

"No. You don't," Euphemia said between her teeth. "Inhale, count to five, hold, then exhale. Works for me when I'm in labour."

At last, they reached the front of the queue. Euphemia forced her lips into a smile as she presented the children, one at a time, to an inspector. The tremor in her hand betrayed her jangled nerves. She followed her own advice: deep inhale through the nose, exhale through the mouth. They were ready with the inspection cards stamped in Liverpool and their vaccination cards pinned on the children's coats. Despite that, inspectors were bound to visually and physically examine each individual: lymph nodes checked, tongues depressed, inner ears prodded with a cotton swab. A man used a steel, hooked instrument to raise each person's eyelids, one at a time. A fear-stricken woman pulled away, begging to know what they were looking for. She received a one-word answer: "Trachoma." Euphemia shuddered. *A bug in the eyes? From the ship? Jesus.* The little ones shrieked. Euphemia struggled to restrain each child, wishing they could refuse. *They use it over and over, like sticking a dirty knife in a jam jar, but what can we do?*

When the metal talon scraped the rim of her eye, Euphemia clenched her fists and swallowed hard to keep from retching. And speaking out. *All that time and money spent for the inspection in Liverpool, for what? Money we could ill afford to waste.* "Are we criminals?" she wanted to scream. "No. Just third-class."

Somehow, she controlled herself, keeping the children in line while shifting Hugh from hip to hip. Then they announced that parents would be questioned, individually. She mouthed, "Oh, God." William found her eyes, shaking his head in disbelief. It obviously meant nothing that Thomas had posted a bond to guarantee his support. For the first time, they heard the label 'LPC: Likely Public Charge.' They saw inspectors holding men on either side, three chalk letters marked on their coats. They'd be sent home, alone, or perhaps with their family, if they were lucky, someone said. Euphemia's heart stopped. *Lucky. This is it. We'll never get by this time. Oh, why did we think we could fool them?*

Trembling, Euphemia entered the examination room. Half an hour later, an officer accompanied her to their bench, exchanging her for William. She watched his stooped shoulders disappear behind the door. Taking Hugh from Henry's arms, she rocked back and forth on the wooden seat. Her eyes stung, and her throat was so dry, she couldn't swallow. A moan escaped her lips.

Henry held out his hands. "Mum, what took so long? We're famished. We've not eaten a bite since breakfast, and there's no food anywhere. Don't they care there are little ones? Someone said you could buy food, but I haven't any money and—" His furious expression became one of fear when he met her eyes. "How was the examination?"

"Oh, Henry, it went on and on. My name, date of marriage, your father's occupation, whether I could read and write, my nationality, state, and history of health. I can't remember… I was that nervous. I hope I made sense." Her teeth ached from clenching her jaw. *Water. I need water.*

"If only we could've practised. I doubt your father remembers his own birth date, let alone our anniversary. I'd've had '1892' tattooed on his wrist in Liverpool. God forbid he should mention the effect of the mine… He's not the best liar, unlike some—" *No, don't say that.* But she couldn't seem to stop talking. "Questions like, 'Have you been to prison?' Good Lord, if I'd been to prison, would I say so? Not bloody likely! 'Participated in anarchist activity?' Such as? 'Complained about taxes?' Everybody does that. 'Are you polygamists?' Ha!" She rolled her eyes. "'Methinks my husband's enough on his plate with one wife, thank you very much,' I'd love to've said, but I kept soft as butter. Pray your father keeps his temper, as well."

"What's 'poli-poli-ig-amists,' Mum?" Edward asked.

"Oh, shut up, Edward." Henry turned around and swatted him. "Can't you ever just shut up, for Christ's sake?"

Euphemia shook herself. Henry was wiping his face on his sleeve; his faery bracelet fell to the floor. John was kneeling, running both hands on the smooth, cold marble. He picked up the bits, rolling the soft threads in his fingers before handing them to Henry, who stuffed the mass in his pocket.

"I need the toilet," Euphemia said. She did. Desperately. She plopped Hugh on Edward's lap and placed him in charge. Ann sucked her thumb and rocked, swinging her feet alongside Tom, who was amusing her with a clapping game. "Come along, Henry. Let's fetch water for everyone."

Out of earshot, she turned and wrapped Henry in a hug. "Oh, my dear boy, I've leaned on you too hard. Forgive me." She rubbed his shoulders and made to dry his tears with her handkerchief. He took a deep breath and stepped back.

"Sorry, Mum. I'll try harder," he said. "I, I… it's just, I'm done up. So tired. And I could gnaw the buttons off me vest."

Brushing his cheek, she said, "We're all perished, to be sure. Soon's your father's passed and paid for our papers we can go, the man said. Costs $16 to get our cards. A 'head tax,' so-called. More bloody expense. What's that in pounds, I wonder."

She took Henry by the shoulders and turned him around. "I'd hate to be in the place of that poor woman. Over there, see?" Gesturing with her chin, she tilted her head. "In the grey dress, look. I heard an inspector say her handbag was stolen." She spoke under her breath. "Thank God your father kept our money safe on his person. What on earth will she do? Can you just imagine fellow passengers robbing you? When we're all in the same boat? God's truth."

She smoothed the front of her skirt, then attempted to tuck a loose strand of hair back into the bun under her hat. No use. She'd have to redo her coif in the toilet. She thrust the hat pin back in hard. *Ouch. Dammit.*

"One of those wayward orphan boys, I shouldn't wonder. I'd search the lot of them." Her urgent need for the toilet pressed her. "Listen, compose yourself, wash your face and hands, and think on the train trip. Won't that be exciting? All the way to the farm. One last hurdle, pet. Then we shall truly be in America. Uncle Thomas is just outside those big doors."

"But, but, Mum, what if—"

"No, don't," she said, grabbing both his arms. "You'll tempt fate, as Nan would say. Say a word to the faeries; I'll keep up my prayers. We've made it this far." She patted his backside. "Now, scoot."

Euphemia wended her way through the crowd. *He's there, on the other side of that huge door. I feel him. I've been intent on getting us through, even though I dreaded this. Henry's the same, fighting for something neither of us wants. We're like sparrows stuck in the chimney flue.* She dropped her head between her knees as she sat on the toilet.

She mustn't sob, lest someone hear. *Henry's right, William ought to have come on his own. He'd never have made it, though. Yet it almost cost our Hugh his life.*

When she leaned over to wash, her hat fell into the sink. She watched the water fill it to the brim.

"Oh dear." The woman next to her reached over to help. "It's straw. No harm done. Such a pretty hat."

"Would you like it?"

"Wha—what? Why yes, if you don't want it. Are you sure?"

"Yes. I never should have bought the bloody thing in the first place. Damn nuisance. You're welcome to it."

CHAPTER TWENTY-ONE

Tra ta'n chibbyr roie ghirrym, ta fys aiu cre ta lattal ushtey:
When the well runs dry,
we know what it is to want water.

AS Henry followed his mother's boater hat bobbing up and down in the crowd, he felt a glow in his chest. Her concern for his feelings surprised and comforted him. He could hear Nan: "She's put on a brave face; you must do as much. You're a man, so."

Pushing aside the heavy washroom door, he bumped headlong into Connor. He attempted to engage him in conversation, but his friend seemed distracted, freckles standing out like measles on his pale cheeks, nose pointed straight ahead. As he brushed past with a quick farewell, he pocketed the pearl-handled knife.

I missed the chance to say goodbye. I'll never see him again. Probably for the best. He stepped into the water closet. The smell of bleach almost knocked him back. *These inspector types think we're all dirty. Well, we're not.* As he reached to pull the chain on the porcelain water tank, he glimpsed a wad of purple material tucked in behind. He gingerly extracted a velvet purse, string handles cut.

Mum said a lady was robbed. Oh. Oh no.

Mum would know what to do. Returning to the bench, he said he'd met Connor, then, after checking both ways, he fished the purse from under his jacket. A faint smell of chicken wafted to his nose. *My coat still bears my guilt.* His cheeks burned.

"Oh my, yes, Henry, we must report it. That woman is alone. She stands to be deported as a vagrant. Poor dear, she must be terrified. Let me see—hmph, just as I feared. No money. I told you boys not to trust that Irish brat!" She wrinkled her nose and waved her hand in front of her as if swatting a fly. "There's your 'lace curtain' Irish and your 'pig in the kitchen' Irish, my landlady used to say. Him and his father are the latter." She grabbed Henry's arm, hoisting Hugh onto her hip. "Edward, mind the children. Come, Henry, we must report this—I hope they catch the blighter!"

Henry stuttered as he spoke to an inspector, while Mum nodded her support. Other passengers in the queue overheard and began pointing. He recognized some of the people from the ship. Cold sweat rolled down his sides. His hands started to shake. *Wish I'd never seen it. Or said anything. Someone else might've…*

The inspector frowned and called for a supervisor, shouting that the purse had been found. When the man arrived, Henry described Connor and his father, discernible by their red hair.

A woman pushed forward in the crowd, shouting, "Say, I remember you. I heard a steward talking to your father, saying how you'd stolen a chicken and weren't allowed upstairs no more on your own. Maybe t'was you stole the purse."

"What's this, what's this?" Mum cried out. "No, you're mistaken. My son's not a thief. He never stole anything in his life."

"Well, he sure looks guilty," the woman said. "Hark at his face."

Tom and Edward exchanged frightened glances. Ann sensed the tension and began to cry. John took Henry's sweaty hand and squeezed. Mum balanced Hugh and whirled in a circle.

"We need your father. He ought to be back by now. Where the blazes is he?" Her eyes were lighthouse beacons, scanning the crowd. She touched an inspector's arm. "Please, sir, you must find my husband, William Carine. He's being examined. We need help."

* * *

Da later told them he'd been detained for a full examination. He'd only just removed his shirt when the excitement began. "The doctor gave me the once-over and sent me back to where people were milling around you, Henry, clapping and shouting. I didn't know what to make of it."

The inspectors discovered money in Connor's coat. The woman described the sum and the silver clasp holding the pound notes. She tearfully pressed a coin from her gloved hand into Henry's icy palm. "Thank you, lad. It's all I had in the world."

Mum shook her head, crossing her arms, shooting a dagger at the woman who'd pointed a finger at Henry. "My boy did his Christian duty, as he's been raised. Your smile is reward enough."

The lady gave Henry her blessing and was led away by an inspector. Faint with relief, Henry smiled and inwardly thanked the faeries. John grabbed his hand. His brown eyes glistened with tears. "I'm glad you're my brother, Henry," he said.

If he only knew. I'd hate for John to think less of me. Edward kens my secret; so does Da. He wished he could erase the past. Maybe this made up for it somewhat.

As they were ushered through the line, Mum grabbed his shoulder and hissed, "What's this about a chicken, Henry?"

Henry didn't turn around. He couldn't face her. Not after all this.

"Never mind," Da said, patting her arm. "Just boys' pranks. All over now." He smiled at Henry just as an inspector handed Mum their identity cards. In a serious tone, the officer said to keep them safe for three years, just in case.

"In case of what, sir?" But the man had already turned away.

"Too late for them to question us anymore, eh, Da?" Edward grinned and tugged Da's sleeve. He expelled a sigh, which prompted a coughing fit.

"Too right, Edward. I thought we were done for when they marked my jacket with chalk. EX. I thought that meant "exit," but it means "examination." An X means mental case. I guess they can tell just by looking. Good thing they can't read minds, for I could've strangled somebody. This rigamarole took forever. It'll be a wonder if Thomas is still waiting for us."

He handed Henry his handkerchief. "Here, erase that chalk, would you, Son? It's like it's burned on my coat." Henry felt Da's shoulders trembling as he rubbed his back. "These little cards are like gold. I'll put them in my bag for safekeeping, love."

When Mum handed them over, he examined them closely. He groaned. Mum jumped. Henry tripped over his feet. *Now what?*

"Christ, they've spelt our name wrong. Carin, not Carine. They went and dropped the 'e', would you believe? Bloody hell. Well, we can't ask them to fix it, after all this," He scowled, removed his bowler, and ran his hand through his hair. With a deep sigh, he shook his head. "Ah well, I guess it's meant to be; a new name for a fresh start. We've lost the oldest name on Man, though. Sad. We mustn't tell Grandad, though."

Mum nodded in agreement, extracting her handkerchief from her purse. "We passed, that's the main thing. Such a trial." She wiped her cheeks and forehead, then dabbed at the baby's nose. "We'll get used to it, won't we, my lamb? 'A rose by any other name…' the saying goes. Oh, peuh!" She waved the handkerchief like a white flag. "Something doesn't smell like a rose, at all. William, I must get Hugh sorted. Ann and I must freshen up. You and the boys go to the toilet, just there, look. Then we'll meet Thomas outside. You're right; he'll think we've died or been sent back. It's been hours. Feels like days."

"Where's your pretty hat, Mum?" John asked. "It matches your tie. I love that hat."

"Oh, I lost it in the washroom. Never mind," she said, brushing his cheek. "Henry, see the boys wash their hands and face. We must look somewhat presentable." She tugged her hair back in its coif, then took Hugh from Da and made Ann hold her skirt.

As her small form walked off, Henry flashed back to Connor. *Poor blighter never knew his mother. It's his father who turned him into a thief. I'll never steal again.* He clenched his fists in his pockets. *Christ, they'll be shipped back to Ireland, or worse, slapped in prison over here. Separated. Connor will be an orphan. Mum said they deserve it. Still…*

He fingered the strands of faery thread in his pocket, silently giving thanks to the *Little Ones. I reckon if it hadn't been for Mum hearing about the purse and me finding it, Da might've been properly examined; they'd have heard his cough, seen his hands tremble…* He shooed the thoughts away like flies on fresh scones. Right out of the oven. His stomach growled.

Scones. Cream. Berry bonnag. *Ach, I'm so hungry, I could eat my arm. And parched. Hot, sweet tea, or better yet, ginger beer… We are starving now, Nan. Truly.*

Chapter Twenty-Two

"FINALLY! I feared they'd deported you!" A shout greeted them as they stumbled out of the huge wooden doors onto the sidewalk, blinking in the afternoon sunlight. A huge man approached. "I was that worried. Been waiting an age; overnight and now more'n half the day. No matter, you're here now, Carine family."

Henry almost gasped aloud. *He's a mountain.* Uncle Thomas staggered forward to throw his arms around Da's shoulders. The embrace knocked him off balance, and his bowler tumbled to the sidewalk. John retrieved it.

The din of the street was louder even than the cacophony inside the warehouse. Henry's ears rang as if church bells were clanging in his head. The ground came up to meet him with every step, and the surrounding buildings seemed to cant side to side. His stomach turned. Or maybe it was just hunger.

Uncle Thomas shook Da's outstretched hand, frowning. "By God, William, I never realized—Mother said, but it's worse—I'd've passed you in the street... me own brother." He hit Da lightly with his fist. "Never fear. We'll have you right as rain in no time. The Michigan air will do you a power of good."

He rocked back on his heels and ran his eyes over Da. "How was the crossing, then, eh? Better than mine back in '95, I'd wager. Stinking foreign vessels! You can't beat a British ship. The *Ivernia* all she's cracked up to be? I should hope so for the cost."

He didn't await an answer to any of his questions, but turned toward Mum, removing his hat. Throwing his arms wide, he whistled.

"Why, just look at you, Pheme. Beautiful as ever. You look a fashion plate in that corduroy suit. Pretty as a picture."

The boys looked around. Who was "Pheme"?

"There you go, exaggerating again, Thomas. I look like I was sent for," Mum said, straightening her skirt and pulling on her blouse. "The journey wore me out, not to mention the trial we just endured. I'm perished."

"Whisht, 'tis fair as a queen, thou art, my lady," he said, bowing to kiss her hand.

Is he making fun of her? What a strange greeting. God, I'm so hungry and thirsty, I could die. Henry longed to sit down, even on the sidewalk. *Pretty clean compared to Liverpool.*

Suddenly Uncle Thomas took both Mum's hands and whirled her in a circle, almost lifting her from the ground. When he stopped, Mum reached for Henry's shoulder to steady herself. A scowl crossed Da's face under the brim of his hat.

"Do you mind not flinging me about, Thomas? I haven't got me land legs yet!" Mum said, leaning over to catch her breath.

"Ah, but it's good to have you here, at last." His voice boomed. Then he shook himself like a dog waking up. "All of youse, I mean. Of course, of course," he said, directing his gaze toward the children. "You're a marvel, Pheme, and no mistake. Travelling with all these young'uns, I can't fathom it! I had enough trouble on me own."

"Is that you or the whiskey talking, Thomas?" Mum said, sniffing the air.

"Yes, well, a fella needed to kill some time. There's a pub close, fortunately. Inspections were over quick when I came but with a whole family… Speaking of which, let me see if I can decipher who's who."

He shifted his gaze to Henry and sized him up. "You're Henry if my memory's any good. About four you were when last I clapped eyes on you, but I'd know you anywhere, all skin and bones like your dad. A long drink of water, as we say. We'll soon get you fattened up." He patted his protruding stomach. "This is mine, all paid for!" He laughed and punched Henry lightly.

Ouch. My sore arm. He's so loud. People are staring.

"As for the rest, I only know your names from Nan's letters. The wee man in your arms, Henry, is the newest addition to the Carine clan, I presume. Hugh, I believe… named for the old man, eh? Good choice." He squeezed Hugh's chubby leg, then bent down to Ann. "I've not had the pleasure of meeting this young lady." He curled a tendril of blonde hair around his index finger. "The colour of gorse in bloom," he said. "Beautiful. What's your name, sweetheart?"

Ann just stared, thumb in mouth, eyes wide. Mum answered. "Ann. She's four. She'll make strange for about two minutes, then you'll never keep her quiet."

"After Grandma Ann. What a little doll."

"Jenny. Jenny Kronchent. The faeries named her, not me," Ann said, displaying her doll.

Uncle Thomas bent backward, laughing as if it were a good joke. Then he reached down to gather her in his burly arms. She didn't kick. *Amazing. She always kicks.* Thomas held her high in the air, gaze fixed on Mum as he spoke:

"Ah, she's the picture of Nan. Same eyes. We call that 'Alice blue' over here, Pheme, for President Roosevelt's blue-eyed daughter. Nan was as fair, I recall. Hard to believe. It's been ten long years—" His voice dropped as he set Ann amongst the younger boys, who stood gathered around Mum, turning their feet and glancing at Uncle Thomas. *You'd think we were meeting The King.*

"That reminds me, we must send the old folks a telegram; let them know you've arrived, safe and sound. They'll have the worry at them. I imagine the goodbyes were hard. When I left—" He yanked a handkerchief from his breast pocket and mopped his broad, sweaty face, then fanned his face with his hat. "God, it's a scorcher."

Despite the humid heat, Uncle Thomas wore a wool suit, with cuffed, creased trousers, a fitted single-breasted coat over a buttoned waistcoat, a white shirt, and a loosely knotted tie. His felt hat, tipped to one side, had a single dent in the crown and a band sporting a striped feather. The ruddy cheeks, thick lips adorned by a long, bushy moustache, and light grey eyes bore little resemblance to Da's pale skin, chiseled features, and hollow cheeks. *Gosh, they might be strangers. Nan says we all 'take after' different people. Edward and I aren't a bit alike, either.*

"Now then, Henry, introduce your band o' brothers. I know names, of course, but can't put them to faces for the life of me. There's a Thomas, I believe… named for some reprobate in the family. Ah, 'tis you, is it?" He poked at Tom's chest.

"I go by Tom, me." Tom crossed his arms, matching his uncle's stance.

"Hmm, my ears were doorstops, too, at your age. Don't worry, your head will grow to fit them, and then you'll be as clever as your namesake!" When he laughed, a flash of gold appeared between his front teeth.

"Well, I won't forget your name, but we'd best call you Tommy, so's we know who we're calling to dinner, eh?" He flicked one of Tom's flaming red ears. *Ouch. Tom hates people remarking on his ears.* Oblivious to the tears brimming in Tom's eyes, Uncle Thomas looked about, as if searching for something.

"I understand we've an apostle among us. John?"

John jumped, interrupted from gazing up at the tall buildings. "Yes, sir. I'm John, sir. Pleased to meet you. Sir. Uncle."

Uncle Thomas leaned down and cupped his ear. "Didn't realize you were so young. The quiet one. Freckles, eh? You'll get even more in the Cheboygan sunshine, Johnny. As will your mother, with her fine complexion, if she's not careful. You need a hat, Pheme."

"You had a boat, Mama. With spots on. Where is it?" Ann asked. Uncle Thomas pinched John's pale cheeks. "You've your mother's eyes. Hark at those long eyelashes. Puts me in mind of a fawn." He glanced up at Mum. She was fussing with Ann's braids.

Straightening, Thomas touched his cleft chin, then snapped his fingers. *His chin matches the dent in his hat. I wonder if he planned that.* "Here's a thought, Henry. What say we call you 'Harry'? Sounds more American, any rate."

"I'm Henry. After Da." His voice cracked. *Dammit, when I needed to sound like a man.*

"So, Harry, with baby here, that makes six if my arithmetic's any good. None of youse were left on the ship?" He returned his hat to its jaunty angle on his enormous head.

"Not quite, Uncle." Edward leapt out from behind Mum's skirt. "Fooled you!"

Thomas indeed appeared startled. "Who's this young rapscallion, then? Edward? A fine-looking young man, like meself, betimes. Hair black as coal, though mine's shot with silver now." He leaned down to examine Edward more closely. "Those eyes—are they grey or blue? Wolf eyes, I'd say. A bit wild, this one, Pheme. Ten, thereabouts?" He picked him up under the arms and whirled him around. "A handsome lad, and no mistake."

When Thomas set him down with a thump, Edward stumbled, bumped into Henry, and fell on his knees. Da pulled Edward to his feet and brushed his sleeve.

"Handsome is as handsome does, Thomas," he said. *Is Da angry, or just tired?*

"Me, too, Nuncle Domas. Me and Jenny wants a turn to fly," Ann begged, raising her arms.

"Righty-o, sweet Alice Blue."

"Where do we catch the train for Cheboygan, Thomas?" Da said.

"Go on with you, William," Thomas said with an eye-roll as he picked up Ann and twirled her, then hoisted her up to ride on his shoulder. Gripping her knees against his broad chest, he shook his head.

"We were never for leaving Boston the day you arrived." Uncle Thomas exhaled a puff of air. "Away with the faeries, now? Ach, we're off to our hotel. You need a cold brew, William, to clear your head."

Henry cringed. *Thomas seems to be mocking Da. How strange.* The sun blazed against the red buildings, setting the colour on fire. *It's so hot. I've never known such heat. We are done up; he's got that right. But an 'otel? Who pays?* He saw Da's notebook with its rows of carefully totted sums. Da was searching for his handkerchief.

"Don't fash yourself, William. I see the worry's at you, but it's all arranged," Uncle Thomas said in a lighter tone. "Listen, Cheboygan's a long way off. You've no earthly notion of the distances here, and you can't expect to undertake a railroad trip directly after an ocean voyage. Believe me, I know. Besides, it's unlikely we'll ever be back in this fair city. I thought we'd show Pheme and the children the sights." He bounced up and down, making Ann giggle. "You're in the most beautiful city in America."

Boston glistened in the sunlight, a newly-minted coin where Liverpool had been as dull as an old penny. Trams and carriages crammed the cobblestoned streets. Pedestrians raced in every direction, seemingly occupied with important business, crossing fearlessly in front of the traffic. The buildings stood taller than the hotels in Douglas and were more lavishly decorated, with striped fabric awnings and hanging lamps. Atop one brick edifice, a red, white, and blue flag caught a slight breeze, attracting John's attention. "The Stars and Stripes," Henry said, remembering a lesson from school. "The flag of America. I don't recall what they stand for."

"You'll learn it in school, boys," Uncle Thomas said. "You're American now."

Henry felt a chill run the length of his spine. *Well, I'm not. I'm Manx. But mustn't say anything.* He gritted his teeth, almost biting his tongue. He felt caught in a whirlpool of sight, sounds, and smells: the ringing of trolley bells, toots of motorcar horns, the clatter of iron hooves on cobblestones, mingled with the fumes of horse manure and petrol. The ground heaved beneath his feet, and he teetered, almost knocking into John. *Christ, I've lost me sea legs, and we're not aboard ship anymore. We need food, drink, and rest. Hark at Da's face, grey as ash. Perhaps I should take his arm; we could hold each other up. That might embarrass him...*

"Land sake's, William, we can't leave yet," Thomas said, striding in a circle like a giant in a faery tale. "Don't you want your young'uns to get an education? We're in the cradle of America, lads. The Boston Tea Party happened right round here somewhere." Gripping Ann's knees, Thomas pointed with his chin. "When the Americans threw the goddam English out. We Manxmen should've done the same. One reason I love America so—"

Mum was shaking her head, a finger to her lips. "Sorry, Pheme. Not used to young'uns."

Henry was taken aback. *Thrown out? At a tea party?* Edward's eyes held the same question. They hadn't learned that at school.

"Ahem, I reckon I'll get used to little pitchers and big ears,"

Thomas said. "Like yours, eh Tom? I'm an old bachelor, me." Ann chortled with delight as he bounced her on his shoulders.

"Speaking of tea—" Mum said. "Thomas, please, I'm shattered. And the children—"

"Inspection was a trial, eh? I'll wager you're as famished as I am. The fish dinners here are almost as good as Nan's, boys. Pft." He blew like a steam whistle. "Your Da wanted to load youse all onto a train tonight."

"Well, I reckoned—"

"Saints alive, Pheme, it's a wonder you manage, what with seven children including our William here." He stopped and turned around. "You, brother mine, need to gather strength for the next leg of the journey. Nine hundred miles. That would make Douglas to Peel, back and forth, thirty times or so, if my arithmetic's any good. You haven't the foggiest notion, do ye? Not your fault; you've never travelled. You'll have to follow my lead."

He pointed with his foot to the carpet bags lying in a heap. "This all you brought?" He glanced at Da. His tone softened. "Good for you; no point dragging stuff from the old country. A fresh start's what you need. Grab a couple of bags, lads. We'll find us a hack." With his free hand, he tapped Edward's shoulder. "I'll call you Ted, after our President, Mr. Teddy Roosevelt. Everyone admires him. Onward ho, Ted!"

He led them down the sidewalk. Ann bumped along, high above. Henry thought she didn't look comfortable, more scared. They passed ladies in bright, shiny dresses, light coats, ruffled blouses, carrying parasols or wearing plumed hats. Edward and Tom stumbled along, struggling to keep up with Uncle Thomas. John stopped to point at buildings twelve storeys high. Tall church spires punctuated the puffy white clouds and suddenly bells rang out—six o'clock. Tears sprang to Henry's eyes. *Seven hours. Not a bite to eat for any of us except Hugh. Poor Mum. If we don't eat soon, we'll drop.*

Uncle Thomas hailed a hackney carriage. They squeezed together on the seats, but within moments arrived at a train station. *A train? I thought he said we weren't taking the train.*

"Come along, Pheme. This here's the elevated railway. You won't believe the sights from Charlestown to Tremont Street for our hotel. Tomorrow, we'll take the subway! Ever ridden a subway, William? We ain't leavin' Boston 'til we've painted 'er red."

Chapter Twenty-Three

Ta dooinney ny ghaa er ve daunsyn as fer elley geeck yn fiddler:
Many a man dances while another pays the fiddler.

Boston
July 31 - August 3, 1905

THEY stumbled down the wide steps from the Tremont Street platform. Throughout the ride aboard the Main Line Electric railway, Uncle Thomas provided details of its construction. Henry thought he sounded like Grandad, bragging about "his" Manx Steamship Company. Same voice, but louder.

"Wait 'til you see the Touraine, Pheme. Finest accommodations in the U.S. of A. Makes the Sugarland in Douglas look a proper dump," Uncle Thomas shouted as they approached a stately red-and-cream-coloured brick building.

"It's like a picture in a storybook," Edward said.

"You're right, Ted. Built to look like a castle, and that's just the outside."

The Hotel Touraine offered all the modern conveniences, Uncle Thomas said, as he whisked them through the glass doors and into the luxurious lobby. "There's even a tub with running water in the basement, which you will enjoy, Pheme." Mum's face turned scarlet. She hustled the children along. At the reception desk, they learned he'd reserved two rooms for the family; one with two single beds for the four boys to share, and one for their parents, with Ann in a cot beside their bed, and the baby in a cradle. Henry asked for a cot of his own. *I'm nearly a man, so. Don't fancy sharing a bed with Edward anymore. On the ship, I had me own bunk.* Mum tapped his arm. Uncle Thomas ignored him.

They were on the eighth floor. Henry let out a groan. *Oh no. More stairs. I'm so tired, and I'll have to carry Ann.*

"You've never ridden in an elevator, I see." Thomas laughed. "Or slept so high up. Like you're in the clouds."

Ann screamed the whole ride up, despite the reassurance of the friendly black man in uniform at the controls. "*The Buganne, the Buganne,*" she cried, every time the doors closed and opened and the small room jolted to life with a whirring sound. She wriggled and kicked in Henry's arms. *How ever will we get her back in to go down? What if it gets stuck?*

Nervous about the boys having their own room, Mum put Henry in charge. He nodded and shut the door. *Finally. Ah, there's a pitcher of water. I could drink the whole thing. Oh, I forgot, there's running water. As much as we want.*

"What do you think of Uncle Thomas, then, eh?" Edward said, bouncing on a bed. "He's jolly!"

"He called me Tommy; made fun of my ears." Tom flopped down and punched a pillow.

"Well, that's only natural," Edward said. "Anyway, he did say his ears were doorstops once. I like him. He calls me Ted. Like the King of America."

"Not the king, you idiot. The president," Henry said. "They threw the goddam English out, remember? At a tea party." He impersonated Thomas' voice and exaggerated gestures.

Tom threw the pillow at him. "You're as good as that old parrot named Jim. Do some more."

Henry opened his mouth, but John tugged at his coat. "What's a 'postle' Henry? He said I'm a 'postle'."

Henry smiled to reassure him. "It's from the Bible. A man who fishes and tells stories. A good man."

"Oh. I like catching fish. And stories. But he calls me Johnny. I'm John."

"And me 'Harry.' I won't answer to it, and that's that," Henry said.

"I do like the elevator," John said. "I wish an elevator could take us home from here. We could go back and forth, quicklike."

"Ah, what a lovely notion, John. I'll dream of that, tonight. C'mon boys, Mum'll be knocking soon. Wash up."

"Yes, I'm starving." Tom imitated Grandad's voice, making them all laugh. "See, I can be Jim the parrot, too!"

And then Nan would scold him for saying it. Henry could hear her. *I wish that elevator could take me home.* He locked the door behind them. Pocketing the key made him feel like a man.

Mum covered Ann's mouth to muffle Ann's screams in the elevator. Warning everyone to be on their best behaviour, Mum led the way into the dining room. The sparkling chandeliers, shimmering crystal glasses, and gold-rimmed dishes kept their eyes open wide and their mouths shut. Ann, pale and shaken, was provided a highchair. She sucked her thumb and nodded off to sleep. Henry saw the exhaustion drawn on Mum's face. He took Hugh on his lap so she could sit comfortably.

Da accepted the menu from a waiter, scanned it, and frowned. "We're not accustomed to fancy food, Thomas. 'Brussels à la Rossini?' 'Boeuf à la mode?' 'Patty de foy grass?' Ye ken?"

"Don't complain, William. You'll be eating nothing but your dear wife's cooking in less than a week," Uncle Thomas said. "You can't teach an old dog new tricks, Pheme, but I'll not deprive you of these tasty comestibles." He ordered breaded veal cutlets, creamed peas and onions, scalloped potatoes, and Boston cream pie for dessert, with beer for the adults and milk for the children. Henry longed for ginger beer but dared not ask. Mum seemed shy, somehow, about asking Thomas for anything.

"What's veal, Uncle?" Edward said.

"Why, it's a calf, Ted. They always write 'milk-fed veal' on the menu, as if it could be otherwise. What's that sorry look, Pheme? Lamb versus mutton. Sweet and tender, you'll see."

Henry noticed both Mum and Da said little; they focussed on their meals and sipped their beer. The steaming dishes of food served on gold-rimmed plates with silver cutlery reminded Henry of the ship's first-class galley. *Some folks eat like this every single day. No wonder Thomas has a big belly whilst Da's a broom handle.* He savoured the creamed peas, the way they popped in your mouth, and slid down with the sauce. His brothers couldn't fork the food in fast enough. Mum daintily used her cutlery and sent the boys a sharp look to slow down.

Thomas filled the silence with information on Boston's history, sounding like a schoolteacher. *He does go on. And on. He's putting me to sleep. We're all dead tired. Ann's lucky.* He squirrelled a biscuit into his pocket to give her later. As soon as the meal was over, Mum said they must be for their beds.

At breakfast, Uncle Thomas suggested they bless their journey by attending a service at the Old North Church. "It's Paul Revere's signal house, boys. He warned the Americans against the god—hmm, the British. It's a beautiful church that—"

Mum protested; the children weren't used to attending church, and besides, she'd nothing to wear. John halted his spoon halfway to his lips. "What do you mean, Mum? What about your new suit and your boat hat? Oh, you lost the hat."

Uncle Thomas waved his hand. "Not to worry, Pheme. We'll visit Siegel's and get you togged out. And these lads will behave themselves in church, or they'll have me to answer to," he said, sweeping the table with a stern look.

A cloud crossed Mum's face. Da's eyebrows knit together. *Boy, one minute he's so nice, and then…* Henry tried to brush the unsettled feeling away like the waiter cleaning crumbs from the tablecloth.

"It wouldn't be proper to accept—No, Thomas, thank you, but no," Mum said, setting her teacup firmly in its saucer.

"Nonsense! We're family. William, you won't object to my making a gift of a new dress and a night out for you both? The night out, I mean, not the dress! Unless you'd like one, too?" Thomas snorted, drawing looks from other diners. Da looked like he had something in his throat that he could neither swallow nor spit out. He wiped his lips with his handkerchief. He made a fist, suppressing a cough, closed his eyes, and made a brief nod.

"That's settled. Now, you go rest with the little ones, whilst I take the boys on a tour of downtown." He made to stand. "You'll see the wonders of Boston, lads. There's a tea kettle, big enough for all of youse to stand up in; hangs outside a shop around the corner. Don't believe me? You'll see." He reached over to pat Mum's hand. "Meanwhile, have your bath, Pheme. Relax with a good long soak, like Cleopatra—"

"Thomas, for heaven's sake!" Mum covered her face with a napkin.

Uncle Thomas chuckled. "C'mon boys. Forward. March."

They marvelled at the giant tea kettle and enjoyed their first taste of an ice cream soda in a drugstore. Then they hopped aboard a streetcar.

"Next stop, Boston Public Gardens." They'd never visited a pleasure garden and were astounded by the flowers, the trees, fountains, and statues.

"I wish I could climb up there," Edward said, pointing to Washington's statue. Just imagine how far you could see—"

"That's why it's on a plinth, to stop scallywags like you doing that very thing." He flipped off Edward's cap, ruffled his hair, and then tossed the cap in the air. "Onward, lads."

John quietly asked if they could ride the paddleboat swans on the lagoon, but Uncle Thomas shook his head. Henry frowned. *So much for the grand tour.* They were back at the Touraine by lunchtime.

After a light meal, Thomas charged Henry with the youngsters while Da rested, and he took Mum shopping. Henry shrugged his shoulders. *Stuck minding the sheep, as usual. Except without Blackie for company.*

* * *

That night, Mum entered the dining room after the family was already seated. She wore a high-collared, cream-coloured gown with a train. White gloves sheathed her arms to the elbows. Her thick hair, piled atop her head, enhanced her oval face and chestnut eyes. Guests swivelled to follow her progress. The children gasped.

"Mum, you look like a queen," John whispered. He started to clap. Ann joined in, and soon the children were all applauding. Some diners smiled; others raised a glass, thinking it was a party.

"Whist, stop it, now," Mum said, gesturing with a new fan. *Her rosy cheeks make her even prettier. Like the lady on posters for soap.* Mum's dimples appeared, and she fluttered her lashes. *She's making a proper show of it. Who knew Mum could look this way? She's Mum.*

Da stood to pull out a chair, lost his balance, and fell toward the table. The motion brought on a coughing fit. He reached for a glass of water, but it slipped from his grasp, tipping onto the tablecloth. A waiter rushed over, and Uncle Thomas looked away. Henry fairly threw the baby on Edward's lap and circled behind the chairs to catch Da's elbow.

"Take me upstairs, Henry. Please," he said, gasping. Mum grabbed his arm.

"No, my love. Stay and have dinner. I'm not up to it this

evening." His voice cracked. He whispered. "You're so beautiful."

Mum's lip trembled. Her smile disappeared. "Edward, give wee man to Tom," she said. "Help your brother." She guided Da around the table. "We'll bring you some soup later, dear. Rest, and don't smoke."

Da seemed to shrink, avoiding the concerned looks bouncing from table to table. "Hurry up, lads. Please."

Henry and Edward helped Da to lie down. Henry propped the pillows and gave him water.

"I ought to stay, Da. You need a hot drink. I'll—"

Da waved them off. "I'll be fine, Henry. Go. Eat. Last chance for that rich food."

Back in the hallway, Henry slid to the floor against the closed door, crossing his arms to ease his pounding heart.

"I don't know, Edward; I don't think he'll even make it to the farm. He looks worse than on the ship, weak as a newborn lamb." His throat was swollen shut. *How could he eat?*

"Nah, he's just tired. C'mon, race you down the hall," Edward shouted. "Last one to the elevator's a rotten egg!"

At the dining room entrance, they slowed. Uncle Thomas' booming voice carried through the doors. *Does the whole room know our business? Da wouldn't like that.*

"Well, that seals it," Thomas was saying. "Such a fine lady must attend a vaudeville show! Keith's Theatre's around the corner. I hear tell these vaudeville shows are quite the—" Mum put her palm out and shook her head. "Now, don't go giving me that look, Pheme. My treat. I'll book another night."

Edward jumped up. "Hurray! A show and another night in the hotel! I love this hotel."

"Don't get excited, Ted. The show's for adults. But an extra day'll give us the chance to ride the subway—the first in North America, ye ken. Johnny here can ride the ducks on the lagoon. We'll take our lovely Alice Blue," he said, tickling her nose with one of her braids. She pulled away.

"Don't, Nuncle. Me and Jenny don't like tickles."

"Yes, I'll treat you to an ice cream soda and chocolate, sweetheart. Boston's got the world's finest candy stores."

The following afternoon, Henry stood before Mum's mirror, pinning up her hair, choking on anger and Da's cigarette smoke. *Now I'm lady's maid as well as nanny.* Mum chattered away. *Why's she so bright and breezy all of a sudden? I'm miserable. I wish we were home.*

"The lady at the hat shop admired my thick hair, saying how most women tuck a rat underneath their up-do to make the pile of hair look fuller. I thought I'd try it."

Henry dropped the brush. Mum giggled at his expression in the mirror.

"Not a real rat, silly!" She tapped his hand. "A hairpiece made of horsehair. See? Tucked in like a bug in a rug." She laughed. "I love this pouffy hairstyle, don't you? Much prettier than a plain old bun." She stood up to remove the lid from a tall, black and white striped box, ornamented in gold lettering. "Hark at this. Real ostrich plumes. Fancy! All the ladies are wearing them." She smoothed the long feather between her fingers. "I wonder how you pluck an ostrich? A bit more difficult than a chicken, I shouldn't wonder." She handed Henry some long pins topped with beads. "Poke them in deep, Henry. I don't want it flying off. There's a frightful breeze between these tall buildings. Ouch, no, no, that's fine. Pain is the price of vanity."

Uncle Thomas had said "Harry" could watch the children while the adults went out. Mum refused.

"The boys are handful enough, let alone a baby and Ann. Henry's never looked after them all, on his own. We need a sitter."

Henry almost snorted, thinking of the hours he'd watched over the baby, and his parents, on the ship.

Da shrugged. "You two go," he said, taking a pull on his

cigarette. "I'd just cough and have to excuse myself. Besides, play-acting doesn't interest me."

When Uncle Thomas arrived at the door, wearing a top hat and carrying a cane, Da stuck his nose in a newspaper. Henry saw Thomas take Mum's arm as she whirled out. At the click of the lock, Da grabbed a whiskey bottle from the dresser, poured a glass half-full, and moved to the window. He opened the curtains and looked down.

"Being up this high, bah. Not for me. You, Henry? I'd rather have me feet on the ground."

This comment came out of nowhere, but Henry agreed. "You're right, Da. It's like being back on the ship. I hated thinking about the deep. This feels the same. I wonder how we'd get out in a fire."

Da strode to the coat rack and popped on his bowler. "Keep an eye on wee man for a bit, Henry. I must go out. I'll put Edward in charge next door. Those rascals better behave. Won't be long."

* * *

Thomas wished Euphemia goodnight downstairs, leaning in to whisper, "Wasn't it just like old times, Pheme? At the Gaiety. You can't imagine—"

She swirled into the elevator, grateful for the presence of the operator. Her stomach remained in the lobby as the lift braked at the eighth floor. She tried to blame the pounding of her heart on the elevator's screeching noise. *The Buggane it is, Ann; indeed, it is.*

She rushed down the hallway, her dress trailing behind her. She set her key gently in the door, thinking she'd sneak in without disturbing William. She found him playing cards with Henry. Hugh slept in a dresser drawer, and Ann was curled in her cot. *Have they checked the boys?*

"And? How was it, then?" William's eyes remained on the cards.

She bristled. *He told me to go, and now he seems—*

"Tell everything, Mum," Henry said, pushing his cards away.

Euphemia moved to pick up Hugh, but Henry shook his head, saying he'd just been changed. *'Course he has. I can rely on him.* She gave him her brightest smile.

"Well, first we attended a vaudeville show at the Keith Theatre and then we dined at The Rathskeller. Thomas says it's the most famous restaurant in Boston," she said, as she gingerly removed her hat pins. Describing the show, she couldn't suppress her delight. She twirled around, singing snippets of a song she remembered. Henry clapped. "What's that tune, you may ask? Why, that's from *Louise Dresser and her Picks.* She has a chorus of little coloured boys that sing and dance with her." She could hear the lilt in her own voice, sure she hadn't sounded so excited in years. "Louise is a blonde beauty—Thomas couldn't take his eyes off her. The show's a spectacle of beautiful costumes, rousing songs, and oh, the music. You should have seen it—"

"All very well for some," William tossed down his cards and moved to the bench in front of the dresser. Leaning down, he spoke to his reflection in the mirror. "What I don't comprehend is, where's Thomas get the money? You say this new outfit didn't cost much. Thirty dollars, I make it, taking into account the petticoat, stockings, corset, and other frippery. A fortune."

"William, for pity's sake, don't get all het up. It'll make you cough. You're spoiling everything." She removed her hat, carefully placing it on the bedside table. Then she flopped on the bed with a deep sigh. "I love Boston. The lights, the motor cars, shops, music halls—"

She stopped herself. *William will be hurt if I say more. But somehow, I feel Boston would suit me down to the ground. Maybe that's what Leeman saw... Oh, God. Perhaps I oughtn't be a wife, a mother. Why did the outing make me happy? Wasn't I happy before?*

"A city's nice, if you're rich, Euphemia. Don't let this frivolity go to your head. Thomas might've covered our train fare instead of this fancy hotel. But no. While you two were out, I checked on tickets at the station."

Euphemia sat up, removed her gloves, and threw them at William's back. "You mean to say you left Henry with Hugh? When I specifically said… Jesus, I can't leave you alone for five minutes. That could've waited 'til morning." She stood up and helped herself to a glass of whiskey. "And I bloody well won't feel guilty about going out. I won't." She gulped and slammed her glass down. "I've not had an outing in fifteen years and am not likely to have another one stuck out in the country. I deserve a bit of fun, after all I've been through. It lightened my heart." She barely stifled a sob. She fell back on the pillow and turned to the wall.

"One, two trains, then an overnight stay in Detroit," William said. "A streetcar, then another train to Cheboygan." He counted off the stages on his fingers. "Eighteen hours, all told. How about that? We've almost gone through our savings even though we're getting five dollars to a pound. Things are so dear, our money's almost worthless." Swinging his legs around to face her, he threw some pound notes on the floor from the pile on the dresser.

Euphemia sighed and roused herself, unpinning her hair.

"Oh William, for pity's sake, it's all relevant, uh, relative, I mean." The rat twirled to the floor. Henry jumped, making Euphemia laugh. Then they both got the giggles and couldn't stop. William kept talking.

"Relative, eh? I could say a word about 'relative.' I can't stomach borrowing any more of his—" he broke off in a fit of coughing. Henry poured him a glass of water and made for the door. Euphemia thanked him for minding the baby.

"I'm sorry you couldn't attend the show, pet. Someday, eh? Maybe there's a playhouse in Cheboygan. Any road, Uncle Thomas arranged for us to be driven to church in a motor car—fancy! A saloon, it's called. Won't that be something?" She felt a lift in her spirits, like being in the elevator. "So many new experiences. It's been a proper holiday."

"Well, we won't be riding First Class on Michigan Central," William said through a cloud of smoke. "We'll be sitting up all night. Best order sandwiches and drinks for the journey, Euphemia, at breakfast. Train leaves at five o'clock sharp. I, for one, will be glad to get moving."

Chapter Twenty-Four

Etshyn ta jannoo ny smoo jiu na v'e,
chliaghtey t'eh kiarail dy volley shiu ny laccal shiu:
He who does more today than usual,
designs to deceive you or fail you.

August 4, 1905

EUPHEMIA pulled the drapes, and Sunday morning burst in. She'd awoken even before Hugh cried. So much to do. Baby needed to be changed and fed, Ann's hair wanted brushing, the boys hadn't been bathed… Henry ushered them into the room. She looked at their tousled hair and crusty eyes and handed him a washcloth.

It seemed only moments later they were riding in the open saloon car, accompanied by the chiming of church bells from every quarter of the city and the ripe smell of horse manure wafting up from the streets.

"Horses will soon be a thing of the past. The city will be much cleaner with automobiles. Progress!" Thomas tapped the side of the car and shouted back to them from the front seat. He held Ann on his lap and pointed out sights along the way.

"Trinity Church, ma'am," the chauffeur announced, swinging the door wide and taking Euphemia's gloved hand to assist her. William opened his door, and the boys tumbled out. Thomas waited for the chauffeur, then lifted Ann into William's arms.

"I'll join youse later," he said. "I've got some business to attend to." He took a roll of candy out of his pocket and handed it to Henry. "Dole them out, Harry. Hub Wafers made right here. Keep the little ones quiet."

Euphemia smirked. *World's best candies, too, I imagine. But it was thoughtful.* William tried to hand her the baby, but she shook her head. *Let Henry take him; it'll spoil my look. The train must flow down the aisle.* She straightened and held her head high, enjoying the weight of her wide-brimmed hat. *I'm as finely dressed as the other ladies. I'm as good as they are.*

The family stood on the church steps, eyes skyward. *It's not the church he mentioned before. It's Catholic! I wonder if Thomas knew that... This doesn't compete with York Minster, but they've never seen a cathedral. Not likely to, either.*

"Is it a castle, Mother?" John asked.

"It certainly looks like one, sweetheart." She looped her arm through William's, and they preceded the children under the portico and through the massive wooden doors.

The dim interior, illuminated only by candles and multi-coloured stained glass windows, vibrated with organ chords and choir song. Euphemia revelled in the music and couldn't wait to sing the hymns. William and the children were stunned to silence by the height of the arches, the gleaming organ pipes, and the richly decorated wooden panels. Euphemia smiled. *This is wonderful to see. Doesn't miss a trick, our Thomas. Where is he? He's missing the show.*

Throughout the hour-long service, the children wriggled on the hard pews while Henry bounced Hugh against his shoulder to suppress his fussy cries. Edward and Tom amused themselves by kicking each other until Euphemia hissed at them. William fanned his face with the service leaflet, ignoring her frown. Ann wouldn't sit still and almost took a tumble. Henry only just caught her by the arm.

"Good job, Henry. Her head would've cracked like an egg on this floor." Euphemia passed Hugh to William so she could hold Ann, and when she squirmed, she gave her a sound slap.

I wish Nan were here; she'd keep them in line. Our John knows how to sit quiet, bless him. He says it's God's house. His castle. She smiled and patted John's knee. He didn't respond; his eyes roved from one side of the altar to the other, up and down the sculpted wooden beams, to the Biblical figures aglow on the rainbow windows. *We'll never get him out of here.*

Despite the annoyances, Euphemia sang out with the choir; she knew the hymns by heart. People in front swivelled to smile and pass her appreciative looks. *How I've missed singing in the choir.* When she knelt in prayer after signalling to the boys to join her, she gave thanks for their safe arrival and prayed fervently that they would thrive in their new home. Especially William. *Please let him be healed, please, please, so that we might move off on our own, away from Thomas. Keep my family safe, my secret intact. For the good of us all. Forgive me my sin.*

As they streamed out with the crowd to the bold strains of the massive organ, Euphemia inhaled deeply and let out a contented sigh. She let Ann down to walk and took William's arm.

"That did me a power of good, William. I do believe I can carry on. With God's help. He's brought us this far, eh?" She squeezed his hand. He stopped in the aisle and faced her. His eyes glistened as he ran his knuckle along her chin.

"You've been very brave, my love. I prayed too, that I'll soon be well enough to help. Please forgive my temper—" She stopped him, putting her finger on his lips and brushing a tear from his cheek with her glove. She hoped he could read all the love she sent him with her eyes.

Thomas didn't attend the service at all. When they emerged

from the portico to the steps, after standing in line to thank the priest, he rushed them back to the car.

"Off you go. To the station." He directed the driver, gesturing with his cigar. "William, once we arrive, you stay with the children and see to the tickets, whilst Pheme and I return to the hotel for the luggage. I bought a good solid trunk so we won't need to deal with those cheap carpet bags. Pheme and I will repack everything. I've asked the hotel to prepare a full basket of sandwiches and drinks to keep us fed for the overnight trip."

"Fine, fine," William said into his handkerchief. "Henry, go along to lend a hand. We don't want to miss the train."

"No, no, we'll manage. Back in two shakes with luggage and lunch." When the driver stopped in front of the station, Thomas handed Ann to Henry, barely waiting for everyone but Euphemia to land on the sidewalk. Thomas placed his arm across her shoulders. Unable to move, she sat stiffly upright, one hand on her hat. *He's managed to get me all to himself. What's he got in mind? Last night better not have given him ideas.*

When they arrived at the Touraine, Thomas asked the driver to wait. He led her by the hand towards the upholstered divan in the lobby. He checked them out and gave orders to the bellboy.

"Bring the luggage downstairs. Throw the bags in the trunk I've set in the hall. Fetch our vittles and drinks from the kitchen. Oh, and I'll need a box of beer. Make that two." His voice carried all the way to her seat. People were staring. He didn't seem to notice.

He flopped down nearly on top of her, removing his hat to wipe his brow as though he'd carried the trunk downstairs himself.

Euphemia shuffled aside, folding her hands on her lap. "I hope he's quick. I hate leaving William and Henry with the children on their own. Besides, we mustn't miss our train," Euphemia said, relieved that they weren't repacking. They wouldn't be in the room alone.

"*Traa dy lioor,* as Da would say. There's time enough, Pheme. Don't fash yerself." He patted her knee, and his warm hand remained there.

She deliberately placed it on his own leg. "Well, I don't hold with that, no more than I believe in faeries. I've never enough time, me, with six children and a household to manage."

"Last night was wonderful, eh, Pheme?" he said, turning to gaze directly into her eyes. "I'm so glad you agreed to come. I've been waiting and hoping, for years. Listen—"

"No, you listen." She tightened her jaw to steady her voice, an old singing trick. She filled her diaphragm with a deep breath. "I don't know what you're thinking, but I've no intention of looking back. None. Understand? I didn't 'agree' to come, any road. What choice did I have? This is Nan's doing, not mine." She clasped her trembling hands together. "I'm determined to make the best of this, for the sake of my husband and children." She started to rise, but he gripped her arm.

"I know, I know. I'll see youse sorted. I promised Mother, and I promise you. Just wait 'til you see—"

She pulled herself free of his grasp as the young man approached, pushing a trolley and carrying a wicker basket. "Oh good, thank you so much. We'll be off now," she said, exhaling a ragged breath and striding to the car, heels clicking. She pressed her lips together and kept silent until they met William in the train station. She greeted him with a kiss, ignoring his quizzical but pleased response, and held his hand while they trooped down the platform seeking their carriage.

William mentioned that he'd paid all eight fares, except for the baby who travelled for free, as he handed their tickets to the conductor.

"Well, I bought the trunk, paid for the car and the lunch, so we're even." Thomas waved his hand as though swatting a fly. "I ken how ye must keep a tally."

Seated on wicker benches that folded forward and back, they settled in comfortably at first. The men removed their hats, placing them in overhead nets.

Euphemia unpinned her hat. "I should've put it in the hat-box at the hotel," she said, glaring at Thomas. "Where'd the box go? I don't want the feathers bent." She peeled off her long gloves. "I should've changed into my suit for the journey and all. My dress will get covered in soot. Dammit." She stamped her foot. *Thomas's fault; his fanciful notion to take them to church, his wily plan to get her alone at the hotel, his wheedling… Well, at least I got the chance to put him in his place. He'd best stay there.*

Strands of her hair came tumbling down. With a grunt, she loosened the rest, yanked off the rat, and fashioned her customary coif. No point in keeping up appearances now. She placed the hat in the net with her new velvet purse, kid gloves, and the rat inside.

"Time to get down to brass tacks," she said, rolling up her lace sleeves. She took Hugh from William. The baby settled against her breast, eager to nurse. She'd deliberately purchased a dress that buttoned at the front to make it easier since she had no maid. *Smarter than I realized, and my shawl comes in useful as a cover.* She started humming.

"Isn't that from the vaudeville show?" Thomas sought her gaze and smiled. She kept humming. "You've such an ear for music. I've missed your singing, all these years."

The boys raced to the windows to see the train pull out of the station, cheering when the whistle blew and steam rushed past their window. A few well-wishers waved from the platform.

"Why do people wave goodbye, Da?" John asked. "They did the same on the ship. We don't know them, so?"

"I've no earthly notion, Son. Habit, I guess." He coughed and started to dig in his pockets for his makings. Euphemia frowned and shook her head. She didn't want to breathe his smoke. He slumped back in his seat. The rocking motion quieted Ann. Seated beside Thomas, she snuggled against his shoulder, hugging her dolly and sucking her thumb. The boys continued to bounce on the seats until hunger overcame excitement. Thomas officiously divvied up the sandwiches wrapped in brown paper.

"We're on rations, boys, like the army. The food must last eighteen hours, minus eight for sleep, so if my arithmetic is any good, that makes ten hours. With you gannets, we'll only just manage. Harry, you keep an eye on them, 'specially this young whippersnapper," he said, leaning over to ruffle Ed's hair. "No filchin' from the basket, eh, Ted." He winked.

"Yes, sir, you can count on me, sir. I'll watch everyone."

Henry narrowed his eyes at him. "And I'll keep an eye on you, Edward. I know what you're like." Edward stuck out his tongue.

Euphemia sighed. "Boys! Enough. Your bickering's getting on my last nerve."

"Yes, behave yourselves, youse," Thomas said, reaching into one of the boxes. "There's ginger beer for the young'uns and real ale for me and you, William. Michigan beer's better—"

"I'd like a beer too, if I may. I'm a man now. Today's my birthday," Henry said, looking at Euphemia under his brow. "It's August fourth. The date was posted on the hymn board."

Euphemia covered her mouth with her hands. "Oh, Henry, forgive me. I've lost track of the days." Her eyes and nose tingled. She wanted to slap herself. *My firstborn son, all he's been through.* Guilt washed over her like a wave on the Douglas seaside. Ice cold.

"Ach, Pheme, I'm surprised you keep your head on straight, contending with this lot," Thomas said. "You could do with a beer. Of course, you may have one, Harry." He yanked out the cork on a brown bottle. It popped. "Ooh, I love that sound. Here, let's have a toast." He raised his bottle above his barrel chest. "Here's to Harry. Many happy returns, and welcome to

America. What's that make you? Fourteen, now? A man, so. If your birthday fell a month earlier, you'd have fireworks every year, for America's birthday. You should just see—"

"It's Henry."

Euphemia was taken aback by the dark tone and angry gaze Henry shot at Thomas. *Damn Thomas and his nicknames. I'll set him straight. The boys hate it. I put up with it. I wonder why.*

A porter stopped to ask if they needed anything. Ann's blue eyes widened. The man leaned down and smiled.

"I have a little girl your age; she loves her dolly, too. What's her name?"

Ann squeezed against Thomas, her eyes stark. She covered her face with the dolly's skirt.

"I'm so, so, sorry, sir," Euphemia said. "She makes strange, she's not used to, I mean—"

"Oh, I understand, ma'am; she ain't never seen someone like me. So tall and good-lookin', that is." He pointed to his chest with his huge, dark thumb. His brown eyes smiled warmly. "Well, you folks don't hesitate to ask for Simon if ya'll needs anything." With a flash of perfect teeth, he moved on to the next family.

What a voice; he'd make a wonderful singer. She closed her eyes to the rocking of the car, transported back to the vaudeville show, thinking how she'd dreamed of singing at the Gaiety. Long ago.

At each station, more passengers boarded. People started opening windows on either side of the carriage for relief from the heat. Smoke and soot filtered in, clinging to sweaty faces. The conductor briskly slammed the windows, muttering, "You English. Always the same." He clicked his tongue and his heels down the aisle.

Tom spoke up. "We're not English, us." Thomas shook his head.

"I just wanted to tell him we're Manx, is all," Tom whispered to Henry.

Euphemia bent down and scrabbled in the basket. "Oooh, my stays are killing me. Why, oh why, didn't I put on my cotton blouse and sensible shoes? Kid leather boots might look smart, but they're totally impractical." *All down to Thomas and his schemes.* "I hope the hotel put in napkins. How ever will I keep us clean?" She found there were neatly folded cloth napkins in the bottom of the basket. She wiped Hugh and Ann's faces before her own, then tossed the cloth across to Henry.

"Wipe your brothers' faces, please, pet. Tom and John, you look like pigs." Seated side by side, the two of them touched noses and snorted. Passengers across the aisle smiled. A little girl giggled.

"You two'll be on the vaudeville circuit someday, I swear." Thomas laughed. Then he reached behind and pinched one of Tom's ears. "Tommy, you'll be an acrobat. Wouldn't even need a trapeze; just stand on a mast and jump. You'd float right to the ground." He motioned with his hands. No one laughed. Tom looked as though he'd been slapped.

"Enough with your personal comments, Thomas," William said, kicking him in the ankle. He dug in the basket for a sandwich and handed it across to Tom.

"It's just teasing. I said mine were the same." Thomas lowered his voice and looked out.

"Aye and you didn't like the teasing, did you?" He returned to his seat, still scowling. "I remember your scuffles in the schoolyard. Show some sympathy."

"It'll help him grow a thicker skin," Thomas said to the window. "Life's tough out here. Not a place for mollycoddled boys."

"He's eight, for God's sake," Euphemia said, handing Hugh to William so she could check on Tom. He hadn't touched his sandwich. "Like a drink, sweetheart?"

Tom gulped, his shoulders shaking. Henry opened a ginger

beer and passed it over the seat. Edward helped Tom steady it as the train swayed on a curve.

"Almost a man in this country." Thomas leaned back against the seat, crossing his feet and his folding arms.

"Let him alone, Thomas. He's my son," William said. He took a beer for himself and split a sandwich with Euphemia.

After a brief silence, Edward leaned over the seat back and said, "Uncle Thomas, you promised to tell us about Chay-bog-gan and the farm, remember?"

"Ah, so I did, so I did, Ted." Thomas sat up, his tone genial. Edward and John sat cross-legged on the floor between the adults' feet. Tom curled up on the vacant seat. William covered him with his coat.

Euphemia studied Thomas' expression. *Does he have a soft spot for Edward?* The thick bread stuck in her throat, and she choked. She reached for the bottle, tipped her head, and gulped. She reached for Hugh and held him hard against her breast. *The beer's good for me, any road; make my milk flow. I'm so tired.*

"Well, for one thing, it's pronounced Che-boy-gan." Thomas was saying, emphasizing every syllable. "Don't ask me what it means. Strange name for a beautiful place. You'll love it, as I do." He flashed his gold smile at William. "Climate's perfect; never too hot nor cold, even in winter, though we get a fair amount of snow. The wildlife, the clear lakes, and the river… and the trees! Millions and millions of trees."

Thomas barely stopped for breath, his voice rising and falling to the rhythm of the wheels. Euphemia couldn't help bending an ear, hoping to learn what he'd been up to all these years. *As William said, where'd he get his money? Out from under somebody's nose, like the peat he stole?*

"It's the trees that took me there from Boston. I'd heard about fortunes to be made from timber, white pine, in particular. She grows two hundred feet; takes four men to encircle her trunk. Wide as this car, matter of fact." he said, stretching out his arms. "Oh yes, Harry, you needn't smirk; it's not a word of a lie. We've nothing like it, so you can't fathom the size. On Man, we lived in the sky, high on the cliff—"

"Underground, more like," William said, furrowing his brow.

"Just so, William, just so. The forest's my home now. You want facts about trees, ask me. For instance, there's two types of coniferous trees, meaning they have cones. Your pine's got prickly needles and your fir, soft ones, so to tell them apart we say: 'friendly fir' and 'prickly pine.' Clever, eh?"

Edward's head bobbed up and down, his grey eyes glued to Thomas. "A good trick. Like some people are friendly and others are prickly, right?"

"Just so, Ted, just so. In the days of the great sailing ships, white pine were called 'mast pines,' they're so tall and straight. Nowadays, they're mostly cut up for lumber. Wood's creamy as milk, no knots to catch the saw, so hard it can be planked up a year after it's felled. Unlike hardwoods." He made a downward slice with his hand. "Those'll crack down the middle. I'm building a mechanical plane to produce shingles. That's where the real money is."

Euphemia barely recognized his serious demeanour. *I thought he'd have no patience for children. He does seem to like teaching them. That bodes well.* She rocked Hugh, trying to imagine her new home.

"How'd you learn so much about them?" John asked.

"Why, that tree's made my fortune. Ye ken how Grandad and Nan revere the giant oaks, the few we have left, that is? Well, that's how I am about the white pine."

"So, it's a faery tree, then?"

"I hope not, Johnny, for we're cutting them down nine to the dozen, and the faeries would be getting awful spiteful. I intend to leave a few, special-like, but we must clear the forests for farmland. The lumber's worth a king's ransom. A man in America can really make something of himself." He lightly tapped William with his boot across the aisle.

Euphemia cast her eyes away from William's angry face. Thomas carried on.

"Started with naught but five pounds, me; became a lumberjack, now I have a farm. And you, Pheme, will soon find yourself living like a lady to the manor born. You'll see. I won't spoil the surprise." He grinned and raked his hands through his salt-and-pepper hair. Then he leaned back, clasped his hands over his belly, and began sawing logs on his seat.

Well, he's shamed William and Tom down to the ground. Henry sees through him. They dislike one another, that's plain as that big nose on Thomas' face, snoring like a lord. This'll never work. I told Nan so. Oh, God. It can only get worse. What's this surprise he's banging on about? I can live without more surprises.

When night fell, William insisted the boys lie on the floor so Euphemia could lie down. Bundling Ann in a coat, he tucked her in at their feet. Thomas roused himself.

"For God's sake, William. You ought to've arranged a berth for Pheme and the babe. I'll catch the conductor. He can sort it."

"Don't fuss, Thomas. We're fine," Euphemia said. Curled up, her head twisted at an angle. She was too tall to stretch out. Thomas offered his coat as a pillow. She nursed Hugh under her shawl. There'd been nowhere to change his diaper; the washroom was a postage stamp. She'd had to lay him on the floor, then wrap the mess in William's newspaper. Head lowered, she'd handed it to Simon.

"No trouble, ma'am. I've got young'uns at home, myself. I'll deal with it." Simon flashed his big smile, the whites of his eyes shimmering in the dark. She touched his sleeve in thanks. *Could've thrown it out the window, I guess, but that conductor would be fashed. Men design these damn trains with no thought for necessities.*

The blue light of dawn peeled back the discomfort of the

passengers' sleepless night. Smoke and coal dust from the steam engine filled the carriage, making more than just William choke and cough. People stood up, groaning and bending over to loosen aching muscles before joining the long queue for the toilet. Euphemia needed William's hand to right herself on the bench. Her legs were all pins and needles, and she could barely turn her head.

"I don't know if lying down was better or worse, William. I feel like a skeleton shaken in a bag." Hugh began to wail and squirm. "His nappy must wait 'til we get there. I'm not going through that again. What are families supposed to do? It's a nightmare."

William nodded, handkerchief against his mouth, about to vomit or faint, or both. His face looked as wan as oatmeal under the stubble of his beard, and his eyes stood out like marbles. *And I'm complaining.*

"Ah, William, my love. You've been up all night; not a wink of sleep, I shouldn't wonder. Sit back; I'll see to the little ones."

The train pulled into the station with a scream of metal brakes and a billowing cloud of steam. Thomas told everyone to hurry, or they'd miss their connection. Euphemia rushed the children down the passageway to disembark. Too late, she discovered that she'd left her hat, her gloves, the hairpiece, and string purse in the overhead compartment. Tears sprang to her eyes. "My beautiful hat. Please let me go back. Simon will've kept it for me, sure." She squeezed William's arm.

"No, we can't, love. I'm so sorry," William said, his voice soft and sorrowful. "We must catch the streetcar for the interurban station. We haven't got our tickets for Cheboygan yet. Perhaps the company would ship it." He made to touch her chin, but she recoiled.

"Oh, I should've brought my hatbox, I just knew it." She slapped William's hand. "You might've reminded me, William." She gestured with her chin. "You two managed to get your hats,

I see." William and Thomas exchanged guilty looks. "I'm expected to think of everything; no one gives a toss about me."

Henry said he could race down the platform, quick-like, and be back in a jiffy. William and Thomas turned and pointed to the station doors. Euphemia clenched her teeth and tugged Ann by the hand, balancing Hugh on her hip. He started to cry, and she bounced him harder. *If only Nan were here. I knew I'd never manage on me own.* Suddenly she remembered the family at their table on *Ivernia;* the woman with twelve children, unable to speak a word of English. *Where did they go, when they arrived in Boston? What about the thousands of others in the Immigration Station, come to that? God help them.*

As William said, we're lucky. So lucky, I guess. God help us. I lost my hat.

PART THREE
HERE TO STAY

Michigan: The Cat Which Stalks Below

CHAPTER TWENTY-FIVE

Ta dooinney berçhagh fegooish giastyllys gollrish billey fegooish mess:
A rich man without liberality is like a tree without fruit.

August 5, 1905

TRAPPED in the hive of the Detroit station, Henry minded the youngsters while Da went to exchange their remaining few pounds and hire a porter. Mum had asked Uncle Thomas to find her the toilet so she could change Hugh. No one had slept properly, and the food basket hung empty on Edward's arm. He and Tom shuffled along, dazed into silence. John tripped over his feet, staring up at the vaulted ceilings. "It's like the church, Henry. But for trains. A church for trains."

"Look where you're going and keep up, John," Henry said, keeping hold of Ann's tiny fingers. He caught sight of Uncle Thomas hailing them with his hat.

They reunited with Mum and Uncle Thomas at the exit doors. Mum's face matched Hugh's flaming cheeks. She looked near collapse. Henry reached out for Hugh. She eyed the boys, then grabbed Henry's arm.

"Henry, where's John?"

Henry counted them off like sheep: Tom, Edward, Ann. No John. "He was here a moment ago. Oh, Mum, I watched him, I did." *My fault—I should've made him hold onto my coat.* He opened his mouth to call him, but his voice strangled in his throat. All he could see was John's sweet face, his trusting eyes. Where could he be? Maybe taken by a stranger…

"How ever will we find him in this throng?" Mum was fairly screaming, swirling around, flapping her arms.

Da raced up, alarmed at Mum's distress. "Whatever's the matter? What's going on?"

Uncle Thomas caught Mum's hand. "Not to worry, Pheme; there's plenty of station officers hereabouts. He's not the first child to be lost in this morass, I reckon. Keep together and stay put whilst I hunt the wee devil."

"I see him," Thomas called over his shoulder, having quickly spied John sifting through the crowd. He lifted him under his arms and dropped him like a sack of potatoes in front of Mum. Then he shook his finger in John's face and yelled in his ear.

"You little blighter! Don't wander off! You might've cost us our connection."

John's face flared. Tears soaked his cheeks, his eyes reminding Henry of a rabbit in a snare. Da clenched his fists at his sides. Mum knelt to wrap John in a hug, hushing him as he stuttered and sobbed. "Never mind, darling, I'm just so glad you're safe. We must thank God in our prayers tonight, eh?" She wobbled on her heels, and Uncle Thomas reached down to help her stand. Edward moved to pat John's back. Tom stood with Henry and Ann, gripping her hand so hard she wriggled loose.

"Thank you for finding him, Thomas," Mum said. "He's a child, remember. Everything's new to all of us." She brushed down her skirt. Henry noticed her hand trembling. "And you must get used to some things yourself. You've taken on a family."

Her lips formed a small smile that didn't reach her eyes.

She encircled John's shoulders and murmured soothing sounds. Her manner reminded Henry of something, as if he'd lived this before. But it was like looking through cobwebs in a darkened room. He shivered, though his body was drenched in sweat.

Uncle Thomas straightened, adjusting his hat. "I s'pose you're right, Pheme. Minding children is more like herding cats, as far as I can tell." He leaned down and took John's trembling chin between his thumb and forefinger. "Sorry to be such a grumpy old bachelor, Johnny. You're no worse for wear. Good lad."

John recoiled. Da swept him into his arms. "We mustn't lose you, John. We love you so. If that ever happens again, find a policeman, eh?"

"Come on, youse." Uncle Thomas said, heading for the doors. "Follow me and stick close."

When he pushed the heavy wooden door open and held it for Mum, Da stepped in front and grasped her arm. Henry gave him a bright smile, then herded the others through like Blackie guiding sheep.

Streetcars whizzed past the station. A porter brought their trunk as far as the street, but Henry and Da were forced to heft it along the boardwalk and hoist it up the two narrow steps to board the car. They had to stand it on end between them in the aisle. Da apologized to passengers who tripped on it squeezing past.

"I knew we didn't need the damn thing," Da said, stepping aside and pressing against the trunk so a lady could move by. He tipped his hat at her, appealing for patience. "Our carpet bags would've done the job much better. He went overboard, as usual."

"Don't fash yourself, Da. They'll never see us again," Henry said. Da's dejected tone made him angry. *Who does Thomas think he is, one-upping Da all the time?*

"I know, Son. It's just… I'm starting to remember—never

mind. There's naught for it now."

Sweat dripped from his chin. Henry took the weight of the trunk against his chest so Da could find his handkerchief. He decided to share a thought he'd had after the church service.

"I've been thinking on what the vicar said in church, Da: 'All will be well. And all manner of things shall be well.' That's a good saying, eh? Same in Manx, isn't it?"

"Yes, if I'd a penny for every one of our proverbs, I'd be a rich man. *Traa dy liooar* means things have a way of working out, ye ken. Long's you're on the right path. Someone turns up to help you out, betimes." he said, covering his cough. "Today, for example, the driver gave us the workers' fare for the bus. It would've cost six cents just for meself. That's a kindness, eh?"

"It's as if the faeries are watching over us, Da. We found John, too."

"I wouldn't mention faeries in these parts, Son. People will think you're daft."

"But Grandad said—"

"We must fit in, Henry. It's a new life we're after." He suddenly pointed out the front window. "Here now, is that the station up ahead?" The driver nodded.

With only minutes to spare, they caught the Detroit and Mackinac connection to Cheboygan. Henry collapsed on the seat, exhausted from maneuvering the cumbersome trunk. He fumed at Uncle Thomas for the trouble he'd caused Da, who could least afford it.

"All aboard for Cheboygan!" Edward shouted, constantly repeating "Cheboygan" until Mum said, "Edward. That last nerve of mine? It's about to snap." Henry sent her silent thanks.

* * *

Within four hours, they arrived at the Cheboygan station, thankful they'd finished with trains. The building was old and shabby. Mum frowned as Uncle Thomas helped her alight.

"Don't be fooled by appearances, Pheme," he said. "There's

thousands flocking in. The city's growing by the day. The stationmaster will mind the trunk. My friend Pete is coming to fetch us. I'm dying for a drink." He looked over his shoulder. "How's that, William? Fancy a cold beer?"

Da's too worn out to answer, but I'd love one. I'm starving and dead tired.

Pete arrived with an open wagon drawn by a pair of heavy horses. Uncle Thomas made quick work of the introductions. Pete nodded at each person's name, even Hugh. "Howdy, folks. Welcome to Michigan." His eyes were kind, though he seemed shy. Once they were seated on benches, he clicked his tongue, and they set off at a smooth, steady walk.

"What does the name 'Cheboygan' mean, Uncle?" Edward asked.

"No idea, Ted." Uncle Thomas leaned over to tap Edward's knee. "Che-Boy-Gan: feels good in the mouth, doesn't it? Michigan State has many a peculiar name: Kalamazoo, Poughkeepsie, Topinabee. Here's a good one: Ypsilanti. They make underwear in that town, warmest there is. We'll order youse all some; you'll need it, come winter. Even you, Pheme," he said, winking at Mum. She shooed him like an annoying fly.

Pete turned around. "Cheboygan's a native word; it means 'shallow.' After the river, see? They dredged 'er in the '70s to allow for bigger boats."

"Imagine that, Pete. First I heard of it. Say, take the scenic route along the riverbank, would you, so's we can have a look-see." He held up his hand when Mum sighed and shook her head.

"You can't miss your first sunset over the river, Pheme. Then we just cut in a few streets for The Ottawa. Best restaurant hereabouts. The farm's pretty close, but we'll stay the night. You look done up." His voice softened. "Have a hot bath, Pheme, get the little ones sorted. William and I will see to the supplies tomorrow." He paused, waiting for an answer. She just shrugged. "Good? That's settled then."

The smoothness of the horses' gait couldn't mitigate the deep ruts in the wagon road.

"Washboard, we call it, ma'am. Lucky it ain't rained recently. Could be worse," Pete said.

"Could be better, too. That last bump nearly knocked my front teeth out," Da said, rubbing his jaw. *Poor Da hasn't shaved in days; he looks old.*

They arrived at the docks just as the setting sun tinted the wide river pink and gold. Two distant lighthouses swung bright arcs into the twilight. Boats of all shapes and sizes bobbed against the dock, and gulls screeched overhead. Henry took a deep breath. *Uncle is right. It is beautiful. If I could take a photograph, I'd write on the back: Cheboygan River, August 5, 1905. Except it would be black and white. There's no way of keeping this view, except in my mind.* He squeezed his eyes and the afterimage faded.

Mum folded her hands and brought them to her lips. She smiled at Uncle Thomas.

"Told you it'd be worth the detour. Grand, eh, Pheme?" he said, grinning like Jinxy with a mouse. "Like a painting. Hark at the wide boats, the ones all decked out with flags? They're ferries."

"Faeries! Where? Everyone says we'll see faeries but—" Ann stood on the seat and squinted.

"He means boats, silly," Edward rolled his eyes.

"Don't." Henry surreptitiously kicked Edward's shin. "Leave off," he said between his teeth. Edward stuck out his tongue and turned around.

"Someday we'll take us a ferry to an island called Bois Blanc, Pheme." Uncle Thomas said, in his proud, teacher voice. "'White woods' in French, that is, for the white pine. I know what that means; it's my treasure." He paused and glanced at Da. "Best hightail it to the hotel before dark. You are fading fast, William. Giddy up, Pete."

The wide main street teemed with cars, buggies, dogs, and people strolling on boardwalks. Unlike Boston, the buildings stood no more than three or four storeys high but appeared stately and solid. Built of red and yellow brick, they glowed softly in the halo of the gas street lamps.

"Everything looks so clean, doesn't it, Mum? Like it's been washed, not in white like the cottage but in colour," John said, gazing around with wide eyes.

"You're right, Johnny," Uncle Thomas said. "You've an artist's eye, and that's a fact." He patted John's knee. John flinched and moved back on the bench.

No good trying to make up now, Uncle Thomas, Henry wanted to say. *John doesn't forget.*

Clearing his throat, Thomas continued. "Pheme, look there. The Opera House. They just rebuilt it, brick this time so it won't burn down again. Like *The Three Little Pigs*, right, Ann? First time I thought of that." He chuckled. "Anyhow, we'll catch a show there like we did in Boston. Pheme?" Mum kept her eyes fixed on the street lamps. Da coughed. Uncle Thomas turned to him.

"No shortage of good dance halls hereabouts, when you're up to it, William. You're such a fine dancer with those long legs of yours." He squeezed Da's knee in his enormous hand. "I can't wait to show you around, William. Tonight, I'll treat you to a taste of our local ale. That'll lift your spirits. It's been a long journey, to be sure. You'll be right as rain in no time." He tapped Pete's back.

"Thanks, Pete. Here's The Ottawa, Pheme. Not quite the Touraine but fine, just the same." He pointed to a three-storey building festooned with window awnings, illuminated within by electric lights. "Settle up with Pete, William. I'll get us registered. They mightn't have three rooms. I'll stay at Cheboygan House, if not. They know me."

Henry took Hugh, squalling now the wagon had stopped.

Uncle Thomas helped Mum alight and propelled her toward the lobby doors, calling to Pete, "Tomorrow, around ten, will do. Come along, Pheme; you'll soon be sitting down to a hot dinner. Tommy, see to Ann. Ted, you carry the basket."

Pete came around to assist. Bouncing the baby on his hip, Henry made his way past his siblings to the front of the wagon, eager to get near the horses. While Da tried to pay Pete, who said tomorrow would do, Henry reached up to pet each horse's nose in turn, gazing into the liquid eyes beneath their blinkers. He marvelled at their huge, shaggy hooves stamping, waiting patiently. Steam evaporated on their broad backs and Henry breathed in their warm, comforting scent. *I love horses. I wish I knew more about them.* When Pete remounted the driver's seat, Henry asked their names.

"This here's Dolly on the right, and this's Fanny. Best team, these parts. Your son's got a good eye for horseflesh, Mr. Car-ine." Pete grinned, and in the half-light, Henry saw that his face bore a terrible scar, and he was missing two teeth. "Most folks just take these beautiful creatures for granted; some want them banned now automobiles are popular. But they'll never replace you, will they, girls?" With a click of his tongue, the team jingled forward. "See you in the morning." Pete's voice rumbled softly in the fading light as he drove away.

Henry turned to follow Da into the hotel. Hugh started to fuss. The boys and Ann were already inside.

"C'mon, Son. I'm famished, aren't you?" Da said, "Look, the lobby's lit with electric lights, like in Boston. Didn't expect that in the wilderness. Then again, I don't know what to expect. I'm glad it's a small hotel. More comfortable."

Henry smiled. *You mean you hate heights, Da, but won't say.* Henry supervised his brothers' ablutions in their room. When they trooped across the hall for her inspection, Mum merely nodded, saying she wished she had the trunk to change clothes; her dress bore the sooty evidence of their journey. She almost choked on the hairpins in her mouth, telling Henry she couldn't comb out Ann's hair.

"My arm's still so sore from that damn injection. Try, please Henry, but if she screams like a banshee, don't bother." She twisted her long hair into a loose coif while warning the boys to be on their best behaviour. "Remember what Uncle says: 'Children are to be seen—'"

"AND NOT HEARD!" The boys chimed in, making Ann giggle and clap.

"Boys, Uncle Thomas says he's friends with the establishment; I won't have him embarrassed on our account."

"Heaven forbid. I've been embarrassed on his account, betimes," Da said.

Wish Da had said it louder. Why does Mum care?

Mum nursed Hugh and tucked him in an open drawer. "He'll be fine until we get back, the lamb," she said, her voice filled with love. "I could curl up next to him. That journey fair wore me out."

As they entered the dining room, Uncle Thomas exclaimed how refreshed they looked, declaring Mum a "miracle worker." He escorted her to a round table set for twelve, bragging to the waiter that he'd brought his family from the Isle of Man to live on his farm. Some diners at other tables gawked at them. A few nodded at Uncle Thomas. He returned smiles and nods, loudly requesting a highchair for "Alice Blue." Mum asked for cushions for John and Tom.

"Of course, Mrs. Carine." An elderly lady came forward, extending her hand. Her grey hair was coiled in a braid atop her head, and she wore a dark dress covered by a long white apron. "Allow me to introduce ourselves. I'm Mrs. Tucker, and this is my husband, Joe," she said, nodding in the direction of a short man with dark, slicked-back hair, wearing a suit and bow tie. Henry detected an English accent. *She sounds like Mum. Maybe she's from Yorkshire, too.*

"Thomas has been on about your emigration for months. We're so glad you're here safe and sound." Her smile lit up her brown eyes as she settled Ann in the highchair. "I understand you've travelled from Boston in less than two days. That's really something, especially with young people." Her gaze inspected each face, then stopped at Mum. "I'll bring dinner in a jiffy."

They attacked the heaping dishes of fish, vegetables, and condiments. After a few bites, Uncle Thomas stabbed his fork in Da's direction. "How's that for fresh fish, eh, William? My treat! The Ottawa's got the finest cook in Cheboygan, present company now excluded," he said, pointing at Mum with his cleft chin.

"Does it come from the ocean, Uncle?" Edward spoke, breaking Uncle Thomas' rule.

"That river you saw, Ted? Right there. Yup, yer pike, bass, trout, pickerel… Cheboygan River's as rich as the Calf of Man—only fresh-water fish, that is. This here's pickerel, my personal favourite. Giant sturgeon over a hundred pounds have been landed here; they can swallow a man whole."

Mr. Tucker stood back on his heels and crossed his arms over his chest. Henry caught his wink.

"Ahem, it's no word of a lie, Joe. I seen a photograph." He gulped his beer and set the mug down, sloshing some on the tablecloth. "I don't fish these parts, though. My farm's near Mullet Lake. Our Ted will wonder why it's called that, I reckon. For the fish, of course. Mullet's delicious, flaky as pastry. Fishing's excellent year-round. Come winter, we'll pitch a tent on the ice and fish through a hole. Buggers practically jump into your net." His eyes toured the table. "Ha! You doubt me, Johnny, but it's true."

John reddened and lowered his gaze. Henry buttered a roll and handed it to him. *John might burst into tears. Uncle Thomas is oblivious. He just goes on. And on.*

"Not to mention the hunting. Deer, elk, moose, creatures of every sort abound in the woods. Wild turkeys, too. Easy to locate; you hear Tom Turkey's gobble a mile off. Noisy fellows, Toms, eh, Tommy?" Looking at Tom, he went 'gobble, gobble,' making chicken arms, rotating his head, opening and closing his eyes. Ann giggled. Tom hid his face in his sleeve. His fork fell to the floor.

"What's a moose?" Edward asked, emphasizing the 'oo' sound. Mum tried to shush him. *Why bother? Edward does just as he likes. She knows that. Gets away with it, too.*

"Like a mouse?" Edward made a disgusted face. "I wouldn't care to eat that."

Uncle Thomas burst out laughing. "Listen to this, Joe. The boy thinks a moose is kin to a mouse."

Uncle Thomas continued speaking at full volume, ignoring Edward's downcast eyes and the dirty looks of other diners.

"Well now, Ted, your moose is one of God's mistakes: legs of a horse, body of a cow, head like a mule, horns shaped like a baby's cradle, the width of my arms. Even has a beard like an old man. I can't draw, but you wouldn't believe me anyway. You'll have to see it for yourself. Ugliest creature on God's green earth, and huge. A single bull will feed us for months. We'll bag us one, come fall." He flourished with his knife, then banged the end on the table.

Stuffing a piece of bread in his mouth, he said, "Which reminds me, William, tomorrow we buy you a gun. D'ye ken how to shoot? An animal on the move, like?"

Mum's hands flew to her mouth. Uncle Thomas creased his brow; his look darkened.

"No arguments, Pheme. William must learn to shoot. Cougars, lynx, coyotes, even wolves roam the woods. For food, defence, and security, a man needs a gun. We hunt or we go hungry in winter." He finally seemed to notice the boys staring, jaws agape. "Not youse, so don't get excited."

Henry's mind swirled like the cream on his dessert with visions of carrying a rifle. He'd only seen pictures in books. *Is it heavy? How do you kill a wild animal? What's it cost?*

Suddenly John overturned his milk. Mum leapt up, anxiously mopping with her napkin. Mrs. Tucker patted her arm.

"Allow me, Mrs. Carine. You poor dear, enduring that journey, all these children—doesn't bear thinking about." She tutted and wiped the table. "Still, you look fresh as a daisy." She handed Mum a fresh napkin. "Please, let me send my daughter Sophie to tuck in the young'uns. We'll sit in my office and have a quiet cuppa. Thomas has told me so much about you, I feel I know you already. A Yorkshire lass? I'm originally from—"

Ann held her doll in the air. "Did Nuncle say about Jenny? This is Jenny Kronchent. The faeries said her name. And me, did he say about me?"

Mrs. Tucker bent down. "No, he didn't tell me about you all, just your Mum. Hello, Jenny. You're lovely. Who made you, then?"

Uncle Thomas answered Henry's silent question. "I didn't know the rest of youse, did I? I knew your mother, way back." His face and ears were as red as Tom's.

Henry couldn't believe his ears. *No mention of his own brother to his friends? Their reason for coming? Leaving Man? Abandoning Nan and Grandad?*

Henry noticed Da scowling at his dessert. Mrs. Tucker filled his water glass when he started coughing.

"Pardon my saying so, Mr. Carine, but you seem plumb tuckered out. You could do with a stiffener. Joseph, take the gentlemen to the lounge." She moved to the sideboard and placed a crystal decanter and three glasses on a tray. "I'm sure you'll feel better after a good night's sleep, and tomorrow you'll be at your new home." She raised a glass of water in a toast. I hope you find happiness in America, Mr. and Mrs. Carine, and your lovely young'uns, too."

"It's C-C-Carin, actually, Mrs. Tucker," Da said, faltering. "They changed our name on our papers. Dropped the 'e.' We're sticking with it." Da shrugged at Uncle Thomas' raised eyebrows. "Save confusion betwixt us. Don't fash yerself, but don't tell, Da, neither." He stood up and pushed in his chair. "Yes, ma'am, I could do with a drink. Thank you kindly."

That night in his own cot, Henry thanked the *Phynodderree* for their new name: 'Carin.' *Maybe it was a mistake or a joke but I like it: Henry William Carin. My own name, so. I must remember to spell it the old way when I write to Nan. Da's right: Grandad mustn't find out. He'd be angrier than Uncle Thomas. Why? As Da says, it separates us. I'm glad.*

Chapter Twenty-Six

Cha vel monney maynrys ec dooinney ta ayns seihll ny lomarcan:
There is not much happiness for a man
who is in the world alone.

Mullet Lake Farm
August, 1905

EUPHEMIA insisted the men haul the trunk upstairs so everyone could change into work clothes before they set off right after lunch. Henry said she seemed more like her old self in regular clothes.

"Old? There's life in me yet, young man." Euphemia said, crossing her arms, pretending to take offence.

William agreed, nuzzling her neck with a kiss and a compliment on her taste in perfume.

"A fine gentleman bought it for me. Can't recall his name at the moment." She lightly pushed him away. "Let's go before I faint with hunger."

She strode down the hallway, Hugh on her hip, a lilt in her step from William's attentions. *Rest has done him a power of good. I, on the other hand, am still exhausted. And famished. And my breasts hurt. Don't tell me my monthlies are starting again.* A moan escaped her lips. *I must wean Hugh soon, though it's hard. Yes, once we're settled.*

Mrs. Tucker greeted them at the dining room entrance. "You're looking more rested, Mrs. Carin."

"Thank you, Mrs. Tucker." Taking her arm, she said under her breath, "I'm so much more comfortable in me own stays. That S-band may be fashionable, but it's torture." They laughed and tapped their heads together. *She's much older, but perhaps she might become a friend, like Jill. Less than a month since I've seen that sweet face, yet it feels like ten years. Will I find such a one again?*

The family settled around the table for a hearty lunch of roast pork with gravy, buttery mashed potatoes, yellow turnips sweetened with brown sugar, and applesauce on the side. The boys enjoyed helping themselves from large china bowls on a revolving platform in the centre of the table. Mrs. Tucker said the turntable was called a "Lazy Susan." At home, Nan or Euphemia portioned the food; seconds were rare. Henry, Edward, and Tom loaded their plates at will and gulped pitchers of lemonade. *That "Susan" isn't "lazy," in my book, and she prevents them from talking. I must get me one.*

"Making up for the rations on the ship, are ye, boys?" Thomas teased, disregarding Euphemia's anxious glance to see if Mrs. Tucker noticed her sons making pigs of themselves. She had.

"Does my heart good to see young'uns enjoying my vittles, Mrs. Carin," she said, leaning over Euphemia's shoulder to replenish her coffee. Then she clicked her tongue. "You've a passel to feed, including Thomas, who eats like a horse."

Thomas patted his distended belly. "Yup, it's mine and all paid for."

"More or less. Settling your account today, then, are you?" Mrs. Tucker raised an eyebrow at him. "I imagine we'll see less of you, now Mrs. Carin will be chief cook."

Thomas shifted in his chair and raised his coffee cup to his full lips, trailing the long moustache. *So, he spends time in town, does he? Doing what? I can imagine.*

Mrs. Tucker placed her left hand on Euphemia's shoulder. "I slipped an American recipe book in your basket, dear, along with egg salad sandwiches and a jar of lemonade. No need to cook tonight."

"Oh, how kind! You put me in mind of my best friend back home," Euphemia said, her eyes misting. *She's a stranger, yet so kind and generous. Mustn't cry, or I won't stop.* She wiped her eyes with her handkerchief. Mrs. Tucker warmed her with her smile.

Thomas' friend Pete had arrived to drive them to the farm. As soon as everyone was settled amongst the sacks of dry goods and the trunk, Euphemia flipped open the wicker basket to extract Mrs. Tucker's gift: *The Settlement Cookbook.*

William reached over and placed a thin metal box atop the book. She recognized the tartan design.

"Toffee! MacIntosh's Toffee! Well, I never. They have it here? Children, Da's bought us a treat." She couldn't break it; it was too soft. "We must wait until we get—" She choked on the word "home." She gulped, then began reading aloud, despite the bumpy road.

"Here you go, Edward, for some funny-sounding words: *Kipfel, Schnecken, Matzos, Kugel.* I can't pronounce the names, let alone cook them. 'American' food? Sounds foreign to me."

"Don't fash yourself, Pheme. Your cooking will be excellent, as always. Better than batchin', right enough. That's what it's called when a bachelor fends for himself, like me and Pete here. Right, Pete?"

No answer. They rode along in silence for a while, but Thomas soon started up again, frustrating Euphemia's efforts to concentrate on the cookery book. *Quiet never lasts long around him.*

"I see you eying your da's new gun, Harry." He put his hand to his heart and intoned, "'Thou shalt not covet thy father's gun,' according to The Bible." He chortled. "Your da seems a bit nervous, and that's a fact. Never you fear, William; you'll be as fine a shot as me in no time." He winked at Edward. "We'll bag us a giant 'mouse' before winter, Teddy boy. Ha, ha." He paused to wipe his brow. "Yes, that joke's a might tired, I reckon."

My word, he picked up on Henry's sour expression. At least he's making an effort with the boys since the train station fiasco. I hope it lasts.

"In Michigan, boys, first thing you must learn to handle, even before a gun, is an axe. Not just for chopping firewood but for cutting down trees and clearing stumps. You must respect it. Abuse an axe and she'll wear your hands raw or open your foot like an over-cooked sausage. Treat her kindly and she'll grow to love you. Like a woman."

Euphemia could feel his gaze, hotter than the sun. She kept her head buried in the book, not daring to glance at William. Thomas cleared his throat, then continued.

"You'll learn to drive a team, too. Pete tells me you've taken a shine to heavy horses, Harry. All to the good. We'll get us a team, eventually." He leaned forward, placing both hands flat on the wooden bench. "You've a great future ahead, now you're here, lads. Not forced down a mine like us, eh, William? Fresh air, sunshine, hard work. 'Every day's a good day above ground,' so they say."

William nodded. "Yes, we miners abide by that. Still, there's satisfaction in hard graft; counting your load at day's end, working beside fellows who've got your back, coming home to a wife and family—" Euphemia smiled when he patted her arm.

"You tend to look for the good, William, but by God, it cost us dear: Ralph, Mel, dead; your health, ruined. I'm lucky I escaped before it killed me. Er, I mean—"

William turned to face Pete's back, staring down at his hands. "I agree, Thomas. When a man's got a choice, best take it. I hope my sons will have it easier, being here. I appreciate your support, case I haven't said."

"*She dty vea, William. Ta, she dty vea,*" Thomas said, barely audible above the wind and the clatter of the wagon. "Soon be there." He shouted to Pete. "Keep these girls at a good clip." Tears stung Euphemia's eyes in sympathy with William's wounded pride. *He's your brother, for Christ's sake, Thomas. I should say he's welcome.*

She inhaled through her nose and breathed out through her mouth to calm her nerves. Once they'd left the city, the road became little more than a track through dense forest. *The air smells like freshly washed sheets dried in the sun; one of my favourite smells.* She filled her lungs to bursting, then slowly exhaled. She'd never been anywhere with no houses for miles. Conifers swept the forest floor and stirred the clouds at the same time. Light danced through the trees, reminding her of people flashing by on the streets of Liverpool. Pete manoeuvred the team around fallen tree branches and deep ruts. Her spine shook like dice in a shaker. The children were continually dislodged from their seats, landing on the full burlap sacks. She hoped one of them wouldn't lose a tooth.

"Corduroy, it's called, for the ruts. Would'a be worse had it'd rained," Thomas said.

"Corduroy. Like your suit, Mother." John looked up at her.

She leaned down to tap his cheek. *The things our John takes notice of.* She returned the cookbook to the basket. *Wish I could ask Mrs. Tucker about these recipes.*

A few miles along, the team turned down a country lane. They pulled up before a large, white house framed by a picket fence and a flower garden. Euphemia delighted at the rows of gigantic sunflowers and multicoloured roses espaliered on trellises. *Sunflowers? Roses? This can't be his.*

"Are we here?" Tom and Edward leapt up, lost their balance, and tumbled down. Thomas shook his head, explaining that they were picking up vegetables from the market garden operated by Mrs. Miller and her husband, Leon. Oddly, he'd stated the wife's name first. He descended the front seat awkwardly, landing with a thump, and turned to wave his hat. A large woman in striped overalls and a battered straw hat was headed their way, followed by a thin, stooped man.

"Hallo, Mrs. Miller. How are you, this fine afternoon?"

"Thomas, you old devil," Mrs. Miller said, pumping his hand, then punching his shoulder.

Euphemia instantly admired her boldness. *Seems strong as a man. Her English accent is refined; she's upper-crust, for sure. Strange. A handsome woman, bright green eyes, sparkling white teeth, a beaming smile… whatever is she doing here?*

"Your long-awaited family's here, at last. Welcome, Carines, to the land of milk and honey!" She spread her arms as if embracing the wagon. "May you find all you seek in Michigan."

An educated woman, to be sure. Euphemia handed Hugh to Henry so she and William could alight and meet them properly.

"Speaking of which, Thomas ordered a goodly supply of milk and honey, as well as butter, cheese, fresh and home-canned vegetables, to start you off. I threw in some smoked bacon, too." She crossed her arms, then planted her feet wide. "I'll tally it, shall I, Thomas, in exchange for that promised cord of wood? Beware this rapscallion, folks," she said, winking at Euphemia. "He's a big talker but a slow walker, as I always say."

Euphemia returned her twinkling smile. *She's got his number obviously. How long has she known him?*

Mrs. Miller removed her hat, revealing wavy brown hair with only a few streaks of grey. She gestured to her husband to do the same. "Introductions, if you please, Thomas." She clicked her tongue. "I'll present my husband, Leon. He built your house, fine carpenter that he is." She gave him a slight, affectionate push, then her warm tone turned officious. "Leon, pull the cart over to load up whilst I meet the young people. Land sakes, must I think of everything?"

I'll bet you do, indeed. Euphemia pictured her lovely, plumed hat, still travelling by train to parts unknown.

Mrs. Miller repeated each child's name in turn, then summarized: "Henry, Edward, Tom, John, Ann, Hugh, oh yes, and Jenny! You're the oldest, Henry, yes? And Hugh here is the newest addition." She turned to Euphemia, wide-eyed. "What a lovely, large family you have, Mrs. Carine! We weren't blessed with children, sadly." She paused, glancing down. "I do hope you don't find it too much, what with… And you're just as Thomas described you: pretty as a picture." Euphemia perceived sympathy in the intent gaze and wrinkled brow. *Is she troubled on my account?*

"We womenfolk must stick together in this wild frontier, Mrs. Carine." She wiped her hands with a handkerchief from her overalls, then squeezed Euphemia's hand. She clicked her tongue again. "You're in need of a hat, my dear." She called over her shoulder. "Leon, fetch Mrs. Carine a sun hat." She patted her cheeks as her smile unfolded from her lined face. "I keep covered up. Prevents sunstroke. And wrinkles."

Euphemia donned the broad-brimmed straw hat and laughed as it slid over her ears. *How kind she is. I hope we'll be friends.*

Mrs. Miller then turned to the children. "I know you'd like to play, but your uncle's in a hurry. Next time you can visit the farmyard and meet my guard-turkey, Tom, yonder." She pointed to a huge white bird the size of a gannet, patrolling the fence. "Better than a dog and twice as vicious."

When Thomas introduced William, she pumped his hand. "I understand you've been poorly, Mr. Carine. I hope the voyage didn't tax you too strenuously. Thomas described the conditions in steerage—"

Class sets us apart, clearly. Yet she seems very down to earth. I must ask Thomas the story of this woman.

William interrupted. "Fair to middlin', me, thank you, ma'am. Pleased to make your acquaintance." He removed his hat and returned her smile. "Our name's 'Carin' now, Mrs. Miller. They spelt it so on our immigration cards, and we're keeping it."

"How clever. Distinguish yourselves from this scallywag," she said, pointing her thumb at Thomas. "Well, Mr. Carin, your closest doctor's in Cheboygan, three hours away. If ever you get hurt or fall ill, why, you come here. I can cure almost any ailment in man or beast with natural remedies I learned from the Indians." She patted his arm while looking expressly at Euphemia.

William tipped his hat and helped Euphemia back into the wagon. Suddenly, she thought of something. "Mrs. Miller, my husband bought the children some toffee, but we can't break it. Could you—"

Mrs. Miller put the box on the tailgate and struck it with the hammer hanging from her overalls. "Problem solved," she said, handing her the crushed toffee. Euphemia thanked her anyway.

The children waved goodbye while the wagon turned a wide circle. As they passed by the two-storey house with its expansive porch and decorated eaves, Euphemia glimpsed lace curtains in the windows.

"Her gardens must be a sight to behold. Quite the unusual character," Euphemia said.

"Salt of the earth," Thomas said, nodding. "You'd never guess, but her father's a Lord in the British parliament. She came out back in the '80s, escaping some scandal, I heard. She never explained, and you can't get a word out of Leon. I'll miss our chinwags once we have our own garden. She invites me in for tea, plays classical piano… Just shows, you can't judge a book—"

"Her husband's pretty quiet," William said.

"Wouldn't say boo to a goose. She found a fellow willing to let her wear the pants. She runs the market garden. Leon's a master carpenter, as you'll soon appreciate."

They re-entered the humid forest and were suddenly assailed by swarms of insects. Euphemia wafted her handkerchief in Ann's face to shoo them away. The boys cupped their hands over their ears and squeezed their eyes shut. Edward lightly swatted one on Tom's face. It left a streak of blood. Euphemia screamed.

"Why, it's naught but a wee mosquito," Thomas said, chuckling.

"A mosquito! Don't they carry malaria? Oh, you never said—"

"Now, Pheme, this ain't Africa, for God's sake." He laughed. "You'll swell up from the sting, then itch like the dickens, but you mustn't scratch. That'll make it worse. Dammit, I forgot lotion of calamine. Oh well, mud'll do."

"Mud, Uncle?" Edward said.

"Yup. We learned that from the Indians. That's why the first settlers called them 'Red Indians.' Fools. For one, this isn't India, and two, their skin wasn't red but smeared with mud for protection against insects." He shook his head and reached over to brush one from Euphemia's cheek. She shrank back, tears in her eyes, swatting at a high-pitched buzz in her ears.

"Calm down, Pheme. A nuisance, but you must bear up. I don't pay any mind, nowadays. Mrs. Miller recommends putting a hot spoon on the bite. Maybe then you just feel the burn," he said, with a snort.

"It's worse for horses, right, Pete? Especially hitched to the wagon, like now. They can't use their tail. That's why horses have long tails, don't you know, Alice Blue?"

Ann flailed her hands, dropped Jenny, and started to bawl.

"Yes, ma'am," Pete said, turning around to talk. "We build a smudge for the horses in the field." He tapped the reins to hurry the team along. "Ah, now we're in the open, the wind'll blow them away."

Suddenly, Thomas asked everyone to look over Pete's shoulder at a wire fence.

"We've reached my land. See up ahead? The lane's cleared of trees." He pointed with a trembling finger. "There she is—the yellow house." He removed his hat, wiping his brow with his sleeve, seeming to struggle for breath. "Our house, now. I hope it pleases you, Pheme."

Euphemia frowned. William rocked backward like he'd been slapped. At their approach, the structure seemed to expand in height and breadth; two storeys, wrapped in a covered verandah. Thomas showed off the gabled roof with wooden shingles. The peak and eaves were festooned with sculpted, white trim. He drew spiral shapes in the air.

"Gingerbread, it's called. Latest fashion. Leon's a whiz at it." He smiled at Ann. "You've a gingerbread house, Alice Blue, like in a faery tale."

Ann had thrown herself on the flour sacks and covered her head. "Jenny and me hates 'skeetoes.' They bite."

Euphemia shifted her gaze between Thomas—the house—Thomas. Overcome, she gripped the side as the wagon hit another rut. *This is twice, maybe three times the size of the cottage. A house? No. A mansion.*

The building glowed like a buttercup in the sun. A wooden swing hung above the veranda. An inlaid stone path led to a tall, wide staircase. Pete slowed the team and stopped at the front entrance. Thomas swung down, raced around behind, and reached for Euphemia's hand, gesturing with the other.

"She's built of planked lumber, every square foot. Biggest house in the county, I'd wager."

The boys sat stock-still. Hugh squirmed on Euphemia's lap. His diaper was filled, and he wanted feeding. She was frozen.

"Well," Thomas said, grimacing. "Here's a fine 'how do you do.' Cat got your tongues?" An orange cat sauntered up and encircled his leg. "Speaking of cats, I have two: 'Ginger' and 'Bread.' Keep the mice down, right, Ginger?" He gathered the cat into his arms. "T'other's pure white, so, 'Bread.' He's 'round here somewheres. Notice the long tail, Johnny? Not stubby like Manx cats." He tugged the cat's tail, and she leapt down.

Thomas brushed his hands together, then spun around left, right, and finally gestured skyward. "Come on, now, Pheme. First impressions?"

"I—I just… don't know… It fair takes my breath away. I'm speechless." Tears were close.

"Ha! Success! When does that happen?" He slapped his knee. "And you, William, what say you? Big change from sharing the cottage with Mother and Da, eh? Come on, all of youse, hop down. Pete, unload the vittles from Mrs. Miller, will you? The boys'll help with the sacks, later."

Thomas reached for Euphemia's hand again, but Henry scrambled down first, and she handed Hugh over. John fell backward when he jumped. William dusted him off, then assembled the boys and carried Ann. Looking around as if expecting to be bowled over, they ventured up the stairs. Thomas unlocked the panelled door inset with stained glass and steered Euphemia inside.

"Been building her three years. Me and Leon, that is. Just needs a woman's touch here and there. That's where you come in."

In the spacious vestibule, she felt Thomas' warm hand traverse the small of her back to her waist. She dropped his arm and sought eye contact with William. His face was pale and sour as a bowl of whey. The children encircled him like a lifebuoy, gawking upward at the high ceiling.

"Shuck off your shoes, everyone. These pine floors mark up something terrible," he said. "Come, Pheme, see the kitchen first. Let Hugh crawl; he can't do himself an injury."

On the left, an archway displayed a furnished parlour illuminated by a large window. A long wooden coat rack and hat sat to the right of the door. Past the parlour, a solid oak stairway led upstairs. Thomas traversed the dark, windowless hallway past the stairs in a few strides and threw open a door. Euphemia followed silently in her stocking feet.

In his salesman's voice, Thomas said, "This, good lady, is a Hoosier cabinet." Doors slammed. "Store flour, sugar, bread pans and such, with a marble surface for rolling out pastry. Latest model. Here, you've cupboards over the counter and a built-in sink." Bang, bang. "A pump brings in water using my own gravity system." Squeak, squeak. "No electrics yet out here, but it'll come. I'll take kerosene and wood over peat, any day."

He zigzagged across the kitchen, sliding on his socks. "Over here's your icebox; solid oak." Thud. "We harvest ice from the lake in winter, keep it buried in straw all summer so's we never run short—" He interrupted himself to unlock the back door. Pete stumbled in, loaded down with a box. Euphemia remained riveted where she stood, barely breathing.

"On the table just there, Pete. Put the milk and cheese in the ice box, would you? Should be nice and cold by now; I put the ice in 'fore I left." He banged his hand on a windowsill. "No more cooling milk here, Pheme. Modern conveniences, eh?"

Pete turned to leave. Thomas slapped his back. "Good man. Catch you next time, eh?"

"Sure enough, Thomas," Pete said, closing the door.

Thomas pointed out implements in a corner of the spacious kitchen. "I've a butter churn and cream separator, there, see, but we'll rely on Mrs. Miller until we get a cow."

He was saying so much, so quickly, Euphemia couldn't keep up. *What is all this? No wonder Mrs. Miller hinted at something. I never dreamed… Three years, he said? He only knew we were coming last year… Something smells fishy.*

"Now, dear madam," Thomas said, sweeping outward. "The jewel in the crown; Clapp's Ideal Steel Range. A reservoir for hot water means no more cooking over a hearth or using the copper. I didn't even buy one."

Euphemia gingerly touched the cold, shiny range. *I haven't the faintest how to cook on this contraption.*

"I'm wondering—"

He swirled her around to face the bare window. "Sit you down, Pheme. I had Leon build this table and chairs just for you. I ken your shock; this here's the best fitted-out kitchen in the county."

Arms mid-air, he noticed William at the door. "Ah, William, come in. Come, all of youse. What d'you reckon? Beats the cottage, eh?"

William clutched his bowler in both hands. Ann held her doll the same way. She popped her thumb in her mouth, breaking the silence. The boys tiptoed in, Henry carrying Hugh at arm's length. The smell was overpowering, but Thomas grabbed Euphemia's arm and headed toward a swinging door at the end of the room.

"The dining room, folks; table for twelve, complete with a Lazy Susan like The Ottawa! I forgot a highchair for Alice Blue and Hugh. Leon can—"

Edward pushed past the adults, clambered onto a chair, and banged his elbows down.

"Let's eat! I'm starving."

Tom and John scrambled beside him. William placed the wicker basket on the table and opened the lid. "These young'uns want feeding, and Hugh's a mess. They need attending to."

"Grandad'll never be dead, as long as you're alive, Ted," Thomas said, smiling. "I know your stomach's stuck to your backbone but let me finish the tour. Quick as a wink, then we'll make short work of Mrs. Tucker's lunch, I promise." His voice became plaintive. "I've waited so long."

Euphemia creased her brow. *So long? A single year? Yet this house took three? I can't make head nor tail of it. William looks equally befuddled. When Thomas calms down, I'll pull him aside… I hope he hurries. We're perished.*

Chapter Twenty-Seven

Myr smoo vees er yn tailley, shen myr smoo veer yn eeck:
The more on the tally, the more the pay.

THOMAS whirled Euphemia around to face the buffet, crowned by a gilt mirror. "Dishes, utensils and such, stored away like Mother's dresser." He rubbed the surface of the cupboard. "But, white pine, best there is. I love it." He yanked open a drawer. "You choose the linen, Pheme. Now to the parlour."

After a glance at the settee and fireplace, she was manoeuvred back to the hall. "Here's a built-in bench. The seat holds winter scarves and such. Leon's idea. Clever, eh? Your knitting skills will come in handy, very soon." He slammed the lid. Henry jumped; Hugh began crying. Euphemia sighed. *William's right, we must stop.* "Thomas, please—"

Thomas was headed upstairs. *Maybe the privy's up here.* She balanced Hugh on her hip and climbed, gripping the wide handrail.

"I expect you're wondering about the sleeping arrangements and the facilities, Pheme."

Thomas took two stairs at a time and stopped on the landing. Behind his head, a circular stained-glass window glowed red and yellow. William's eyes widened as Thomas pointed out the design.

"My tribute to the old country. Da'd be pleased, eh?" He took his handkerchief from his pocket and wiped his eyes. "I commissioned a *ny tree cassyn* from a Boston artist. He'd never heard of our three-legged man, would you believe? The glass came in a barrel of molasses so's it wouldn't break. Got good molasses out of it, too. Clever, eh?"

William nodded, a glint of moisture in his eyes. John rubbed his small hand around the carved ball atop the newel post.

"Ah, trust you, Johnny, to appreciate Mr. Miller's handiwork. We installed the banister after the furniture was in. Just a few weeks ago, in fact. Wait'll you see the tub in the bathroom, Pheme. Like the Touraine. Unfortunately, we don't have running water yet. The privy's out of doors."

Euphemia clutched the banister as if aboard *Ivernia*, dizzy with nausea. Thomas motioned to everyone.

"Come see your room, boys," Thomas said.

He led them to a room outfitted with two bunk beds, one single, and a washstand. One wardrobe occupied the corner.

"Just like the ship, Mother," John said.

Euphemia brought a hand to her mouth, bit down, and swallowed the sweetness rising in her throat, while Tom and Edward fought over the top bunks.

"There's an extra for Hughie," Thomas said, chucking Hugh under his chin and smiling into Euphemia's eyes. Then he pinched his nose. "Uh-oh. Best keep moving."

"Where's your room, Uncle?" Edward asked.

"Oh, I'll kip in a bunk under the eaves behind the stairwell. Don't need a fancy room, me. I'm used to roughing it."

Are you, indeed? This is "roughing it?" Euphemia blew out her cheeks. *If I don't get to the privy soon, I'll burst. I'm going down. We can tour after lunch. Not as if we're going anywhere.*

Thomas took Ann by the hand. "Across here, a little room

for you, Alice Blue. Mummy's right next door—you needn't fret. I've a surprise —" Ann rushed in. On a table next to the curtainless window stood a miniature two-storey house, painted yellow and trimmed in white.

"Mr. Miller crafted a model, planning the house. I wanted your little girl to have it, Pheme."

Euphemia stared at him, astounded. *He considered a child he'd never met? He's changed that much in ten years?*

Ann stood, examining the dollhouse, while Thomas led Euphemia to a room occupying the back corner of the house. The other boys were bouncing on their beds, but Henry was nearby. William remained in the hall, shifting his feet, watching Hugh crawl about.

The door opened into a furnished bedroom with a double brass bed, a large dresser with an upholstered seat, a wardrobe with mirrored doors, and a washstand complete with a blue and white bowl and pitcher set.

Henry's eyes glittered. "Your room in the Touraine, Mum," he said. "Only better."

Thomas spoke in low tones, as though they were in church. "I forgot a crib, but an apple box will suffice. I had help purchasing sheets and towels… I hope you're comfortable."

He lifted Hugh's booted foot and held it in his palm, his grey eyes fixed on hers. *It feels like a dream. Unreal.* She passed Hugh to Henry and collapsed on the bed. Her mouth was parched, and heat rushed to her face.

"Water, please. I need water."

Ann padded in. "Jenny says faeries live in the little house, Mama."

"Such good news, sweetie," Thomas said, his voice falsely bright. He backed out, half-closing the door. "Introduce me to them, won't you? I've never seen faeries in these parts. At home, neither, come to that. They must've followed you across the pond." He put his finger to his lips. "Let's give Mummy a moment. There's a chamber pot under the bed, Pheme. Henry, fetch your mother some water."

"Hugh needs a change, Mum. Should I—" Henry looked as lost as she felt.

"Oh, just strip him down for now. I'll deal with it later. Keep him away from the stairs," she said, unable to move. "Shut the door." Her ears were ringing. She shifted on the bed, unbound her hair, and draped it over the pillow, fanning her face with her hand. Hot tears slid down her cheeks, and her head reeled as though she were drunk.

What in God's name's going on? Nothing's right. This grand house—he never built it for us. He didn't know we were coming. We escaped being deported by a hair. What was his plan if we didn't get through?

She sat up and pressed the pillow to her chest. *There's someone else, sure. I sensed a problem, from Mrs. Tucker and Mrs. Miller, both. They felt sorry for me. My God, Nan, a fine kettle of fish you've dropped us into. Where can we go with not a penny left?*

Euphemia half-smiled at Edward's voice in the hall. "We found the chamber pots too, Uncle. Can we eat soon?"

Best get up. Inhaling a ragged breath, she rolled over and noted the white lace counterpane. *Impractical as hell. Who purchased that, then? Never Thomas.* She got up to wash her face. No water. *Of course, who'd have filled it? Get hold of yourself, woman. There's time enough to find out, as Grandad would say.*

She could hear the firm tone Thomas used on the boys. "You'll be emptying the pots, every morning. Lots of chores on a working farm—"

Bang. Euphemia jumped, nearly dropping the pitcher. *What the hell was that? Oh, God, Hugh fell down those bloody stairs. What's the commotion?* Henry was calling for help.

"Mum, come quick! Da, Da, what's wrong? Oh, Mum, I think he's fainted."

Euphemia flew out the door. Her bones turned to water. She knelt as Henry raised William to a seated position against the wall. William groaned, opened his eyes, and coughed.

"What is it, William?" Euphemia felt his forehead. "You're soaking wet. Edward, run, ask Pete for water if he's still here. You'll never manage the pump. Is it the heat, William?"

"It's too much. It's just too much." William's voice quaked.

"I know, darling, such a hard trip. We made it through, my love… and now… Oh, God, we must get him to bed, Thomas."

"Of course, of course. How can I help you, William? Are you ill?"

"No," he said softly. "It's this, all this. This… house. It's too much. How? How will I—" His head lolled back as he fought for air, flailing his arms, pounding his sock feet on the floor.

Is it a fit? Euphemia wrapped him in her arms, swaddling him, shushing him like a baby. "Don't talk. Good job, Edward," she said as she took a mug of water and held it to William's lips. "Let's get you settled, shall we, and I'll bring you supper. Goodness, the sun's going down. You're past it, my love. We all are."

Thomas' face drained of its usual ruddy colour. His eyes expressed genuine concern. *He seems abashed, as he should. Perhaps he'll appreciate how very ill William is and leave off unmanning him at every turn. Oh, God, don't let this be the end.*

"Thomas, help me. We must make him comfortable. Tom, remove his shoes; don't soil the counterpane. Henry, feed the children, whilst I see to Hugh. We'll have an early night. There's been enough excitement for one day."

Chapter Twenty-Eight

Down by the salley gardens
my love and I did meet;…
She bid me take love easy,
as the leaves grow on the tree;
But I, being young and foolish,
with her would not agree.

William Butler Yeats, 1889

FOR everyone but William and Hugh, the next day's dawn marked the beginning of work. Ceaseless work. Thomas acquired a cow, a rooster and laying hens, and an ox he called Samson.

Euphemia, Thomas, and the boys rose before breakfast to begin the daily chores.

"No dilly-dallying, boys," Thomas said. "We must get this operation underway before winter. There's no time to waste. *Traa dy liooar* means naught in these parts."

Euphemia fed them porridge every morning, with fresh milk and raspberries from Mrs. Miller. "If oats keep Samson strong, it's good enough for us," Thomas said, dismissing Tom's request for fried eggs. "This wee man is thriving." He laughed and chucked the rolls under Hugh's chin.

Euphemia hoarded eggs for baking or hard boiling, keeping a worried eye on the larder. Somehow, she produced simple but filling meals for them all, plus Mrs. Miller and Pete who often came to help. She resumed serving the plates like back home.

Home. After only six weeks, life in the little white cottage with its cheery red door seemed like a dream. Euphemia recalled fondly how she and Nan accomplished their daily routines, cogs in a well-oiled machine. They'd smile in mutual admiration at day's end, as the family gathered 'round the hearth. She'd sing through her work while Nan chattered on, to herself or the faeries, one couldn't be sure. At three o'clock they'd stop, often joined by Jill or one of Nan's friends, for tea, scones, and gossip. Now, all alone, she shouldered all the household responsibilities.

William remained bedridden, barely able to raise his head from the pillow without help. His teeth ached, he couldn't hold a teacup, much less keep down food. At night, he thrashed about in a cold sweat, moaning and coughing so much that Euphemia finally took to sleeping on Thomas' cot in Ann's room. Thomas slept on the parlour settee, for some peace, he said. They'd called the doctor, who recommended rest, chicken soup, more rest. With downcast eyes, he handed Euphemia a vial of laudanum to help William sleep and quell his outbursts. *Maybe I should use it myself,* she almost said.

She mounted the flight of sixteen stairs multiple times a day to tend to him, between preparing meals, washing clothes, sweeping floors, baking bread, and… everything else. Her dresses began to hang like gunny sacks on a clothesline; she simply tightened the ties on her apron.

Of the boys, only John stayed with her; the others worked on outdoor chores Thomas assigned, dawn to dusk. John would do little jobs, then lay on the floor with the cats and draw on brown paper or nap. She set Ann to turning the cream separator, gathering eggs, fetching things, with Jenny in the crook of her arm. *At least she's quit sucking her thumb; there isn't time.* She laughed to herself. *If there were, I'd take it up. What would Thomas think of that?*

Thomas. A few days after their arrival, she'd cornered him in the kitchen once she'd settled William and the younger children upstairs. Henry was reading one of Thomas' magazines in the parlour.

Every cord in her throat longed to scream, but she was determined to remain calm while speaking her mind. "What's this all about, Thomas? As William says, this house makes no sense. Were we an afterthought? Was, or is, there another woman? There's been a change of plans, sure? D'you think we're daft and can't see?"

"No. I swear. I built all this for you, darling. It's you I want, you I've been waiting for, working for—"

"Thomas, get this straight, once and for all: you mustn't say such things. I'm your brother's wife. Besides, how could you know I'd come? It's the last thing I wanted—" She smacked her hand on the counter. "That's far-fetched. I reckon you planned to marry. You built this house for a family. Then Nan wrote and bullied you into taking us in. The timing still makes no sense."

"Lots of things make no sense, Pheme. Your marrying William, for one. But I knew, from Mother's letters, that things were becoming impossible for you, that you'd be a widow soon… Perhaps it's for the best."

She shrieked and jumped as though stung by a bee. Thomas clapped a hand over her mouth. She longed to bite it, draw blood. She wrenched away and pulled at her hair, sending pins flying like moths.

"For the best? Did I hear that? Jesus Christ, your brother upstairs at death's door. For the best? That fits your plan, doesn't it? I might've guessed it wasn't brotherly devotion that made you so eager to help us—" Her tongue became a flannel rag stuck to the roof of her mouth. She could barely swallow, but at the same time, she gagged. "I could puke." She leaned over and almost did. "So now you've a fine house, a ready-made family, complete with a cook, labourers… Christ, I've been blind, so blind." Tears coursed down her cheeks. *Poor William. He's been duped. That's the worst of it.*

Thomas seized her shoulders. "But in Boston—in Boston, it felt like old times, didn't it, Pheme? I got the impression, I dared hope—" He attempted to embrace her; she shoved him.

"Boston? Boston was a dream, Thomas. This is reality. The man I love is dying, I've six children—" Her voice cracked. *God, I need water.* She grabbed the water pump.

"Never mind, never mind, now. Shhh, hush, darling," he said, restraining her. She shrugged him off hard and began pumping the handle.

Thomas cleared his throat and wiped his sleeve across his brow. "Listen, Pheme. I'm sorry William's ailing. I hate to see him suffer. Blood's thicker than water, as Mother used to say. I want him to recover, I do. He may."

"Liar! You know goddamn well there's no cure."

Hopefully, William can't hear. Or Henry. Never mind. She grabbed a ladle and pitched it at him. He ducked.

"Well, he's better off here; so are you and the youngsters. Mother got that right. There's no future on Man. We'll make a good life. As one family." His tone and eyes softened. "Please, don't fash yourself, Pheme. I intended to help, not hurt you." He reached for her arm. She turned and let her water glass fall into the porcelain sink. It shattered.

By God, we're stuck, but so is he. He paid our bond. He's responsible. She straightened her back and turned to face him, brushing the front of her apron with her palms.

"'Fash this, fash that!' Fash you, Thomas." She lifted her chin and glared at him. "You get me a girl like you did for your mother, once upon a time. I've a sick husband, a baby, six children, this huge house to manage… I can't cope."

"There's an orphanage in Cheboygan—"

"Christ almighty! No bloody orphans!" This time she couldn't restrain herself. "Might as well have another child. No, goddamn it. I need a maid of all work, and that's that."

"Where would we put her? All the rooms are full."

"Well, you might've thought of that, Idiot. A woman wouldn't have made such a blunder. You built a grand two-storey house with no thought for running it afterward. It's all for show. Didn't even install a dormer." She shook her head at his blank expression. "You haven't a clue. A house this size wants a servant, and I'm not it, whatever you may think. Took me all day yesterday to wash sheets, never mind clothes. I was half-dead when we arrived, I've had not a moment's rest…"

She tended the Clapper, which, like Hugh, needed constant feeding. "The maid can kip beside Ann. Bring the dollhouse downstairs. I'll take the empty bunk in the boys' room; Hugh can sleep in a drawer."

"You've got it all figured out," Thomas huffed.

"Well, somebody bloody well has to," Euphemia said, releasing her frustration. "I'm at the end of my tether. Get you to Cheboygan. Perhaps Mrs. Tucker's daughter, Sophie, would—"

"I doubt it. She's needed in the hotel, and besides, why would a young lass want to live way out here?"

"I've asked myself the same question, Thomas. Indeed, I have. Any road, I'll have help, or I swear, I'll move us to Cheboygan. Least there, I can work for wages. And don't you 'darling' me, ever again."

CHAPTER TWENTY-NINE

Te ny share dy ve boght as onneragh na dy ve berçhagh as breagagh:
Better to be poor and honest than to be rich and lying.

Mullet Lake Farm
August, 1905

"THAT'S it, Harry, lean in. *Jean shoh.* Now pull. Hard. Whack his ass with the quirt." Uncle Thomas directed Henry's efforts to remove a tree stump while resting on his shovel. Henry gripped the chains in one sweaty hand, gingerly whipping the ox to persuade him. He stumbled and promptly fell face-first into the mud. Uncle Thomas gave him a hand, but as soon as Henry righted himself, pushed him. He sprawled backward, prompting a hearty guffaw. Henry ground his teeth, using his fists to clean his eyes.

"You're a right mess, Harry. Good timing; it's lunchtime. Wash up in the trough. Drop your duds on the porch. Mustn't track through your mother's clean house."

Henry bent to unwind the chain on the stump. Uncle Thomas kept talking. "Feels good to work into your heat, eh, Harry? Builds an appetite for your ma's fine cooking." He rubbed his stomach. Henry didn't understand the expression but was too filthy and tired to care. Uncle Thomas adopted his "teacher" voice: "That's what they say here when the sweat pours down your back like cold water. Makes you hungry as a horse and horny as a bull. Say, have you ever…?"

Henry's ears blazed. Thomas snorted. "What with all this hard work, you're getting as powerful as Samson, not the bag of bones you were even a few weeks back. You'll look more like me in no time." His sleeves nearly burst when he flexed his biceps. "After lunch, we'll make better progress, so long as one of us doesn't decide on a mud bath like goddamn Cleopatra." He threw his head back to laugh, then directed his gaze to a small structure next to the barn.

"I'll see how our Ted's getting on, shingling the chicken coop. That boy doesn't know how to work like you do. Bone idle. Probably talked Tommy into doing it. I'll give him the fear of heights all right. I'll put the fear of God into him…" He smacked his gloves against his side and left.

Henry stumbled across the rough ground, leading Samson by a rope attached to the ring in his nose. After watering the ox, he washed his hands and face in the trough, visited the outhouse, then tore up the back steps. *I wonder what's for lunch. I'm starving. Oops, sorry, Nan. You'd scold me. I must write her tonight to send with Mum's letter. She'll be anxious for news. I'll make it sound good. Let the faeries tell her the truth.*

Shucking his muddy boots, he began peeling off his overalls. He opened his mouth to ask Mum for clothes when her voice penetrated the screen.

"It's just no good, Thomas."

How'd he get here so fast? He said he was checking Edward. His boots aren't here. We're not allowed to enter by the front. But it is his house…

"We've been here for weeks, and I still can't get ahead. There's too much to do. Mrs. Miller says I must "can" vegetables and fruit for winter. How on earth am I supposed to do that?" Her voice creaked like the wire clothesline in the back-yard. "You insist we prepare for winter, but how? I dread it. At home, we hardly noticed the seasons. No snow, for one. It's so different here." Her voice sounded whiny, like Ann's when she didn't get her way.

"Yes, you are right. Da was always saying: '*Traa dy-liooar:* time enough. Don't let the worry at you; work'll get done, all in good time.' Nice, but here it's more like: 'Never enough time.' But don't fash yourself, Pheme." He cleared his throat, cough-ing slightly. "You're doing your best."

"I'm out of my depth. Wish Nan were here to help."

She misses Nan, too. I'm so homesick, I can barely swallow. Until food gets in front of me.

"Well, I, for one, am glad she's not." He said, emphasizing the *not*. "She'd boss everyone day and night. Listen, I'll ask Mrs. Miller to gather the implements, bring fruits and vegetables, and teach you how to make preserves. There, there, don't cry."

Henry hardly recognized the soothing voice. *He never uses that on us boys.* He peeked through the screen just as Thomas took Mum in his arms. Stifling a gasp, he watched him raise her chin and attempt to kiss her. She didn't slap or push him away. She turned her face aside and drew back. Henry dug his finger-nails into the wooden doorframe. He wanted to fly back down the stairs and vomit. His legs were stumps. They wouldn't move.

"Stop, Thomas. I am William's. I chose him a long time ago. I regret—past mistakes."

"A mistake? That's all I am? And why didn't you tell me? About Edward. I knew, the minute I clapped eyes on him. I had the right to know." His fierce tone became frightening. He kicked a chair. *He'd better not hit Mum.* Henry searched the porch for a weapon and grabbed a muddy boot.

"Why would I? When I know what it's like to be an orphan, not knowing who your father is? I never, in my wildest dreams, thought you'd find out. Never." Mum sobbed. Her cheeks were shiny with sweat and tears. She took Thomas' hand and brought it to her chest. "Let it be, please, Thomas. William's his father. He raised him. No one knows any different. Besides, William needs me, now more than ever." Her eyes were pleading with Thomas.

"And I don't? Wasn't it me who found you in peril, came to your rescue?" He wrenched his hand away and gripped her shoulders. "I'll never understand why you married him. You were mine. He never deserved you, couldn't provide for you the way I can. This house is proof. The fact you came is proof."

Mum shook herself and rubbed her arms. Henry sensed her discomfort, especially at the injection site. Then anger began to curdle his stomach. *How dare he hurt Mum? What's he on about? Thomas and Mum? Before Da? It can't be.*

He crumpled to the floor. The doormat cushioned his fall. A memory appeared behind his eyes. Shadows, shouts, his body shaken hard. From a dream? A nightmare?

"I thought you'd changed your mind that time we… I thought you'd see sense and come to America with me." Thomas' voice was pitched low. "Then you dropped me again, like unwanted baggage. Did you consider my feelings? The grief you caused? No."

Henry peeked around the door frame. *Is he crying?*

"Mother and Da don't know why I left. We never even had a proper farewell."

Mum pushed her hand downwards, then put a finger to her lips. "Not so loud, for pity's sake; William might hear." She slapped his chest with an open palm. "You planned to leave, any road, Thomas. How dare you twist it around and blame me." She shook out a handkerchief from her sleeve. "I reckon Nan knows everything. She's not daft. She's also practical. Like me."

Uncle Thomas reeled like a drunkard and dropped backward onto a chair. "But… but she never let on. Always writing with news of every birth, every death. 'Twas a couple years ago, she let on William was poorly. Then, she suggested… but I'd begun preparing for you to come. Once, that is—"

"You mean to say you planned for… William's death? Jesus Christ." She turned her back and supported herself on the sink.

"Well, I ken the milk reek, Pheme. Lead poisoning. The miner's curse. There's no cure; it's in the bloodstream."

What? No cure? Why're we here then? Thomas lied. He said—

"Why'd you reckon I'd come here, even so? I might've gone back to Douglas, or England, had Nan not interfered."

"Well, I did say Michigan's climate is a curative. That's a known fact. He might rally."

He pushed himself up and filled two glasses of water. His hand shook as he handed one to Mum.

"William needs fresh air; I told him. He's so goddamn stubborn. He's locked himself upstairs. I know what's eating him—pride. Coming from under Da's roof, not a pot to piss in nor a window to throw it out of, slaving in the mine 'til he was too sick to work. Now, seeing all this—" He swept his arm in a circle. Water sloshed on the floor.

"Jesus, Thomas. You seriously thought I'd come running to you? Without being forced?" She whirled on him. "You're so full of shit, it's coming out your ears. One of your expressions, but Nan would say 'away with the faeries.'"

"Well, I haven't done so bad for myself. Look around, why don't you? That's your trouble, Pheme; you've no imagination."

"I could never afford one," she said.

"Not to worry, I've enough for the both of us." He laughed slightly and put down his glass.

"There is no 'both of us,' Thomas. Let that sink into your thick skull." She snapped a tea towel at him. "Where's the maid you promised me? I'm drowning in work."

Her voice grew cold. Henry felt it, like closing the door on the icebox. He struggled upright and dropped his boot on the porch to announce his presence. Mum jumped, her red face betraying agitation. She quickly recovered and waved at him with the tea towel.

"Ah, Henry. Good. Glad you're here. Lunch is ready. You must be famished. You're not used to such hard labour." She glowered at Uncle Thomas. "Anybody'd think you'd been down the mine, you're so filthy. Go upstairs and change. You can't sit at the table in your drawers." She handed Henry a tray. "Deliver this to Da, would you? His favourite—shepherd's pie."

Avoiding his uncle's penetrating gaze, Henry grasped the tray with shaking hands. His stockinged feet silently mounted the stairs. He forced a smile as he balanced the tray against his hip and turned the door handle.

"Good to see you, Da. *Kys t'ou?*" He struggled to keep his face neutral, hiding dismay at his father's pallor. *What if he dies? And we're forced to stay here, with Thomas… and now, Mum…*

"Good to be seen, Son. Fair to middlin', me." Da smiled back. In his undershirt, his bony chest reminded Henry of a chicken ready for the soup pot. His hair hung lank over his glistening forehead. The grey stubble on his face emphasized the purple circles beneath his eyes. *He looks hot and uncomfortable. One thing's sure; he does need air. This room's stifling.*

"What in God's name happened to you, Henry? You're filthy as a pig. Best not soil this bed cover or your mother'll kill us both." He wheezed and attempted a chuckle.

Henry crossed to open the window. A bird was sitting on the sill, looking at him.

"Oh, a beautiful bird, Da! A spotted breast, a long, curved bill, and a red spot on its head. Wonder what it is? I've never seen one at home."

He stepped aside so Da might see. When he turned around, Da's face was white as a sheet.

"A bird at the window means death, Nan always said."

Henry quickly raised the sash to scare it away. He took a

deep breath and searched for a cheery response. "Look, Mum's made you her specialty." Removing the bowl covering the warm plate, the smell of pork assaulted his nostrils. Not the sweet scent of ground lamb. *This is cottage pie, not shepherd's pie. Dammit. Nothing's right here.*

He set the tray on the dresser, propped Da up with pillows, and told the story of taking a mud bath with Samson, minus the shove. Meanwhile, a realization twirled in his mind, creaking like the windmill in the yard.

"That goddam thing wakes me up, all hours. You likely don't hear, your side of the house. It's the *Buggane*, Ann says."

* * *

August 5, 1905

Dear Henry,

I'm writing you a separate note to say hello from the faeries and wish you a belated happy birthday. I am sure you miss our walks up to Cronk Howe Mooar, and I know the Little Ones miss you, too. Themselves have been rather quiet of late. Good. I long for news of the family. I wish we could easily stay in touch. There's a telephone now at the pub, but will we ever be able to talk across the Atlantic Ocean? Not in my lifetime.

We find the days long, I'll admit. Much less to do. Not much news to share, except that Jill has married. She asked Grandad to stand in for her father. Grandad never thought he'd give a bride away at all. He's done it twice: once for your mother, and now for Jill. We are delighted. I'm sure your Mum won't mind her borrowing the wedding dress either, so in a way, it's lucky youse couldn't take it. Her husband is an upstanding man. Treats her like gold, which she is. A greengrocer, him, so he won't be going down the mine. Thank God.

Speaking of the mine; good your father decided to leave. Bradda Mine is indeed closing. So many families destitute. It's best to take your fate in your own hands rather than be at the mercy of changing tides. Remember that, Henry.

The telegram from Thomas said youse had a fine crossing. I hope to hear of your journey sometime. I imagine it is very busy on the farm with much to learn. You'll be making yourself useful, as always. I've asked your mother for news of your da (and the rest of youse, of course). I doubt she will be totally honest. Speak true, Henry. Is your father getting better? How's he adjusting to the farm? The climate? How is it between him and Thomas? The pair of them never got on. Not like Ralph and Mel. The twins were two peas, one pod.

And you? Is your new life exciting? Grandad and I hope you are happy. The Loughtans miss you, I think. Do you have sheep to tend? Is Thomas good to you? I hope you're not working too hard. Is Thomas adjusting to the family?

Enough questions! I look forward to your letters. I kiss the photograph of youse every day. I'll write and ask Thomas to arrange another photograph of the whole family for Christmas. My love is flying across the ocean to you, dear one. Dybannee Jee oo. God keep you safe.

Yours ever,

Nan

P.S. I forgot to mention Blackie. She still loves going to tend the sheep with Grandad and has claimed your spot around the chiollagh. Does Thomas have a dog? Oh dear, I promised no more questions! Write soon.

P.P.S. Grandad hopes you're keeping up your Manx. Ta graih aym ort. So much. We love you so much.

Chapter Thirty

Ta ny danjeyryn smoo ain lhie follit ayns reddyn beggey:
Our greatest dangers lie hidden in little things.

LATE August, Thomas gifted Henry and John a week at Mrs. Miller's to acquire gardening skills. Mrs. Miller was pleased that John wanted piano lessons, proclaiming him 'a natural.'

"He takes after our grandfather," Henry said. "He makes the fiddle sing."

To his surprise, he found nurturing plants much like caring for newborn lambs. Sweating under his shirt as the sun pounded his straw hat, he hoed rows and rows of potatoes, happy to be shed of Thomas, Mum, and Edward. At night, exhausted, he burrowed into an upstairs bed and devised plans for him and Da to leave, as soon as Da was up to it. Too soon, he was back pulling stumps.

Henry complained to Mum that Edward and Tom went off fishing or snaring rabbits every afternoon while he was constantly put to work. "They're children, Henry. You're going on fifteen. You wanted to be a man, you said. Besides, think what you're learning: gardening, clearing land, using heavy implements… It'll come in handy someday."

When Uncle Thomas brought home a pair of heavy horses, Henry almost clapped with delight. "Introducing Buster and Slick, a willing team; Slick's willing to work, and Buster's willing to let him," Thomas joked. "Like you and our Ted."

Henry ventured to suggest that something dignified would better suit such beauties.

"Nope. They're used to their names, Harry. Can't teach an old dog new tricks, nor an old horse neither, come to that," Uncle Thomas said.

Henry walked away, kicking the dirt. *Didn't stop him from messing with mine. Giving us all nicknames, even Mum. How dare he say "our" Ted? When it's "his" Ted.* Though he'd searched Edward's face, he couldn't see the resemblance. Edward threatened to tell on him for staring. He stopped.

Following Uncle Thomas' directions, he began driving the team while manipulating the twelve-inch one-bottom plough called a "foot burner." Next, he learned to run the drag harrow, then the chain harrow. Meanwhile, Edward and Tom cleaned the garden plot, raking tree roots, filling baskets of stones. Progress was imperceptible until Pete brought Dolly and Fanny to help. Henry was eager to learn as much as he could about horses from an expert.

"It's all in care and management, Henry," Pete said. "Always tend the team before yourself. Check their hooves and brush 'em down. Keep an eye out for ailments like sweeny or gall." Henry frowned. "I'll lend you my vet book. It's got pictures."

Pete pressed his fingers on either side of Slick's jaw, inspecting his teeth. "I'm a horse dentist, too. No worse'n pulling my own, which I've done on occasion. Hate dentists." A stream of tobacco juice made his point. Henry laughed. Considering his relaxed attitude to personal hygiene, Henry figured Pete didn't balk at any dirty chore.

Pete taught him to rig and care for the harness, the name for each snap and buckle, and when to use "Gee haw," "Giddy up," and "Whoah."

"Once you learn the horse's language, Henry, they'll never let you down. Unlike some folks I could mention, close to hand, and all. You're a mite young and green to be lookin' after a team. Thomas—well, you are a tall drink o' water, but you gotta be strong to manage heavy horses. Man died here a while back. Team run off… Oh, never mind."

Worried about getting kicked, Henry tip-toed past their behinds, eyes glued to their boxy hooves.

"Nah, your Percheron's the smartest, most lovin' horse there is. Buster and Slick weigh nineteen hundred pounds apiece, I'd wager. Perfect for dainty work. Won't tromp all over the young trees while you cut down bigger ones. A good outfit: seventeen hands high, give or take, well-matched in style and colour. Do you proud." Patting one of the huge rumps with his broad hand, Pete smiled his gap-toothed, crooked grin.

"Good thing Buster has a star on his forehead and Slick has white socks, to tell them apart," Henry said as he ran his hand along Buster's neck and coiled his fingers in the dark mane, inhaling the scent. The dark, liquid eyes fringed with luxurious lashes drew him in like a bottomless well. "But, how ever will we feed them, especially in winter? We haven't a hay loft, nor a ready supply."

"I reckon Thomas didn't consider that. They'll each require forty pounds a day, more if they're working. I'll have to deliver from my place a while yet." Pete spat. "Paid in advance, from now on."

One day, standing together in the horses' stall, Pete asked Henry about his home. "Ain't never heard of it. Why's it called 'The Isle of Man,' anyway?" Henry readily shared the history Grandad had instilled, as well as customs like the wedding horserace, where the winner would break a cake over the bride's head. Pete doubled over, laughing. *His laugh sounds like a horse. A good, kind man. Like Grandad.*

"Sounds a fine tradition. The race I mean. The gal mustn't like it much. Gets a powerful headache, I reckon, if the cake's anything like my mother's was." He snorted. "Are you homesick at all?"

Henry's throat closed. Words wouldn't come. Buster nickered softly. Pete handed over a currycomb from the bib of his overalls. Standing on an apple box, Henry began combing Buster's mane. "It's not what we expected, Pete."

"Yes, I imagine it's different to Man Island. And Thomas works you pretty hard."

"Oh, it's not the work I mind," Henry said, not wanting to give the wrong impression. "Miners start at my age, and most boys are on the washing floor at nine or ten. Grandad always said, 'Hard work never killed anybody,' though I wonder if that's true. Especially with Da…" His eyes blurred. He leaned his forehead on Buster's solid neck.

Pete cleared his throat. "Is your Pa on the mend?"

Henry buried his nose in the thick, soft fringe and shook his head. Pete attached the feed bag to Slick's nose and patted him loudly. The crunching of oats and the smells of horses and hay filled the stable.

"Your Ma's such a nice lady," he said when Henry lifted his head. "Her apple pie's a treat. Old bachelors like me don't mind helping when there's grub like that on offer. Gals 'round these parts couldn't cook bait for a bear." He blew out his lips and exaggerated an eye roll. "Maybe why I never married. Too late for me now. I've a face only a mother could love, as they say. My own ma wouldn't recognize me nowadays."

Henry burst out laughing. "That's a good one, Pete. 'Bait for a bear.' Never heard that before." His voice quaked. "It's great having you for lunch."

"Careful. Makes it sound like I'm on the menu."

"You know what I mean." Henry grinned. "I love your stories, like the one where the rich man asks his friend to bury him with his money, but when it comes time the friend says, 'Why bury the cash? I'll write him a cheque.' So funny! Another one, please, Pete."

He curry-combed Buster's hind quarters, smiling as he recalled Pete's conversation with Mrs. Miller one lunchtime. The midday meal was always interesting when Pete and Mrs. Miller joined them. She'd asked Pete about his scar, with her usual: "… if you'll forgive my boldness."

Without hesitation, Pete described the accident. He'd been repairing a shingle plane from underneath. "Just got 'er runnin' smooth like shit through a goose—ahem, sorry ladies—when the goll darn saw falls down on my head. Other than this scar, though," he said, tapping his gouged, puckered cheek, "I ain't suffered no ill effects." His brow creased as his fingers searched the back of his rough-shorn head, usually covered by his hat. He let out his horsey laugh. "All 'cept for this hole, back here. Who knows? That was likely there all along."

That brought on uproarious laughter all around. Mrs. Miller offered to fix the hole with tarpaper and glue if it worried him. "Reminds me of the song, 'There's a hole in my bucket.'" She then regaled them with every verse until the last, when the lament started again. They clapped with delight, especially Edward, who compared Henry to the hapless character too stupid to fix a bucket. Tom begged her to teach him the words.

That night, Edward whispered to Henry, "Uncle Thomas doesn't yell or curse when they're around. It's nicer."

Henry nodded. "He puts on a good face for company, all right. He's the one who should be in vaudeville. Wish he was."

When it was just family, everyone except Hugh ate supper quietly, which suited Uncle Thomas. A flask found its way from the breast pocket of his jacket to his lips at regular intervals. The parlour fire wasn't even lit afterward. "No point wasting wood in summer. We'll need it, come fall," Thomas said. No songs and stories around the hearth eased their path to bed. After final chores, Mum settled Ann and the boys while Henry checked on Da. Then he'd head across the hall and flip about in his bunk, struggling like a fish on land. *How long can we keep this up, with Da needing constant care? Mum's worn out; she doesn't even sing anymore. Nan would be heartbroken if she knew. Perhaps the Little Ones had said something; her letter sounded worried.* He couldn't write and invent happy stories. There was never enough time.

Once he'd prepared the garden plot, ready for next spring, Uncle Thomas made him drive the team into the forest. It "wanted" cutting. Neither the squirrels' ceaseless protests nor the biting black flies could dissuade him. Henry silently mourned the fall of every giant. He hated the loud crack just before it whooshed to the ground, never to feel the sun warming its branches again. And then followed the brutality of stump-pulling, as he told Da.

"A shame, Henry, but 'twas no different our side of the pond once. Man, Scotland, and Ireland; their woods all became moors for sheep. Farming demands open land." He sighed. "Wish I could help youse. I've never cut a tree in me life."

Henry deplored that birds, insects, squirrels, even the wind, would soon have nowhere to live. One-hundred-fifty-foot trees became lumber, then cash. The *mooninger vegewere* must've abandoned this land when settlers came. No faery thread nor flashes of light appeared in the woods. Henry's faery bracelet had fallen apart. At night, he imagined ascending Faery Hill with Nan, collecting thread from gorse bushes. Solitary oaks dotted the hillsides, worshipped as faery trees. He smelled the salt air, pure and bracing. He felt as if his strides could devour the countryside and take him across the Irish Sea, like Manannan. Yellow gorse and purple heather bloomed on fields of browsing sheep. Skylarks rang bells in towers of clouds.

When he squeezed his eyes, memories appeared like illustrations in a book. *John's handy with a pencil. I'll get him to draw Faery Hill, the cottage, the Calf of Man on the horizon... before we forget.*

Ravens squabbling and squawking in the canopy brought him back to the stifling forest. He cricked his neck, mindful of falling limbs and swooping ravens, struggling to keep pace with Thomas on the cross-cut saw. He worked into his heat with the two-man saw, the bucksaw, and the axe.

The strip of remaining forest brooded like a displaced ogre. Beasts lurked in the shadows, which Thomas promised they'd hunt, come fall. Henry both wished and feared they might show themselves. *Are they vengeful like Red Caps? Who'd blame them?*

In addition to driving the team and other chores, Henry replenished the wood pile daily. He learned that wood burned cleaner and smelled better than peat, but the stove gobbled it like ducks eating bread. Appreciating care for tools, he began using the foot-peddle grinding wheel. Alone in the woodshed, he'd peddle for hours, mesmerized by flying sparks, humming to the song of steel against stone. Mum teased that butcher knives were becoming paring knives. He relished the time to think.

Pete had mentioned steamships leaving Cheboygan and crossing Lake Huron. Always looking for stokers. Brutal work but good pay. Henry weighed the possibility. *I'll get me a job, come spring, long as Da is up and about. Mum likely will have to stay for the little ones, but I'm gone.*

The devil's voice grated on the wheel. *How will she cope; she can barely manage as it is with your help, idiot. How'll you get to Cheboygan, stupid? What about money, fool? And what would Nan say about you abandoning Mum after you promised…?*

Thoughts revolved like records on Mrs. Miller's phonograph. *Does Da see that Edward's like Thomas? Nan did say that. She knew, Mum said. Then why'd she make us come? It's a disaster if Edward finds out. Or worse, Da. Edward: always trying to get on Da's good side; same with Thomas. That asshole. Christ, I hate, hate, hate him.*

Sparks illuminated spiderwebs. Stone sharpened steel.

CHAPTER THIRTY-ONE

Sleep, O babe, for the red bee hums
The silent twilight's fall:
Aibheall from the Grey Rock comes
To wrap the world in thrall.

Gartan Mother's Lullaby
(Traditional/Seosamh MacCathmhaoil)

Autumn, 1905

SEPTEMBER sprinkled poplar leaves over the pine tree standing guard in the driveway. The earthy scent of fallen leaves freshened the air, and slanted sunlight made working outdoors easier. Euphemia relished the cooler temperatures and rain, which reminded her of Man. She and Mrs. Miller canned, jammed, and jellied every fruit and vegetable the market garden produced. They even canned roasted chicken. The kitchen roared with heat from the range and steam from the canner. The children kept busy, fetching, peeling, and cleaning… while Euphemia suffered pangs of guilt. *They ought to be at school.*

She reminded Thomas that the school year had started. Edward, Tom, and John missed having chums. *Compared to work-*

ing on the farm, school would be a breeze. They might even learn something. She hadn't taught Ann to read; Tom still struggled. "Thomas, you promised they'd learn American history, remember? They need to make friends, start fitting in—"

"How'll we get them back and forth, Pheme? Ach, it won't hurt to skip a year or two. Maybe they'll even build a school hereabouts. They can make it up. Our Alice Blue's bright as a new penny, Ted's sharp as a tack, Johnny charms the birds from the trees and can draw them, too. As for Tommy… well, there's plenty to learn here, more valuable than book learnin'."

He rubbed his hands together and donned his hat. "Next year, Pheme. We'll be better fixed by then, maybe with a small-er wagon and another horse. We can't spare the team. Besides, we'd need a sleigh for winter." The screen door slammed.

Next year. Always "next year." Mrs. Miller spoke rightly when she was here, canning. I'm glad she took two apple pies so I could repay her kindness.

"I'm no good at pastry, Mrs. Carine. Mine comes out tough as old shoe leather. They'll keep in the root cellar but won't last long around Leon."

"We all have our talents, Mrs. Miller. Making pastry's noth-ing to me, just as growing vegetables comes easily to you. Sadly, I've little time for pie-making these days. Thomas still hasn't hired the maid. I'm fair worn out. Even the new shoes I bought in Liverpool are grumbling." She attempted a laugh.

"Well, his promises are like your pie crust, Mrs. Carine. Easily made, easily broken. Though I don't hold with that first part." She chuckled.

"I know. And woe betide anyone who doesn't meet his ex-pectations. He drives the boys as hard as Samson the ox. He ignores me when I mention school, though he said they'd go." She slammed the rolling pin on the ball of pastry. "By the way, it's 'Carin,' Mrs. Miller, but please, call me Euphemia."

Mrs. Miller's openness spurred her on. "This house, Mrs.

Miller. What's the story of this house? The construction time, up against our decision… it simply doesn't add up."

She waited, fluting the pie crust with her thumb. Mrs. Miller sat running her large, workworn hands across the oilcloth, seemingly enamoured by the pattern. The pies were done. Euphemia took a seat and refilled their teacups.

"What did Thomas tell you?" Mrs. Miller avoided Euphemia's eyes.

"That he built it for me. But he didn't know we were coming."

"There's your answer, Euphemia. I can't say more."

* * *

In the evenings, if she wasn't too tired, Euphemia's fading strength was spent helping the boys read from the Bible. Henry and Edward read well, but Tom stuttered. Thomas would sigh, mouth the words, then head for the porch. Tom would retreat upstairs. She made Ann copy her name, and Jenny's, with a carpenter's pencil. *It's a start.*

Hugh didn't get cuddled before bed; there was no rocking chair. While the boys cleaned the kitchen, she dozed on the settee, too exhausted to knit. Henry would rouse her, check William, and turn in. She'd haul herself upstairs behind him, tuck Hugh in his drawer, and squeeze next to Ann. She hummed her favourite lullaby, enjoying her daughter's warmth, the smell of her hair, the beat of her heart, her regular breath. *My angel. Who kicks like a mule and steals the covers.* Euphemia rocked slightly, rubbing her belly, sensing the fluttering life inside.

She'd known for a few weeks. She'd blamed her nausea, headaches, and lack of appetite on the sea voyage, the inoculation, fatigue… until the buttons on her skirt popped and she recognized the soreness of her breasts. She counted back, remembering when she'd distracted William from his cares. Unfortunately, nursing didn't prevent pregnancy. This spring there'd be another babe, with Hugh still in diapers, perhaps.

She silently sent a prayer and love to the baby. She flipped over and then: *What if Mrs. Miller knows a way, with native plants, herbs and such…* She tightened her jaw. *No. Mustn't think that. You'll go to Hell. Perhaps I'm there already. Mrs. Miller guessed last week, I'm sure.*

Mrs. Miller had been surveying the newly cleared garden plot. "Rain and snow will break up the soil, Euphemia. Come spring, I'll show you what to plant. After corn-planting moon in May."

Euphemia reflexively placed her hands over her stomach. *About when this baby's due.* Noticing Mrs. Miller's surprised expression, she felt heat rise to her cheeks. *Dammit. I must keep William in the dark for a while yet. He'll guess, soon enough. Not like it's the first time. I'd hoped by spring he'd be up to leaving. Now, oh, God.*

She'd begun to pace the hall at night after checking the boys and William. Once, Thomas surprised her.

"Jesus, Pheme, you scared the shit out of me," he said. "I woke up and saw a figure in white at the top of the stairs. This house is too new for ghosts."

She whirled away from his outstretched arms and clicked Ann's door closed. Heart pounding, she leaned against it, sensing his hand on the other side. She felt him breathing on her neck, kissing her bare shoulders, moving up to her lips.

"Pheme." Had he whispered? Her hand clutched the glass doorknob. What if she turned it? Her groin throbbed, her breasts ached. She slid to the floor and curled into a ball, tucking her icy feet under her nightdress.

She jolted awake. Ann shook her arm. "Did you have a 'night mere,' Mama? You weren't with me."

"Yes, yes, I did, sweetheart. Oooh, Mama's stiff. Must've been there all night. Let's get porridge on, shall we?"

* * *

In October, the warmth Thomas called "Indian Summer" gave way to fresh, cool temperatures almost the same as at home, much to William's relief after sweating in bed for three months.

"Who cuts down all the shade trees?" He complained to Euphemia one lunchtime. "You'd think he'd have spared more than one white pine, for God's sake. This yellow house cooks like an egg in a goddam frying pan. Not like there's fresh ocean breezes, hereabouts."

"I know. Funny, isn't it? Such a big house and yet it feels empty, though we've filled it to bursting." She set a damp cloth on his brow. "How ever did we manage? We'd be shocked if we stepped through the red door again." She felt her eyes stinging. "Sometimes I wake up at night and can't remember where I am. You, too?" She paused, rubbing his arm. "I miss Nan, Grandad, Blackie, Jill, even my old Brown Betty. Can't make a decent cuppa to save my life. Must be the water's different, too." Tears spilled from William's blue eyes onto her hand. "Oh dear. Forgive me, love. I shouldn't have said—I'm trying to be strong. I am. I want you to know, I'm not impressed by all... this. You're twice the man Thomas is. I acted the fool in Boston. When you're better, we'll leave, make our own way. Agreed?"

William rolled over, throwing the cloth on the floor. She picked it up and stepped out, gently closing the door. After composing herself, she descended the stairs.

She joined the table in time for one of Thomas' speeches.

"Now's when God takes his paintbrush to the leaves, Alice Blue. Red, yellow, purple, orange, you won't believe the colours. We'll buy a scrapbook so's you can press some. A single maple leaf can be as big as this plate by fall."

"Really, Nuncle?"

The boys' poorly hidden smirks anticipated his answer.

"No word of a lie."

Her eyes smiled into Henry's, sharing the same thought. Then she dropped her teacup, nearly breaking the saucer, when Thomas said, "Now, time for you boys to learn the manly art of hunting."

Her stomach lurched as if she were riding the overhead train. A shiver ran down her spine.

"Don't be frightened, Pheme. It's worse if they don't learn to use firearms. Here folks hunt to put food on the table. Ted and Tommy are fishing, but we must have a supply of meat. We can't get to Cheboygan in winter, even if we could afford it. Naught but salt pork and canned chicken for six months? That'll never do." He leaned into his hands on the table. "That's settled."

Euphemia resumed feeding Hugh, propped on her lap. Still no highchair. *At least he's weaned. I'd better commence toilet training.* She listened with half an ear to Thomas' lecture on marksmanship.

"D'youse ken why we wait 'til late fall to hunt big game, boys?"

"It's cooler? Maybe easier with no leaves on the trees?" Edward said.

"Good guesses, Ted, but no. One, males are fat and healthy by then; two, we need ice to preserve the meat, so that's November."

Edward used his knife to mime pointing a gun across the table at Tom. Tom aimed and pretended to fire.

Thomas slapped the knife out of Edward's hand. "First lesson: don't point a gun at nobody. And no, Tommy. You won't be hunting yet. The rifle's as long as you are tall. The recoil will land you on your arse. Or take out your eye." He pushed away from the table.

Euphemia saw Tom's temper rising to his face and ears. She tried to catch his eye and noticed Henry's frown. Thomas stood up and gulped the last of his beer.

"You and Johnny'll use the slingshot to pick off squirrels, weasels, birds—only what we can skin or eat, mind. Kill as many crows as you want, gophers too, come to that. Nasty varmints.

Only Harry, Ted, and me will hunt this season."

"I don't want to hunt, me. Nor use a slingshot, neither. I like—" John said.

"I'm bigger than Edward. Stronger too," Tom said, crossing his arms over his chest.

Thomas shook his head. "It's not just size, lad. It takes co-ordination. *Traa dy liooar.* There's time enough. Next year. That's final." He turned toward Edward and Henry. "I'll show youse the basics with my 30-30 Winchester, but I'll get youse a .22 caliber for small game, rabbits, turkeys, squirrels, and such. It takes practise to balance. There's loading, cleaning, sighting, and breathing to get a handle on."

"I know how to breathe, for Christ's sake," Tom said. He threw his knife on his empty plate and balled up his fists.

Euphemia halted Hugh's spoonful of potatoes; he threw his head backwards, bumping her chin. *Ouch, that hurt, dammit. What did I hear? Thomas'll box his ears. He'd better not; I'll deal with Tom, later. He must learn respect, no matter what.*

Thomas continued speaking. "We'll need us a sand crib behind the chicken coop for target practice. You start on your belly. Later on, whilst I hunt, youse'll observe and help with transport and dressing."

Thomas passed behind Henry and reached over his head for the toothpick holder. He squeezed his shoulder. Henry visibly winced.

"A rifle's worth three months' wages, Harry. Don't say I haven't paid you."

Oh, God. He must've heard Henry complain to me about working for no pay. He's never shirked, even so. She glared at Thomas. He shrugged, pointing his toothpick at Edward.

"C'mon, Ted, we'll build the crib. I'll teach youse to iden-tify animals so's you know a mouse from a moose." Edward rushed to the door. "Harry, keep working the team on my shin-gle plane." He sucked the toothpick. "Damn fine contraption, if

I do say so myself, that bale hitch hooked to the horses. Might apply for a patent on the bugger."

"Ahem. Language, Thomas," Euphemia said as she ran a spoonful of mashed potatoes across Hugh's lips. "Who likes his tatties, then, eh?"

She smiled, enjoying her baby boy. The rush of contentment made her pause. *It will be nice for Hugh to have a playmate. Stuck way out here, Ann getting older every day; he'll have no one close to his age. It'll work out, Nan would say.* Her mind drifted as she imagined the new babe in her arms, a feeling she loved.

"Sorry, Pheme. Don't pick up my bad habits, Tommy." He ruffled Tom's thick brown hair.

"It's TOM!" His chair crashed behind him as he stormed toward the door. Euphemia jolted, startling Hugh.

She hoisted Hugh to her shoulder, intending to reach Tom before Thomas could.

"Thomas Percy Carin, get back here this instant and apologize. I won't have such displays of temper."

Tom turned back, eyes downcast, ears aflame. "Sorry, Uncle. It's just, I am bigger than Edward and it's not fair—"

Thomas waved him off like a bothersome fly. "There's a fortune to be made selling joists and shingles, Harry, soon's the horses are trained. You're just the man, Pete says. *Gow shen.* Target practise starts once the crib's ready."

My, but this gun business has preoccupied him. Otherwise, he might've thrashed Tom. He'll go to bed without supper, any road. We're stuck here for a while yet. We must go along to get along.

Chapter Thirty-Two

Moyll yn laa mie fastyr:
Praise the fine day in the evening.

THE famous "Moose Hunt." Henry groaned as he tugged on his mud-encrusted boots. He'd no desire to stalk a wild animal and couldn't guess the nature of a "crib." Since asking meant a long-winded explanation, he didn't bother. He preferred working with the horses, only wishing Pete would come over.

When Edward appeared at the shed, flushed and shouting, Henry dragged his feet. *What if you shoot and miss? Might it attack?* He'd never killed anything bigger than a goose. *What do you do with a dead moose?* At home, sheep and cows were butchered. *Is that what Thomas meant by "dressed?" The filthiest job, no doubt.*

As Uncle Thomas demonstrated, Tom and Edward watched in silence. John had wandered off. Henry smiled at the tiny figure stravaging beside the garden plot, waving a stick. *I wish there were faeries in the garden. I felt them, betimes. Like Nan.*

"Safety first and foremost, lads." Uncle Thomas was saying, walking with the gun barrel pointing downward, bolt open, unloaded, push-button safety engaged. "Never, ever hunt alone; you stick together. Clearly identify what you're shooting at and what's behind before pulling the trigger. Never hunt in the dark, or even at dusk. Shadows can fool you."

Hefting the gun to his shoulder, he displayed the proper stance. "Brace yourself, bend at the knees, take a deep breath. Next, just a light flick on the trigger. Pull 'er even a little and your shot'll go wide." Thomas placed the gun in Edward's hands. "You try, Ted. Don't worry, she ain't loaded."

Edward immediately lost his grip. Henry jumped, expecting an angry curse, but Thomas remained calm.

"See, good thing she wasn't loaded or you'd've blown your goddamn foot off. My old '94's a bit heavy, I know. The .22 will be lighter." He returned the gun to Edward. "Now remember, Mr. Flibbertigibbet, you mustn't talk while stalking an animal. Just like fishing. Keep yer mouth shut. Focus. Breathe slow and steady-like." Thomas inhaled loudly, then continued in a whisper, looking off into the distance. "You'll sense the animal's presence before you actually see him. Stay downwind or he'll run off."

Placing his arm around his shoulder, he covered Edward's index finger with his own and squeezed. Henry held his breath. The trigger clicked. Edward flushed and grinned. Henry could envision the animal crashing down.

"It'll be a while before we're hunting on our own, I guess," Henry said, hoping so.

"Depends," Thomas said. He extracted a small box from the bib of his overalls. "All it takes is dedicated practise, like any skill. Don't get cocky, mind. You gotta know your gun, how to sight, load, and clean 'er. You must hit the bull's-eye at fifty feet before I allow you out. Watch and learn." He used the round end of the bullet as a pointer. "You only load one bullet at a time, even though she'll take two," he said. Slipping the bullet into the case, he clicked the barrel. Raising the wooden stock to his shoulder, he closed one eye and aimed at the circular target nailed to the side of the sand crib. "One, two, deep breath, then breathe out as you give a light touch." The shot cracked; the target shuddered. Edward tore off to check the paper circle. Henry glimpsed Mum at the clothesline, covering her ears.

"About this much from the bull's-eye, Uncle," Edward called, indicating an inch or so with his fingers. He whistled.

"Get your ass back here." Uncle Thomas shouted. "No running until the gun's safely stowed."

Edward slumped back, head down.

"Never do that again, you. Might get your fool head blown off." Thomas raised the gun to his shoulder. "Next, we'll set our sights."

"Must be where the expression comes from. 'Setting your sights on something,' Uncle?" Edward said.

"Good thinking, Edward. I'll bet you're right." A voice came from behind them.

"Da," Henry shouted. "You're up!" A surge of joy rushed from head to toe.

Edward and Tom vied to encircle Da's waist. He rubbed their shoulders, smiling at Henry. *Da. Out of bed. Today. I'll never forget it.*

"A man can hardly sleep with a gun blasting off next to his bed, now, can he?" He laughed his old laugh. "Besides, I don't want to miss all the fun. I brought mine down. Show me, Thomas?"

Da couldn't hold the gun steady, but Thomas supported him and showed him how to get a bead on the target and pull the trigger. After just one attempt, Da leaned against the fence post, wheezing. He praised the boys' efforts to shoot from a prone position, although they mostly hit the sand. Thomas even helped Tom. His shot actually marked the paper, to everyone's astonishment. *Except Tom.* Henry sent him a wink.

When William joined the family at dinner, Uncle Thomas came across as pleased as punch. "You're looking more like yourself, William. I knew you'd be right as rain with a little rest.

Now all you need is good Michigan air and sunshine."

John applauded and Tom led the children in a chorus of 'For He's a Jolly Good Fellow,' breaking Thomas' rule.

"I wish you'd told me you planned to come down, William. I'd have made berry bonnag, your favourite." Mum smiled, wagging her finger.

"*Lurg roayrt hig contraie,*" he said, reaching for her hand.

"Does that mean you're getting better, Da?" John asked, brow furrowed, eyes focused on Da's face. "We don't talk Manx anymore. I forget."

"No, no, your dad's a typical Manxman, Johnny. Daren't enjoy happiness for fear it will be snatched by the *Phynodderree*. It's a proverb: 'After spring tide will come neap,' meaning 'Don't get excited over good fortune; a reverse may come.'" He sighed. "William, after what you've been through? Let go of Manx superstitions."

He stood and raised his glass, motioning everyone to join him. "A toast: *Jean traagh choud as ta'n grian soilshean*: Make hay while the sun shines!" He encouraged the children to clink their glasses. Tom and John tapped so hard they spilled their milk. Mum laughed. Ann giggled.

Da's face lit up. "It certainly feels good to be part of the action again."

"We're all so pleased, aren't we, children?" Mum said. "You must try to come down as often as possible, William. We've missed you so." Mum's voice caught in her throat. Her brown eyes were liquid, like horses' eyes. *She's beautiful. She looks like herself again.*

Thomas said, "Look around, brother, and say you haven't made the right choice. Life's good in Michigan, as I told you." He leaned over and poured beer into Da's glass.

"Careful, Thomas. He just got up." Mum said.

"Balderdash! The man needs a drink! Listen, William, come spring we'll take us a ferry to Mackinac Island for a special outing. It's a faery isle like Man, Alice Blue. There's a faery archway they fly through. We'll have us a picnic with the *Little Ones,* eh?"

He looked at Mum. "Next summer, I promise, Pheme," he said, draining his glass.

Mum fussed with Hugh in his new highchair. Henry's jaw tightened. He held his breath and waited for something. Da's cough.

Chapter Thirty-Three

Gow shiu aggle ynrican dy yannoo meechredjue:
Fear nothing but unbelief.

October-November, 1905

WILLIAM'S health rallied. He looked less haggard, more robust. Euphemia credited the crisp, fall air and prescribed daily sunshine. She forbade him from smoking, despite Thomas having supplied the makings. After lunch, she'd tuck William in a blanket on the porch swing to observe the bright woods past the house. Ann cuddled beside him with Jenny and her new puppy. Euphemia began taking afternoon breaks, as of old, to enjoy tea and scones with William, and play with the fluffy, speckled bundle of joy. Later, she'd return to find Ann's blonde head resting on William's chest, both lost in blissful slumber, the puppy at William's feet.

Henry had asked Thomas for a dog, saying it could guard the house. Euphemia knew he longed for a four-legged companion. Thomas brought home a black and white English Cocker Spaniel. With great fanfare, he presented the puppy to Ann. As the tail-wagging, barking, four-legged whirlwind chased a giggling Ann around the kitchen, Henry spoke up.

"I'm the one who wanted a dog," he said. "How's a five-year-old supposed to train a huge dog, judging by the size of those paws? Plus, you said to mind the pine floors. Hark at the scratches already. Dogs should live outside, like Blackie."

His eyes implored Euphemia to make Thomas relent. She knew it was a lost cause. Thomas favoured Ann, petting her blonde hair, admiring her clothes, buying her treats. Euphemia suspected each gesture was meant for her. His gaze always sought hers. Unseemly. Causing shortness of breath. *Am I angry? Why do I feel so…? He's spoiling her. She has him wrapped around her little finger.* One day, she stuck a dandelion clock under his nose and ordered him to blow the "wishing flower."

"A wishing flower? Why, t'aint nothing but a plain old dandelion."

"The faeries say it's a wishing flower, Nuncle. Close your eyes, make a wish, and blow. If all the fluff flies away, you get your wish."

He blew hard, staring at Euphemia. She heard his wish as if he'd spoken aloud. He smiled, as every seed took flight. *He persists, no matter what.*

She sighed, crouching to help Hugh contend with the jumping, licking puppy. "It's the family's pet, Henry. I'm sure you'll train him, like Blackie."

"She's a bitch, Pheme," Thomas said, scratching the puppy's ear. "Won't need much training either. Your Spaniel's a natural retriever, bred for hunting. What's her name, Alice Blue?"

Looking vacantly upward, Ann crossed her arms and pronounced, "Sally. Sally Fwaykway."

"What kinda fool name is that?" Thomas snorted with laughter. "A dog must come when you call. 'Here, Sally Fwaykway?' I think not."

"The faeries say that's her name," Ann said, pursing her lips. "So, it is."

"It's not so strange," John said, reaching over to stroke the soft fur. "Your name's different, Mother, and it's nice. She likes it, don't you, Sally?" He hunched down and received a lick on the nose. Euphemia giggled. *This dog's a balm to our hearts. Thomas gets it right, now and then.*

"'Sal, then," Thomas said, shaking his head. "Keep it short. Now you mention it, Johnny, 'Euphemia' is a strange name." He quickly added, "In a good way, I mean, Pheme. Unique. Where's it come from?"

"Sister Michael at the orphanage named me," she said. She pictured those kind eyes, the sparkling smile. "After a Christian woman, she said, in Roman times. Deemed a saint because the lions refused to eat her, so they set her free. I ought to have said before now. It's a nice story, though I hated my name. Then Nan said it with her lovely accent and told me it means 'of good repute' in Gaelic." The puppy rolled over for a tummy rub. "I'm happy with it. Sally will get used to hers."

"What's 'repute' mean, Mother?" John asked.

"It means 'of good reputation.'"

"What does—"

"Never mind," she said, collecting the bundle of flailing legs. "Go, fetch a boxful of straw. She must sleep in the kitchen at night. Bring extra for the floor."

The boys wanted the dog to sleep with them. Ann insisted Sally be in her room. The fight was on.

Sally barked at a knock on the screen door. Mrs. Miller entered, motioning for someone to follow.

"Good day, Euphemia. Here's Sophie, come to see if she can be of help."

"Oh, Mrs. Miller, how kind! Come in. Of course, I remember you. Thomas said you wouldn't come way out here, leave the hotel—"

"Mrs. Tucker's my friend, helped me when I arrived," she said. "When I told her how hard it is on you, what with Mr.

Carin bedridden and you managing on your own, she insisted. Trust me, Sophie's a fine girl and a hard worker."

"Oh, I'm sure, Mrs. Miller. Sit, please Sophie. I'll pour you a cuppa. Let's get acquainted. Then I'll show you the house. It seems gigantic but there's only room for a cot, I'm afraid—I do hope the sleeping accommodations will suit your—"

"Please don't worry, Mrs. Carin," Sophie spoke in soft, slow beats, looking at the floor. "I don't take up much space. I'll work for room and board; send my wages to Mother."

"Goodness, I hope this boisterous clan doesn't frighten you. We've six children, as you know, and one—" She cleared her throat, avoiding eye contact with Mrs. Miller. "—puppy. A brand-new puppy, to boot. Meet Sally Fwaykway," she said, smiling at Mrs. Miller's puzzlement. "That's faery language. 'Sal,' for short."

Sophie knelt to embrace the puppy and received a sloppy kiss. Ann gathered Sal into her arms.

"My doggie."

"She's everyone's friend, Ann," Euphemia said, tapping her arm lightly. "Mrs. Miller, would you arrange with Thomas about the pay? You know best." *Thomas will be fair if Mrs. Miller sorts it. Help, at last. I could cry.*

She lifted Hugh. "Youngest of the family, Sophie. You met him at the hotel. Hugh likes nothing better than to crawl about stark naked. The rest of us are much more restrained, I assure you," she said, laughing, hoping to put her at ease.

She reached for the baby and surrounded him with her arms. "I love babies. We'll get on fine, won't we, Hughie?"

* * *

As the fall colours deepened from yellow to gold, violet to maroon, red to crimson, William's health steadily improved. Unable to work but at least mobile, he spent his time gathering rainbows of leaves with Ann and playing catch with the boys in the afternoon. Euphemia was thankful he minded the youngsters while she and Sophie worked out a routine. *Lucky for me, she's nowhere near as green as I was at the Sugarland. She's about sixteen, I'd wager.*

The quiet girl willingly undertook any task and saw what needed doing, a rare quality Euphemia appreciated. The house breathed easier. Euphemia found herself singing as she prepared meals. She finally enjoyed William's company, morning, noon, and night. They'd chat as he peeled potatoes or shucked peas. Like newlyweds.

"It's the most time I've spent with your father our whole married life," Euphemia confided to Henry one evening as they did the dishes. "I hate to say it, but I'm glad he's housebound for a while. He never complains when you all go out, though I know it bothers him."

With Sophie's cot in Ann's room and William's cough subsiding, Euphemia returned to their bed. She spooned his back, not wanting to entice him, knowing his shame at previous failures. A few nights later, he embraced her. His erection swelled against her back.

"William! Are you sure? I'll do anything…" she whispered.

He gently shuffled her atop him, wriggling his nightshirt above his hips. "You lead, darling. I'll follow. A different dance, eh?"

Her heart rose to her throat as she straddled his hips, grasping the brass rail for support while rubbing herself lightly across his stomach. The coolness of his skin lit her desire. She wriggled, trying to slip his cock inside. He shook his head.

"No, slowly, love. Take your time. *Traa dy liooar.*"

She giggled at the expression. *Don't take too long, William.* Then she leaned down, blowing his nose, his mouth, his closed eyes. She drove her hips back and forth, slowly at first, then faster and faster. Gasping for breath, body trembling, she felt a gush of liquid flow onto William's belly and trickle down her thighs. *Dammit, no towel.* Leaning on his chest, she pushed herself upright… *Never. It's never happened with him.* She urged him to enter. "Now, now, harder, harder." She was past caring if anyone heard. Her mind flew out the window, back to the little white cottage, their own room, embracing under shafts of moonlight to the sounds of waves below the cliffs. *There, yes, home. In bliss.*

They lay together, spent and warm, in white sheets crisp with sunlight. Hearts pounding, they clasped hands. William buried his face in her hair. She whispered in his ear, "I can taste you in my mouth." It was as if his blood coursed through her veins, vibrating with memories of fifteen years of love, laughter, even sorrow and pain. *Doesn't matter, it's all rich. We're rich. Please, please, don't let it end. I need him so.* She pleaded with God or the faeries, whoever would listen.

William gently rolled her aside. "Time to wash, love."

The woman's penance—washing up afterward. She hated leaving the warm bed, but she used the bowl and pitcher, then whisked a sheet from the cedar chest. Side by side once more, she haltingly shared her news. She couldn't stop the tears and sobs. William leaned on an elbow and smiled his crystal-blue smile.

"I've known a while, love. Think this is my first go around?" He chuckled, then kissed her cheek. "I hope it's a girl, a playmate for Ann. It's hard on her, the only girl. *Foddym gra gyn danjeyr dy bee dy chooilley nhee dy mie.*"

"I know that means all will be well, William. Nan's saying. As if—as if everything's—" Her damp hair fell into her streaming eyes. William stroked her chin with his index finger, shushing her like a child. Voice quaking, she finally said, "I'll try to believe it, for you, William. I hope the children will be excited."

Henry won't. A babe ties us here longer. He'll have to accept fate; we all do.

"William, I need some things. I know we haven't much money left—"

"Never you mind. You've given me everything I could ever

want, my love. I only wish I could give you more."

"I've the family I always wanted. And you." She lay back, warmed by the beating of his heart. Her breathing slowed. *We last made love in June. Another lifetime. Five months ago. I didn't even know how much I missed him, and we've only just discovered what could be, between us, if only…*

* * *

November's howling winds and torrents of rain forced them all to keep indoors. William lounged in the parlour, playing games, reading to Ann and John, singing Manx songs for the children of an evening, while Henry stoked the fires. Euphemia smiled down at her knitting. *It feels more like home now that William's downstairs. With rest and good food, he'll be better by spring. We'll plan our own future. Far from Thomas.*

She worried over their stores with ten mouths to feed. Glass mason jars of fruit and vegetables, pickled eggs and canned chicken lined the pantry shelves; potatoes, turnips, carrots, and apples nestled in sawdust in the root cellar; meat hung in the icehouse. Thomas had bagged a moose and a deer. The boys had learned the meaning of "bagged" by carrying heavy, dripping slabs of meat in canvas bags to the stone boat stationed in the field. When Thomas was away in Cheboygan, Henry described how he'd directed Pete to dress out the kill while he leaned on a tree and smoked.

"Undress more like," Edward said, explaining how Pete had removed the hide with his bowie knife and butchered the animal. "Not pretty, Mum."

Euphemia shrieked in horror when the moose's head floated down the driveway on the stone boat. "It's hideous. Bury that! You don't expect me to do anything with it, I hope."

Thomas roared with laughter. "He's a beauty in my eyes, Pheme. The taxidermist in Cheboygan will make me two fine trophies, a bull moose and a buck, to display above the mantle. The parlour will look like a proper hunting lodge, English

Cocker Spaniel on the rug and all. Like the goddamn King of England, eh, boys? I might just commission me a portrait."

Euphemia shuddered at the thought. *Why do some men revel in killing? Meat's one thing, but there's no pleasure in it.*

John took one look at the bull moose's severed head and fell to his knees, sobbing. *My sweet John. He just can't adjust to life here.*

"So that's a moose," Ann said, popping her thumb out of her mouth, emphasizing the double vowels. "Jenny and I don't like it." She stuck out her tongue. "We won't eats it."

"It's a strange creature, I warned you, but it looks damn fine on a plate. You'll eat when you're hungry, I reckon," Thomas said, shrugging at Euphemia's scowl.

"Well, I've no earthly notion how to cook such a beast, any road," Euphemia said, pressing her apron with the flat of her hands. The bump responded with a kick. She inhaled sharply and exhaled, relieved. *The first one.*

"Don't fash yourself, Pheme. No different than beef. You add onions and bacon to tame the wild taste is all." He dropped his cigar and rubbed his stomach. "Delicious!"

Euphemia leaned over and lost her lunch. Humiliated, she stood up and wiped her mouth with the handkerchief in her sleeve.

"Never mind, Mrs. Carin," Sophie said, bouncing Hugh. "I can preserve and cook the meat. Mother taught me."

* * *

A few days later, when the temperature dropped below thirty-two degrees, the family experienced snow for the first time. The sparkling crystals swirled like fairies, Ann said. The lightly dusted trees matched the gingerbread on the eaves. The icy air stung the nostrils with every intake of breath and puffed out like clouds on the exhale. Euphemia and William held hands and delighted at the snow sculptures in the yard. She'd experienced winter in Yorkshire, but never snow this deep, this heavy.

Beautiful and frightening, all at once.

Now Thomas enthused about Michigan winter. He demonstrated how to make "angels" in the fresh snow. Startled to see him tip backward and splay out on a snow mound, Euphemia said he'd do himself an injury. Everyone stared, jaws agape, as he swept his long arms and legs in wide arcs. Then he put out a hand for help.

"Careful, I have to get straight up, otherwise I'll ruin the impression." Thomas huffed, frosting his moustache.

Sophie, Tom, and Edward struggled to lift him. William was laughing and coughing too hard to assist. "You've made an impression all right, Thomas. I don't think we'll ever forget it," he said, tears streaming down his face. He brushed snow from his brother's back. Euphemia smiled. *Maybe harder than truly necessary.*

"Haven't done that since the loggers first showed me when I was in forestry. Makes me feel young again," Thomas said, smacking his legs.

Ann pointed. "Looks a fat faery," she said, frowning. "I'll make a proper angel, Nuncle." She flopped back and made a delicate imprint with her long, wool coat. Henry took both her hands to help her up.

"That's a lovely faery, Ann. Never forget the faery folk are all around you. Fly, my angel." He twirled her, making her coat bell out in a circle. He drew her close and they pressed their foreheads together. Ann giggled and thanked him for "flying" her.

Euphemia felt a rush of love and pride for Henry. *Such a good son and brother. A credit to us. They're all growing up nicely despite—*

"Faeries live in my little house, Henry. I hear them. They don't like it here. They want out."

"I understand, sweetheart. Ach, I will miss you so much." His voice cracked and he squeezed Ann so tightly that she squirmed. Euphemia eyed him. *Did I hear rightly?*

"Miss me?" Ann knit her brows. "Where am I going, Henry?"

"Never mind, never mind, sweet one. Ooh, your hands are like ice. You forgot your mittens. Let's go in."

Ann wriggled out of his arms. "I wants to play in the snow with Sal."

As soon as Ann dropped to the ground, Edward ploughed headfirst into Henry. He landed backwards in drift.

"That's it, wave your arms and legs, Henry. Make us a scarecrow!"

Thomas joined in the snowball fight, and Sal bounced for joy, catching snow in her mouth. William was drawing in gulps of air, saying he found it bracing, like aboard ship.

He doesn't cough, though the air's frigid. Winter's not as bad as I feared. We'll survive.

Chapter Thirty-Four

Tra ta'n laa gaase liauyr, ta'n feayraght gaase ny stroshey:
As the day lengthens, the cold strengthens.

December, 1905

ONCE she'd absorbed the shock of bone-chilling temperatures and learned to dress everyone in layers, Euphemia appreciated winter, a respite from constant work. Daylight slipped away in peace and quiet. Everyone relaxed in the warm parlour, listening to the crackling fire and the click of knitting needles. Sophie introduced popcorn, a delicious treat.

Thomas amused himself by teaching William and the older boys to play poker using matchsticks as betting chips, dismissing Euphemia's protests. "It'll help their arithmetic, Pheme. Mine's excellent." Ann watched in fascination, whispering to Jenny. John preferred lying by the hearth, copying the Sears Roebuck catalogue. Sal rested her head on the small of his back and dozed. Though they weren't tired from exerting themselves, they went to bed shortly after supper; no use trying to sew or read in the half-light of kerosene lamps. Mornings began slowly for everyone except Henry, who got up before dawn to stoke the kitchen stove, milk the cow, and feed the livestock. There was nowhere to go, not much to do, day in, day out.

"This is almost a holiday. We've 'time enough' at last," Euphemia said one night over dessert. "*Traa dy liooar.* Am I pronouncing it properly, William?"

"That's right, Pheme," Thomas said, nodding. "It's the pace of life here. That expression means what counts is the task itself, not the time it takes. On Man, the seasons weren't as harsh. Here, it's the story of the ant and the grasshopper." He pointed his spoon in Ann's direction. "Ye ken, Alice Blue? I'll get you a book." He dipped into his bowl for another taste. "In Michigan, you must 'make hay while the sun shines.' Then you've the fruits of your labour all winter, like these raspberries. Delicious, Pheme. More, please."

William smiled at her. "I'm that proud of you, Euphemia, for all you've learned and accomplished in such a short time. Nan would be mighty impressed. You worked like a Trojan, whilst I was flat out in bed."

Euphemia put a finger to her lips and refilled his teacup. "We're just glad you're getting better."

"Spring'll be here in a few short months, William. Your job now is to rest and recover. Let us look after you. Then I'll put you to work, never fear. We've a barn to build."

Euphemia sighed. *He has to be top dog. William oughtn't to open himself up that way.*

She swivelled to retrieve a sheaf of paper from the buffet. "Sign this letter to your mother, please, William. I've had no time to write since we arrived. I'm sure they're anxious, poor dears. What'll they think of our news, eh?" Avoiding Thomas' grey stare, she cradled the baby bump. "Add a few words, if you're up to it, my love. Your mother would be pleased."

"You've your good news to share and all, Da," Edward said.

"I'll send some drawings, Mother," John said. "I've drawn

a moose. Nan won't believe it."

"And I'll copy out 'There's A Hole in My Bucket' for Grandad," Tom said, humming. "It's better than 'The Phynodderree.' Pity he can't hear the tune. Wish I could write music."

Thomas shook his head. "Well, your grandad couldn't read it; he plays by ear."

"Let me send a picture, too, Mama. I can sign my name and Jenny's," Ann said. "Oh, and I could make Sal's paw print with my paints and send some pressed leaves and flowers—"

"Goodness, I'll need a box," Euphemia said. "Lovely ideas, children. Everyone should send a little something, even you, Thomas." He shrugged and lit a cigar. "Think of your poor parents, all alone now. Why, I'd even send a bone for Blackie, if I could. I'll hurry and finish Jill's tea cozy. I wish I could have attended the wedding. How long do you suppose a parcel takes to get there?" She counted on her fingers. "Horse, then train, then ship, then train, then horse again, Cheboygan to Port Erin. Makes my head spin."

"And to think, we did it in reverse, all by ourselves, Mother," John said.

"Well, the faeries came along too, right, Henry? You said so." Ann said, bouncing Jenny on her knee.

"Aye, they did, at that. We wouldn't have made it through, without them." Henry patted her arm and smiled.

Thomas blew a cloud of smoke. Da coughed. "Ach, drop those Manx superstitions, Harry. They don't belong in the New World." Thomas curled his lip. "Say, I just remembered, Christmas is coming. What would you like from Santa Claus, Alice Blue?"

Henry pushed his chair back from the table. "I'll be for my bed, Mum. First, I'll *smoor* the hearth in the parlour. *Oie vie as caddil dy mie*, Da."

Euphemia's stomach burned. *Why can't Thomas just let him be? Everyone believes in something. Though, I think Thomas only believes in himself.*

* * *

By January, snow drifts as high as ocean swells engulfed the house and outbuildings. The boys spent hours shovelling narrow pathways to the barn, woodshed, chicken coop, out-house, and back door. Henry didn't mind; working outdoors invigorated him. He loved returning inside, the warmth setting his extremities alight. His red flannel underwear stuck to his skin under his heavy coat. After peeling out of his damp clothes and hanging them to dry in the kitchen, he'd relax until late afternoon with Uncle Thomas's collection of Popular Mechanics magazines.

The stars emerged early. Henry would finish evening chores, then remain outside for as long as he could bear the cold, staring upwards. Grandad had taught him to identify several constellations. The Plough, scraping the northern horizon, reminded him of ploughing the garden plot. *Brutal work. This year will be easier with Buster and Slick. I wonder who'll do it.* He easily picked out The Hunter. *I don't think I'll ever make much of a hunter, me. The whole bloody business makes me sick. I like working with animals, not killing them.* Deep down, he knew he couldn't compete with Edward's marksmanship. *Takes after his father, I reckon.*

Pinpointing each star in The Hunter's belt, he reached The Dog Star. Canis Major twinkled, a lamp in a distant window. *Is Grandad seeing the same stars, Blackie by his side? I wanted a dog. Then he goes and buys one for Ann. To spite me. Bastard.*

Millions of diamonds shimmered on a scarf thrown over the night's counterpane. King Orry's Road, *Mooar Ree Gorree. Are Grandad and Nan seated on the bench, drinking tea? Nan's will be cold. He'll tease her… Lucky she's not here; it'd be frozen solid.*

After stargazing, Henry often visited Da at his bedside. He'd roll the single cigarette Mum permitted as they discussed the day's events or reminisced about Man. He'd acquired Da's habit, and they enjoyed a companionable smoke, Henry talking, Da suppressing his cough. Then, with an *Oie vie*, Henry would turn down Da's lamp and head for his bunk.

Sleep came in fits and starts. He'd bang his pillow, seeing that mouth pressed against Mum's, hearing once more the truth about Edward. His sympathy for Mum's plight had evaporated like snow off the roof. *She said her name means "of good repute." Ha! She slept with Thomas. It felt like a dream, him hitting me, but it really happened. Can't Da see? God forbid he should find out.* Finally, he'd drift off, entangled in knots, twisting like a nest of snakes. He'd wake up covered in sweat, despite the frigid room.

By day, he planned for the future. *We'll leave, Da and me. He hates him, that's plain, he just doesn't say so, blood being thicker than water and all that. Why stay once he's better? Bastard won't even send the young ones to school.*

One night, shovelling the paths took longer than usual. Sheltering from the wind, he stood beside the privy, savouring the tobacco taste and smell of his cigarette. January's full moon, Wolf Moon, Mrs. Miller said, shone silver as Grandad's signet ring. *It even has an inscription, though you can't read it. I'll learn the Indian names of all the moons. They mean something—*

A scream pierced the darkness. A fox? He'd learned that the screams of foxes sounded like someone being murdered. Ann said it was the *Buganne*, as usual. Foxes were hibernating now. *Maybe Thomas is strangling Mum. Nothing would surprise me with him.*

He palmed his smoke, collected his lantern, and followed the track around the house, down the slope to the chicken coop. Screams assaulted his ears. In the arc of light, a tall, round figure was silhouetted against the wall. *Mum?* Henry jumped as another scream erupted.

"Oh, God, Henry, you scared me." Mum clapped her mittened hands over her mouth.

"I scared *you?* You scared the hell out of me! It sounded like someone being throttled. What in the devil are you doing out here alone? And in the dark too. It's dangerous. There could be wolves, Thomas said.”

“I come out at night and scream sometimes, Henry. I thought no one could hear. I scream and scream. Until I can’t. Then I go in.” She puffed out a cloud of mist and met his eyes. “It helps.”

“Oh. I see.”

He did. Mum waddled forward and touched his cheek. *She’s so big. The baby might arrive at any time.* He remembered Hugh’s birth in the cottage, Nan helping Mum, how scary it was. *Why’d she want to go have another one? Now of all times?* Anger burned in his throat. He took out his matches, cupped his hand, and re-lit his smoke.

“How’re you holding up, love? You don’t say much, these days, though you never were much of a talker. Like your father. You’ve taken up his habit, too, I see. I wish you wouldn’t.”

He took a drag, blew out the smoke, and found her dark eyes, barely visible in the lantern’s soft glow. “It helps.”

She dropped her gaze and sighed. After a final puff, he flicked the butt onto the snow. They watched the orange tip fizzle.

“It’s a lot harder than we thought, isn’t it? We reckoned life would be easier compared to home. Winter, for one thing. Thomas said—”

“I hate him, Mum. I hate his bloody guts. I want us to leave.”

“I know,” she said, her voice pitched low. “It’s obvious. To everybody. Can’t say I blame you. Where would we go? How would we live? We’ve no money.”

“I can earn money. At least I’d get paid somewhere else. When Da’s better, I’m gone.” His words formed a misty cloud between them. He stamped his feet and clapped his hands for warmth.

“You think yourself a man now, Henry. You certainly work like one. But there are many ways to be a man. There’s thinking of others before yourself, putting your family first, like Da. That's a real man." Her eyes brimmed. She gripped his arm. "You know we can't leave, especially not now—" She rubbed her hands across her belly, protruding from her unbuttoned coat.

"Is it *his*?" The rock flew. He couldn't stop it. Nor reel it back. The splash resounded in his gut.

"Wha—what did you say?" Mum stumbled backward.

"I heard you arguing. Then I remembered you and Thomas together; one of my earliest memories, in fact. Plain to see, now I know. Edward takes after him. Even Nan said so. I'm ashamed of you—"

His cheek barely stung from her mittened slap, but he recoiled. Then she pushed him down and began kicking him in the ribs, screaming and sobbing at once.

"How dare you? How dare you judge me? I'm your mother." She shrieked and kicked. Kicked and shrieked. "You know nothing about it. If you breathe a word to your father, or Edward, or… or anyone—"

She collapsed on the snowbank and retched. The smell of puke reached his nose. Snow melted on his face in the snow. His spine felt shaken like a bag of jacks. He gasped for breath.

"I won't, 'course I won't, Mum. I'm sorry, I'm sorry." Words spilled into the snowbank like clotted cream. *Oh, God, what have I done?* He peeked under the arm covering his head. Her round face reflected the moon. She hunched beside him on her knees and used a tone he'd never heard before. Ice cold. Not a trace of warmth.

"When you finally do become a man, Henry, you'll learn that people, even your parents, make mistakes. I'm paying. Don't make your father or Edward pay, too. They don't deserve it."

She hid her face with her mittens, shuddering. Her scarf dropped. Henry crawled over to place it around her shoulders. Struggling upright, he tried to lift her. Atop the drift, they tottered and fell against each other. The bulge pressed against him. With a rush of shame, he saw himself sinking like that cigarette butt. To steady her, he grasped her forearms.

"Forgive me, Mum. I'd no right—I'll never tell anyone, I swear."

She stepped back, holding his arms, shaking and breathing hard. Her eyes riveted him in a coal-black gaze. They made a pact. But something had broken. He heard a jug smash on a slate floor. He shook like a wet dog and his teeth began to chatter.

"Move before we freeze to death."

As they started back, Henry glanced up. The Plough had disappeared. The moon hid beneath a shroud. He swung their lanterns to light their way.

* * *

The next day, Mum went into labour; Henry blamed the argument. Sophie flew up and down the stairs whilst Da, Uncle Thomas, and Mr. Miller paced the parlour floor. The children huddled in the kitchen. Henry tended to Hugh. Mrs. Miller remained at Mum's bedside. Pete undertook the fifteen-mile ride on horseback to fetch Dr. Harding despite the weather.

It took ten hours for the doctor to arrive. Mum had laboured for twenty. After seeing her, Dr. Harding, his face solemn, led Da away. Henry's nails dug into his clenched fists. *Might she die? Or the baby? Both?*

He did his best to distract the children: serving hot soup, setting up a blanket tent with chairs for Ann, playing jacks and knucklebones with Edward and Tom. *I'm back on Ivernia. The floor is moving, and all. We're in a storm.*

At some point, he dozed off in Mum's easy chair and dreamt he was lying atop the stone boat underwater. Fish surrounded him. A body draped loosely in a shroud floated his way. He awoke with a start, heart pounding, just as Mr. Miller burst through the door. "The babe's arrived. It's a girl."

Ann crawled out from under her tent. "Mama, Mama, I want Mama."

"And Mum? Is she—" Henry could barely swallow, let alone speak.

"She's fine, Henry. Resting," Mrs. Miller said, encircling Henry's shoulder. He wanted to collapse against her. Instead, he hugged Hugh until he kicked him.

"Let's get supper on, shall we?" Mr. Miller said, rubbing his hands together like sandpaper. "The women are plumb worn out. We menfolk think we know what labour is: toting bales, ploughing land, chopping wood, but let me tell you; we ain't got a clue. Not according to Mrs. Miller."

Chapter Thirty-Five

Oh hush thee my dove, oh hush thee my rowan,
Oh hush thee my lapwing, my little brown bird,
Oh fold thy wings and seek thy nest now,
Oh shine the berry on the bright tree,
The bird is home from the mountain and valley
Oh horo he ri ri Cadul gu lo.

The Manx Lullaby, Traditional

February-June, 1906

THE winter days dragged on. With a newborn crying all hours, the two men became restless. Thomas said Mullet Lake was frozen, ready for ice fishing. Da said he felt up to it. Henry wanted to go, both to escape the noise and try fishing that didn't involve a boat. Edward and Tom were eager to learn.

Thomas hadn't exaggerated. They'd no sooner bored a hole than fish bounced into their net, nineteen to the dozen. Da easily made friends with other men huddled in cozy huts on the vast ice sheet, warmed by fires smouldering in Dutch ovens. As the pile of fish rose with the temperature in the hut, so too did the body odour, the laughter, and the volume. The men joked, smoked, and shared flasks and fish stories into late afternoon. The boys delighted in the company. At sunset, the fishermen hefted their overflowing baskets and sloped away, vowing to return the next day, weather permitting.

Da became jovial on the way home. He led the boys in one Manx tune after another, recalling how harmonizing helped the miners trek seven miles, twice a day.

"Singing lightens the load, boys. Ach, you can't imagine how it feels to contribute to the table again. And to have some mates."

Henry threw his arm around Da's shoulder, surprised they were the same height. *You can't imagine how good it feels to see you enjoying life again, Da. You're coming back.*

Then came the spring thaw. Da's energy melted with the snow. By April, most days found him wrapped in a blanket on the porch swing, dozing. The baby kept Mum busy, though they shared afternoon tea. She assigned him little tasks, fixing broken clothes' pegs, cleaning fresh eggs, things he could do seated. Once the frost had lifted, Da began taking slow walks with Ann, John, and Sal. They strolled the woods past the garden plot in search of faeries.

One day in May, while tilling the soil, Henry's focus on the team was shattered by a loud crack. *What the hell? Did a tree fall? Da's over there with the little ones.* Ann stumbled out of the woods, Sal on her heels, barking wildly. She waved and called for help. Henry dropped the plough. He ran. Fell over a furrow. Got up. Tripped. Fell again. Nearly doubled over to keep his balance, he chased Sal across the uneven ground. He discovered John kneeling on the ground next to Da. Ann came up behind Henry and crumpled against him. She pointed, sobbing. "Something came flying from there, Henry. It knocked Da down."

Da lay prostrate, groaning in pain. His eyes were squeezed closed, and his heart throbbed in his throat. Henry crouched down but couldn't find blood. As he lifted Da's head, he saw

Edward racing toward them, gun over his arm, a dead rabbit in one hand.

"Da, did I hit you? Da?" Edward screamed, eyes wild, like a cornered animal. "I tripped over a rock; the gun went off by itself—"

Henry jumped up and kicked Edward's shin. "By itself? Idiot! It was loaded?" Henry smacked his forehead. "You put in two bullets, didn't you, you stupid asshole. When Uncle Thomas specifically said never, ever—"

"Oh, shut up, shut up! Leave me alone. Da, are you hurt?" Edward fell beside him, dropping everything. Sal sniffed the rabbit. He turned and flew at her, hands outstretched like claws. "Go away, you goddamn dog!"

Henry smacked the back of his head, knocking his hat to the ground. "Don't you dare hurt Sal, you son of a bitch, or I swear—"

Da moaned. His words came slowly, barely audible. Henry had to lean down to hear. Da winced. "It's my shoulder, Henry. Edward, you stay. Henry, take John and Ann. Bring Thomas. Just a scratch, but I daren't shift meself, lest I start to bleed. It burns—"

* * *

A few days after the funeral, Henry drove the team to Cheboygan alone. They still needed to eat, Uncle Thomas said, his expression brittle as his words. Mum made a list. Henry noticed her hand shaking when she dipped the pen. *She's not the woman in our photograph in that lovely boater hat. The photographer said we mustn't smile. Will we ever smile again?*

"Stop at Mrs. Miller's," she said as she straightened her shoulders and yanked her lank hair into a coif. "She'll have fresh asparagus already, I shouldn't wonder." Her hair slipped loose again. "I'm tempted to cut this damn mop. Bloody nuisance." She fairly growled, handing over the list. *She barely looks at me these days.* Sophie passed him a little smile as he closed the kitchen door.

When he jumped down off the wagon, Mrs. Miller pulled him in for a long, pillowy hug. She invited him to stay for tea. "I'm sending extra preserves, a ham, and bacon, too. Stores get low this time of year. Leon, load the wagon. Come, sit you down, Henry. We need to talk."

She asked him to describe Da's last days, taking Henry's hand across the table, excusing her boldness. He faltered at first, but once he started, he couldn't stop.

"Crossing the ploughed field to reach him was like trying to run through waves in the sea. When first I got there, he seemed all right. He thought it was a flesh wound. I ran for help. Edward couldn't move."

"Shock. The shock might've killed the boy, Henry. Poor lad. Terrible, just terrible. Where was Thomas?"

"Flat on his back in the shed. Out cold, when I found him. Later he said he heard the shot, looked up from the shingle plane and the baling hook whipped off and hit him in the head. Strange how that hook came loose." He shook his head. *The Phynodderree?* "He says his ears are still ringing."

"Lucky he didn't lose an eye. I noticed the red mark on his forehead at the funeral. And Pete? Where was he?"

"At his place. I unhitched the horses and sent Tom on Slick to fetch him. Pete made straight for Cheboygan. Sophie saw to Uncle Thomas whilst I found Mum upstairs with the baby. Maybe we should've tried to lift him, but Mum's still weak, and I feared hurting him more."

"No, you did right. I wish Tom would've stopped here, though I've no experience with gunshot wounds. That took much too long. Six hours at least. My God. What did Doc Harding do?"

"Removed the bullet. Sophie and I helped. Da passed out—"

"Thank God for small mercies. Sorry, go on." She rubbed

the tablecloth with the flat of her weathered, knobbly hand. Her tanned, wrinkled face looked older. Her blue eyes clouded over. "There was so much blood. Mum, well, she, she couldn't—I acted as nurse. Sophie's awful good. Doc Harding said the bullet had struck the liver. Two days of suffering. The laudanum helped…"

When he began to weep, Mrs. Miller lifted him, like hoisting Hugh out of his highchair. She hugged him until his shoulders relaxed, then poured more tea, adding two heaping teaspoons of sugar. Henry wiped his face on the fresh hankie she extracted from her sleeve.

"Did he say anything? Or see anyone, people who have passed?"

"What?" A chill raced down his spine. "How did you know? He spoke to his brothers Ralph, Mel, and Arthur. Said they were in the room. And he saw Nan and Grandad too. They're alive, as far as we know, but they came. *Themselves* were there, he said. He had told me he didn't believe in the *Little Ones* anymore—" His voice broke.

"I've seen it before, Henry," Mrs. Miller said, handing him a slice of cake. "Comfort comes at the last to ease our passage."

"He spoke to each of us, alone. Gave me Grandad's ring, said I must be my own man, and that he was proud of me." Tears spilled from his eyes. His left hand trembled as he held out the silver ring on his little finger. "It was too loose on Da. He'd gotten so thin. Grandad was a big man."

After a deep inhale and a gulp of sweet tea, he continued. "Then he asked for his old flask from the trunk, saying he wanted to be buried with it. Thomas made a stupid joke at the funeral. I knew why; it contained peat. I was there, the day he collected it."

He shuddered, remembering how he'd thought stuffing a flask with peat was insane when that was all he'd taken to remember home. His throat contracted, stoppered like Da's flask.

Mrs. Miller rubbed his arm. Tears rolled down her face. She took back the handkerchief.

"Poor Da. He hugged Edward in front of us all. He told him not to hold it against himself. Said for us not to blame him either. You can't believe it, but he kind of laughed, saying as how he didn't have long anyway; it was the milk reek that got him, not the accident. He spent time alone with Mum, then Thomas. A long time, that one. Then we gathered 'round, and he passed."

Henry choked back more tea. He needed to finish. "I never saw anyone die before, Mrs. Miller. He let out a soft sigh, and then his head dropped to the side. He had a smile on his lips. Thomas came over white as a sheet. Mum howled. A wolf crying at the moon can't sound as mournful, Mrs. Miller. I hope never to hear that sound again."

"I know, Henry, I know. Your poor, poor Mother. And she's a newborn to care for. Thank God Sophie's there."

"We all cried. Even Thomas. Everyone except Edward. He hasn't said a word since. He barely eats."

"Oh, dear. I'll come over tomorrow. I'll make up a tonic to help him. This could ruin the boy's life." She smoothed the tablecloth, brushing crumbs into her hand. "Thank you for telling me everything, Henry. That was hard, but better to get it off your chest. Bottling things up only makes them worse." She pushed back her chair and collected Henry's hat from the table. "Best be off, or you won't get home before dark. Longest day is coming. Strawberry Moon."

As he jiggled the reins, Mrs. Miller caught his arm. "You must write to your grandparents, Henry. Tell them everything, just as you told me. His mother will want to know. Especially that his kin came from the other side." She took another handkerchief from the bib of her overalls and blew her nose.

"Thomas sent them a telegram."

"Cold comfort. Promise?" When he nodded, she patted

Slick's neck. "You're head of the family now, Henry. Not an easy row to hoe. Take care of yourself."

"We say *'Cair Vie'* in Manx. Means 'safe travels,' Mrs. Miller. Thank you for the tea."

"*Cair Vie*. Good lad."

CHAPTER THIRTY-SIX

"There's a hole in my bucket, dear Liza, dear Liza
There's a hole in my bucket, dear Liza, a hole…"

American Traditional

August, 1906

DEAD. Euphemia squeezed her fists together, pounding the pillow, kicking beneath the covers. Her greatest fear had come to pass. Not in the way she'd expected. No. Much, much worse. *He might've rallied again, as before, with a bit more time, more rest, good food, sunshine… Or he might have quietly slipped away. That would have been sad, but I could've accepted it. But at the hands of his own… of Edward? My Edward.*

She flipped over and buried her face in his pillow, breathing in. She'd prevented Sophie from changing the sheets. Damn the counterpane; she didn't care if the stains ever came out. Burn it. She wrapped herself in one of his sweaters, the blue one she'd knitted, back home. She tugged the shawl collar over her face and let her tears flow like a river. Her hands and feet were ice. *If William were here, he'd take my hands and blow on them, then warm my feet between his calves, and then…*

Her breasts responded. Milk rolled down her sides, soaking her nightdress. Eliza's tiny face flashed before her. *She's hungry, I shouldn't wonder. I must get up. I'm so tired. Where is she? Oh yes, Sophie put her in Ann's room so I could sleep. Did I? I don't remember. Maybe she cried and I didn't hear. My new lamb. I'm neglecting her.*

Guilt forced her up. She began to pace the floor. *What am I to do? I can't leave, as Henry insists. Go? Go where? With seven children including a newborn? Oh, my chest hurts.* She bent over and pressed her arms against her swollen breasts. *My heart's in two jagged pieces, like the Valentine's cards I once thought fanciful. I finally understand Nan's breakdown. Back then, I'd never lost anybody. I had no idea.*

She sat down at her dresser and stared into the mirror. *My hair's a right mess. I'll frighten everybody looking like this.* She began brushing, imagining Nan and Grandad collapsing when they received the telegram with no family to comfort them. There would be no tombstone with his family name inscribed like the many others at Kirk Christ Rushen. *I know. I'll make Thomas send Nan money for one so she can spend time with it on Sundays. I'll never tell her what happened. Not ever.*

When we married, I said, "'Til death do us part," not knowing what that meant. When the vicar sprinkled earth on the casket, my feet lifted, and I almost threw myself in. I wanted to follow you, William. I can't face the future you laid out, at the last.

"Marry Thomas, Euphemia. It's the only way, my love. I thought about it all the while I was in bed. I knew I was past it. You must raise the children here, and you can't be unmarried. It won't do."

She couldn't restrain herself from arguing, even then. "Never mind what my feelings are, then, or what others might think? Not to mention Henry, especially. He'll never forgive me. He's furious as it is. Anger's changing him." She couldn't tell him why.

"Henry will understand. He's almost fifteen. A man," William said, his ragged voice straining, thick with blood rattling in his shallow chest. "Think of the youngsters, Euphemia. Thomas'll do right by them; his pride won't permit otherwise. We must face facts."

She wanted to scream, "Facts? Face facts, William? You don't know the half of it."

"I know he still loves you."

Euphemia's head shot up. *Did I speak aloud? How does he know? And what does he know?*

"I agreed to come here for your sake and the children's." He traced her chin with his index finger, catching a tear. "Ach, I've been that angry at the unfairness of it—Thomas, a single man, not a care in the world, hale and healthy, and me just over forty, a family to raise, letting you down. Some days, I wanted to chew off me own hand. I know I was cold to you. I'm sorry. Then I rallied for a time. A sweet respite, eh? But *Themselves* don't lie: *Goll sheese ny liargagh.* They told Nan rightly. I'm not afraid, Euphemia."

His eyes overflowed with concern. "Please, be sensible, love. You can't fend for them by yourself, nor go home. Think of Eliza especially."

Our Eliza. Named for the American song we love. Dear Eliza. We laughed, teasing Henry that he was that stupid boy, unable to fix a leaky bucket. Who can fix this?

"I was terrified for you and the bairn at her birth," William said. "So terrible. But my girls survived. You don't see the woman you've become, Euphemia. I do. Back home, you did your duty, following in Nan's footsteps like a puppy dog. Now, you can stand on your own. I have faith in you."

At his words, she came undone. Like a row of knitting, dropping off the needles. Falling to the floor.

Eliza's birth. Breech. So much pain. Eliza nearly died. Euphemia fought on, thinking of the children, imagining them left with Thomas. *Thank God for Sophie and Mrs. Miller. Dr. Harding arrived too late.*

"This child's your last, I'm afraid, Mrs. Carin," he said. "A pity; you're still a young woman. I'm sorry."

I'm not, Doctor. Not in the least. Her pelvic bones ached to the marrow. Her backside was split in two; she could barely sit down, even still.

"I'm glad the bullet hit me, not Ann or John," William said. "We were lucky. Don't look like that. It is a blessing really, love. Quicker this way. I'm so tired…" He asked her to light him a smoke since he couldn't move.

She regretted her constant fussing, restricting the only thing that soothed him. *What a waste. Cruel, though I never meant it so.* Hastily retrieving the makings from his bedside table, she rolled a cigarette, lit up, inhaled, and coughed so hard her bladder let go. William laughed through his nose.

"I see why you like it so much, William," she squeaked, spitting out bits of tobacco, placing the end in his mouth. She propped his pillows, smoothed his thin hair, allowed her fingers to play at his temples. *When did his beautiful raven hair turn dove-grey? I can't even recall. He's only early-forties.* She pushed herself up from the bedside and rubbed her hands across her apron.

"We never should've come, William. I said so, over and over; you wouldn't listen. We'd have been better off to stop at home. Nan, Grandad, even Jill could've helped. You'd've come good without the stress of being with Thomas. Didn't help me, either."

William's eyes glittered. "We didn't emigrate for us, Euphemia," he whispered. "We came for the children, remember?" Blood dribbled from his mouth. His forehead was clammy and damp. She wiped his face and said the baby wanted nursing.

"Send Thomas in, would you? I've a word to say to him."

Their last argument rang in her head as she lit a cigarette and dragged deeply. She didn't cough. It calmed her nerves. Henry was right about that. She blew a question into the mirror. *Did our coming really help the children, William? They've no school, no friends, nothing but work. Not to mention putting up with Thomas. You said I'm stronger than I realize. I'm empty as that bucket in the song, William. The one with the hole.*

* * *

Driving to Cheboygan, Henry's heart lifted, and he found himself whistling the "bucket" song. He tied Slick and Buster to the hitching post, handed the shopkeeper Mum's list, and walked down to view the boats anchored in the harbour. The cool river breeze cleared his lungs of the humid, mosquito-infested forest air. He breathed deeply, gazing at the active harbour.

A wooden steamship, bearing the name *Topinabee* in gold letters, bobbed gently in the lock. He sounded out the word, wondering if he'd pronounced it right. With its double deck and shallow white hull, she seemed friendly compared to the massive *Ivernia*. Her freshly painted iron grill enclosing both decks lent an air of security. A man in a dark uniform, wearing a white cap, stood directing people and carts up the gangplank. On a whim, Henry approached him.

"Excuse me, sir, you taking on hands?" Though his voice cracked, he straightened his back and removed his hat.

"Who wants to know?" The man's voice was muffled by a full, curly moustache.

"Name's Harry, sir. Harry Carin." The hated nickname popped out of his mouth. He wished he could correct himself, but felt he'd look a fool. The man's piercing blue eyes assessed him, stem to stern.

"Well, you're a strong-looking young fella, I'll give you that. Long drink o' water. You know your way around the business end of a shovel, by the look of those big mitts. Think you could keep the engines stoked on this beautiful vessel?" The man extended his hand. Henry shook it vigorously. Grandad always said, "Never trust a man with a weak handshake."

"Captain George Hamill, at your service. I'm the grandson of the great Chief Petoskey." He covered his mouth and said, under his breath, "Not really, but the tourists lap it up." His eyes twinkled in his ruddy face. "The *Topinabee's* the most popular steamer on the inland waterway."

Henry grinned. *He pronounces the ship's name in capital letters, for all the world like he's speaking to a crowd instead of just me.*

"Stoking's hard work and seasonal, but the pay's good. You'll see all the sights: Oden, Pon-she-wa-ing, Alanson, Sagers Resort, Columbus Landing, Indian River, stop at Topinabee for dinner, then back here and on to Mackinac Island." The words rolled off his tongue like Mum's shopping list. "Ever been any of those places, young man?" Henry shook his head and closed his mouth, becoming aware that he'd been gaping like a caught fish. "Thought not. Follow me."

Questions whirled in Henry's mind. *I'd see all those towns? Does it travel close to shore or cross Lake Michigan? Not like crossing an ocean, I reckon, but still...* He stepped aboard. As he viewed the luxurious deck with its leather chairs, carpeted decks, brass railings, and gilt-framed mirrors, Henry realized that the upper decks on *Ivernia* might've been similar. He smelled the stolen roast chicken pressed against his chest. A rush of shame set his ears and cheeks alight.

Captain Hammill patted his shoulder. "You are duly impressed. Never seen the likes, have you, boy? Quite something, eh?"

Henry nodded, unable to formulate a reply. *My Lord, the air itself smells of money. It must cost a fortune to travel aboard this ship. What'm I thinking?*

The captain led him down to the engine room. "No fear for safety in here, I tell you. I'm the best goddamn navigator there is. Ask anybody, right, Joe?" A fellow nearby surreptitiously threw a wink at Henry. Captain Hamill raised his arms. "As you see, this gal measures seventy-two feet long with a twelve-foot beam. The bridge at Alanson's a tight fit, but I ain't never put a scratch on her, have I, Joe?" He slapped the man's back.

"Mind you, it's stokers keep 'er moving. The real engine of a steamer. Wood and coal, both. Sure you're up to it? You are sixteen? Not married?" He tapped Henry's shoulder, threw his head back, and laughed heartily. The stokers joined in.

Henry filled out the paperwork, subtracting a year from his birth date, swallowing his fear. He drove the horses as fast as their eight legs could carry them. To the jingle of the harness, he invented words to the "bucket" song:

"I'm leaving, you bastard, you bastard, you bastard.
I'm leaving, you bastard, you bastard, I'm gone."

CHAPTER THIRTY-SEVEN

Ta cooinaghtyn yn chree ny share na cooinaghtyn yn chione:
The remembrance of the heart is better
than the remembrance of the head.

HENRY unloaded the wagon, helped Sophie re-stock the larder, then bolted upstairs. He decided to pack and ask Pete to drive him to Cheboygan. Retrieving an old carpet bag from the closet, he threw in his few clothes, then tiptoed into Mum's room where Eliza slept in her new cradle. He wanted only one thing: the family photograph. He sat on the bed and fingered the silver frame. His hands were so sweaty, he almost lost his grip. Holding it to his chest, he stared at the image, then squeezed his eyes shut. A yellow and black print appeared for a moment. He set the photograph back next to the one of Ann and her Jenny. *Mum needs them more than I do. I'll remember.* Then he bent down, kissed the tips of his fingers, and planted them on Eliza's soft brown head. She stirred, sucking her thumb.

"*Moghrey Mie Mooinjer Veggey, my chree,*" he said. "If we were home, the faeries would steal you, Eliza, for you are a beauty. Mum's neglected the iron tongs across your cradle. *Slaynt as shee as eash dy vea, as maynrys son dy bra.*"

"

He barely slept. At cock's crow, he descended the stairs in the dark and placed his bag by the front door. After morning chores, he entered the dining room. Afraid to sit, for fear of losing his nerve, he inhaled deeply and said, "I'm leaving. I've taken a job."

Mum blanched. "No. Henry." Her voice squeaked as though someone were standing on her foot. She covered her mouth with her hands.

Edward, Tom, and John stared, eyes wide. John whispered, "Don't."

"I can't stay, John. I'm sorry but—" The pain in those sensitive eyes cut him to the quick.

"Sorry?!" Thomas flew out of his chair and leaned across his plate, sweeping his arms. "You goddamn, ungrateful, selfish wretch." The flash of his gold tooth emphasized his rage and solidified Henry's resolve.

"Me? Me? You're a no-good, cheating, lying bastard. You can't hold a candle to Da or Grandad. You're using us. That was your plan all along. Soon even Hugh will be put to work." He struggled to tamp down the quake in his voice. "Well, I, for one, would sooner shovel coal on a ship and be paid for it, than shovel your shit. I can't stand the sight of you." He wished he could spit but his mouth was too dry.

Thomas roared, threw a glass at him, and flew around the table. Ann screamed. Sal barked. Sophie intercepted Thomas, holding the water pitcher in front of her. Glimpsing the butcher knife on the buffet, Henry grabbed it.

"Just you try and touch me. This knife's razor-sharp, as you well know."

Mum stood up, smoothed the front of her dress, and spoke slowly. "Don't you lay a hand on him, Thomas. I'll deal with this. He's my son."

Edward ran from the room. Tom stood next to Henry, arms crossed. Sal jumped and yipped. Henry pivoted and covered the hallway in two strides, stopping for his bag. Ann followed him. Pushing Tom out of his way, Thomas ordered Ann back to the dining room.

Ann grabbed Henry by his belt. "Wait up, Henry. Don't you love us anymore?"

Not daring to make eye contact, he threw open the front door. Pete had just arrived for work and was circling the team in the driveway. *Thank God. In the nick of time.* Henry slammed the front door and rushed to throw himself in the back of the wagon. Pete turned, eyes wide with surprise, then quickly pulled on the reins. Henry clambered up to the front seat, his trembling right hand still gripping the knife. He yanked the reins away from Pete.

"Gee haw! Gee haw!" The team moved ahead. "We gotta go, Pete. Right now."

He glanced back at the porch and saw Ann peering through the parlour window. Then she disappeared. The house sat silent as a broody hen. *Has Thomas locked them in?*

"What in tarnation you on about, Henry?" Pete frowned, retrieving the reins. He pulled hard. "Where in hell is everybody? Why've you got that knife? What's going on?"

"Jesus, Pete, please move," Henry pleaded. "Before—"

Pete scanned the porch. "Where's your mother? I want a word."

Henry grabbed his arm. "Listen, Pete. I've hired on with *Topinabee* and she's about to weigh anchor, see. I must get to Cheboygan today. They're expecting me. Please drive me, Pete. I'm done up."

"Done? Up? What in hell's gotten into you, Henry? Your ma—"

"I can't take anymore, Pete. With Da gone, there's nothing for me here." He leaned over, trying to spit the way Pete did to make a point. He tasted metal. Fearing he might puke, he sat up and focused on the horses' shiny backsides, willing them to move forward.

Pete removed his hat, wiping his bald head with his dirty sleeve, frowning. "Nothing? What about Buster and Slick? Percherons attach to folks, you know. You're training a fine team. Who'll look after them?" His voice came out thick as molasses as he gestured toward the new barn with his switch. He turned his horse-brown eyes on Henry. They were brimming over.

They jumped as Sal bounded onto the porch with Thomas. He had his gun. "Get your arse down off that goddamn wagon, you somma bitch. You're not going anywhere."

Henry's stored-up venom spewed forth. "You'll shoot me? That's rich. You'd lose your slave, one way or the other, Bastard. You oughta be shot, you, with a ball of your own shit." He snorted. "There's one of your sayings for you. My parting gift." He glowered at him, exuding all his hatred.

Thomas thundered down and grabbed Henry's arm with his free hand. "I don't give a damn if you leave, you little prick, but your mother wants you here, so move your fuckin' ass. Now. We'll see who's boss."

"Hold on there, Thomas. You won't hurt the boy," he said. His tone was the one he used to drive horses. No arguments. He clicked his tongue. The team shuffled ahead.

"Stay out of it, Pete. This here's family business." He jumped as the back wheel slipped next to his foot. Henry smiled as Pete turned toward the lane.

"Fine. I won't shoot you." Thomas yelled. "I'll shoot this fuckin' dog. Right here, right now. Alice is watching from the window."

"You wouldn't dare," Henry said, his voice faltering. "Keep moving, Pete. Gee haw." The horses kept plodding forward.

"Go then, you shit. Don't come back. And don't you dare ask Nan for money. I'll write and tell how you betrayed your mother."

"I? Betrayed her?" Henry wrenched around. He screamed at the top of his lungs. "It was you who betrayed her. Da too. I know all about it. And Mum knows I know. So there. Rot in hell, Bastard."

Thomas set the rifle on the ground, then pounded toward him, hands outstretched. "I'll wring your neck, you somma bitch. I'll throttle you. After all I've done—"

Pete shook the reins, and they were off. Henry's heart pounded like the horses' hooves hitting the road. Sweat stung his eyes. Before they'd cleared the forest, there came a shot. Then a howl. It sounded human. Henry twisted around, seeking Pete's eyes. Pete tapped the quirt and gave Henry a sorry look.

"He wouldn't shoot Sal. Would he? Mum would never forgive him. Ann's heart would break. Not even he—"

Pete shifted the wad of tobacco in his cheek and said, "Hold on to your hat."

"Bastard!" Henry hollered and twisted to look behind. His voice disappeared in the crowd of white pines, silent spectators. Another shot rang out. A black form spun to earth. A raven's shriek pierced the sky. Someone screamed. Henry knew it wasn't a fox.

With a final backward glance, Henry watched the gabled roof of the yellow house disappear into the trees. The wheels crunched gravel. Pete slowed to a walk. They clopped along awhile, then he handed Henry the reins. Fishing his pocketknife from his overalls, he cut a tobacco plug. They hit a bump, and he nicked his finger. Popping his grimy thumb in his mouth, he sucked, spat, and then, his voice muffled, he said, "For one thing, you hate boats, Henry."

Henry thought he might laugh. Or cry. *He's picked up the conversation where we left off. Casual-like. He doesn't seem to—*

"You said so, many times. I can't believe… Why, just think of your ma. Who'll she turn to now?"

The horses pulled the dust along behind them. Henry

hoped to make Cheboygan by noon, but when Pete wanted to talk, you couldn't rush him. They were at a safe enough distance now. *Thomas won't come after me. Too proud. But what's going on back there? I've left them in a right mess.* He swallowed his guilt. *There's nothing for it. I had to.*

"Season's short, you know, Henry. Pleasure boats quit end of September. Then what'll you do? Come back?" Pete's voice lifted.

"Not bloody likely," Henry snapped. Then Pete's stricken look gave him pause. "No, no, Pete," he said, keeping his tone gentle, like speaking to a horse. "I intend to strike out, find me an island to live on. I hate the forest; I can't breathe."

"Say, what about Bois Blanc? That's close by. They cut timber all winter. Leastways then you could visit. I'd put you up at my place." He ran the back of his sleeve across his eyes. "Sun's heating up."

"No, I'm never coming back. I'll get work on a freighter. Captain Hamill says they cross Lake Huron into November. Bois Blanc may be an idea. Means cutting trees, though." He glanced at Pete's crumpled face. "Don't worry, Pete, Thomas trained me for hard labour. I'm used to it. I'll miss the little ones and Sophie, too, of course. And Buster and Slick. Ginger and Bread. Sal. And you, too. I'll write, but don't pass my letters on." He gripped Pete's forearm. "Promise?"

Pete shook his head, looking down at the reins. "Can't read nor write, neither one."

"Tom or John will read them for you. Don't show Edward."

Pete hunched his shoulders and jiggled the reins. "Don't see how your ma'll get on, Henry. A new baby, all them young'uns, Edward in a right state—"

"I do pity Edward. I wouldn't be in his place, for anything."

Henry pointed to the road with his chin. Pete took the hint. Suddenly, Connor's small, pointed chin flashed into his mind. He remembered how he and Edward had played with the top,

Edward dancing with glee as he reeled it off. *Edward promised he wouldn't tell about the chicken. I don't think he ever did. Still, I hate him.*

"Edward killed my father, Pete. I can't forgive him. Edward is… Thomas is—" The wagon jolted over a bump. He bit his tongue. And tasted blood.

"Whoa, hold up there, Henry." The horses heard "Whoa" and halted. Pete laughed at himself and clicked softly. "Sorry, ladies. Didn't mean it." He turned to Henry with a solemn look. "T'ain't fair of you, understand? Edward's mired in guilt. Might never get over it."

"Pete, if Ann hadn't been leaning down to pet Sal at that moment, she'd be dead. Da even said so. And John; why, the shock nearly killed him. Typical Edward; out hunting, by himself, toting a loaded rifle. He never listens to anyone. Ever."

"Bad things happen in life, Henry. No use placing blame," Pete said, leaning over to expel a sluice. "Don't swallow poison expecting the other fella to die. Anger rots you from the inside. You're too fine a fella—"

"Well, they'll have to get along without me. I'm sick of being bossed around. I can't stomach the sound of his voice. 'Teacher voice,' I call it. Know what I mean?"

Pete smirked a little. "Sure do. Still, you're what, fifteen? Mighty young to be—"

"I'll not darken that door again."

Pete fell silent. They rattled and sweated through the morning's journey, arriving at the dock perished with thirst. Henry jumped down and pointed out *Topinabee* fluttering her flags brightly in the cloudless sky. Henry gave Pete a handshake, connecting with his dark brown eyes. Pete wrapped him in a tight hug.

"Bye, Pete. Thanks for teaching me about horses, and so many things besides." Henry said into Pete's shoulder. "You've been a true friend. I'm lucky you were there." Then he took a step backward. "Pete, you don't think… he didn't… shoot Sal, did he, Pete?"

"Na, prob'ly shot in the air to scare you. He's mean, not crazy. I hope." He scrambled in his pockets and extracted a few crumpled dollar bills and a tin of snuff. Henry thanked him, aware of the gift's value. When he handed Henry a fuzzy humbug, he popped it in his mouth and headed for the gangplank.

* * *

Henry took to stoking like a duck to water, as Mum would've said. Hatred propelled his shovel. Sweat rolled down his back, cooling his anger. He smashed unburnt cinders to dust, envisioning a certain fat head. The roar of the engines drowned his fears and his memories. When Captain Hamill heard that Henry planned to apply on a freighter, he enticed him with a bonus, even allowing him to mingle with guests as long as he wore his uniform. During stopovers, Henry became an errand boy, but whenever they docked in Cheboygan, he stayed aboard and played poker with Joe, the boiler engineer.

One day, the captain clapped Henry's naked shoulder just as he heaved a shovelful of coal into the boiler. "I've been watching you, Harry. And the boys've been talking about you."

Henry jumped. The shovel clattered down. *Is he firing me? What did I do?*

"You're the best goddamn stoker we've seen. You could work for the devil himself," he said, laughing.

He expelled his breath loudly and smiled. "How'd you know, Captain? I did."

Hammill raised his eyebrows. "Well, don't wear yourself out, Harry. Stoking'll break your back if you ain't careful."

Later, in their quarters, Joe peppered him with questions, but he resolved to keep himself to himself. *No use stoking gossip.*

Despite his fear of ships, Henry loved *Topinabee*. She mostly hugged the Michigan shoreline and calmly traversed the Straits of Mackinac, Captain Hamill's steady hand at the wheel. Four-hour shifts hardened his palms and emptied his mind. During breaks, he'd sprawl on his bunk, his ears ringing, or sit alone in the mess composing his letter, as promised.

> *Dear Nan and Grandad,*
>
> *I hope this letter finds you well. I'm sorry I haven't written. ~~Mum probably told you~~ I have left the farm. I am working on a steamship, ~~a beautiful vessel that plies the waterway~~ I'm sure you know about Da. He saw you before he died. He said so. And Uncle Arthur, Ralph, and Mel came too. Da gave me Grandad's ring before he died.*

The words on the page swam, replaced by Mum's tearful cries, Thomas and the gun, Ann's small face peeking out from the lace curtain… Every moment came rushing back like water under the prow. His throat tightened. He'd left Mum, baby Hugh, his precious Ann, who heard the faeries like Nan. *Whatever will happen to her, and tender-hearted John, and Tom, boiling with rage? I'm not there to comfort them in Manx, nor share stories of home. Eliza will never even know me. Nan mightn't forgive me for leaving. I can't tell them Edward shot Da. They're sorrowful enough. Does Nan really know that Thomas is Edward's father, not Da…*

After several attempts, he tossed his scribbles into the river. He watched the pages bob on the water like seagulls. *Wait 'til I get settled. Then I'll write with good news.* He closed his eyes and saw a green meadow, dotted with sheep. A fence. A gate. A black dog. A log cabin with a sloped view down to the water. Not an ocean, but a wide lake. One lone tree stood on the hillside, a faery tree. His farm. *I'll bring John, Tom, and Hugh there, someday. Ann and Eliza, too. We'll make a new life together. But not Edward. Or Mum. They can stay with Thomas. They deserve each other.*

Chapter Thirty-Eight

Prairie Land, hand in hand, lovers stand,
close together as the sun goes down,
Hear him say 'Come away, don't delay,
you'd look sweeter in a wedding gown…
When he said 'Let us wed,' o'er his head
flew the echo of her Ha! Ha! Ha!

"Prairie Bird Wedding Song,"
Jack Drislane, 1909

June, 1907

"WELL, Pheme," Thomas said, encircling Euphemia's waist from behind as she stood at the kitchen counter, preparing lunch, "It's been almost a year; time to uncover the mirrors and get married, with William's blessing. People talk, you know."

"What people?" She pressed her lips together and rolled her eyes. "We don't associate with anyone who doesn't know us. I don't give a damn, any road," she said, slamming a pot, making Sophie jump and Sal bark. "Forgive me, dear. Let Sal out, would you? And please, call the boys."

"The kids'll be teased at school if we ain't married," Thomas said, pinching a carrot from a steaming pot. "Besides, I'd like a proper ceremony in Cheboygan, and a 'do' with all the trimmings at The Ottawa. Mrs. Tucker puts on a fine wedding feast."

Sophie dropped the mason jar she was holding. Peaches and juice sprayed across the floor, though the jar didn't break on the wooden floor.

"Aw, that's too bad," Thomas said. "A sweet treat for you, Sal. You'd like to visit your folks too, wouldn't you, Soph'? It's been two years if my arithmetic's any good."

Sophie ran from the room. Euphemia frowned as she smacked his hand. "Teased? At school? When do you reckon that will happen? It's way past time for Ann to be in school. Tom's lost interest, and Edward... well, if he speaks again, that would be a start."

She bent down to scoop the peaches into a bowl. "No, Sal, this isn't for you. What's Sophie upset about? Not like her to leave a mess. I'll let her calm down for a bit. Strange."

Thomas shrugged and opened a bottle of beer. He raised his eyebrows, asking if she'd like some. She nodded, spooning a helping of mashed potatoes onto plates. "There is something I've been meaning to tell you, Thomas. Mrs. Miller wants to take in our John. He'll attend school in Cheboygan, and work in the garden for room and board. She wants to continue his piano lessons. What do you think?"

"Fine with me," Thomas said, taking a long swig. "That one's not suited to heavy work, and she's taken a shine to him. He might just inherit her money; she's no children to leave it to." Thomas tapped her bottom and whistled.

Euphemia whirled around and glared at him. "Jesus, Thomas, I'm thinking of his future, not plotting Mrs. Miller's demise." She looked down, choking back her emotion. "He mustn't think I'm giving him up. That's what worries me. I'd be losing another son. I miss Henry so."

She tossed salt into the bubbling gravy, tossing some over her left shoulder, like Nan, for luck. "Why can't I trace him? Pete knows more than he's telling. I just want to know he's safe."

She carried the roast chicken into the dining room. Ann was struggling to set the table. Sophie had obviously been crying. She lifted her up, cooing, "Let Sophie help, sweet one."

Hugh sat on the floor, banging a pot with a wooden spoon. Thomas yanked it away. "How youse can stand that racket is beyond me," he said. "Can't hear meself think."

Hugh screamed, picked up the pot, and threw it against the wall. Ann dropped the forks and covered her ears.

"It's been a year since Harry left, Pheme. Pete says he's fine but won't say any more. I ain't interested. He'll come back one of these days, wagging his tail behind him, like the rhyme, eh, Alice Blue? You must get over it."

Sophie cleared her throat, bouncing Ann on her hip. "Excuse me, Mr. Thomas, but a body doesn't just 'get over' things," she said, her voice unusually firm.

Thomas opened his mouth. Euphemia poked his chest lightly with the meat fork.

"Oh no, you don't, Mister. You'll not shut her down, Thomas, like you do the boys. She's practically a grown woman, a full member of this household." She paused. "And my friend."

Thomas plumped down in his chair, tucking his napkin into his shirt.

"You were saying, Sophie?" Euphemia smiled at her.

She set Ann down. "Well, to my way of thinking, somehow you 'get through' sorrows, but you don't 'get over' them, Mrs. Carin." She moved to the buffet. Euphemia noticed her hand shaking as she poured a glass of water.

"I agree, wholeheartedly, my dear. Take Nan, for instance. She never 'got over' losing her three sons; that didn't make her weak. She was the strongest person I've ever met. William was just one heartbreak too many—" Euphemia's voice caught in her throat. She motioned to Sophie for water.

Nan's death, right on the heel of William's. Who will visit the faeries and Arthur, I wonder? Perhaps Grandad, with Jill, and her new babe. He must feel so alone. "Poor Grandad. Try telling him to get over her death, Thomas."

Hugh toddled over and tugged at her skirt. She balanced the platter on the table edge and pinched off some breast meat.

"What will your father-in-law do all alone?" Sophie asked, placing Hugh in his chair.

"He's going to live with our friend, Jill. He'd never manage on his own; he can't boil water, bless him. I'd love to care for him here."

"He'd never survive the journey, Pheme, let alone the winters," Thomas said, crossing his arms over his belly. "And how'd he come up with the money? Proceeds from the small hold wouldn't be half enough." He buttered a slice of bread and stuffed it in his mouth. "Besides, he's my father, not yours."

"Not fair. They were the only parents I had, you know right well." She blinked away the mist clouding her vision as she placed the roast in front of Thomas. She handed him the second-best butcher knife. "I only pray Nan is at peace with her sons. And the faeries."

"Our faeries are gone, Mama," Ann said, retrieving Jenny from Hugh's highchair. "They left with Henry. We don't hear them anymore, do we, Jenny?"

A chill ran down Euphemia's spine. *That must mean they're watching over him. Nan too, I reckon.*

"That's nice, Alice Blue," Thomas said, beginning to carve. "Dammit, this knife wants sharpening." He grunted. "Hmm. I'll get to it, later." He flopped slices of meat onto an extra plate. "So, Pheme? I'll book the preacher, shall I? Mrs. Tucker can plan us a to-do." His voice rose with the colour in his cheeks.

The spring on the screen door squeaked. Tom, Edward,

and John were returning from the barn where they'd been clean-ing stalls. They dropped their mucky boots on the porch, but their socks bristled with straw as they straggled in.

"Ah, you reek to high heaven." Euphemia pinched her nose and made them go back to the porch while she filled a washtub with hot water. They flopped on the floor like rag dolls and gingerly removed their socks. Their feet were as black as their rubber boots. All three stood in the tub and splashed their feet. Tom and John kicked at each other in fun, but Edward quickly dried off and made his way to the table.

"Smells so good, Mother," John said.

"Yes, I'm starving, Mum," Tom said, rubbing his belly.

"Guess what, boys?" Thomas said once they'd all sat down. "Your mother and I are to be wed, soon's I get everything ar-ranged. What've you got to say about that, then, eh?" He raised his glass in a toast. "Cheers. We will return your name back to the real McCoy, or rather 'Carine.' He guffawed. "It'll be the big-gest shindig Cheboygan's ever seen. Maybe I'll invite the mayor."

The boys looked at one another, then resumed eating in silence. Sophie asked to be excused.

"Well, don't get excited or anything," Thomas said, sweep-ing the table with a glare. He stopped at John. "Say, I have other news, just for you, Johnny. Mrs. Miller wants to adopt you. Im-agine that."

John's lips formed a silent O. He blanched. Edward bolted out of his seat and ran into the backyard, barefoot.

"Bu—but she—she can't," Tom stuttered, shaking his head. "She just can't."

Euphemia rushed to put her arms around John. His whole body trembled. "Jesus Christ, Thomas, that's not how I meant to tell him. Why open your big mouth? Listen, darling—"

John stood up, kicked his chair, then stumbled into the hallway. Tom and Sal followed.

Euphemia collapsed onto her chair, overturning a glass of

milk. Ginger skittered to lap it up. Her hands dropped like bricks into her lap. She put her forehead on the table and sobbed. Ann and Hugh started crying. Upstairs, Eliza joined in. *She wants feeding. Oh, God. Three sons gone from me: Henry, Edward, and now, John. I could scream.*

* * *

Sitting at her dressing table, Euphemia wielded her sewing scissors—snip, snip, snip. She smiled into the mirror, holding each lock between the index and third finger of her left hand, humming a tune. *Oh, that's from the vaudeville show "Louise and Her Picks." I can still picture that buxom blonde singing her heart out; Thomas, smitten as a barn cat. Fancy that coming back.* She set the scissors down, took a puff of her cigarette, then swept the remaining waist-length hair into a Gibson swirl. *I can't believe I gallivanted off to a show leaving William behind, sick as a dog. Wasting precious time. Thomas did that deliberately, I see now. William allowed me to enjoy myself; make a fool of myself, more like.* She grabbed another hank of hair, pulled it tight, and chopped.

She envisioned Thomas' face when he saw her hair, two days hence, when she'd walk down the aisle. Perhaps he'd thought she'd wear her wedding dress. Jill had cleaned out the cottage and sent it wrapped around her Brown Betty, likely unaware that Grandad had tucked money inside the material. She'd squirrelled away the English pounds from half the dispersals. *I must get to the bank and change the money. Are women allowed an account here?*

She smirked into the mirror. *Doubt he's given my wardrobe a second thought. Off he trots to Cheboygan, nary a question as to my wishes. No, he'll arrange everything. Ha! Perhaps I'll come as Lady Godiva. That'd have them talking!* She pulled a face, making herself laugh.

Sophie had helped with alterations to the dress; after Eliza, she'd gained weight, and she didn't intend to wear a corset. Standing on a stool in her room, handing out pins, she'd confided her reason for marrying Thomas. "Merely to stop tongues wagging. I don't love him."

"I know, Mrs. Carin." She looked directly at her and asked a personal question, "Do you miss your home? Sorry, maybe I shouldn't—"

Euphemia paused, formulating a truthful answer. "Well, I'm an orphan, dear. I've no childhood home. I reckon that's why I became so attached to William's family. I miss the people more than the place. I never spent much time out, so occupied with the children, helping Nan run the house. Isle of Man could've been anywhere." *Until I left it.* "Our Henry hated leaving; he's Manx, through and through." She touched Sophie's arm. "And you? You must miss your mother."

Sophie's face fell. Her lower lip quivered. Euphemia stepped down to put her arms around her. The hazel eyes filled with tears. "I'm so sorry. We should've sent you on a holiday before now. Thoughtless of me—"

"I don't want to see her, ever again. She stole my baby."

"Wha—what? Stole? Your baby?"

Sophie's voice juddered in sobs. "I never even got to hold it. Was it a boy or a girl? I'll never know. She whisked it away like a stray cat, the minute it was born. I hate her."

Jesus, Mary, and Joseph. Mrs. Tucker? Kind, generous Mrs. Tucker? Now I see why she's skittish. After Leeman, I was the same. She went through something even worse. I'd never have guessed.

"I'm so, so sorry, dear." She waited. *If she chooses to tell more, she will.*

"We were in love, Tony and me. He worked in the kitchen. We planned to elope. Then Mum found out. She locked me in my room. I never saw him again." She looked up, her eyes brimming. "We were both sixteen. We could've been married. But no. She only cared about her reputation. The hotel. It's everything to her." She was twisting Euphemia's dress in her fingers. She started and let it go.

"I couldn't get out of bed for a while. After that, I refused to work. When Thomas offered me this job, I jumped at the chance. I never want to see her again."

Euphemia took her chin. "You've a place here as long as you want. I'll make us a home, as I learned from Nan, the mother of my heart. I'm determined."

She squirmed in her dress, unable to breathe. "Too tight." She snapped her fingers. "I know. You could wear it! Would you be my maid of honour, Sophie?"

Sighing now, she cut another lock of hair. *Sophie's my only friend in this godforsaken place. Who cares about the age difference? She works hard and is sensible like me. Bet she first thought me a lady, with this house and all. Appearances are deceiving. The cottage impressed me too, once. I struggled to understand Manx ways and expressions. Sophie must think we talk funny. I've forgotten what it was like.* She took a puff.

Yes, I'm homesick, but not for the place; for the past. She shook out her bobbed hair and brushed her hand across her face. She stubbed out her cigarette, glimpsing the framed photograph. She smiled, recalling the boys chasing the parrot. She silently blessed each face and pressed her lips to the glass, then slipped it in her underwear drawer, next to her reticule. She left Ann's picture alone.

She took a sip of cold tea, swallowing her bitterness at how readily John had agreed to leave, when she'd thought to convince him. "You'll attend school in Cheboygan, love, keep up your piano, learn a trade… It's wonderful, yes?"

"You forget the most important thing, Mother," he said.

"What's that?" She started. "It pains me—"

"No more Uncle Thomas."

His voice was ice cold. She pressed her lips together and yanked the brush through her hair, hard. *Yes, sweetheart, you gain your freedom. This is for the best; John's too sensitive to be around Thomas. He and Tom were born too close; I was weak as a calf. I'm stronger now. I must plan for the future. I doubt Thomas has made a will. He might've been killed by that baling hook. I'll see to it, right after the wedding.*

She pulled her shoulders back, stretched, and yawned. *There's time enough for me to get things sorted. My children are all that matters. As for conjugal rights, he shall have them. Funny, he's not selfish in bed.* An instant body rush burned her inner thighs. *Maybe he'll calm down, be softer on the boys, stop going to Cheboygan…*

Admiring her uneven bangs, she glimpsed the girl she'd been; wild brown curls, sparkling eyes. Men's eyes followed her, and she didn't know why. She'd thought herself ugly. She pictured Leeman's face, smelled his breath. *Such a ninny. My girls will know the facts of life, by God. Then Thomas swept in. I was a seashell; he was a wave. Still, if I hadn't gone with him, I'd never have met William…*

Snip, snip, snip. *William would say to do as I liked whenever I threatened to cut my hair.* Her eyes gleamed in the mirror, imagining Thomas' reaction. *Thomas and William. Chalk and cheese. I chose William for the songs, the picnics, the kindness, and the children we both hoped for.* She stroked her chin with her knuckle. *Oh, William, I'm stuck here with Thomas, and it'll be no picnic. He's never even taken me on a single one. I'll sign the register, 'Euphemia Michaels Carin.' Our American name. For you, William.*

Tossing her head, she revelled in her short curls. *A bit raggedy; I love it. Should've cut it years ago.* She leaned in, creasing her brow, smoothing the bags under her eyes. Her glass bottle of violet perfume caught the light. She dabbed a bit on her wrists and behind her ears, eking it out. *There'll be no more.* Grabbing the tweezers, she plucked a few offending grey hairs.

"Ouch! Ah well, you're mid-thirties; can't stay young forever, lass," she said aloud.

The floor behind her creaked. A breath of air brushed her neck. She shivered at a feather-light touch on her bare shoulder.

"Don't fash yerself, my love. You're so beautiful. Always will be." *William. Plain as day.*

CHAPTER THIRTY-NINE

Oh, waltz me around again, Willie.
Around, around, around.
The music is dreamy, it's peaches and creamy
Oh don't let my feet touch the ground.

"Waltz Me Around Again, Willie"
Will Cobb, Ren Shields, 1906

July 13, 1907

THE strains of the wedding march penetrated the church doors. Euphemia heard an organ and—a violin? Grandad? Her heart leapt. *Has Thomas brought Grandad over?* Her bouquet of sweet peas trembled in her hands. A pair of ushers, young men she didn't recognize, opened the doors and she stepped across the threshold, accompanied by a squeaky note. *Grandad's not here.*

Transformed by her dress and floral crown into an elegant young lady, Sophie preceded her down the aisle. Euphemia, wearing her corduroy suit and leather boots, strode with more confidence than she felt. She smiled at the collective intake of breath. Leon grabbed Thomas by the arm, preventing him from toppling over. *Is he shocked or drunk? Why is Leon standing up for him, not Pete? Oh, Pete's looks.*

Her only escort was the scent of her bouquet. She was giving herself away. A crown of daisies graced her head. No veil. *Bless our Ann, strewing petals from her basket so seriously. Her matching crown makes her an angel. Thomas does cut a fine figure in his morning coat. My face must be red as a beet. It's so hot. My suit seemed a good idea at the time, but I mustn't faint. Breathe. The aisle's as long as York Minster's. Well, not quite.*

At the front right pew, she sought to connect with the boys. John and Tom stood side by side; Edward remained seated, head bowed. Tom held Eliza, swaddled in Hugh's christening gown. He lifted her tiny arm to wave. *No Henry. Pete couldn't contact him, then. Or maybe he did.* John's eyes met hers. He smiled and began to clap, elbowing Tom. Pete joined in, encouraging Hugh to imitate him. Ann set down her basket and clapped, too, without smiling. Euphemia looked left for Mrs. Miller. She and Mrs. Tucker offered supportive smiles.

She deliberately shifted her gaze to Thomas. His eyes glistened. *One final step.* As the minister directed the congregation to be seated, Thomas brushed his bearded lips on her ear, "I've always loved you, Pheme. This is the happiest day of my life." His hand trembled as he took hers. His grey eyes drew her out of the moment. The waves on Douglas Bay. Their first kiss.

"Your hair suits you."

Her knees buckled. *Why'd he have to say that? William, help me.* When the time came to repeat "love, honour, and cherish," she inwardly crossed her fingers. Leon handed Thomas a gold ring. It slipped and rolled on her finger. She frowned. *Way too big. He might've measured with a string like William did. He'd plenty of time.*

He pulled her close before the minister pronounced them "man and wife." She returned the kiss with a measure of thankfulness and relief. Hands clasped, they faced the congregation. She exhaled as though she'd been holding her breath for a year.

Scanning the faces swimming before her eyes, she recognized only a few: the Tuckers, the Millers, Pete, Mr. Dennis, the shopkeeper, no one else. One person stood out: a tall, broad-shouldered woman with blonde hair piled under a feathered hat. Euphemia noticed the fine lace of her dress and the kid gloves clutching the pew. Startling blue eyes met hers with an unwavering stare. *Rude. Who is she?*

She wanted to ask Thomas, but he steered her as if they were strolling the Douglas promenade. The congregation met them on the portico, forming a reception line. Thomas spoke too loudly, and Euphemia accepted enthusiastic compliments. She searched for the blonde woman among those gathered at the foot of the steps while Thomas hollered for everyone to head to the hotel. He asked Sophie and Mrs. Miller to accompany the children.

"We're going to the photography studio. Shouldn't take long."

Euphemia knit her brow. "What? Why not the whole family? I'd like an up-to-date photograph of the children. Why didn't you ask me?"

"Just us. The more poses, the more it costs."

Euphemia followed the photographer's instructions. She didn't smile.

At The Ottawa, Euphemia had to credit Thomas with the preparations in the reception room: bunting, linen, china and crystal, a three-piece orchestra to boot. *He does things up proper, I'll give him that.* Glad she'd foregone a corset, she relished Mrs. Tucker's feast; she didn't have to cook. Thomas and Mr. Miller toasted her with champagne, which she'd never tasted. She downed glass after glass, giggling at the tingle. The music pleased her even more. She couldn't wait to dance.

In advance of the wedding, Mrs. Miller had offered dancing lessons, Leon manning the gramophone. Thomas huffed, saying dancing was for sissies, but he would do the first waltz.

Euphemia had never learned and dreaded making a fool of herself. Tom trampled on Mrs. Miller's feet, but John picked it up quickly, though he barely reached Euphemia's shoulders. Edward stayed home.

Dancing with John now, she wished she could've danced with William. *He'd have waltzed me 'round and 'round and 'round, like the song.*

"Dance me over to Pete and Mr. Miller, please, John."

She wanted to catch Pete alone; Thomas was standing at the drinks table. Startled, Pete polished his bald head and wrenched on his knotted tie. His face turned red as a raspberry when she pulled him aside.

"Con—congratulations on your marriage, ma'am, Mrs. Carine," he said, extending his hand.

She shook it and returned his crinkled smile. "Thank you kindly, Pete. I wish to request a wedding present from you."

"Sorry, ma'am, I ain't got much cash, so I thought a load of cordwood, ahem, now that Henry—"

"Exactly. Now that Henry's gone. Thank you, Pete, but my gift is you telling me his whereabouts. A mother's got a right—" she broke off, summoning tears. *He won't refuse—the Gaiety didn't know what they were missing.*

"But I promised… I—I mean to say, I guarantee you he's well, ma'am."

"So you say, Pete, but I must know. I can't sleep for worrying. It's been so long, not a word from him. Please, I beg you." She grabbed his arm, as if about to collapse. Pete caught her elbow. She glimpsed Thomas heading their way. "I won't tell Thomas, I swear."

"Well, he's a stoker aboard the *Manitou*, runs Chicago to Mackinac Island. He passed the winter logging on Bois Blanc."

"A ship? But Henry hates ships. Can you ask him—"

She felt Thomas' hand on her waist. He swivelled her around in a dance move, chuckling.

"C'mon, Pheme. You ought to be mingling with the guests."

She wrenched herself away. "Why would I? I don't know half these people." She scanned the room for John, not wanting to waste any more good music. *Henry's alive. I want to dance, dance. John's too short; maybe Leon would—*

"True. Come, I'll introduce you to folks."

The blonde woman came up from behind and tapped Thomas's shoulder with her fan. "Starting with me, Thomas."

Thomas pivoted, bumping into Euphemia. *Good Lord, he looks like he's been sent for. White as a sheet. I didn't see her come in. Whoever is she?*

"I startled you, Thomas," the woman said. "Forgive me. I didn't mean to give you a turn, and on your wedding day, too." She offered Euphemia her gloved hand. "I'm Alice, Alice Pomeroy. I read the bans in the paper. Thomas and I are… acquaintances. Isn't that so, Thomas?"

Her mellow voice flowed like treacle. Euphemia appraised the pale, creamy skin, rouged cheeks, thick blonde hair piled high, astounding blue eyes fringed by coal-black lashes. Blue eyes. "Alice" blue. The expression popped into her mind. Thomas always claimed Ann's eyes resembled Roosevelt's daughter's… Suddenly the music blared out.

"Don't just stand there gawping, Thomas; introduce your bride. Cat got your tongue?" Her red-painted lips made her teeth even whiter. Euphemia's shoulders dropped under the weight of corduroy, dull and brown compared to an ivory tea dress, with a lace overskirt and shirred long sleeves. Delicate as a wedding gown. Alice dipped her head, slightly.

Thomas stammered through an introduction, then whirled Euphemia away, pretending to lead her in a dance. Threading across the floor, he handed her off to Leon and scuttled away like a beetle in a house fire. Euphemia glimpsed him fishing out his flask as he headed for the French doors. *Rude, even for him. Something smells fishy.*

Her eyes swept the room, but the bouffant hairstyle was nowhere to be seen. She gulped another glass of champagne. By midnight, Euphemia and Thomas were both inebriated. When they collapsed on the bed, Thomas lurched toward her. She swatted him away.

"Who is she, Thomas? That woman. A former sweetheart? Or a current one?"

Her words slurred. She retched and scrabbled for the chamber pot. Then to ease the burning in her throat, she propped herself on a pillow. Thomas rolled over and passed out.

Alice. Alice P—something… Had she turned up to claim this god-awful ring? She twirled it on her finger; it dropped on the sheet. She screwed it onto her thumb. *He made a vow. I'll see he keeps it.*

* * *

A full bladder nagged her awake. The smell of the chamber pot made her gag. *What time is it?* She staggered over to draw back the heavy brocade curtains. Sunlight stabbed her eyes. *Oh, Christ. The children will be awake, wanting…*

She threw on a robe and staggered down the hall to the Tucker's residence. Sophie opened the door, Eliza on her hip. The baby reached out and she took her, apologizing to Mrs. Tucker for the hour.

"How are you, this morning, dear? Not to worry," she said, smiling. "The others are with the Millers and Pete, viewing the river boats. Sit you down on the sofa." She pulled over an ottoman. "Here, put your feet up."

Euphemia forced a smile. "So kind. I could murder a cuppa, if it's not too much bother."

"Of course, I was just thinking the same. Sophie—"

Eyes averted, Sophie left the room. Mrs. Tucker glanced at her retreating back, folded her arms, then looked at Euphemia. "Was the reception to your liking, Mrs. Carine? The cake was an old family recipe."

"I'm over the moon," Euphemia mumbled before she could stop herself. She settled Eliza at the breast and attempted levity, laughing at Thomas' reaction to her outfit. "Though now, I regret my choice. Corduroy? In July? But the feast, Mrs. Tucker, and the band! All wonderful. Thank you for everything." She lifted her gaze to Mrs. Tucker. "I'd dance every day if I could. I didn't know many of the guests, though. That woman with the big blonde hair, for instance. Friendly with Thomas, cold to me. Do you know her, by chance?"

Sophie delivered tea and biscuits. The cup rattled in the saucer as she handed it to Euphemia. Their eyes met. Sophie shook her head and shrugged her shoulders.

Mrs. Tucker reached for the teapot. "See to the little boy, would you? Keep him occupied." Waving Sophie out, she came to sit on the sofa. Euphemia winced when she squeezed her hand. The ring pressed into her thumb.

"Oh, Mrs. Carine, it's too big." She shook her head. "Mrs. Miller and I, we were of two minds about telling you. We went over it and over it... Thomas and Alice Pomeroy, well, you see—"

A knock. A bellhop tipped his hat. "Morning, Mrs. Tucker. The guest in Room 25 asked me to fetch his wife. Urgent, he said."

Euphemia flew up, handed over Eliza, and cinched her robe. The hallway swayed like *Ivernia*. Thomas flung open the door just as she touched the knob. She stumbled in, tripping on her robe. He grabbed her arm.

"What the hell took so long?"

He was wearing his suit and hat. His eyes were bloodshot, and his breath reeked of whiskey and stale smoke. Euphemia twisted away.

"Get you dressed, sharpish. She's downstairs. Waiting."

"Who's waiting? That blonde woman? What's she want?"

"Not sure." He crossed the room in two strides. "Meet me

in Mrs. Tucker's office." The door slammed.

Jesus. Mrs. Tucker was about to explain… She washed her face, threw on her suit, and combed her curls with her fingers. Her empty stomach churned as she tripped down the stairs.

The sheer curtains on the glass office doors revealed Thomas, gesturing wildly. Alice was a statue. Head turned, like a marionette on a string, when Euphemia entered.

"Hello, Mrs. Carine. Allow me to introduce myself properly this time—Mrs. Carine, at your service." She paused. "Oh, I see. You had no idea. Thomas already has a wife."

Euphemia swayed. Thomas steadied her, gasping as if he'd run down a flight of stairs.

"Listen, Pheme, it wasn't deliberate, I swear. I thought—"

Alice laughed. A sparkling, hearty laugh. "You thought what, exactly, Thomas? That you could leave me in Boston, and never come back? All that talk about building us a house once you'd visited your folks in England—" She poured a glass of water from the pitcher on the desk. "I thought you were dead. I wish you were, you bastard."

Euphemia collapsed. Thomas moved to support himself against her chair.

"So, here we are then, the three of us." She handed Euphemia a glass of water. She took it, spilling some on the carpet. "Lucky for me, a friend here in town saw the bans in the *Democrat*." She folded her arms under her ample bosom. "I could charge you with bigamy, Thomas. A man in Boston just got seven years. The law don't look kindly on abandonment. I've the papers to prove we're wed, though my wedding ring's been misplaced." She curled her red lips and tipped her head toward Euphemia. "What solution do you propose, Thomas? After proposing to both of us?"

Euphemia felt his fingers dig into her shoulders. He expelled breath like a deflating rubber balloon.

"It's money you want, then. How much?"

"Well, I've asked around, even took a drive out to peruse the fancy house you promised. Very nice. Perhaps I'll make you keep your word, force an annulment." She smiled down at Euphemia. No warmth lit the crystalline eyes. "What do you say, Mrs. Carine? You're awful quiet."

Euphemia twisted her icy hands, barely able to swallow the water. Her mind raced. *If our marriage were annulled, what happens to us? Where would we go? How would I support the children? They need a home.*

Alice smirked and waved her hand. "Oh, don't worry, sister, I don't want him back. You're welcome to him. I do believe I'm entitled to something, however. Say, three thousand?"

Thomas pounded his fist on the back of the chair. "Are you mad? I don't have that kind of cash. I could pay in instalments over time."

"Trust you. To pay. Over time. Ha! No fear. 'Once bitten, twice shy,' Thomas. Find the goddamn money, pig, or I'll set the law on you. I swear to God."

Euphemia pushed herself up on the arms of the chair and turned around. Her voice shook as she addressed Thomas. Only him, not Alice.

"I have two thousand five hundred English pounds with me. My deceased husband's legacy, meant for his children. I didn't make it to the bank, so I've no idea what that is in American, but enough, I expect." Her eyes were welded to Thomas. "You'll hand over the marriage license and sign a statement swearing never to bother us again. Mrs. Tucker will witness. She knows what's going on."

Thomas didn't blink, though his grey eyes watered. The spider veins on his cheeks stood out like lines on a map. His moustache trembled. "No," he mouthed, shaking his head.

Yanking at her thumb, she swung around. "Here's your ring, Alice." She placed it on the desk. "Melt it down for all I care."

PART FOUR
TIME WAITS

"Time and tide wait for none."
Geoffrey Chaucer

Chapter Forty

Shegin da'n dried kiarail eu ve jeh nyn gree hene:
Your first care must be the care of your own heart.

August-September, 1909

FROM the ship's stern, the wake left a perfect V of buttermilk. Seagulls swirled above the foam, squabbling like brothers. *Like Edward and Tom.* Henry leaned on the metal rail and stared at his white knuckles. The familiar urge overtook him. To jump. *I left a mess in my wake, too, for others to clean up.* He pictured Ann's face at the window, heard her sobs. "Why, Henry? Why are you leaving us?" *She probably cried for many nights afterward, hugging her Jenny. I hope the faeries came to soothe her.*

A wave struck the prow, and he banged his hip. *Swore I'd never leave shore again after Ivernia, and where do I end up? I've lost Tom, John, sweet Ann, little Hugh, baby Eliza. Edward's the oldest now. Not much use to Mum. How're they getting on? Wish I could take that elevator in Boston, the one John imagined would bring us home, to sneak back and see.*

Sunlight glinted on the ring he wore on his left hand. Grandad's signet. A bit tight now. He could see Mum removing it when they laid Da's out. She'd tucked it in his palm and wrapped his fingers around it, anointing him head of the family. He'd thought about wrenching it off his pinky and tossing it overboard. He couldn't. It was all he had left from home.

He recalled Joe on *Topinabee* asking why he never sent or received letters. He'd brushed him off. "Got nothing to say."

"Shucks, you've no trouble chatting with the ladies topside. They bat their pretty lashes and send you off like a drone. Instead of nectar, you're bringing in tips. Busy Bee." He laughed and punched his arm. "What're you, sixteen, Harry? I'll take you into town, find you a girl—"

"Got me eye on a little filly, Joe. Just need enough money to afford her." *Old Nosey wouldn't guess, but I do mean a horse.*

Like many a steamship, *Topinabee* plied the Inland Waterways, traversing three rivers and three lakes, from Lake Huron to Lake Michigan and back. Henry never rested easy, fearing he might drown or be burned alive in one of the notorious steamship fires, but he looked forward to the stops along the forty-two-mile route from Cheboygan to Oden. Every small town had attractions and girls to admire. He saw more of the country than he'd seen after a year at Mullet Lake.

When the tourist season ended, he headed for Bois Blanc where logging continued all winter. He grudgingly gave Thomas his due for teaching him to operate a shingle plane, which meant working in the shed rather than the forest. Lodging at The Pines, a summer resort, seemed promising until he discovered that the owner was the off-season chef. Henry's shirts soon hung like laundry on the line. When he soaped his face to shave, he looked like Da.

Come April, he gladly returned to stoke for Captain Hamill, who knew stokers were the ships' true engines and fed them accordingly. He supplied Henry with two sets of new clothes. "You're a scarecrow in those rags, Harry. You'll frighten the ladies. We must fatten you up, or you'll be down on your tips!"

Henry admired Captain Hamill's skills and camaraderie. Joe was still maintaining the boilers, working his jaw in time to the pistons. They enjoyed a last smoke together on the upper deck before the season's first sailing.

"You seem a little worse for wear, Harry," Joe said, glancing at him sideways.

"Wintered on Bois Blanc with a Mr. E.T. White. Somabitch couldn't cook bait for a bear. Damn near starved to death."

"Ha! 'Bait for a bear.' Funny! You been drug through a knothole backward, I'd say. Stoking again? Careful. A stoker needs a cast-iron back with a hinge in the middle, they say."

"Pay's good, so here I am. My plans for the future cost money. Maybe, by next year—" *Oh, God. Hope I don't take after that bastard. Be careful is right.*

"Know what I'd do, Harry? Get me a job on the *Manitou*. She's steel, not like this quaint old tug. Hundreds of passengers, longer season. Sails between here and Mackinac Island across Huron. You'd get to see Chicago. The buildings there are a sight, now I tell you. They're constructing one so high, a so-called skyscraper—"

"I've a brother interested in architecture, but not yours truly." He knew if he didn't interrupt, Joe would recount his visit to the Chicago World's Fair for the umpteenth time. "I hate cities, me. Homes for rats. Liverpool put me off for life, bloody hellhole. I like *Topinabee*. Big ships make me twitch."

"The *Manitou's* unsinkable, they say. Steel bulkheads in the hull. Toured 'er this winter."

"Then why don't you—"

"Me? Nah, I'm too old. Three engines to maintain. I'd burst a blood vessel. They've four Scotch boilers so they want strong stokers like you, I reckon. Wages gotta be better than Hamill can pay," he said, glancing around. "The *Manitou's* a floating hotel. Swankiest crew's quarters I ever seen." He looked down to the water. "Wooden ships, bah! A thing of the past, mark my words.

Like the horse and buggy."

Joe pinched his cigarette and tucked the butt in his pocket. "Hamill's orders, you know. Prevent stray cinders alighting on deck."

"See? I like Captain Hamill. He's mindful of safety. Besides, he's hired me back. I can't quit on him."

"He'll give you a good reference, sure. Stokers come and go, Harry. It's a young man's game. You'd earn a load of cash in just one season."

"Thanks, Joe. I'll consider it. I'd like to earn enough money to—" Joe's curious look made him change tacks. "What'd you do this winter?"

"Stayed the right side of the grass, me." He laughed and encircled Henry's shoulder. "Down we go, back to the fires of hell. Never you mind about Captain Hamill, Harry. A man's gotta think of himself in this world."

* * *

After calculating the glacial accumulation of his savings, Henry applied for *Manitou*.

"You sure about this, young man?" First Mate O'Connell's eyes fixed him like steel rivets. "You're eighteen, you swear? We don't stick to shore like *Topinabee*. 'Tis three hundred nautical miles, Chicago to Mackinac. You can't change your mind halfway across."

Henry twisted his cap in sweaty hands. "I'll do my best, sir."

"Captain McIntyre's a Scot who maintains stern discipline, mind," the First Mate said.

"Suits me," Henry said. "Long's he's fair."

"Fair-minded and cautious, too. Never lost a life yet."

Lost a life. Blood rushed to Henry's feet as he remembered the funeral service he'd witnessed. *Everybody says Lake Huron's a ships' graveyard, but what choice've I got?*

He joined The Black Gang, a member of five teams of

four. They worked shirtless in one-hundred-degree heat, shovelling to the rhythm of the stoking indicator in four-hour shifts. He learned what his father had meant about a group of men performing hard graft. Like miners, the gang watched each other's backs. A drink and a smoke together at day's end sealed their bond. The daily ration of rum numbed aches and pains. Henry acclimatized to the noise, the heat, the repetitive motion that cramped his hands and twisted his spine. The bell drove him on.

At night, closing his eyes, he silently begged the faeries for protection: "*Fastyr mie, gura mie eu, Mooinjer Veggey.*" In the morning, he'd leave a small glass of rum at his bedside, always gone when he returned. He remembered the steward on *Ivernia* fingering his talisman. Each safe crossing meant one less for him; his savings grew.

Henry was pulling his last shift of the season when a late September howler of a storm barrelled across the Straits of Mackinac headed straight for the *Manitou*. Between bouts of vomiting and crashing to their knees, the stokers were hard-pressed to keep the ship aright. Henry's stomach heaved like the floor. *This is it. We're going down, for sure.* He recited the Lord's Prayer in time to the stoking bell, remembering that Nan believed in God and the faeries, both.

A purser appeared in the boiler room shouting Henry's name. He tossed him a white shirt and commanded him topside. His team protested.

"He's needed to help. Take a breather, the rest of youse. We're near enough to Mackinac but the captain daren't make harbour. C'mon, boy, make it snappy."

The staircase bucked like a wild horse. The hull creaked and screamed. *The Buggane, Ann, come for me, sure.*

The purser hollered over his shoulder. "We must get passengers to their cabins. Stateroom's a mess; broken glass, smashed furniture. Someone's liable to get hurt."

Henry bumped against the iron door and nearly toppled.

Looking up, he glimpsed a woman's skirt rising like an open parachute as a wave swamped the deck.

"Oh my God," he yelled, just managing to grab her hand. She clasped his neck in a stranglehold. He coughed, asking for her cabin number. Gripping her like a runaway horse, he tugged her along, fighting the waves. Finally propping her against the correct door, he grabbed her shoulders.

"You'll have some nasty bruises, miss." He shouted above the wind and the roaring waves. "Sure you're alright?" Another jolt tossed her into his chest. Grasping her around the waist, he took in her red hair and green eyes, stark with fear. She pushed him away, collapsed, and vomited at his feet.

"Oh," she wailed, "Your shoes. I'm sorry, I just couldn't—" She retched again.

He tried to lift her, but they rolled sideways like dice. Henry reached for the door handle and fairly pushed her inside.

"Safe and sound, miss. You must stay put. Can I do anything more? Only, I must get to the stateroom. I'm under orders."

Her hair was a cascade of dark, wet curls. Freckles stood out like ink spots on her pale cheeks. Through chattering teeth, she said, "My sister. I'm travelling with her." She clutched her stomach and crawled onto one of the beds.

"Her name? And yours, miss?"

She raised her head, her eyes brimming. Shaking with sobs, she said, "Nell. She's Nell. I'm Mary. Last name. Smith. Water... I can't... it's coming—" She rolled over and vomited down the side of the bed.

He looked around. "Oh, I would only... only, the jug's broken." He wiped her face with the edge of the sheet and propped her up. "I'll find your sister, miss."

Henry shuddered. On *Ivernia* they'd been warned that, during storms, people sometimes choked on their vomit or died of shock. *I watched out for that. She shouldn't be alone.*

"Nell. Please."

"Yes, of course, miss," Henry said, yanking a blanket from the other bed. "You must sit up. Stay warm. I'll send someone if I can't find… Nell?"

She nodded. Her lips were blue. He could hear her teeth chattering. "Your name."

"Henry. Henry Carin. Someone will be here, soon."

Waves washed his shoes as he fought his way forward. At times, he crawled on all fours. When he finally reached the chaotic stateroom, he spied an officer with a megaphone and stumbled over to explain the urgency of finding a Miss Nell Smith. He was immediately recruited to clear the stateroom of hazards and assist injured passengers. *Have they found Mary's sister?* He assured passengers they'd be safe, though he knew Lake Huron's bed was as littered as the stateroom floor. With bones. Thousands and thousands of bones.

* * *

Morning dawned, clear and calm, as if the storm had never happened. Despite his exhausting night of work and terror, Henry returned to the engine room; he couldn't let his mates down. Mary's name slipped off every shovelful of coal. *Did she survive?*

First Officer O'Connell descended the stairs, shouting Henry's name. The team stopped and stared. Someone handed him a towel. His shovel clanged on the metal floor.

"Well, men, Henry Carin's quick action saved a passenger from being swept overboard," O'Connell announced, above the engine's roar. "He also worked all night, clearing up, assisting passengers. In gratitude, Captain McIntyre is awarding the Black Gang a day's leave, with pay." He stopped and grinned. "The rest of the crew must clean the entire ship."

The Gang cheered, while the engineers grumbled. Everyone took a turn shaking Henry's hand. First Mate O'Connell didn't hesitate, though he removed his white glove.

"What a night, eh, boys?" He hated being the centre of attention.

"We've suffered no loss of life, once again, due in large part to this young man. How's it feel to be a hero, Henry?" Mr. O'Connell said. "A close shave, and no mistake. We've no structural damage, as far as we know. Only minor injuries." He stopped and his tone changed. "We've word that several ships were lost."

A chill ran the length of Henry's spine. Heat rose to his face and ears as he mumbled that any one of the Gang would've done the same.

"Don't be bashful, son. Captain McIntyre's most grateful you kept his record unblemished. He's the best mariner on the lakes."

"I believed that honour belonged to Captain Hamill of *Topinabee*." Henry laughed slightly, keeping his eyes on the floor.

"Ah, we men all exaggerate, don't we now?" O'Connell said, his eyes twinkling. "In more ways than one. Speaking of which, there's a lovely young thing topside, asking for you, Henry." He elbowed him lightly, handing him a coin. "Half a dollar from Captain McIntyre himself. Say, why don't you take the girl for a ride on a bicycle built for two, if you know what I mean?"

He snorted. The men chuckled and raised their eyebrows. Henry shook his head, uncomprehending. "You must get out more, lad. Listen, take the gal to the music hall, or out for a meal. Enjoy yourself."

"She's from money, sure," someone said. "At what this trip costs. You might be lucky, Henry."

"Ach, leave him be, lads. I've not seen such generosity from the captain in my ten years, not likely to again. You're a credit to the *Manitou*, Henry."

CHAPTER FORTY-ONE

The die has been cast.
Julius Caesar

September, 1909

EUPHEMIA, jaw clenched, straightened tablecloths, re-folded napkins, rearranged cutlery. *Dammit, Edward's usual half-assed job laying tables. This is a dining room, not a borstal. And where's Thomas? The fire needs tending. We must keep the customers warm. Christ, if I don't do it, it doesn't get done.*

Ten o'clock. Lunch service is just around the corner. Tom worked in the kitchen, prepping vegetables. He'd taken to cooking like a duck to water. He helped with the cooking while Sophie cleaned house and minded the toddlers. Running Phe's Roadhouse, the only diner near Mullet Lake, took time, organization, and energy. Euphemia loved it.

The dining room doors swung wildly as she marched into the kitchen calling Edward. He was slumped in a chair, wiping silverware. She waved her hand in his face. He turned away but sat up straighter. A knife fell to the floor. *That means a fight, Nan would say. Well, it's constant in here, any road.*

"Edward! The rooms want sweeping. Land's sake, how many times do I have to tell you, polishing can wait 'til afternoon? Guests are arriving soon." She wanted to kick him, despite her guilt over his lassitude and self-imposed silence. Perhaps because of it. Every time she looked at him, a carousel of dark thoughts wheeled in her mind. *If only I'd been more strict about the guns. I knew Edward never listened. I should have… I shouldn't have…*

The screen door hinge squealed. Thomas shuffled in and dropped the slop bucket. He'd shucked his boots off on the porch, but his socks were caked with mud.

"Thomas, I won't have you traipsing through the dining room leaving a mess. And how many times have I told you to oil that goddam hinge? It gets on my last nerve."

"Don't fash yerself, Pheme. The fishermen come for your pie, not clean floors," Thomas said. "And your winning personality, of course." He put a hand on Edward's shoulder. "Just the job, Ted. Why, I can see my face in that spoon."

Euphemia heard wagon wheels crunching on the gravel drive. "Edward, run see to the fire in the parlour." Euphemia rushed to the front door. "Ah, it's the Millers, look. John's with them, and all." Her mood lightened as she stepped on the verandah, straightening her apron. "Thomas, help Leon unload. I've business with Mrs. Miller and I must see John." She called behind her, "Tom, make the tea, would you." She smiled down as Mrs. Miller slowly ascended the stairs.

Euphemia led her into the vestibule, eager to show her the dining arrangements for paying guests. "I started with two tables and now, well, I can hardly believe it." She spread her arms to encompass the foyer, parlour, and dining room. She pointed to a table set for four. "Please, sit. Tom's bringing lunch."

"You have done well, lass. All down to your excellent cooking. Word travels fast when the food's good."

"Yes. I've had to resort to the veranda, some days. I'm

thinking of taking in boarders. Hiring a tutor for the children. Thomas never arranged schooling. Promises, promises. Pie-crust, as you said, Mrs. Miller. Speaking of which, would you like pie? My own rhubarb, rooted from yours." Tom poured tea. "Thank you for the sunflowers. Thomas says fishermen don't care about frippery. Tourists do, though. Besides, I like things nice."

"Bah! What's he know? Men! It's your business like the garden is mine. Leon wouldn't dare stick his oar in. Thomas does seem a bit, uh, subdued, may I say, since—"

"Yes, he minds his P's and Q's, all right. He knows I've the papers Alice signed. Almost burned them in a fit of pique, but then I thought better of it. The farm's in my name now so she can't take it, should she show up again wanting more. The tables have turned."

"Many tables, to be sure," Mrs. Miller said, smiling, lifting her teacup in salute. "To 'Phe's Roadhouse!' Great name. You're not farming at all now?"

"No. To hell with it. Pete's renting the land. I sold the team; Pete said they weren't being looked after properly. Thomas works on his shingle plane contraption. Tom cooks, Ann clears tables, Hugh washes dishes; they all help, but I want them educated."

"Funny you should say that… It so happens, I've a proposal for you. Regarding John."

"Sounds ominous. Is he behaving himself?"

"Good as gold. In fact, I sent some of his drawings to my cousin George in London. We agree; the boy has real talent. He found an art school that accepts boarders. I'd like to send him. He'll be a bit behind but will soon catch up. He's clever, but any longer will be too late." Euphemia lost her grip on the teacup. Mrs. Miller's eyes pleaded with her. "Euphemia, his gifts are wasted, here. He'll learn to paint, spend holidays with George's family, travel abroad, Paris, Rome—

Euphemia put up her hand, then brought it to her chest. "No, Mrs. Miller. So generous of you but absolutely not." She shook her head. "My sweet boy. He's twelve. Cross the ocean again, on his own? It was bad enough—"

"Of course not. I'd accompany him. First class is, well, a lot different than—anyway, time I visited family after twenty-some years." She brushed the tablecloth with her open hand and sought Euphemia's eyes. "I'd see him settled, dear. He's like a son to me."

Euphemia took a sharp intake of breath. "With respect, Mrs. Miller, he's not though, is he? He's mine. I'm an orphan, as you know. I always swore to keep my children by me." She looked left and right, lowering her voice. "I imagine you know what Mrs. Tucker did; orphaned her own grandchild. For what? Foolish pride. Reputation, bah! 'The father's Italian, they're too young.' She's ruined Sophie's life. My mother abandoned me, too. I never forgave her."

"With respect, Euphemia, perhaps you should."

John swept aside the velvet parlour curtains, carrying a vase of sunflowers taller than himself. He'd obviously been listening.

"I want to go to England, Mother. Da went down the mine at my age." He set the vase on the sideboard.

"You've no idea what it means, love, leaving kith and kin. You were too young to understand—," she said, her eyes smarting, "—the parting side of goodbye." She put a napkin over her mouth. Her blurry eyes fixed on Mrs. Miller; she could only see Nan, Grandad, and Jill. Then Henry. *He left me. My temper got the better of me. It's my fault. He hates me and Thomas, both. I'll never see him again. I can't bear for John to leave, too.*

"I'll send letters, drawings, photographs perhaps, I promise, Mother. I'm going. It's my life." John said, beginning to arrange the flowers.

Euphemia clenched the tines of her fork in her palm. "Fine. Go then. You're a man, now." She stood up. "As you say.

Thank you for the flowers again, Mrs. Miller. I must get lunch ready."

* * *

At breakfast, Sophie said, "The foxes were near last night. Did you hear them screaming? After the chickens, I'll bet."

Chapter Forty-Two

"Daisy, Daisy, give me your answer do.
I'm half-crazy, all for the love of you.
It won't be a stylish marriage,
for I can't afford a carriage.
But you'll look sweet, upon the seat
of a bicycle built for two."

"Daisy Bell,"
Harry Dacre, 1892

September, 1909

HENRY washed from the waist up with cold water. He borrowed a fresh shirt and a wool jacket, both a bit tight. His own white shirt was soiled from the night's work. He slicked down his hair before placing his cap, then took the stairs two at a time. He hoped Mary wouldn't notice his fingernails.

"Mr. Carin, is it?" A tall, rather plain-looking woman approached. Her dark brown hair was swept in a coif atop her head. A cameo adorned the collar of her striped poplin dress. "I'm so pleased to meet you." Her right hand was bony and withered. Henry tried to show no reaction, shaking it gently.

"I understand you pulled Mary from the jaws of Neptune last night. She was in such a state. I'm the long-lost sister, Nell." Her smiling brown eyes reassured him.

Mary stepped up from behind her. "Hello, Henry."

Henry held her hand a bit longer than was proper, distracted by her bright red hair lying in a thick plait over her shoulder. Her eyes were the colour of a sunlit lake. The pallor of her cheeks and a bruise on her cheek testified to her near miss.

"I can still see the wave, sweeping you away, Miss Smith. Glad I was there at the right moment. I barely nabbed you." He felt suddenly dizzy, as if the wave were upending them both. Heat rushed to his face, and he remembered to remove his cap. Mary's eyes dropped to his hands. He tried to hide them, too late. Sweat beaded on his forehead and trickled down his neck. They'd figure him for a stoker. He suspected they would politely close the conversation, maybe offer a tip. He'd refuse. Knowing he'd saved a life, Mary's life, was reward enough.

"So are we. You were heaven-sent," Nell said. She turned around. "We must send Uncle a telegram, Mary. I heard ships were lost overnight. Duncan and Grandad will be frantic. We won't mention your close call." She touched Henry's arm. "May we treat you to a meal in gratitude, Mr. Carin? The least we can do."

"Oh no, just 'Henry,' please, miss. That's very kind, but no need. I—"

"Fiddlesticks," Nell said. Henry smiled at her spunk. "The steamship company is billeting passengers at the Grand Hotel while they repair the ship. Please join us. Have you ever dined there?"

Henry shook his head. *Not bloody likely. They wouldn't look at the likes of me. Still, a chance to get to know Mary better? I'll take it, not to mention a meal at The Grand Hotel. Fancy, Mum would say.* He picked up their bags and led them down the gangplank.

Amongst the dozens of horse-drawn carriages dockside,

he spied his friend Paul's team, standing quietly in their traces. Every trip to Mackinac, he'd visit the carriage rank, willingly grooming the horses, and chat with the men. "Motor cars are banned on Mackinac, ladies. Just so. The two don't mix in my opinion," he said, and went on to share details of Percheron care and training. Mary nodded and smiled, while Nell spoke to Paul.

Suddenly he reined himself in, embarrassed by his chatter. Helping them into the open carriage, he decided he'd leave them at the hotel. He was out of his depth.

They clip-clopped down wide thoroughfares lined with stately buildings and tall trees draped in fall rainbows. The light September breeze carried the crisp apple scent of autumn. Sunshine warmed their shoulders and set Mary's hair to shimmering in the tiny curls that edged her braid. She smiled across at him, pointing out palatial homes and charming gardens until they arrived at the Grand Hotel. As he assisted the ladies, Henry clenched his jaw, trying to steady his nerves and keep his mouth shut. He could barely feel his feet on the ground.

The gleaming white structure seemed to float upon a lake of grass. Landscaped gardens swept up to the famous porch where people wove in and out like spectres. On stopovers, Henry had admired the six-hundred-foot verandah, but only from a distance. Tall windows punctuated the high walls. The building's white pillars lent the appearance of a wooden steamship, topped off with an elevated crows' nest flying the Stars and Stripes. Mary and Nell seemed awestruck. They stood at the foot of the red-carpeted stairs, clutching their reticules, staring at the front door. Paul waved goodbye, and still, nobody moved.

Nell was the first to shake herself. They reached the lobby, and she headed to the desk while Mary and Henry sat as upright as churchgoers on the porch's easy chairs. Henry was too nervous to wait inside, thinking people would mock his ill-fitting clothes. He might even be asked to leave. *Should I tell Mary I can't stay?* Gazing out at the gardens bursting with colour, he could smell flowers. *When will you get such a chance, again? Take your luck where you find it, Joe would say.* He felt Mary's eyes on him. *She can likely tell I don't belong here.*

"Where do you hail from, Henry?" she said, smoothing the chair's upholstered arm.

He kept his voice low. "Isle of Man. Do you know it? Most folks don't."

"Oh, I thought your accent might be Scots, but it's a bit softer. My mother's family originates from the Isle of Colonsay. They came by the *Henry Clay,* in '59. Out of Liverpool."

He smiled, excited at the connection. "We came out of Liverpool too, by *Ivernia,* in '05. You're an islander from across the pond, too."

She grinned. "That was nearly fifty years ago, Henry, unless I look young for my age." She primped her hair, plainly teasing. "No. My mother was actually born on the ship, and they named her after it." A smile lit her eyes. "They called her 'Henrietta' though." He looked down with embarrassment. "My family left one island for another, so we're islanders, I guess. I was born—"

Nell rushed toward them, full tilt. "Well, we've no view and one double bed, but Mary, wait 'til you see the linens, the carpets, the striped wallpaper, and plush furniture. Oh, Mary, the colours, the style! To stay in this famous hotel! I'd never have dreamt… something good came of that trial. A silver lining, so to speak."

She paused to fan herself with her hand. "Gosh, it's hot. Maybe it's just me." She laughed. "Our meals are covered; no tipping allowed the bellboy said, a bit snootily. I'm so hungry, aren't you?"

The waiter led them to a centre table in the vast dining room. They readily tucked into a savoury lunch of soup, roast beef, and blueberry pie. To make conversation, Henry shared the Mackinac history he'd picked up. The women leaned over their plates to hear above the chatter.

"Like Isle of Man, Mackinac is a faery isle. There's a giant hole in Arch Rock near the eastern shore where they are known to fly. A beautiful spot—"

Mary's green eyes widened. "You believe in faeries, do you, Henry?"

"We do on Man." He answered softly. *Is she scoffing at me?* "It's part of life, there. Maybe faeries only exist on islands, like the Isle of Man, Ireland—" He cleared his throat. "There are other spirits here, too. The first people's Great Spirit once lived in a cave. A friend said they once came here from all around to honour 'Gitche Manitou.' Our ship bears his name."

"As does our island," Nell said.

Henry's head shot up. "Excuse me? Aren't you from Chicago?"

"We're from Manitoulin Island, or *'The* Manitoulin,' as it's called, though I've never known why. Mary and I will return to Chicago tomorrow, and then go home to Canada." With a shudder, she rubbed her arms, twisting her right hand around her shoulder. "Though I fear setting foot aboard."

"I do understand, Miss Smith, believe me, but please don't worry. Captain McIntyre's the best. He's never lost a passenger, not a one."

Nell toasted him with her teacup. "Thanks to you, this time."

Henry brought the teacup to his lips, extending his pinky, aware of Mary's intent gaze. He carefully set the cup in the saucer. *Mary's chin is as fine as this gold-rimmed china. Da used to trace Mum's chin with his knuckle. I'd forgotten that.*

Nell dabbed her lips with the linen napkin, covering a yawn. "Would you accompany Mary to buy souvenirs, Henry? I must have a lie-down, soon's I send the telegram. This whole experience has worn me to a frazzle."

She patted his arm with her left hand. "Since you saved her

life, we'll trust you," she said, smiling into his eyes.

She'd read his thoughts. *Was this seemly?* He promised they'd come straight back.

"Oh, dinner time's fine. Go. Enjoy yourselves."

During the carriage ride back to Main Street, Henry left commentary to the driver. He drew in his shoulders, avoiding contact. Glancing at Mary's dress, he took in the plain blue sateen, the hand-embroidered bodice. No hat. No gloves. Simple hairstyle. Nell had mentioned the "free" hotel, and her dress was cotton, decorated with buttons and bows. He recalled Mum's embarrassment about her brown suit in Boston. His heart lifted.

"Let's get fudge, Mary. Fresh-made, creamy and sweet. Ever had it?" He helped her alight and twined his arm in hers, escorting her like a lady.

"Yum! We make it with maple syrup and cream at home. I love it."

They visited souvenir shops, many selling Chippewa handicrafts. She admired the flower designs in porcupine quills on birch bark boxes but opted for a braid of sage and cedar.

"The scent will remind me of Mackinac," she said, pressing her nose into the twisted herbs. "I'll keep it in my 'hopeless' chest, as Verna calls it." She snorted, tapping Henry with it as they turned to leave. He opened the door with its tinkling bell and showed her out.

"Wait there a moment, please, Mary."

The shopkeeper bit his half-dollar when he paid for the box. When he rejoined her on the boardwalk, Mary's delighted exclamation startled him. "Look, Henry! A bicycle built for two! I've always wanted to see one."

She began to hum a tune. He raised his hands.

"Gosh, I'm surprised you don't know it." She sang a few bars in a warm alto. "Nell plays it on the piano. I'd love to—" Her eyes tracked the bicycle.

"You've a lovely voice, Mary. You would 'look sweet upon

the seat,' but the fact is, I've never driven a bicycle. I'd topple us in a trice. Let's have tea, instead. My treat, this time." Henry guided her toward a teashop he'd visited on occasion. As they crossed the threshold, he glimpsed a tiny, yellow poplar leaf on the sill. He slipped it in his pocket.

Over strawberry scones with clotted cream, Henry focused on Mary's history.

"Well, we're on Manitoulin Island. Straight across from Michigan as the crow flies. Except a crow couldn't fly that far," she said, with a slight laugh. "Largest fresh-water island in the world, if anyone cares to know. Surely you've heard of it, being on the lake?"

"Yes, I've a mate told me about it." He tried to sound casual.

"Papa's family's Scottish, like Mother's. He and his brother, Jim, built the church and the schoolhouse since they were the first white settlers in Campbell Township, in '76. Mother's family emigrated on the *Henry Clay*. I think I told you. 'Henrietta' was her middle name. Everyone called her 'Etta,' but to Papa, she was 'Kate,' for her given name, 'Catherine.' Funny, eh?"

"I know nicknames." He deliberately rolled his eyes. "Had an uncle who called everyone by a nickname. Mine was 'Harry.' Hated it. So, your mother's… passed?"

"Yes, I barely remember her." She blew on her tea. "I was four; Nell, nine. Nell had polio when she was little, but I don't remember. We've a brother, Melvin. Mother's family adopted him after she died in childbirth. Her folks blame Papa. How was it his fault? There's no doctor nearby." She looked down at her lap, fingering the braid beside her plate. "Papa always says he adored her. Just twenty-eight, she was." Henry sensed that she was lost in memories. He didn't want her to stop.

"Mother's brother, Duncan, calls our father 'the old boar.' That's mean. My Uncle Jim, on the other hand, Papa's brother, is downright cruel. He beats his wife, who is my mother's sister. She runs away but always goes back. A right bunch." She took a bite of scone and dabbed her mouth. "Grandfather says my mother married the devil and her sister married the devil's brother. He's got no use for either one. Two brothers married two sisters. Strange, eh?"

"Happens, I guess." Henry shrugged. "But your father can't be the devil; my uncle, Thomas, took that job."

She laughed, displaying small, straight teeth. Her green eyes sparkled in the light from the lace-covered window. *Her laugh's as musical as that bell above the door. Her eyes match the Irish Sea. A rare colour—*

"There's more than one devil in this world, I'm betting." Mary looked down and swirled her tea. "Grandma tells fortunes from tea leaves. I wonder what ours say." She tipped the dregs toward the saucer.

A waiter scurried over to lift the teapot. Henry hurried to refill their cups. "My Nan could hear the *Little Ones* give warnings, though we didn't always listen. Seems the old ways run in both our families. How'd you get from Manitoulin to the *Manitou?*"

"Well, Duncan, Mom's brother, left Manitoulin to attend the Chicago World's Fair in '93, opened a restaurant, and came to riches. Now, every fall, he sends a train ticket for me and Nell. They say I look like my mother. I can't tell. We've only the one photograph. They want us girls to live with them. I would, but we can't leave Papa." She pressed her lips together. "We're not happy, though. We're stuck there with Papa's wife, Verna, and our bratty stepbrothers. She rules the roost. We never go anywhere except once a year. This time Uncle Duncan added a treat, the trip to Mackinac. So lovely, until the storm came up."

"We were homebodies, too, not by choice. I've only seen more of the world by working on steamships." He turned the conversation back. "Why'd your family settle on Manitoulin in the first place? Seems awful remote."

"Cheap land. All the land belonged to the native people, then the government took it and sold it off. Not many folks have come. Land still goes for fifty cents an acre."

Henry clattered his teacup in the saucer. "You're pulling my leg, surely."

"It's true. Several Colonsay families went, hoping to better themselves. Colonsay's desolate, I've been told, but what did they get? An island, sure, but no faeryland, believe me, Henry. Isolated. Lonely. Papa has to work in the bush, logging all winter, to keep the farm going. Nothing there but rock, wild animals, and trees. You seem interested. What on earth for?"

"I'm saving to buy a farm. We Manx believe in faeries, as I said, and I want to return to an island." He paused. *I hope she won't think me daft. In for a penny…* He plunged ahead. "My mate, Joseph, is Ojibwe. He says his people call Manitoulin 'Spirit Island.' I'm curious since you're from there—"

"You think there's faeries there?" She shook her head. "Well, I've lived there my whole life, and I've never seen a one. Or heard tell of one, either."

"P'rhaps you don't know where to look. Besides, I wouldn't say there's nothing there." Henry searched her eyes, hoping she understood his meaning. Her face flushed. She removed the napkin from her lap and made to stand. The waiter pulled out her chair. Henry rose, swallowing hard. She excused herself to go to the powder room while he paid the bill. When she joined him outside, he hastily extinguished his cigarette.

The return trip passed in awkward silences broken by attempts at conversation begun simultaneously. At one point, Mary laughed at their simultaneous interruption and the driver gifted them a smile. Mary blushed again. *He thinks we're sweethearts. I've made a right mess of this.* He fingered the tiny box in his pocket.

The Grand Hotel seemed to stretch its arms in welcome. Asking the carriage driver to wait, he walked Mary up the red staircase, stopping before the massive front doors.

He let out his breath and said, "Forgive me, Mary. Being too forward, I mean. I don't step out much…"

"No need to apologize. It's just that I… I'm—"

"Still in shock, I expect. I'm so sorry for—for your frightful experience."

"Henry, you saved my life. I'm in your debt." Mary took his arm and squeezed it gently. "Please come say goodbye?" She smirked. "Nell's taken a shine to you. We'll find her in the lounge, I expect."

Nell was seated in an elegant, wing-backed chair sipping a brandy.

"Nice to see the roses in your cheeks, Mary. Sit, have a sherry." She gestured for a waiter. "Verna, our stepmother, never lets us imbibe, Henry. Let me offer you a drink." Henry arranged the chairs. "Are you bound for home, Henry, at the end of the season?"

"No, ma'am. I work winters with the loggers on Bois Blanc."

"Can't you find something else?" Mary said. "Papa hates logging. Says it's brutal."

Nell clucked her tongue. "Mary! You mustn't pry. It's none of our business."

"So's stoking coal, Mary, but it's a living," he said. "I'm saving for a farm."

"Do you have family, Henry? You mentioned an uncle. Where are they?"

"Land's sake, Mary. Can't you see you're making Henry ill at ease? Let's change the subject. Would you like pie with ice cream? I love ice cream, don't you?"

The waiter arrived. Still standing, Henry slid the two glasses toward Mary.

"Thank you kindly, Miss Smith… Nell. Best get back. My free day's over. Thank you for the lovely meal. It was a pleasure meeting you both."

He leaned down to shake Mary's hand, capturing her gaze. "I'm glad you're safe, Mary. '*Cair Vie*,' we say in Manx. It means 'Go safely.' I hope you get to ride a double bicycle, someday. I'll remember the song always."

She broke eye contact but kept hold of his hand. He slowly let go, nodded at Nell, and replaced his cap.

"Nell, would you please see me out?"

Chapter Forty-Three

"Lovely Kitty – Ben-my-chree – I am your most
devoted admirer, your slave. In me you see no
mortal, but a fairy mannikin, whose heart has for
long past been truant to his race, and devoted,
oh, I cannot tell how truly and intensely fixed
on thee."

The Phynodderree: A Tale of Fairy Love
Edward Callow, 1882

September - October, 1909

MANITOULIN. Manitoulin. Just a few more weeks of stoking, and he'd go there. Locate the Smiths. See if Mary had any interest in him. He hummed the bicycle song. It lent strength to his arms, back, and torso as he shovelled. Imagining himself around the hearth, swaying to Grandad's fiddle, he started singing a favourite song:

The Phynodderee arose at dawn.
He threw the grass toward the left...

Soon his team joined in, keeping time with the stoking bell. They picked up the words, enamoured by a tale of faeries and elves. Then some men launched into songs with words as filthy as the smuts on their faces. Laughter blazed like the furnaces; four hours flew by. Word spread. Lieutenant O'Conner dubbed them 'The Singing Stokers,' and the captain awarded them a half-dollar as encouragement. Henry squirrelled it away with his poker winnings. Thomas' teachings came in handy again.

Man-i-tou-lin. He rolled the word around in his mouth like Macintosh toffee. He'd never noticed the word's similarity to Man, short for Manannán. *Both islands were named for a god. Are there faeries, too? I'll be able to write Nan and Grandad once I've found a home.*

He dared to approach First Officer O'Connell when he appeared for his next inspection. Hesitantly, he asked about freighters crossing Lake Huron to Manitoulin. "For work after the season, sir," he hastened to add.

"There's plenty. *Presque Isle*, she's a fine vessel, now. We'll give you a good reference, Henry, when the time comes. Mind you debark before November, though."

"Why? Does Huron freeze over?"

"Rarely. She's fed by both Superior and Michigan, so currents flow continuously. But our latest September squall was nothing to the November witch. 'Bitch,' I call her; thirty-foot waves, cyclone-force winds. Legend says there's a monster underwater near the mouth of the Serpent River responsible." He brushed coal dust from his sleeves. "There's a ships' graveyard out past the straits."

Oh, God, after that close call, dare I chance it?

"Not to worry, son. There's plenty of work on the docks in Owen Sound. 'Little Liverpool,' they call it. You've been to Liverpool, yes?"

Henry made a sour expression, remembering the stench, the rabble, the rats…

"Well, it's not that cesspool, but close. Lots of pubs. My favourite's the Bucket of Blood. Can't miss it. Wild as hell. Ha! When the town declared prohibition, a few years back, 'twas a boon to the bootleggers." His eyes twinkled. "There's good fun to be had in all four pubs on Damnation Corners. Watch out for the ladies, mind. Keep your eye on your wallet."

The lieutenant shook his hand, wearing his glove. "Best of luck, Henry. You're a fine young man. You'll be missed."

* * *

In Owen Sound, he hired on with Canadian Pacific as a stevedore. Wages were good, so he stayed put, fearing Huron's storms. Besides, Mary had said her father was in the bush all winter; it wouldn't do to arrive unannounced, her father absent. Now that his goal was in sight, he relaxed and made friends. After ferrying cargo around in the bitter wind all day, the stevedores frequented the "restaurants," where strong spirits were served in coffee cups. The men could not entice him upstairs, however. He'd sip a drink for a while, then return to his rooming house, walking alone down quiet, snow-bound streets. He bought a violin in a pawn shop, determined to learn to play by ear, like Grandad. Picking out tunes like the "bicycle" song, he tried not to disturb fellow boarders, fearing eviction.

He perused the landlady's collection of magazines, admiring the motto of one: 'While there's LIFE, there's hope.' He knew John would appreciate the cover art, especially August, 1907. Two lovers flew heart-shaped kites, strings intertwined high in the clouds. The girl had red hair like Mary. She lounged on the grass, her smile beckoning, wearing a lacy dress. *That's what Mary ought to have…*

Lying in bed, he snapped the lid on a small, blue velvet box. Open, shut, open, shut.

"Buy the best you can afford, young man," the pawn shop owner had said. "You never get a second chance to make a good first impression."

How does a man go about asking a girl to marry him? If only I could ask Da. I wish I'd asked him so many questions.

When January dropped its heavy cloak over the harbour, Henry could barely get out of bed. He moaned and groaned like an old man as he donned layers of clothing and shuffled to the dock. In his heavy boots, his legs wobbled with exhaustion. *Don't tell me I'm going down the slope like Da.* He consulted his best mate, George.

"Perfectly natural. Happens to the best of us come winter. We won't see the sun 'til May," George said. "Nine feet of snow coming yet, minimum." He narrowed his eyes at Henry. "Start a hobby, Henry. This climate's depressing. Me, I weave rag rugs to sell. I'll teach you if you like."

The nights seemed interminable. He imagined the family passing the winter nights in the parlour. *Mom's knitting, John's drawing, Tom and Ann are playing checkers, Eliza and Hugh are asleep upstairs. Sophie's making popcorn. And Edward, what's he doing? Can he talk, yet? Is Sal dozing by the fire, or… not? And Thomas.* He clenched his jaw. *I hope he's dead.*

Trolling Damnation Corners, he discovered back rooms in taverns like The Pig's Ear, where poker games earned him cash faster than braiding rugs. One night, a dark-haired girl attached herself to his shoulder, commenting on his luck. He avoided her, but she followed him out to the privy.

Henry held up his hand. "Listen, miss, I'm not looking for… I've got a girl, see—"

She clicked her tongue and smirked at him. "Look, I'm just warning you; one of those fellas is a damn cheat. Watch your back. There's been knifings, hereabouts." She tucked her long black hair behind her ears and pointed with her cigarette. "The big one with the beard? You're pissing him off. Don't cross that sonovabitch. Take your winnings and skedaddle."

"Oh, thanks, I guess, uh… I'm Henry," he said, extending his hand. "Much obliged. Too bad I can still be duped, though

I learned poker from the best liar there is. Jesus Christ!" He scrunched bills into his pocket and caught her gaze. "Sorry, miss. I've worked the docks too long."

"Bah, I'm no gilded lily," she said. Her red lipstick emphasized the dark stains on her teeth, but her smile warmed her brown eyes. "Name's Tina."

"Can I buy you a drink, Tina? Least I can do."

"I should say so. Gotta earn my keep in this dump."

Her elbows stabbed the polished mahogany bar where she leaned over her mug. As he reached across to pay the barkeep, he glimpsed her spine, a row of clamshells beneath a thin, cotton sheath. The bony hand clutching her glass looked older than her face. He was curious about her age. He knew her occupation.

That night, he talked and drank beer for hours, while Tina listened, nodded, and smoked. Followed by the next and the next. His spirits lightened, anticipating the day's end. Her bubbly laugh, dark eyes, and the smoky scent of her hair when she tossed it back, all intrigued him. People would call her a "loose woman:" unbound hair, no corset. He didn't care. Her company at the bar cost money in drinks for them both. No matter. Always more where that came from; he'd pull an extra shift, pick up a game, braid a rug, even, just so they could pass the time.

"I ain't surprised you got a sweetheart, Henry," Tina said one night. "You stand out in more than height. Hair black as a raven. Those eyes. Mercy! Is everyone so pretty in your country?"

He laughed at the word "pretty." He hunched over the bar and spoke into his beer glass. "Well, Mary's my sweetheart, she just doesn't know it yet." Then he threw his shoulders back and straightened to his full height, six foot four. "As to the Manx, well, yes, we are a fine-looking lot. My father was the handsomest man I've ever seen. My mother's an orphan from England and never knew her kin. She was—is, I mean—yes, she's all right, I guess. My nan says everyone 'takes after' a relative. Who are you like, Tina?"

"Dunno. My father could've been anybody. My mother wasn't—well, the johnnies don't mind your face. I grew up in a brothel." She paused to remove a bit of tobacco from her tongue. "No history."

Henry took a long drink, thinking of his childhood in a cottage filled with love and comforting traditions. "Mum said her childhood was 'no picnic,' so I understand a little, Tina. Must've been—"

"Least I'm never homesick. Coulda' done with more schoolin' though," she said, taking a puff. She leaned against his arm. "Talk about Manx, Henry. I love your stories of the faeries."

He happily described the daily pilgrimage up Faery Hill with Nan, who could understand the faeries. When he said the *Little Ones* stole things, even babies, unless given their due, she nearly dropped her cigarette.

"I thought faeries were always nice, granting wishes and such. I know what I'd wish for."

Suddenly the man on the next stool elbowed his ribs. "Who you callin' fairy? Step outside, asshole. I'll show you a thing or three." He swung and knocked Henry off his perch.

Tina helped Henry to his feet. "Jesus, Matt, he wasn't talkin' to you. Bugger off."

"Shaddup, slut. Obvious what you're after." The man shoved her aside.

Henry clenched his fist and smashed the man's chin. He'd never slugged anyone. His right hook knocked Matt over. Nose spurting blood, he smashed a bottle against the bar and brandished it. Henry's foot slipped when he swiped the bottle away from his face. Matt lunged. Tina threw out her leg and kicked him in the balls.

"Fuck off, Matt. I mean it. C'mon, Henry." She grabbed Henry's swollen, bleeding hand. "That needs bandaging."

Henry flinched, tasting bile. He followed her upstairs. She

unlocked the door with a key from around her neck. Directing Henry to sit on the bed, she lit the coal-oil lamp. She pulled the drapes shut to close out the snow patting the window. Henry shivered, his ragged breath forming clouds in his face. After starting the kerosene heater, Tina poured water into the basin on the washstand. She dabbed his knuckles with a wet cloth. He winced.

"Ice-cold. Brings the swelling down," she said, in her low, smoky voice. He apologized for dripping blood on her floor.

"This ain't the Ritz Carlton, for fuck's sake." She wrapped his hand in a scarf she yanked off her mirror. "Your first bar fight, I assume. Coulda been worse. Matt's a goddamn brute. 'El Dirty,' they call him; don't fight fair. You've bested him now. He'll steer clear."

She lifted his wrist to her lips. "Better? You're no worse for wear."

Henry trembled. From the cold, the aftermath of the fight, or the kiss?

She drew back. "Relax, I won't eat you." The sideways grin and raised eyebrows startled him. "Get those wet things off, then crawl into bed. You stink like a brewery. I'll hang your clothes above the heater."

"No, I won't stay. You've been very kind, but it wouldn't be right—"

"Says who? Your ma keep tabs on you, does she?" She paused. "Listen, it's a blizzard out. Do as I say." She clicked her tongue. "It's like you was born yesterday. You really are from somewhere else."

He shed everything, even his underwear. The sheets were damp. He curled into a ball.

"Shove a bum, chum. Move over. Straighten out." Tina lay down, fully clothed, tugging on the counterpane. She wrapped him in her arms. Her hands and feet were ice, but her body generated more heat than the tiny stove.

When his teeth finally stopped chattering, he rolled over. Her eyes gleamed in the lamplight. Lifting her head with his undamaged hand, he kissed her. She began to kiss his neck, his shoulders. Her lips were soft, her hands stroked his sides, avoiding his erection. She wriggled out of her dress and bloomers, making a tent of the blankets. Immediately the chill made them both shiver. He sneezed. With a laugh, she swivelled, draping the counterpane across her back as she straddled him. The quilt pooled around her hips when she sat up.

"We don't have to, you know. If you're worried, that is," she said. "I can satisfy you without—"

Henry moved to put a finger to her lips, then squealed as his bandage bloomed. He encircled her waist and sat up, hoisting her into his lap. She tasted of smoke. Her straight brown hair brushed his smooth chest. She pushed down, arching her back. For the first time in forever, he was warm.

Chapter Forty-Four

Faggys ta my lheiney aghny sniessey ta my chrackan:
Near is my shirt, but nearer is my skin.

April - May, 1910

ASKING around, Henry learned that the earliest steamer crossing to Manitoulin was *Macassa*, bound for Toronto, with a stop-over at Manitowaning on Manitoulin. He was impressed by the ship's beauty and extraordinary length. Tina was not when he told her.

"So, you're really going then? Off to find your 'sweetheart.' When I'm right here." They lay on the bed, having just made love. She twirled her fingers in his hair, playfully at first, then yanked his forelock and sat up. "We've been together all winter." Her voice broke. "You were using me, like all the rest." She smacked his arm. "I took you for better. More fool, me."

Henry reached up to hold her. He smoothed her tangled hair, feeling her heart racing against his chest. Her shoulders heaved as she sobbed into his neck. He gently pushed her back to find her brown eyes.

"I did tell you, Tina, from the start, that I intended to leave, come spring. I'm not cut out to be a stevedore. Stoking will kill a man. I want a farm." He tucked a strand of hair behind her ear. "What do you want?"

"To go to Toronto. Become a dancer, even a waitress, in a decent place… We could take *Macassa* together—"

"See? We've each got our dreams. But they're different." He shook his head. "I could never live in a city, Tina. Never. Even if Mary won't have me, Manitoulin's my chance to buy land and get a foothold somewhere. I'm coming on for nineteen. Time's a wastin.'"

"What the fuck?" She flew out of the bed and picked up an ashtray. "I was a waste of time, was I? Get out, you prick. Don't you ever come back, or I'll sic Matt on you." She hurled the ashtray and then his shirt at his head. She grabbed his pants hanging on a chair. "Payment's due. Never charged you a dime, though I get a good price." She pelted bills on the bed.

Fighting the counterpane, Henry struggled up. "Go ahead, take it all, Tina. I want to help you. I never offered because I thought, well, we're friends, it didn't seem right—"

"Friends?" she shrieked. "Well, Friend," she said, sneering. "This ain't enough. Gimme your watch and that ring, too. Wha'd you say, 'bout them faeries? They steal unless they get their due. Too bad you didn't see my wings. Right here." She smacked each shoulder.

"Not the ring." Henry covered his left hand. "Please, Tina. It was my grandfather's—"

"Cry me a river. Turn it over, or I'll scream the place down."

✳ ✳ ✳

Aboard *Macassa*, Henry became a passenger for the first time since *Ivernia*. *What would Mum think to see me dressed in a suit, bowler hat and all?* He'd splurged on several purchases before leaving Owen Sound. Having followed Lieutenant O'Connell's advice, his savings were safe. Tina didn't get the lot, though she'd taken enough. He touched his pinkie, feeling for his missing ring. The deck heaved, and he lost his footing.

"You all right, sir?" a young crewman asked.

"Oh, yes. Fine, fine. Got a nasty list, don't she? The lake isn't even rough today."

"Five years ago, they added 23 feet to carry more freight. Makes her unstable," he said, putting a finger to his lips. "But you didn't hear it from me, mind."

"No, I don't mind. If I have my way, this'll be my last time on a steamer." Henry said, widening his stance.

"Where you headed, sir?"

"Just Henry, please. And you are?"

"James, James Marshall. Glad to know you, Henry."

"I'm bound for the Manitoulin. To purchase land, I hope."

"Oh."

"And?" Henry frowned at the subdued response, as another roll took him off-guard. "What is it?"

James steered him to the rail and stood alongside, glancing over his shoulder.

"Mustn't be caught fraternizing," he whispered. Henry nodded. "You do know Manitoulin's haunted?"

"So I've heard. What do you know about it?"

"My friend Richard's got family over there. He says the settlers' diseases killed so many of their people, the survivors burned everything and made tracks. Nobody lived there for over a hundred years. Except ghosts."

"How terrible." The hairs lifted on the back of his neck. *Not faeries. Ghosts.*

"Then some government joker got the bright idea to resettle all different tribes together. 'Civilize' them away from whites. Complete disaster. Now the government's pretty much giving the land away. Why do you think it's so cheap? 'If it sounds too good to be true, it is,' the saying goes. You're really set on the idea?"

Henry frowned. "I've got my reasons. Still, I appreciate the information, James."

"Well, back to work. Best of luck, Henry."

Using his sea legs to steady himself, he carefully extracted a paper from his breast pocket. He'd written Pete from the rooming house, sharing his location and plans. Just before his departure, the landlady had given him an envelope.

April 15, 1910

Dear Henry,

> *Pete give me your letter, as you know. Good to here your news, Henry. How you bin? Four and half years since you left, I rekin. John, Ann and I missed you a lot. Pete told me Mum asked about you. He told her you was alive. Hard to tell all that's gone on in a letter. Sad news first. Nan died. The cottage is sold. Grandad lives with Jill. Mum and Thomas are married. That sounds bad, but things is different here now. I wish you'd come home. Please. We could hunt and fish. Edward won't hunt. He don't do much a-tall. Hugh, why he's just seven and Ann's a girl. Guess you know that. John doesn't live here anymore. Eliza cries a lot. I still hate Thomas. Please come back. If you go again, take me. My birthday's April 10, case you forget. I'm a man now.*

> *Your brother*
> *Tom*

Nan and Grandad, gone? Mom married that bastard? Edward, still not right in the head? John left home? At twelve years old? Maybe I ought to go back, get the low-down from Pete and Mrs. Miller, grab Tom, find somewhere else to live. Maybe Manitoulin isn't the best place, after all...

He re-folded the letter and tucked it away to the sound of the ship's horn.

Chapter Forty-Five

Foddym gra gyn danjeyr dy bee dy chooilley nhee dy mie:
All will be well and all manner of things shall be well.

MACASSA moored at Manitowaning only briefly to exchange passengers and crates. Henry was surprised to see live turkeys being loaded aboard. *Mrs. Miller's guard turkey Tom wouldn't have stood for that.*

Standing on the dock, seeking his bearings, Henry heard his name shouted from the gangplank. James and another man headed toward him.

"Glad I caught you, Henry. This here's my friend, Richard. He'll help you. His auntie has a rooming house in town."

"Thank you kindly. Good to meet you."

Richard displayed his filthy hands. Henry grabbed the right one in his shovel-handle grip. "Ha! I'm a stoker, too. *Topinabee* and *Manitou.* We're from the Black Gang, the both of us."

"I knew you wasn't a toff, Henry," James said, slapping his back. "Say, listen, we've got a few hours off. I'm starving. Your auntie serves food, don't she, Richard?"

Henry booked a room with Auntie Irene for a month. Distances here didn't compare with Man, he learned, and there were no trains. Mary's township, near Providence Bay, was some thirty miles from Manitowaning. One night at dinner, he met Ted, a carter who delivered goods along the concession roads.

"I'll bring you, son. Takes no more'n a day, even with stops. Faster by boat, but this way, you'll see the countryside."

"Exactly what I'm after. I'm looking to purchase land."

"You don't say. You're kinda young—you've family there, do you?"

"No. I am slightly acquainted with the Smiths."

"Oh."

"You sound… skeptical, is it? Is their place haunted? I heard stories on *Macassa*."

"Depends. John Smith, or his brother, Jim?"

"Don't know. There's Mary and a sister, Nell."

"Ho, ho, so that's the attraction." He snorted, almost expelling a mouthful of food. "Well, well, they're nice girls. Mary's pretty as a picture. Old man's a miserable old cob, though. Tough as owl shit. First haw-eater out that way."

"Haw-eater?" The table of men burst into laughter, elbowing one another. He shrugged. "What's so damn funny?"

"You ain't run into that expression yet?"

The landlady interjected as she leaned over Henry's shoulder to pour tea. "Nasty saying. Why, if it hadn't been for hawthorn berries, we'd have died come winter. It's the only fruit we had. This jam you like so well? Haw berries."

"Oh, you mean hawthorn? They're on the Isle of Man, too. Bad luck to fall them, we say." *Because the faeries live beneath their roots.* He held his tongue.

"Smith must'a chopped down plenty, then." Ted lit a cigarette, rocked back in his chair, and studied Henry. "His first wife died young. The one he has now… Cripes! Mean as a barn cat. Sure you wanna get mixed up with them?" He reached over to collect a toothpick. "His brother Jim's even worse—"

"First thing tomorrow?"

* * *

As they trundled along, Ted's continual banter distracted Henry from his fears. Somewhat. *Smith has a mean reputation, not just amongst his family but also the islanders. Maybe he'll come at me with a gun.* He tried focussing on the scenery. Silver birch trees shimmered in the rising sun, their freshly minted leaves scenting the air. Overhead, a hawk's cry reminded him of wheeling skylarks over Port Erin. Beside a small lake, they ate a sandwich and admired colourful ducks and black and white loons bobbing on the clear water. Henry pointed out a blue heron, hiding in the cattails.

"Did you know herons use bait? They drop worms or dragonflies on the water, wait for the fish to investigate, then, whoop, quick as you like…" Ted swept his hand into a fist. "Watch. Smart as ravens."

Like a Mackinac cabbie, Ted readily offered his knowledge of Manitoulin's people, animals, and plants. Henry started to relax. *His team is well-trained and cared for. Seems a likely fellow.*

"Lucky I ran into you, Ted. Amazing to meet someone acquainted with the Smiths on such a huge island."

"It's big but small, if you catch my drift. I know pretty much everybody, hereabouts. Job's easy, except in winter. I get treated to meals and distribute mail, so folks often share their news. What's your story, Henry?"

"I met Mary aboard the *Manitou*. Decided to look her up." He hoped his face didn't reveal too much. "And Nell too, of course."

"Sure. You come bearing gifts." Ted eyed the brown paper envelope on Henry's lap.

"Just some material," Henry said, covering it with his hands.

"Methinks you are crafty as that heron." He laughed, displaying stained teeth, before launching a stream of tobacco juice over the side. *Like Pete. Filthy habit.* His stomach rumbled.

"Good idea bringing supplies, not showing up empty-handed. Say, is that your stomach I hear? Still hungry? Ah, to be young again." He clucked and the horses picked up the pace. "Keep your shirt on, boy. Next stop Mrs. Macneil's, and a damn good feed. Here, a chaw of tobacco'll calm your nerves."

Henry waved his hand. After lunch, as the horses clip-clopped into the afternoon, Henry's head dropped on his chest, and he snoozed in the sun. Suddenly, Ted shook his arm. "We're here." He grinned sideways. "I'll come help smooth the way."

Through a cloud of dust, Henry recognized Nell hanging clothes on a line in the yard. He stood up and waved. As the wagon grumbled up to the house, she came running, shouting for Mary.

"Henry! Henry Carin! What're you doing here? I never thought to see you again."

"Holy cow, Henry, I didn't realize you were so—" Ted pulled the reins. Henry jumped down.

"Mary, look who's here," Nell said, eyes sparkling.

Henry stood straighter as Mary emerged from around the clapboard house pushing a wheelbarrow. She dropped the handles, squinting at the wagon. Her jaw fell open. A giant of a man appeared from the other side.

"Uh, oh. Here comes trouble. The old man." Ted motioned with his thumb. "I'll unload the dry goods."

Mary came up, head tilted, looking at Henry from beneath her eyebrows. She extended her hand and smiled up at him. Her father lumbered up behind.

"What's all this, Ted? I ain't ordered groceries." His voice boomed. Henry's stomach flipped.

"Well, John, it's like this—"

"Papa, this is Henry," Nell said. "The young man who saved Mary's life on the ship." She spoke quickly, her voice off-key, her laugh breathy.

"Oh, well then, I'm obliged to you." Henry returned his

strong grip. "Why're you here? And these groceries? Not charity, I hope."

"No, no, sir." From the corner of his eye, he glimpsed Ted's smirk. "I—I'm from a farm myself in Michigan. I know it's hard to get supplies. It's flour, sugar, tea, just the basics."

"Oh, that's all right, then. I'll compensate you." He raised his voice. "Nell." Everyone jumped. "Tell Verna to put the kettle on. The least we can do is offer you fellas a drink."

Ted dusted his hands and bounded into his seat. "Not me, thank you kindly, John. Gotta make tracks 'fore dark. Oh, your mail." He handed Mary some letters and tossed Henry's things aloft. "Nice knowing you, Henry. Don't forget your bait."

Henry feared a humiliating race to catch up if Mr. Smith took offence. *Couldn't Ted bloody well wait? He said there was no rush.*

"Just what're your intentions, eh?" Mr. Smith's eyes bored into him. "Where're you staying?"

"Well actually, I was hoping—"

"I see. You presumed. Going a bit far, eh? We ain't got room with three young'uns in the house."

"I could sleep in the barn, sir, if I may. Just a few days. I'm hoping to purchase land."

"Please, Papa." Mary touched her father's arm. "Henry's a good sort, a hard worker. He saved my life. We do owe him a debt of gratitude."

The screen door creaked, then slammed. A woman stepped on the porch, arms crossed. Her body filled the door frame.

"S'pose it won't hurt." Mr. Smith said, slapping his gloves on his open hand. A smile appeared on his bearded face, lighting up his green eyes. "Come along, Henry. Verna's got tea ready."

Holding her father's arm, Mary skipped toward the stairs, turning to beckon Henry. Verna still blocked the entrance. Her grey hair was pulled back in a tight bun. She gave Henry a damp handshake, then wiped her hand on her apron. Her eyes protruded in her round, blotchy face. She openly gave him the once-over, like a buyer judging a horse. Henry straightened his shoulders and met her gaze.

"C'mon in," she said. "Nell says you're Mary's saviour. Nice shoes. Leave 'em on the mat."

Everyone trooped behind. Henry bent to untie his new shoes, hiding his smirk. *She's a broad-beamed steamboat.* He hung his hat on the hall rack, setting his carpetbag and parcel on the wooden seat. They proceeded down a narrow hall, past a parlour on the left and a dining room on the right, into a large kitchen that smelled of chicken soup and fresh bread. Despite his big lunch, his mouth watered.

An oval table covered with a checkered oilcloth was set with seven places. Mr. Smith thumped into a chair and the floor creaked. A baby sat burbling in a highchair near the massive stove. Two boys about age twelve peered at Henry through ragged bangs of blond hair, then resumed slurping. Nell grabbed a tea towel and snapped it at them.

"Stand up, you two, and greet our guest properly. It's impolite—"

Verna wrenched the towel from Nell's twisted hand. "They're hungry, is all," she said. Then her voice took on a sweet tone. "Mr. Carin understands." Nell huffed as the boys said hello to their bowls.

"Lorne and Fred," Mary said. "Twins. Can't tell them apart." She circled the table and lifted the baby from the highchair. "Meet our Florence. Can you say hello to nice Mr. Henry, sweetheart?" The baby's face lit up as Mary kissed her head. She cooed, "Hi, hi, hi." Florence copied her. Mary's laugh provoked the baby's giggle. Henry leaned in, smiling, thinking of Ann.

"Lovely name, don't you think, Henry? Nell and I saw Florence Lawrence in Chicago, a fine singer. Canadian, in fact. We might call her 'Flo,' or 'Flossie' for short." She handed Florence to him. "She's heavy, a bouncing baby girl, aren't you, Flo?"

"No. I'd stick with 'Florence.' A lovely name. You named

her, Mary?"

"No one could think of one and I… I had it ready." Mary turned to lift the tray on the highchair.

As he handed Florence back, the exquisite chair impressed him. He rubbed the polished wood, admiring the craftsmanship. Verna drew his attention to the table and chairs, also finely turned and upholstered.

"My father's work; Vern Stanley, maker of fine furniture, Toronto. I inherited his masterpieces. You know woodworking, Mr. Carin?" Verna's voice was as smooth as the table.

"Henry, please, ma'am. Mr. Carin's my father." He chose the brightness of his smile. "No, ma'am, my only experience is with lumber. I'd love to make furniture someday. My Grandad did for our family."

"Well, appreciation is the first step in acquiring a new skill. Please, sit, Henry." Verna encircled his shoulder and sat him down. "There's soup, fresh bread, and butter. I'll show you more of my furniture after tea." Verna patted his back.

That night in the barn, Nell remarked on Verna's uncustomary friendliness. They were getting Henry settled in the hayloft.

"She's taken a shine to you, Henry, and she hates everybody," Nell said, filling a flour bag with fresh straw. "You could charm the birds out of the trees."

"No, that'd be my little brother, John." Henry pictured the sweet face. "She seems alright."

"Hah! You don't know her as we do," Mary said. "She's our wicked stepmother in real life. She unfolded a wool blanket. *She's so pretty, with that braid on the side, plaited with green ribbon. Say, I believe she added that after supper.*

"Speaking of faery tales, you seen any faeries yet?"

"Just one. A rare beauty."

"Goodness, that's more than I've seen," Mary said. "Tomorrow we'll tour the area, right, Nell? Maybe Henry can find us one." Her eyes sparkled as she smiled at Nell.

"No guarantee. They're shy creatures. I certainly know where they live, though." Henry put a finger to his nose; they didn't seem to be catching on. He shrugged and pushed open the hay loft doors. "A bit stuffy up here. Say, listen, I want to make a good impression on Mr. Smith, Mary. I'll milk the cow, groom the horse, clean stalls, chop wood…"

Nell swatted Henry with the pillow. "Oh, so that's how it is. Maybe you won't want old Nell along, after all."

"Papa would never let us go off on our own," Mary said, reaching around to tug Nell's apron strings. "Besides, who's going to drive while we spoon?"

Henry felt blood rush to his face and ears. *Is she suggesting…?*

The women completed the arrangement of toiletries and towels atop an apple box. "Snug as a bug in a rug," Mary said, filling a small pitcher from a water bucket. "Mind you don't smoke anywhere near the barn." She wagged a finger at him. "That'll impress Papa the most. There's been fires—"

"You forget, I'm a farm boy, Mary," Henry said. "I slept in a loft my whole life on Man."

He helped Nell descend first, then held Mary's hand a bit longer than necessary. She leaned her chest against the first rung and whispered, "I'm so glad you're here. I still have it, you know."

She reached down to her apron and withdrew the birch-bark box. "These precious things were very dear. I love the hummingbird design on the lid, and look, the yellow leaf inside is still fresh. Nell told me what you said when we parted. I embarrassed you. I'm sorry." She pocketed the box again and put her free hand on his cheek. "Sleep well, Henry."

As they left the barn, he overheard their expressions of excitement and wonder. The scent of hay filled his nostrils, and he drank in the comforting smell of the animals shuffling in their stalls below. He sat on the door ledge watching them cross the yard, arm-in-arm. Silhouetted against the golden pink sky, their skirts belled like flowers in the breeze. They looked as if they might lift off the ground.

He sprawled on the straw mattress and sighed. *Nan, I've found a faery island. Send me your blessing, Nan. Mooninger vegewere, ta mee maynrey. I'm so happy.*

Chapter Forty-Six

I can hear the fairies calling
from the king-cups all a-sheen
Through a mist of white spray
falling down a glen of flickering green…
Fairies, if I heed your calling,
if I take your out-stretched hands,
Will you lead me through the sunrise
to your wondrous golden lands…

"Manx Song,"
Mona Douglas, 1915

June, 1910

IN the morning, Henry completed numerous chores while Mary and Nell scurried about to free themselves for the afternoon. Henry hitched up the buckboard, pitying their horse Betsy, a sway-backed nag with bad hooves. He patted her nose, promising to help. They'd hardly passed the gate when Mary asked Nell to stop along the road allowance. She hopped down and motioned to Henry.

"I don't know about faeries, Henry, but Manitoulin's wildflowers are special. Look—Lady Slipper orchids. Smell. Vanilla, hmm? The pink ones are Ramshead orchids. See, just lean down, turn it gently to the side, see the shape? Oh, mustn't pick." She tapped his hand. "Wildflowers need their own soil."

"You sound just like my nan. She knew plant lore, too. Wish I'd paid attention... some of these look familiar."

From her perch in the driver's seat, Nell said, "Papa made friends with an Ojibwe family. Mrs. Odjig showed him medicines, edible mushrooms, and haw berries. Settlers depended on such knowledge."

"She's been a mother to us," Mary said. "Look... hawthorn, watercress, mint, chives, wild rose bushes, St. John's wort... Mrs. Odjig taught me which plants cure snake bites, cool fevers, staunch wounds. Even what's poisonous." She narrowed her eyes at Henry in mock seriousness. He feigned terror. Their laughter drew a quizzical look from Nell.

Seated again, she continued to name trees and plants as they rolled along. Henry found the road pretty smooth compared to Mullet Lake. They passed a grassy meadow. A maple tree stood like a sentinel. Henry jumped up.

"Stop, Nell. Go back."

He led them down the ditch, over the fence, and across to the tree. While Mary set out their picnic, Henry examined the grass. He found what he was looking for; a plant with long, spear-like shoots. He plucked some leaves, verifying by scent as it was too early for flowers.

"Ha! This is surely a faerie mound."

Mary and Nell leapt off the blanket. Henry grinned. "Don't worry, ladies. 'Tis vervain, the herb of enchantment, marking an entrance to their home." Henry shared their enthusiasm. *I can't believe I found this sign. I must listen.*

"Goodness, I've never seen this plant," Mary said. "Or if I did, I had no idea..."

Henry offered her a few stalks, plucked from the top, not

pulled. She recoiled. "Yikes, should you touch it? May be poisonous. Or cursed."

"On the contrary, Mary. I'll weave a bracelet from it to protect you from evil." He said a quiet word to the *Little Ones*. "I'm overjoyed." He breathed out. "*Ellan Vannin.*"

"Who?" Mary said, raising her eyebrows.

"That's Isle of Man in Manx." He laughed. *Was that jealousy?*

Henry wrapped his arms around the tree, then propped himself against the trunk and began fashioning the bracelet. Mary leaned her head on his shoulder. Nell dozed, laying on her stomach, hat perched on her neck. Sunlight filtered through the branches, dappling the women's skirts with impressions of maple leaves. A cloud of blackbirds descended as one, then suddenly shapeshifted away like smoke. A hawk circled overhead, plying the thermals. Dandelions snuggled with wasps and bees. A pair of ducks raced neck and neck, arguing over the distance to the next lake. Fortunately, it was too hot for mosquitos. They could relax.

Henry's fingers moved of their own accord, squeezing the smell of lemons from the herb. A breeze caressed his damp neck and fingered his hair. Soft voices tickled his ears. The world softened into the pastel shades of the magazine illustration. *All that's missing is the kite. I wonder what it's like flying one. Maybe you'd feel like a bird.* His mind wandered aimlessly, a loose dog. Finally, he took Mary's hand.

"Your wrist, please, miss." He kept his voice low, lest he disturb… anyone.

She gingerly touched the twisted bracelet, searching his eyes. "You said we'd see faeries, Henry."

Henry laughed out loud, then clapped his hand over his mouth. "Oh, you sounded exactly like my sister Ann. She confused ferries, the boats, with the *Little People*." He shook his head. "No, I didn't promise we'd see them, Mary, but they're here. Listen. There, on the breeze. Close your eyes. See with your feelings, Nan would say."

He leaned back and squeezed his eyes to capture the moment. Life was tingling within him, from the ground up. Then he felt a softness on his lips. He reciprocated, ever so gently. When she stopped, he opened his eyes, took her face in both hands, and kissed her. He stopped after a moment, noticing the awkward angle of her head tipped upward. He gestured for them to lie down.

With a sideways glance, Mary lay on her side and smoothed the blanket for Henry to join her. He kissed her again, blew on her face, caressed her earlobes, brushed his lashes against her cheek. "Faery kisses for you," he said. *Where'd that notion come from? They're playing with us.*

Mary explored his lips with her tongue before fully opening her mouth, breathing into his nose while she continued to kiss his cheeks and eyelids. Henry's body responded. Unable to think, he caressed her shoulder and rubbed his bent knee lightly against her legs. He fought the urge to go further. Instead, he dipped his nose into her neck.

"You smell like the lady orchid," he said.

"You smell of fresh hay, one of my favourite smells."

Then she placed her hands against his chest to lean upright. "We'd better stop. Nell might wake up." She curled her legs under her gingham skirt, straightened her cotton blouse, and tidied her coif. As she retrieved her hat from the edge of the blanket, he noticed her hand trembling.

"Gee whiz," she said, taking a handkerchief from her skirt pocket to wipe her lips and the back of her neck. She tilted her head; under her hat, her eyes were forest green. "You must think me bold; we hardly know each other."

Henry jolted upright. "Not at all. I think you're a… miracle." He feared she would find his words silly, manipulative even, but he plunged ahead. "You're *my* miracle. It's a miracle I was there in the storm, isn't it? And I was planning to come to

Manitoulin anyway, and you're from here. We were on the same ship—it's all, well…" He closed his eyes, afraid to look at her. "I think it's fate. I haven't been able to stop thinking about you. I loved you the moment I held you in my arms, soaking wet. Even when you threw up on my shoes." *I made her laugh. Still, she might think I'm daft.*

She stroked Henry's arm then cupped his chin with her small hands and smiled into his eyes. She sat back against the trunk and rotated her wrist, admiring the bracelet. Her veins were visible beneath her pale skin. *Mooinjer Veggey, you are here. Thank you for the vervain to protect her.*

"Tell me about yourself, Henry. Your family, too. You keep mentioning brothers and a sister, but where are they? What about your parents? And your nan, where is she? Why are you here all alone?"

He began with descriptions of Nan and Grandad. "It's almost as if Nan were here with us now. Her voice comes to me… I wish—" Then it all came out. Everything. When he told how he'd left home, he couldn't keep his voice from breaking. "I never found out Nan passed until Tom's letter. I'm disappointed I didn't feel her. I feel her here, now."

Nell jumped, seeming unsure where she was. Sitting up, she looked at Henry. "What's wrong?" she said, rubbing the crease between her brows. Mary shook her head slightly. Henry wiped his wet face with the back of his sleeve. He knew Mary would explain later. They shared everything. He loved her for that, and more.

All to the good. I like Nell. I trust her. Do they believe I'm the genuine article, too?

Chapter Forty-Seven

"And when I feel, fair creature of an hour,
That I shall never look upon thee more,
Never have relish in the faery power
Of unreflecting love—then on the shore
Of the wide world I stand alone, and think
Till love and fame to nothingness do sink."

"When I Have Fears That I May Cease To Be"
John Keats, 1818

July, 1910

FOR two weeks, Henry, Mary, and Nell held to a routine: morning chores, afternoon drive. Mr. Smith didn't seem to mind; Henry had treated Betsy's sore hooves, repaired the shingles on the barn, fixed the eaves troughs to gather rainwater. While cleaning the barn, he'd found a cockerel weathervane with a lightning rod. He offered to mount it on the roof.

"My mother wouldn't be without one, Mrs. Smith. Lightning terrifies her. Might as well wash the upstairs windows while I'm at it. Sling us up a bucket, would you, Mary?"

That night in the loft, Mary expressed her amazement at

Henry's skills with Verna. "You've got her wrapped around your little finger." Mary pinched his nose for emphasis, followed by a kiss. "She's been easier on us, lately, thanks to your magic. You want to watch those eyes of hers. Nell and I can tell which way the wind blows by the colour of them. Better than your weathervane."

Henry shrugged. "You catch more flies with honey—"

"Speaking of honey, I could do with more of your sweet kisses. Dust me with some faery ones, right here." She offered him her cheek. He preferred her lips.

Once the family turned in, Mary would sneak out of the house to join Henry. He prepared anxiously for her arrival, slicking back his hair, brushing his teeth, smoothing his face with the straight razor while holding the hand mirror. Mary caught him shaving once as she peeked over the top of the ladder.

"You should go into vaudeville, the faces you can pull." She laughed. The mirror landed on a straw bale. Mary retrieved it.

"Whew, didn't break. We just missed seven years bad luck!"

"I hope so. Hold it, would you? Mustn't scratch those sweet cheeks."

They petted. They kissed. Until, hearts pounding, they paused for breath and made themselves stop. Henry smiled as he ran his fingers through Mary's fine red hair, soft as down. She always climbed into the loft barefoot. While lying on his chest, she rubbed her tiny, arched feet along his legs. He couldn't hide his erection as he rubbed her breasts through her clothes. In time—just—one of them would call a halt. Then they'd sleep, Mary's instep resting in the arch of Henry's foot. Henry floated on the vanilla scent of her hair mingling with the homely barn smells of hay and warm animals.

One or the other would awaken with a start, hearts thumping for fear they'd overslept. "Your life won't be worth a plug nickel if Papa finds me here," Mary said, shuddering. She'd slip silently down the ladder and through the barn, followed by Betsy's soft nicker and Henry's desire.

At breakfast, they'd avoid each other's eyes and shy away from accidentally touching as they passed the dishes. Nell, who shared a bed with Mary, would pass Henry a surreptitious smile.

Sometimes Henry's feelings of guilt at deceiving her father extended to memories of Tina.

He'd tried to erase their time in bed and her accusations from his mind. *She said I was using her, but she was using me, too. If only she hadn't taken Grandad's ring. I hate her for that; let her have the money. That's all she cared about. She's nothing like Mary.*

Henry's work began at sunrise with regular chores and any other task Mr. Smith assigned. The worst was picking rocks.

"Seems they push up out of the ground overnight," Mr. Smith said, tapping the bib of his overalls. "Maybe your *Little People* put them there to annoy us."

Probably so, but isn't it nice to have someone clearing them, Mr. Smith? Why aren't your sons doing it? Henry wished he could ask. He tried giving the boys little jobs, but they would down tools and run off. Unlike Tom, about the same age, these two had no gumption.

"Why aren't they in school, Mary? They must be what, twelve?"

"We lost our schoolteacher, Mr. Bradley. He deserted us." Keeping her gaze averted from his, her voice came out sharp like a honed blade. She leaned over to collect Florence from the floor and began curling the baby's light red hair around her finger.

"As for those brats," she said, "Verna spoils them rotten. The twins are hers. She was Papa's housekeeper. He married her, thinking she would replace our mother, I suppose. Ha!" She rolled her eyes. "No fear of that. They're useless. Nell and I offered to help, once the teacher—they refuse to learn."

She pressed her forehead against the baby's. "You'll be different, won't you, darling?"

"Ma, ma, ma," Florence babbled.

Henry eyed the two of them, locked together. A feeling nagged at him. *There's something odd about Mary's attachment to her baby sister. Verna seems to take no notice of Florence at all.*

The next day, helping Mr. Smith build a fence, he hoped fellowship would permit questions. It had worked for Old Nosey Joe.

"Snake fence, you call it? How can a fence keep out a snake? Or in, for that matter." Henry laughed at his own joke.

"Means it snakes along the countryside," Mr. Smith said, motioning him to lift the next rail.

"Yeah, I figured," Henry said, hoping he didn't think he was daft. "These stack-rail fences are like ours, but cedar'll last a lot longer. The logs split so nice, you don't even need a plane. I work a shingle plane, me." Fearful of blathering on, he resumed work.

The sun drilled into his cap. Sweat stung his eyes and trickled down his back. *Working into my heat again.* He offered Mr. Smith his canteen. He paused for a swig of water.

"You've a nice place, here, sir. I hope to do even half as good on farming as you. I must convince two of my brothers to live with me. Did you and your brother work together at first?"

Mr. Smith hoisted another rail. Henry grabbed the end.

"Nell and Mary are fine young ladies. I feel privileged to know them. Lorne and Fred will be helpers, and you've another lovely daughter, Florence. A good name, Mary picked." Henry couldn't read Mr. Smith's eyes under his battered hat. They dropped the rail in place. "D'ya think they'll hire another schoolteacher? My mother's anxious for our young ones to go. I left school early, myself, but—"

Mr. Smith wiped his brow on the back of his sleeve and fixed Henry with eyes as green as the barn cat's.

"Time you bought your land, Henry. Frost comes early

here." He removed his gloves, smacked them on his overalls, and headed for the buckboard.

That afternoon, Nell suggested they visit Providence Bay. They walked the beach barefoot and picnicked close to the docks, admiring the fishing boats. The lighthouse gleamed like a toy against the clear blue sky. Nell said so many ships had been wrecked on the point that survivors had named the bay "Providence."

"I hate boats, me. I'll stick to dry land from now on." Henry said, taking Mary's hand. "Think what might've happened if you'd been swept…"

"I know, Henry, but sometimes water travel can't be avoided. Besides, look what came out of that trip," Mary said, knocking his leg with her knee. "Find the silver lining, Nell says. Don't you?"

Nell smiled at her. "Come on, up you two! Let's buy some fish. Bring Verna a salmon, Henry, and she'll never want you to leave."

"Ah, but your Dad's getting anxious. I think he's worried I may corrupt one of his two lovely daughters." Henry squeezed between them to walk, swinging their hands. They lightly smacked his cheeks. "Seriously, ladies, I need to buy a place. Let's ask at the General Store."

The storekeeper drew him a map to a piece of land on offer nearby. Eight hundred acres. Henry settled on a small parcel since he might need to clear it alone. His throat swelled with excitement. They drove out and looked around, examining the trees, assessing the view from a hillock that seemed favourable for a house. Henry made up his mind.

The storekeeper acted as land agent, registering the sale. Henry remembered his father lamenting the exchange rate of English pounds to American dollars. "Canada's on the gold standard, so I can't lose," Henry said, signing the papers and a cheque. "I love this country. In more ways than one." He looked at Mary. Her smile travelled from her eyes to his heart. *Land, my girl, a family… it's coming together. I knew it would.*

The storekeeper grinned, giving him a hearty handshake, happily supplying a tent, tools, and dry goods. Henry wanted to be well-stocked to establish himself before winter.

"I'll be needing a pocketknife, too, sir. With a sharp blade."

"I've just the thing, called a Swiss Army knife. Even comes with a can opener. Handy as all get-out."

Standing outside, he removed his hat and put his face to the sun. He squeezed his eyes, trapping the memory. *Gura mie ayd, mooinjer vegewere. You've watched over me, again.*

* * *

When Mary peeked her head over the ledge that night, Henry motioned for her to sit. He'd placed two stumps side by side and turned the coal oil lamp down low. Her hair clung to her forehead, soaking wet. Rain was pelting down. She rubbed her arms and twirled her bare feet. Henry placed a towel over her shoulders. Straw dust tickled his parched throat. He was used to it. Still, he could barely breathe as he placed the brown package in her lap. She struggled with the twine. He grinned and produced his red-handled knife.

She revealed a thick bolt of material. "Oh, my goodness," Mary said, her voice barely a whisper. "Shot silk. It shimmers. And this, delicate lace. Gosh. For me?"

"Who else? For a tea dress. I don't think you have… I thought the colour would match your eyes. I hope the lady in Manitowaning cut enough. Look further."

Her eyes widened. "I've always mooned over kid gloves." She slipped one on her left hand, turning it this way and that. "Perfect fit."

"There's more."

"A velvet box?" Henry swallowed hard, his mouth as dry as the straw underfoot. "I just love the colour. So blue. I'll keep it with my quill box." Her hand trembled as she smoothed the velvet lid. "Beautiful, thank you."

He gently took the box in two fingers. "It opens." He knelt at her feet.

Her eyes widened. Tears sprang to her eyes. "Oh. Henry. No." She put her hand on his shoulder and shook her head. "I… I just can't."

Henry fell back on his heels, nearly toppling over. The anticipation wound in his gut now unspooled like a broken watch spring. "No? You mean, you… you won't? I waited, Mary, to be sure you felt as I do." He ran his hand through his hair, then extracted the ring. "It's Celtic, the jeweller said. Scottish. See, woven yellow and white gold means us, together, always. I thought you'd like it—" His words disappeared into the high ceiling. The wind slammed one of the loft doors. A clap of thunder startled them both.

"It's beautiful, Henry. No, don't—" When he touched her face, she turned and went to shut both doors. "I just can't. You don't know me. I'm not—"

"I do, though. Know you. We've been together every day for weeks." The rain on the roof roared in his ears. "Nary a cross word between us. On Man, we say: *Sooree ghiare, yn tooree share:* 'A short courting, the best courting.' Grandad teased Nan with it; they married young. And were happy, I believe."

He poured two glasses of water. Lightning tore a strip between the doors. Mary shrieked and jumped back. "Damn good thing I installed that rod; oughta be one here." The horse neighed and the cow mooed, at another thunderclap. "Maybe we should go in, Mary." Tears streamed down her cheeks. "You love nature, like me, like Nan. You're kind and gentle, so good to your sisters. I want to build a home here, on Manitoulin, with you. I waited until I had prospects, my land. Please, reconsider."

"Have you spoken to Papa? Does Nell know? Say you haven't told Verna."

"No, never." He jumped to his feet. "I wanted to ask you,

first. I thought we'd have a picnic tomorrow on my land. I can't believe I'm saying, 'my land.' I plan to set up camp tomorrow, start building a cabin—" He perched on the stump, twisting the pinkie finger where Grandad's ring used to be.

Mary rubbed his shoulders from behind. Barely above a whisper, she said, "I do love you, Henry. I am sure of that if nothing else. I'd be honoured, lucky, to become your wife."

He twisted around. "Well, you're not exactly over the moon at my proposal. Why? You seem… afraid. Is it homesteading? I'm strong and can do most everything myself. I'll work all winter at the sawmill, planing lumber. I won't go into the bush and leave you, ever. When I get my brothers here, why—"

She smiled. "I do hope they come. Tom and John? I understand why you don't want Edward, but maybe he's changed. I long to meet them. Your mother, too. I want her approval." She collected the other glove from the parcel.

Henry shook his head. "Her opinion makes no—never mind. I do wish you could've met my grandparents, though; they'd have loved you." He dropped to his knees, seeking her eyes, his throat aching. "Then you will? Marry me? You're sure?"

"Yes, but—"

Henry shook his head. "No 'buts.' Just one word."

"Yes, then."

"That's two."

She laughed. Henry lifted her up. Wind rattled the doors. Henry felt as if they were aboard *Manitou*, clinging together for dear life. She leaned against his chest, shivering. He grabbed a blanket, motioning for her to lie down. She bent to gather the paper and twine, re-wrapped everything, and made for the ladder.

"Good night, Henry. We won't sleep together again until we're married."

After a fitful night, Henry opened the shutters to watch the sun crest over the house. He smiled at the lightning rod glistening on the roof. It had kept them safe. His new family. The rooster crowed, inspiring robins to launch the morning chorus. He packed his carpet bags, tucking the ring box deep inside, and ferried everything except the mattress down the ladder. He'd bought a camp bed. "There's snakes on Manitoulin," the shopkeeper had said. "Best not sleep on the ground in a tent."

Henry smirked, remembering how Mary had rolled her eyes. "Well, I've never seen one." *She's never seen faeries here either. But I have.*

"Gura mie eu, mooninger vegewere: The road's clear ahead." Henry said. At the sound of his voice, the cow mooed. "All right, Bossy. I'm coming." Maybe Verna would finally teach the boys to milk once he'd left.

The barn cat jumped down from the cow's back. She meowed for her squirt of milk. Henry leaned his forehead against the cow's smooth flank and began his double-time, thinking, thinking, with each squeeze. *I'll buy me a cow, first. Then a horse. Chickens. Build a henhouse, first. No, the barn must come first. Right after the cabin.* His excitement mounted until the cow kicked in protest. He realized his bucket was full. Whistling, he swung toward the house, leaving a trail of white droplets.

Chapter Forty-Eight

Jean traagh choud as ta'n ghrian soilshean:
Make hay while the sun shines.

August, 1910

AT breakfast, Henry asked Mr. Smith to meet him alone. Verna raised her eyebrows, the boys giggled and punched each other, Nell smiled, and Mary pretended to fuss with Florence. Mr. Smith merely rose, filled his teacup, and strode down the hall. Henry followed, slopping tea on the floor. He erased the wet spots with his socks and backed into the parlour. Standing against the closed door, he said, "I wish to ask for Mary's hand in marriage, sir."

"It comes as no surprise," Mr. Smith said.

It seemed safe to take a seat, though Mr. Smith remained standing. He perched on the edge of a straight-backed chair and clasped his hands. He hoped Mr. Smith couldn't smell his sweat. Bushy eyebrows knitted, he looked intently at him. *Oh, God.*

"Mary *has* told you—"

"Oh yes. She accepted. Long's you approve."

"Right, then, I'll not stand in your way. Time she was

married. She's twenty. You're what, nineteen?" Henry nodded. "Close enough. Nell's an old maid, twenty-five, and no callers. You know how to work, and you've made a plan. All to the good."

"We'd like to marry as soon as possible, sir. I've got my land and—"

"Out of the question." He leaned forward, one hand planted on the sideboard. "Unless there's some reason—"

Blood inflamed Henry's face, envisioning their lovemaking.

"Oh no, sir. It's just—with the farm and all—we thought—"

"Good. That's settled." Mr. Smith cleared his throat. "You must build a decent house and a barn. I won't have my girl sleeping rough. I'll help. I'll hire Jim, too. And there'll be a proper Colonsay wedding with a piper and all the trimmings."

He tossed his head and shouted, "Verna!"

Henry jumped up. Everyone tumbled into the room; Verna first, Mary last, carrying Florence.

"The young folks are engaged. Reckon you know. Bring out the whiskey, Verna. Youse'll be married here on the hill. The reception'll be in the house." Henry heard a lilt in Mr. Smith's voice. Nell's eyes sparkled as much as Mary's. Lorne and Fred looked at their feet. Verna blew out her cheeks like a horse.

"Our nuptials were simple, John, not even a dance. Why the fuss?"

Mr. Smith beckoned Mary, opened a drawer, and extracted a wooden box. "You ain't Scots, Verna. We'll follow tradition, in honour of her mother." Running his fingers through a deep bed of coins, he extracted two silver dollars.

"One each, to wear in your shoe on your wedding day."

"Here am I, saving my egg money, while you—" Verna stamped her foot.

"You'll have a dowry, too, Mary; a new bed with linens and a spinning wheel. Jim and I'll help Henry build the house. What crops would suit that land? Potatoes to start—"

"And just where'll we get a spinning wheel, might I ask?" Verna's voice squeezed like sour milk from between her pursed lips. "She's not having mine. Father made it, for me."

"You never use it, though, do you? Never mind, Mary; I'll have one made. Verna, you'll make a wedding cake to put the wishes in—"

Nell raised her hand. "I'll make the cake from Mom's cook-book," Nell said. "I'm a better baker than Verna, anyway."

Verna scrunched up her face. *She'd spit at her if she could, like a barn cat. Her eyes have changed colour.*

Mary hugged her father and kissed his cheek. "What's 'put the wishes in,' mean, Papa?"

"Everyone in the house takes a turn stirring the batter, lass, and makes a wish for the marriage. They did so for your mother."

"Poor dear wasn't so lucky, though," Verna said, as she handed glasses to every adult but herself.

"She gave me two beautiful daughters, Verna. And a son, our Mel—" Mr. Smith's voice hitched. He pulled a handkerchief from his pocket, wiped his eyes, and blew his nose.

Henry's throat tightened, tears stinging behind his eyes. *Not such an old boar, after all. He's grieving yet, like I do for Da and Nan. Maybe heartache never heals.*

"Here's to Henry and Mary," Mr. Smith almost shouted, as he raised his glass. "July 12th today. One year hence, you shall be wed. With my blessing."

He tossed back his whiskey, then shook Henry's hand and kissed Mary's cheek. Verna's glass sat empty. Mr. Smith scowled.

"Toast the young people, Verna."

"You know I don't drink."

"Put water in it then. Raise a glass to their health and hap-piness."

She poured an ounce of whiskey. "Here's mud in your eye," she said, giving Henry such a cold look that he shivered. "Good luck to youse. You'll need it."

"Ach, a dram may do you a power of good, Verna. We can only hope." He turned to Nell. "Pack a lunch, please, lass. We're off to Providence Bay. I want a looksee at your land, check the drainage. You didn't consider that, did you?"

Henry shook his head, unsure what he meant.

"Thought not. You're green, but you're willing to learn. Those mitts of yours'll stand you in good stead, farming."

"Thank you, sir," Henry said, feeling buoyed by the compliment. "I'll get Betsy hitched right away. Chores are done."

"We'd best stop over to Jim's, share your news, introduce you. Mary, gather some supplies for them."

"I'm not giving my preserves to that lazy wench—" Verna said.

"Quiet, you. Bring what they'll need, Mary."

"Can Florence come? Please," Mary said, hoisting the child to her hip.

He shook his head. "We don't know how long we'll be. Probably have supper in town. Don't wait up, Verna."

"Oh, don't worry, I won't." She turned on her heel, shooing the boys out ahead of her.

Henry stumbled down the back steps, blinded by sunlight. His hands trembled as he donned his cap. *Mr. Smith accepted my proposal and blessed us. And Verna's reaction, whew! I thought she liked me.* Now he understood Mary's hostility, bordering on hatred. He felt the same about Thomas. *We've that in common, too.* He gently placed the bit in Betsy's tender mouth. She nickered. *Poor old thing should be put out to pasture.* Rubbing her neck, he resolved to respect Mary's opinions more. *If Da had only listened to Mum, we'd have stopped at home. I know there was more to it now, but still. The twists and turns of life, sometimes forward, sometimes back. What's it mean?*

Ready to load the buckboard, he mounted the steps two at a time. Verna's voice pierced the screen. He decided to see which way the wind was blowing.

"So, it's to be a grand ceremony, is it? The JP was good enough for us but, oh no, not for the daughter of the sainted Catherine. A piper, no less." Verna's tone was bitter as cold tea. "Where does he expect to find one of those? Gore Bay Hotel? What a laugh." A pot banged on the stove.

"And who's to sew the wedding dress, may I ask? Nell showed me that silk. You can't handle such fancy goods, Mary."

"I will," Nell said. Henry grinned at her excited voice. "I'll use Mother's dress, make a pattern. It's in my trunk."

"Your hopeless chest, you mean. Fine, long's you don't expect me… Meanwhile, what am I to do, Miss 'Pure As The Driven Snow,' once you're wed?" She paused. "Raise your bastard child for you?"

Henry gasped, then clapped his hands over his mouth. Too late. Mary swung the screen door open and shrieked. Then she whirled around, dropping a bottle of preserves. It rolled down the steps and smashed. Florence wailed.

"You witch! God damn bitch! I hate you! Why did Papa marry you? You've made our lives a living hell. Now look what you've done."

She stumbled onto the porch. Henry caught her flailing arms as Nell rushed to her side and half-carried her to the swing where she collapsed. The screen door banged as Verna emerged and planted her feet, arms crossed over her chest.

"Well, leastways now you know, Henry. I didn't mean for that to happen. That's what comes of listening at keyholes." She gave a sideways head-toss toward Mary. "Still want to marry her? She ain't a virgin."

Heat coursed through his body. He clenched his fists at his sides. "Please don't speak of my fiancée like that, Mrs. Smith. 'Course I knew. It doesn't matter. I love Mary. Nothing, no one, can alter that." He took a breath, then keeping his tone light and even, he smiled at her. "No harm done, ma'am."

He moved across to the swing. Nell hauled Mary to her

feet.

"That's right, Henry," she said. "Come with me, you two. Papa's all fired up; mustn't keep him waiting."

Henry and Nell helped Mary down the steps between them. Mary clutched Henry's arm so hard that he winced.

Nell bent forward to look at him. "You put her in her place, by God. Well done." She kissed Mary's head. "Come on, sweetheart. It's all right. Don't cry anymore. Papa will notice you're upset. I don't think he heard, leastways I hope not. Don't let on. Let's just go to Providence, right now. Papa's so happy."

Sobbing into Henry's shoulder, Mary whispered, "I'm not coming."

Nell passed Henry the handkerchief from her sleeve. He wiped Mary's face, cupping her chin, looking into her swimming eyes. He wished he could ask why she hadn't said…

"No, Mary," Nell said. "Papa expects—wait, I've got an idea; we'll say you're overcome from the excitement. Not a lie, exactly." She nodded, approving her own plan, and turned Mary toward the path around the house. "Sneak upstairs. Have a lie-down. We'll bring fudge."

Henry lightly kissed Mary's lips and squeezed her hand. "Yes, we will, my love."

"I'm sorry," she mouthed.

Nell steered her toward the front of the house. She lurched away. Nell found Henry's gaze, following her. "You didn't know, though, did you? Mary told me she hadn't—I did warn her—anyway, she'll explain. Believe me, it's not what you think."

"It never is," Henry realized he'd been holding his breath. He inhaled. His hands were dead weights. "Verna's right about one thing; I must stop listening at doors. Brings nothing but trouble."

Nell patted his arm, shushing him. He felt as drained as an empty bucket of milk. His eyes roved the farmstead. The buildings seemed smaller, disheveled, in need of paint. *One old horse, one cow, Mr. Smith, away all winter; a hard-scrabble life. Is this really what I want?*

Lorne and Fred stepped onto the porch and stared at them. Henry felt their eyes boring into his back. Nell waved them off.

"Get inside." Her tone was the one reserved for them. "It's none of your beeswax. Not a word to Papa, or I'll horsewhip the both of youse."

"We need the privy."

"Go around. Through the house."

Just then, Mr. Smith called, "What's the holdup? The buckboard ain't even loaded."

"Coming, Papa," Nell called. She turned to Henry. "I'll get the lunch." She scowled. "Oh, yes, and supplies for Betty."

Henry tossed his carpet bags in the wagon, asking to borrow the lamp. Mr. Smith frowned. "What're you on about, Henry? You'll be here awhile yet. I'll lend you my kit when the time comes. We'll get more supplies. First, you need a horse." He clicked his tongue as he climbed up beside Nell. "Green, green."

Henry sat on the wagon's floor with the lunch basket and a box of supplies. *Good thing Mary didn't come; she'd have been uncomfortable.*

"Drive straight through, Nell. We'll picnic on the beach, stop at Jim's after," Mr. Smith said. He kept up a rolling commentary, sharing his breadth of knowledge on homesteading. Henry thought back to Ted's depiction of the Smith brothers. *Not exactly right where John was concerned; he just took some getting used to. Maybe Jim's not so bad, either. But meeting family, today, of all days…* A sigh escaped before he could stop it. At Mr. Smith's startled look, he imitated a smile.

"About the soil, Mr. Smith. 'Alvar,' you say? What's that?"

432

Chapter Forty-Nine

Cronk ghlass foddey voym: lhome, lhome tra roshym eh:
A green hill far from me: bare, bare when I reach it.

THE beach bristled with gulls hastening along the shore in search of buried treasure. Their cries overhead sent Henry flying back to Port Erin's shores. Pretending the sparkle on the water was affecting his eyes, he forced down his egg salad sandwich.

"Everything tasting all right for you, Henry?" Nell said.

"Nell, I would take your picnic lunch over a meal at the Grand Hotel, any day. I'd choose it for my last meal in prison." He toasted her with the sandwich. *Her fussing reminds me of Nan.*

"As if you'd be in prison," she tutted, pouring his lemonade. Her right hand held the flask awkwardly, but she didn't spill a drop.

"Aye, she's a fine cook, our Nell," Mr. Smith said. "Excellent seamstress too. Why, she picks a dress, a coat, even, in the Eaton's catalogue, copies the pattern and it looks store-bought. Both my girls make me proud." He reached across to pat Nell's knee.

Nell blushed. "Our Mary's a gem. Never shirks a task,

hardworking and cheerful. The best sister a girl could ask for."

"You'll be next, lass. Some fella will be a lucky man." He brushed his hands together. "Now, best make a mile if we're to inspect this land of yours and make it to Jim's." He groaned, struggling to unfold his legs. "God's beard, I'm not used to picnics anymore." Nell and Henry helped him to his feet.

"Thank ye, laddie." His green eyes smiled directly at Henry, for the first time. *His accent sounds stronger? Does he hear mine?*

When they arrived, it seemed Mr. Smith wanted to assess the whole property. Nell stayed behind with a book. Henry struggled to keep up with Mr. Smiths short but quick strides as he moved from a grove of trees to a sandy knoll to a meadow.

"No crick. Hmm. We'll hire a douser to find water, dig a well." He pointed to a stand of tall trees. "Sugar maples. Come March, the syrup'll add a pretty penny to your income. Nectar of the gods. That's a lucky find."

He pounded his booted instep down on the narrow-bladed spade he'd brought to take a soil sample. Extracting a core, he spread the dirt in his palm, sifted it through his fingers, watched it blow away in the breeze, tasted a pinch. Henry couldn't take his eyes off him. Then leaning on the handle, a hand supporting his lower back, he pulled himself straight. Sad eyes and furrowed brow disclosed the verdict. Henry's stomach flipped like butter in a churn.

"As I feared." He shook his head as he dusted off his trousers. "Soil's no good for crops. Sand. Rocks. See those dips over there? Depressions that hold rainwater, but don't drain. I wish you'd waited for me."

Henry ground the soil under his boot like he was putting out a cigarette. "God damn it! I worked so hard. Spent my savings. Christ, with all these trees, it looks so fertile. I want a proper farm, crops, maybe a market garden—" Henry kicked the dirt, waving his arms.

"This land's fooled many folks, Henry. Even the experts

thought crops could grow anywhere here. They were wrong. Not to worry—" Mr. Smith said, pointing out various trees. "White spruce, see? King of the forest. There's cedar, basswood, pines, silver birch, all here. Timber for every purpose: a house, out-buildings, fences, the lot. This soil will do for potatoes and raspberries. Folks hereabouts are raising turkeys. Why, the steamship route to Chicago's called the 'turkey trail' nowadays—"

He put a hand up. "Thank you, kindly, Mr. Smith. I'm grateful. My Grandad always said: *Moyll y droghad myr heu harrish:* Don't count your chickens before they hatch. My worst fault." His throat closed. His tongue stuck to the roof of his mouth. He stomped to the wagon and vaulted into the back, avoiding Nell's startled glance. Mr. Smith tossed in the shovel and motioned that she should drive.

The trip to Jim's passed in a blur of trees, trees, trees. Determined to make a good impression, he offered Jim his hand. The handshake was limp. Since Damnation Corners, Henry could recognize a heavy drinker: rheumy, bloodshot eyes, bulbous, veiny nose, oversized gut. Elizabeth's baggy dress was covered by a ragged, dirty sweater. She flashed Henry a grin, and tossed back her lank blonde hair, pulling Nell into a hug. When Nell announced Mary's engagement to Henry, she whistled.

"Mary's caught herself a big, tall drink of water, and no mistake, Nelly. You must be so jealous," she said, eyeing Henry up and down. "I'll get you to make me a dress for the wedding. I'm all thumbs, with a sewing machine. You're a whiz, even with that gammy arm; I don't know how you manage it."

"Where do you want this?" Nell pointed to the box of supplies.

"In the kitchen, of course, Silly Nelly. That's her nickname, Mr. Carin." She mewed and touched Henry's hand. "You'll stop for tea, won't you? So's we can get acquainted?"

"No, we can't," Nell said, her voice flat as the wagon bed. "Verna'll have supper on. Carry the box over, please, Henry. I hope Papa doesn't jaw with Uncle Jim much longer." She tapped her foot, letting out an exasperated sigh when they rounded the corner of the barn. "Oh, here you are. Finally."

"Cool down, Nell," Jim said. "Don't turn into Verna. Oh, I meant to tell you, John, I run into Bradley, the schoolteacher, over to the hotel in Gore Bay. He asked about youse."

"Don't go mentioning that son-of-a bitch." Mr. Smith slapped his palm on his thigh. "I thought he was gone to Toronto. Don't you say a goddamn word of our doings to that… man."

Elizabeth crossed her arms and leaned toward Jim. "Nelly's making them go."

"It's my doing, Mrs. Smith," Henry said, trying hard to smile. "I'm done up after travelling, and there's my chores yet. I'll just use your privy, if I may."

"I go by Betty to my friends, Henry. Next time, you must tell me about yourself." She turned her pale blue eyes on Nell. "Jim will pay for the goods."

Nell waved one hand behind her back as she yanked her father's arm with the other.

* * *

Dinner progressed with a clattering of dishes and a scraping of plates but no conversation. While Nell prepared a plate for Mary, Henry helped Verna with the dishes.

"I'll miss your excellent cooking, Mrs. Smith. My mother cooked for tourists in a fancy hotel, back home."

"I hope to meet her one day," Verna said. Her voice and manner were subdued. She dismissed the boys from the kitchen, then headed for the porch, letting the door bang. Nell jumped, nearly dropping the tray.

Alone in the kitchen, Mr. Smith slipped a flask from his vest pocket. "Here, a wee dram, Henry. The future'll seem brighter by morning." He took a swig and handed the flask to Henry, closing it in his grasp. "Take it with you, tonight. You've had a blow, to be sure, lad. Nothing we can't fix. There's bad luck and there's bad judgment. You've had a bit of both; there's a solution, never fear." He clapped Henry on the back. "Buck up and don't get too down."

"I'm not so sure, Mr. Smith," Henry said. He opened the screen door. "Thank you for your help. You saved me from a fall, I reckon. Good night, sir."

"Night, Henry," Verna said as he passed her, swinging in the dark.

Chapter Fifty

Boayl nagh vel aggle cha vel grayse:
Where there is no fear there is no grace.

HENRY wrenched open the barn door, straining his arm. He grabbed the lantern and shuffled past Bossy's stall. He went to visit Betsy and rested his forehead against her neck, letting his pent-up emotions flow. She whinnied softly, raising and lowering her head, consoling him. *Horses know. Horses are faeries with four legs.* Mounting the ladder as if climbing a mountain, he threw himself on the straw mattress, not bothering to undress. His belly felt cinched tight, like a saddled horse. He rolled his shoulders and raised his arms, inhaling the dusty air as deeply as he could. The flask in the bib of his overalls beckoned.

He crawled over to sit on one of the stumps. Taking a gulp, he coughed, but he savoured the warmth coursing into his gut. His chest was hollow as an empty barrel. *Goddammit. One fucking disappointment after another. Can't seem to win. First Mum; finding out about her and that, that bastard Thomas. Then Da... Damn Edward to hell.* He took another swig. *Then finding the two of them kissing, for Christ's sake. I wanted to die.* Heat coursed upwards, from his belly to his ears. *Then, Tina, what she did...* His thumb twined behind his fingers, feeling for Grandad's absent ring. He heard a silent reprimand. *Goddammit. I'm sorry I lost it, Grandad.* He rubbed the calluses on his right hand. *All that stoking, shifting freight, penny-pinching, and for what? Naught. My foolish dream of a farm. Were you mocking me, Phynodderree?* He dropped his chin to his chest. Tears coursed down his stubbly cheeks.

Now this with Mary. He tipped the flask again, silently toasting Mr. Smith's generosity. *He's worried about me. He doesn't know the half of it. Maybe he does. Pretending Florence was her sister? Christ. I knew it. Was she going to tell me? Or keep on lying? Is she deceitful like Mum?*

"Henry?"

He jumped. Mary was balancing on the ladder, arms extended. He pocketed the flask and brushed his face with his sleeve.

"Nell told me you'd come." He reached for her hands. "Up-se-daisy."

"I can explain, Henry. I—"

"I knew, deep inside. You and Florence can't hide your bond, Mary. She favours you, Nan would say—a beautiful baby. I just hoped, if it were true, you'd tell me. I thought you trusted me."

She scrambled up and faced him on her knees. The lamp illuminated her red-rimmed eyes and mottled cheeks.

"I could kick myself. I should've told you the truth. I feared you'd judge me like everyone else. Except Nell. As hard as I judge myself." She faltered. The only sounds were the soft cooing of the pigeons above, and the shuffling of Betsy and Bossy below. The cat leapt up beside Mary, startling them. Mary sat cross-legged and settled it on her lap. Contented purring filled the loft. She looked up.

"It's no excuse, Henry, but he—the schoolteacher, Mr. Bradley—he wasn't honourable. He boarded with us for a year in '07. Papa wanted the income, and he took the boys to school with him." The purring was louder than her voice.

"Charming, he was. Educated in England. Seemed to know everything. Told me I was smart, said I could be a schoolteacher, though I was gone eighteen. Told Papa he'd prepare me at night for the Normal School exams. He taught me all right." She began to cry, shaking and sobbing. Henry passed her the flask. She threw it back and gulped.

"I thought I loved him, Henry. He didn't, you know, violate me. No, I worshipped him. He said he'd take me with him back to Toronto. I could teach school. Get off this rock. Away from Verna. Then I discovered I was pregnant; well, Verna figured it out before I did. That was a moment, now I tell you. Almost as bad as today."

"I can imagine," Henry said softly. He was trying hard. To imagine. Loud purring had invaded his brain.

"Can you, Henry? Imagine? Can you see why I kept quiet?" Her voice roused a pigeon. It fluttered down to the floor. The cat pounced. The bird flittered off, as Mary rose and began to pace.

"Verna made it seem dirty. It wasn't. He was gentle. Claimed he loved me. Made me want to… Told me I was beautiful. Verna said it was lucky I was smart since my red hair would put men off, like Nell's withered hand, saying we'd both wind up spinsters. When Mr. Bradley said I had brains and beauty both, I wanted to believe him. I couldn't wait to tell him about the baby, thinking we'd get married. And then we'd leave." She kicked the mattress. "Someone left all right. The very next day."

She flounced down on a stump and sobbed into her apron. Henry crouched, brushing a loose curl off her shoulder. "I love your red hair, Mary. You are a beauty, but more than that, you've a good head on your shoulders. He took advantage of your loving, innocent nature. It's him that's wrong, not you. I'd throttle him with my bare hands."

He took a breath and tipped back on his heels. "There's

something I must tell you, though, love, so's you'll understand my reaction."

He took another shot, for courage. "I told you I hate my Uncle Thomas as much as you hate Verna, but I never said why. What you don't know, Mary, is that my mother deceived my father with his brother. I found out by accident. Listening at doorways. Like today."

His knees flamed against the hard floor, reminding him of the pews in church. He stood, looking into her wide, startled gaze. "Edward, my brother, who shot Da, is really my half-brother. Da never knew, I don't think. I hope not. I can't forgive Mum. The man's my uncle, for Christ's sake. I had to live under his roof while Da suffered in bed, then, he… died. Now I just learned, she's gone and married the bastard. Makes me sick." He tasted bile, or maybe the whiskey was coming back on him, burning his throat. "So, the thing is, what I'm wondering is… did you intend to tell me?"

"I planned to, Henry," she said, taking his hands. "Time and again. But then I feared… you wouldn't want me." Her voice and icy hands trembled. "Verna said no man would raise another man's bastard. She started the lie, telling the neighbours she was expecting a baby. We both stayed out of sight near the end. She's so big, no one could tell. She swore Papa to secrecy. He wanted to hunt Bradley down and drag him back to marry me or kill him. Florence was born here." She pointed to the house as if Henry didn't know. "I was so scared, thinking of Mother, how she died. Nell and Papa were, too. Mrs. Odjig helped. Thank God for her."

She crossed her arms over her stomach. Her face was so pale, he feared she'd faint. "Verna made out like the birth was a miracle at her age. Made a big to-do of the shower. Now, she neglects Florence entirely, like she's a nuisance. I hardly let her out of my sight. I'm afraid she'll turn on her, same as she did on me today. You saw. She blows hot and cold." She looked over at the rim of the loft.

"When you came back today, so quiet and sad, Nell and I both figured you were angry—"

Henry moved closer and touched her knees. "Oh, God. I'm sorry you thought that. I actually was just… distracted. Angry, too. No, not at you. Did he tell you? Your father said my soil's no good. For crops. For farming." His voice hitched in his throat. He dropped his gaze. "I'm down at heart, Mary. My dream—"

"Oh. So, you're leaving, then." She said, eyes downcast.

"No," Henry said, catching her sleeve as she pushed herself up to leave. "I intend to keep my promise."

She lifted his hand. "You mustn't feel obliged, Henry. Florence and I, we'll be fine. I intend to move, maybe to Chicago—"

"Oh, I'm not saying this right. I wish you'd told me is all. Even though I guessed. When I said I knew, I didn't lie."

"Neither did I. I just didn't… tell. No one else knows, besides Papa, Nell, and Verna. Maybe the boys, but I doubt it. I'll understand if you can't forgive me."

Henry wiped a tear from her chin with his knuckle and continued the motion up to her ear. Back and forth, he caressed her face, remembering Da. How much he loved Mum.

"I don't mind what happened before, Mary. All I care about is now. And you." Henry encircled her waist and pulled her into an embrace. "I won't ever let go." He inhaled the perfume of her hair.

"Really, Henry? You still want me? Florence, too?" She sounded out of breath as if she'd been running. "Because I never considered leaving her, no matter what Verna said. Especially not with… her."

"Course I do. She's a faery like her mother. You know how I feel about faeries." His chest wasn't hollow anymore. He kissed her cheeks and sat down, pulling her onto his lap. "But I have to tell you, I can't face cutting down that forest as your father suggested. Felling trees hurts me inside. I avoided it in Michigan. No, I'll try to sell the land, but if not, so be it. I'm nineteen; there's time to make up losses. *Traa dy liooar,* we say."

Mary laughed. "I love it when you speak Manx. I'm so happy. So relieved. I might sprout wings and fly out of this loft right now, like one of those pigeons."

Henry slapped his leg. "I know, let's move to Providence Bay. It's so pretty there. Pretty as a picture. Like you." He kissed her softly. She leaned in, then rested her head on his chest.

"I love that notion. Nell will be so pleased." She took his hand and kissed the soft part between his thumb and index finger. That gesture soothed his racing heart. "Do you think… is it too much to ask? Nell... We're a package."

"Nell must come, of course. Besides, who will drive the buggy while we smooch?" Henry pinched Mary's nose. She slid off, grabbing his arm for balance. He rose, also unsteady on his feet. *We must've emptied the flask between us.*

Chapter Fifty-One

Slaynt as shee as eash dy vea, as maynrys son dy bra:
Health and peace and length of life and happiness forever.

Manx Wedding Blessing

THE next morning, Nell and Mary showed up in the barn where Henry was trimming Betsy's hooves. Their appearance surprised him; all three were usually occupied with their own doings until lunchtime. The women climbed up and leaned on the stall.

"You've helped her so much, Henry," Mary said. "You've a way with horses."

"Horses need attention. And love. Same as people," he said, letting Betsy's foot rest on his knee. "What's going on?"

"Papa told us, Henry," Nell said. "I'm sorry. You're wise to quit while you're ahead, I think. Mary said you two are… sorted. Good. You're meant for each other." She squeezed Mary's shoulder and smiled down at Henry. "I've been pondering the idea of a move to Providence Bay. I'm all for it. I could start a sewing business or teach piano. You wouldn't have to support me."

Henry opened his mouth to protest. She waved him off,

along with a bothersome horsefly. He patted Betsy's rump and took a seat on a bale.

"There might be another option, though. We've been talking, and I recalled a poster in the store showing homesteads on offer. Out west. Ten dollars, one hundred sixty acres. Just imagine!" Her voice had a lilt, and her eyes gleamed.

Henry smiled inwardly. *As brown as Betsy's or Mum's Brown Betty teapot.* The sudden association sparked a familiar pang of remorse. *How's she managed without me? Even around here, they struggle, and they don't have six children—*

"The picture of a farm is so beautiful, Henry, just a drawing, mind you, but one thing's sure; not a tree in sight. Open prairie, in the new province of Saskatchewan."

"Sas-ka-tch-e-wan? Funny, like 'Ypsilanti' or 'Poughkeepsie.' Is it far?"

Mary shook her head. "We don't know the distance exactly, but it shouldn't be hard to find out. Just think, Henry; no trees. What a boon! We could leave straight away. Married, of course. If a man has a family, he can be under twenty-one."

"Whoa, wait a minute. Let's think this through. What about Florence? She needs a home. We wouldn't have a house for a while, I don't imagine. Where will we live? Are there towns, stores—"

"Bah! Other folks are going," Nell said. "It looks like paradise. The poster says, 'The New Eldorado.' Be a shame to miss out."

"But your father'd be heartbroken, Mary. You said you couldn't bear—"

She climbed into the stall and hugged Betsy's neck. "He might come, eventually, but I'm sick to death of Verna, and her brats, especially after… Why Papa married that harridan, I'll never know."

"It's so true," Nell said. "I don't fancy waiting on those three the rest of my life. It's been long enough. Papa's foul temper wears me out. Not to mention, the men in these parts don't interest me. I'd like a home of my own someday."

Henry laughed. "You've plenty of reasons for leaving. Believe me, I understand. Well, can't hurt to look into it." He stood up. "Back to work. I do my best thinking when I'm busy, me. How about you?" He exaggerated a wink.

"Leave off, you bugger. What's your saying: 'Time enough?' The laundry'll get done. If not, it'll be there tomorrow."

Henry opened the stall door, showing Mary out. "Well, best get done what we can and head to Providence Bay this afternoon, then. See if I can cancel the sale, maybe."

"I can just picture it, can't you? Fields of wheat, fat cattle, a big garden with lots of medicinal herbs, even vervain. The faeries will want to set up housekeeping, too, I imagine. They seem to be wherever you are."

"Yes, though I sometimes wonder whose side they're on. I reckon we say *'Themselves'* for a reason."

* * *

After the supper blessing, Verna loudly announced that the young people had news. Mr. Smith halted the carving knife. Mary gasped. Nell dropped the serving spoon full of mashed potatoes. They stuttered through the Saskatchewan plan. Mr. Smith's face turned pale, then red, as he listened.

"Don't say that. Don't say that. I'd never have agreed to your marriage if I'd had any inkling… No, I won't have it." He stabbed the air with the meat fork, glaring at Henry.

Henry gulped, wondering how to justify something he'd only considered for a morning. *God, I hope he doesn't think I had this in mind all along. How did Verna find out? Hmm.*

Nell spilled gravy on the tablecloth, prompting Verna's dirty look. "There's this poster in the store, Papa. It's too good to—"

"Be true. Yes. Well. Been through that, myself. Henry, too, just recently."

"—pass up, I was about to say. It's the government and the CPR, Papa. They can't lie."

"Ha! Never heard that before. Just what do you expect to live on, with no income, maybe for years? Even if they are giving land away." His fork clattered on his plate. "To take my grand—my, my Florence—" He stopped, his eyes fixed on the baby. He picked up his napkin and wiped his eyes.

"It's alright, Papa," Nell said, shaking the gravy ladle at Verna. "Henry knows. About Mr. Bradley running off, leaving Mary in the lurch. Verna let it slip."

"Accidentally on purpose," Mary said. "Yes, Henry knows Florence is my child. Not Verna's. He'll be her father once we're wed." Mary smiled, spoon-feeding the baby. "We'll move the wedding ahead now we're leaving." She glowered at Verna, who shifted in her chair.

"Accidentally on purpose, accidentally on purpose…" Lorne repeated. Then Fred joined in, mimicking him.

"Belt up, the two of youse," Mr. Smith said, banging his fist on the table, making the china rattle. "Eat. On second thought, this conversation is not for little pitchers… Verna!"

Head down, she motioned at the boys, then poured herself tea.

Mr. Smith shook his head at her, anger smouldering in his eyes. Then he aimed his knife at Henry. "That land cost your savings, you said. My girls got no money. How'll you prove up?"

Henry opened his mouth. Mary raised her hand. "Not exactly, Papa. Uncle said we'd receive Mother's legacy upon marriage. What's mine is Henry's."

Henry felt the blood drain from his face. *She never said—*

"You know about this, Henry?" Mr. Smith said, sitting back in his chair. "News to me. Why didn't Duncan tell me?"

"You know why, Papa," Nell said. "Since I'm not likely to marry, given my age and this—" Her eyes shifted down. "I'll take my money now. Where Mary goes, I go."

"And train fare? That'll cost youse a pretty penny, crossing the whole country."

"I'll cover that," Verna said. "I also have some money from Father. I'll help youse on your way."

Shock flashed around the table like lightning. The room filled with the ticking of the clock.

Verna hoisted the teapot. "Tea for you, John?" She smiled, her tone matter of fact. "You seem surprised, dear. You know it's a trial for me with these two constantly bickering. I'd rather hire help or do the work myself in peace and quiet."

Nell blew out her cheeks. "That's rich, Verna. You hardly lift a finger around here. It'll serve you right, keeping up without us."

Verna shifted her cold eyes to Florence, burbling in her chair. "Besides, I've no interest in raising a child not my own."

"You've got it all figured out for yourself, eh, Verna?" Mr. Smith ran his hands through his grey hair and leaned over his empty plate. He pushed his chair back to stand.

"We won't travel straight west, Papa," Nell said. "We must go via Chicago, bid farewell, which will be hard, and make arrangements with Uncle Duncan."

Mary's eyes sought Henry's. "Yes, and Nell and I were thinking, Henry; since we must go through Owen Sound anyway, we ought to visit Cheboygan."

"What? You're traipsing off to Cheboygan, then Chicago? The cost—"

"Damn the cost, Papa. I want to meet Henry's family. It's our only chance." She reached for Henry's arm. "Listen, Henry. You must say goodbye. We're not likely to see any of our folks again."

"We go through Duluth, anyway, for the train," Nell said.

"Worse and worse." Mr. Smith leaned forward in his chair. "It'll cost a fortune. I doubt you factored this in, Verna."

"You cover half, John. There'll be no big wedding," she

said. "They must leave before winter, so there isn't time."

"You're mighty anxious to get rid of us, Verna," Mary said. "Just out of curiosity, what'll you tell your W.I. ladies about Florence?"

"That youse adopted her. Lots of folks do that, too many mouths to feed. Like with your brother, Mel. It doesn't hurt."

Mr. Smith raised his arm as if to strike her. "You know goddamn well that's not what happened, Verna. I couldn't care for a baby, way out here, with two young'uns, no wife…" He collapsed back in his seat. "I regret—"

Mary rushed to her father's side. "Shut up, Verna. Just shut the hell up, you bitch." She rubbed her father's shoulders. "You're in a rush for *us* to leave? We can't bloody well wait."

Verna set down her teacup and sauntered out. Mr. Smith expelled a rush of air and took Mary's hand on his shoulder.

"Listen to reason, Henry. You're set up here. I'll help you clear that land, figure out how to make a living. Don't go West. Take my three girls." His voice broke. Eyes downcast, he said, "I know they were at war with the Métis, just a few years back—"

"Twenty, Papa. Twenty years ago. Not yesterday," Nell said.

"Well, people died, for Christ's sake. God knows what the conditions are now." He reached forward and stabbed the roast chicken. "What've you got to go on, eh? A poster, proclaiming a land of milk and honey. Land's cheap on the Manitoulin, ain't it? You learned that the hard way, Henry… how'll you homestead, just you and the girls? Jim and I, we were two men, and it took years… now we have our own places, thank God."

Brothers. Not always a boon. Mr. Smith was right; we'd need help. I can count on John and Tom. Mary's right, we must stop in Cheboygan. They'll come. Henry's tongue was a flannel rag. He could barely swallow. *Wish I'd brought back the flask. I could use a drink.*

"I don't want you thinking it's all my idea, Mr. Smith. We took the notion together, all at once. The girls made up their own minds—"

"Oh, I know, I know. They're like their mother, God rest her soul. Pioneering? Ain't this family been through enough?" He left them to the uneaten dinner and headed for the parlour.

* * *

Wedding Bells

"On Saturday, August 25, at Providence Bay, the Rev. J. Gilbank officiating, a quiet but pretty wedding was solemnized when Miss Mary Catherine Smith, youngest daughter of Mr. John Smith, was united in wedlock to Henry William Carin, originally of Port Erin, Isle of Man. The bride's dress was green silk with a white shawl. Her bouquet was pink roses and baby's breath. She was attended by her sister, Nell, who wore a dress of maroon satin. Mr. Jim Smith, uncle of the bride, stood up for the groom. Only the immediate family of the bride were in attendance, at the Presbyterian Church. Mr. and Mrs. Carin will proceed to Saskatchewan, where Mr. Carin intends to homestead. Many Manitoulin families are leaving to do the same."

452

Chapter Fifty-Two

By vie lhiat daunsey lhiam:
Would you like to dance with me?

September, 1910

EVENING milking done, Henry carried the buckets to the front porch where Mary and Nell were drinking tea with their feet up.

"Say, my beauties, what's all this lallygagging about on the stoop, then, eh? Do you imagine yourselves aboard ship? Or being waited on hand and foot at the Grand Hotel? With me your servant, delivering warm milk?" He laughed and a bit more milk spilled from the buckets. He shrugged. "My mother always said, 'No use crying over spilt milk.' So, I won't. It's good, you have a cow. First livestock we'll get in Saskatchewan."

"Come wash up," Nell said. "You must be starving after working with Papa all day. How's the packing going? Seems he's sending us with everything but the kitchen sink." She fanned herself with her hand. "We're just taking a break from the heat in the kitchen."

"Yes, we deserve a rest," Mary said. "It's not just you menfolk who work yourselves to the bone, you know. I've been at the laundry all day. My back's killing me."

"And don't mention the *Manitou*, Henry," Nell said, opening the door for him. "I'm worried about all the steamships this journey."

"Believe me, Nell, I sympathize." Henry nodded at her. "Swore I'd never board another ship, me, after our crossing; ended up a stoker. Never say 'never' I guess. Lake Huron isn't the Atlantic, but the waves are just as wild in a storm. Still, it's the gale that brought us together."

Mary smiled, following him inside. "I've had an idea, Henry—"

"Oh no. Grandad would say, 'Means more work for me!' when Nan said that." He set the pails down next to the butter churn. "That pie smells so good. Can't you wait 'til after supper?"

"No. Big Ears is off to her Women's Institute meeting. Talk about listening at keyholes; she's the worst." She frowned as she grabbed a tea towel. "Just one thing before she gets back. I know you said we'd stop to pick up your brothers in Cheboygan, but I want to meet your mother, too. I want her to know me, Nell, and Florence. And also, I think you two need to reconcile. She's your mother, no matter what."

"I know. Since all this, well, I have given it plenty of thought. She deceived Da, though. If I forgive her, I betray his memory, is how I see it."

"Maybe you see wrong. He's gone. Your good memories are set. I never even knew my mother. You'll regret it your whole life if—"

"You've been cogitating on this awhile, I see. But I can't just waltz up to the house, you see. Thomas swore to kill me. He's so violent, I'm lucky I escaped with my skin." He gathered his cigarette makings from the windowsill. "I could arrange a meeting, maybe, through a neighbour. I'll never set foot in that house."

"One more thing—"

"That's two. You're impossible." He laughed and lit his cigarette.

"There's a dance coming up, over at the Gore Bay Hotel. I'd like to go. I could say goodbye to friends, wear my lovely dress, and celebrate a bit since we had no formal wedding." She added quickly, "Oh, I don't mind, don't get me wrong. A shindig would be nice, though." She kissed his cheek, and he encircled her waist.

"I'd love to take you, but be warned, I can't dance."

* * *

"C'mon, Henry," Mary said when he'd sat down for a breather. Mary had taught him the polka and he loved it, but he couldn't keep up with her.

"You'd think stoking'd make a fella more fit." Henry leaned over his knees, gasping. "Maybe I should quit smoking."

"C'mon, don't waste this music. I love dancing; it sweeps me away so I haven't a care in the world." She tugged him toward the dance floor, then suddenly dropped his hand, eyes riveted on a man near the door. Her freckles stood out on her flushed cheeks. She pivoted and almost stumbled.

"Oh, God. It's him. What's he doing here?"

Henry gripped her arm. "Who, what? Whatever's the matter, Mary?"

"Bradley. Over there," she said under her breath, pointing with her chin. "I hope Papa hasn't seen him."

A well-dressed man was making a beeline for the mahogany bar where Jim had been leaning most of the night. Henry took in the dark slicked-back hair, bushy sideburns, full moustache, broad, stooped shoulders, and long legs. Jim waved at Mary. The black coat was now swooping toward them.

Mary looked frantic. Her hand and voice trembled. "Let's

455

get out of here. Please."

Bradley planted himself in front of her just as she was yanking Henry toward the door. "Why, hello, uh, Mary. You're the picture of a blushing bride." He spoke above the music, his nose held upwards as if sniffing the air. "This, I assume, is your husband. Bradley's the name." Rather than extending a hand, he dusted his sleeves. "I read the announcement in the *Expositor.* So nice to know how my protégée is faring."

Henry straightened his shoulders, towering over the man, crossing his arms to show his biceps. *So this is the one who deceived Mary. He'll be lucky I don't clean his clock.*

"Protégée? What d'you mean by that, then?" Mary seethed. "You abandon me, and now you show up? You're on the island? Not in Toronto?"

"I'm the director of the Normal School here in Gore Bay. No more teaching farm brats, though the young ladies are almost as troublesome." He smoothed his shiny hair and twisted back his neck. "I've an assignation here at the dance. I didn't expect to see you. The newspaper said you were—"

"Bradley!" Mr. Smith shouted from across the room. Jim and Elizabeth rushed over from the bar.

"Please, Papa, don't make a scene." Mary interceded, eyes stark. "People will talk. Let's just leave."

Henry slapped a stoker's grip on Bradley's thin arm, thinking to escort him out by force. Verna barged into their midst carrying Florence.

"Oh, hello there, Mr. Bradley." She had no trouble being louder than the fiddler. "You've made yourself scarce." She hoisted Florence into his face. "Meet the newest member of the family. Born after you left. Imagine that."

He backed away. Everyone seated nearby watched the disturbance. The music died.

Florence kicked her feet and wailed. Mary wrenched her from Verna's grasp. "Nell, where's Nell?" She whirled around, asking ladies seated nearby, "Have you seen Nell?"

"Come with me, man," Henry said, "You're upsetting my wife." Henry steered him by the shoulder to where the wagons were parked. The dance was held during the harvest moon so folks would find their way safely home. Henry could clearly see Bradley's face, grey as a photograph. His arms were flailing as though he were drowning. Henry clenched his fists at his sides.

"You must get an annulment. I'll marry her. I didn't know. The child is mine," Bradley's voice was hoarse, but he spat the words one at a time like bullets.

Henry shoved him backward. "Says who? We're married; that's an end to it. I've adopted the child, whose name is Florence. Don't come near Mary again."

Bradley lay there, his gaze fixed on the moon. "I loved her. I thought I did anyway. At the same time, I didn't want to be tied down. At the last minute, I cut and ran. Scared, I guess. Now I've seen… Florence, you say?"

Mr. Smith thundered up, fists raised, eyes bulging. "Get up, you swine. Stand up, you bastard, so's I can knock you down again. Then you won't get up." Spittle was spraying from his mouth. His feet kicked the dirt, just missing Bradley's face. "You betrayed my trust, right under my roof. Took advantage of my girl. I so much as see your ugly face 'round these parts again—"

Henry put his hand on Mr. Smith's pounding chest. "Come on, sir, let's shed this baggage and enjoy our evening." He turned to spit where Bradley was struggling to his feet. "Shove off."

Henry led Mr. Smith, panting and grumbling, back to the hotel lobby. Mary raced to his side, followed by Nell, holding Florence in her arms.

Mary searched his face. "You alright? He's gone? You're sure?"

Nell reached for her father's arm. His hands were still clenched fists. "Did you attack him? Papa, are you hurt?"

"No, Henry stopped me. Lucky for that bastard, I didn't

have my gun. I do believe Henry's driven him off."

They wended their way back to their table and collapsed on the wooden chairs. Mr. Smith took out his flask and offered it to Henry. Nell took a swig after him before her father retrieved it. Verna sat sideways, sipping coffee. Elizabeth was ensconced in a far corner with a group of women. Jim had returned to the bar. The twins were crawling under tables.

Mr. Smith narrowed his eyes at Verna. "Just wait 'til I get you home," he said. "There was no call for him to know. None at all."

Verna sniffed. "Huh. Well, I thought—"

"You 'thought,' did you? That'd be nice, for once. Get your coat, woman. We're going."

The music sounded off-key. *My head's about to explode. Mr. Smith might've had a heart attack.* He put his jacket around Mary's shoulders. She looked as pale and weak as the night he'd rescued her. He half-carried her to the wagon.

* * *

Silence reigned over the breakfast table, marked only by the boys' slurping. Mary rocked Florence on her knee, staring into space. Nell stared at her untouched bowl of oatmeal. Henry toyed with his spoon. Verna hadn't come down, and Mr. Smith had taken his bowl into the parlour. Nell lifted her chin and looked past the open door into the hallway.

"Are you two thinking what I'm thinking?" Nell said. She placed Florence in the highchair. "Here's a cookie, baby. Boys, scrape the plates into the slop pail. Start the dishes. Keep an eye on Florence." She motioned to Henry and Mary and led them down the hall.

Mr. Smith was facing the sideboard, his pipe between his teeth. He started when Nell touched his shoulder. "Jesus, Nell, you made me spill me dram."

"Sorry, Papa." She took the bottle. "A bit early, isn't it?"

Her eyebrows lifted. "I'll take one, too. We came to tell you, we're going. Right away."

Mary nodded. "I can't stay here anymore, Papa. I'll be looking for him at every turn. I thought he'd gone to Toronto. He might come for Florence."

"Take no notice of him," Mr. Smith said. "Henry showed him what for, isn't that right, Henry? Oily coward. Wouldn't even get up after Henry knocked him down." He laughed. "Stay, at least until spring."

"It's not just that, Papa," Nell said. "It's Verna. She makes our lives a misery. She's no care for any of us, including Florence."

"Yes, I know. That was unforgivable. I asked for a divorce, but she won't. I can't just throw her out, considering the boys…"

His shoulders sagged. His hand trembled as he lit his pipe. Henry, Mary, and Nell exchanged concerned looks.

"I'll make a go of it, Mr. Smith, I promise," Henry said. "It's virgin land, just waiting for cultivation. I've broken ground with a single-blade plow—"

Mr. Smith clicked his tongue. "That ain't the right ploughshare; you need a 'coulter.' I looked into it." He exhaled loudly, wiping his eyes with his handkerchief as if the smoke was bothering him. He spoke to the window. "You'll want a team and good harness. Wait, please. It's coming on for winter, and you've a detour… Where will youse live? It'll be too late to build."

"I'm sure there's some sort of accommodation, Papa. It's the government in charge," Nell said.

"All the same. Spend the winter in Chicago then. Or with your folks, Henry? Then set out with the season ahead. Your timing's off."

Henry shook his head. He'd never spoken of his family's troubles and wouldn't do so now. *It would only make things worse.* "No, we must get there soon, have a looksee, find the best land before it's snapped up. I won't make the same mistake twice."

Mr. Smith put down his pipe and lifted Mary up from the sofa. "Don't cry, lass. I'll see youse sorted."

Mary wiped her sleeve across her cheeks, though her lip still quivered. Henry wished he could kiss her. He put his hand on her shoulder instead.

"Thank you, sir. I'll do my level best for your girls."

"Aye, I believe you'll give it your all. We'd best finish packing the crates, Henry. They'll go Fort William straight through to Saskatoon. Rail line just opened. You girls pack your clothes. Only the essentials, mind."

"I'm worried about the cost of shipping, Mr. Smith," Henry said. "Wouldn't it be cheaper to acquire implements there?"

"Let me worry about that." Mr. Smith straightened and pointed. "Meantime, never you fear, Mary; Bradley shows up, why, there's a loaded gun in that closet."

"No, don't." Henry was unable to stop himself. "Don't leave a loaded gun about, especially with these boys. They've no experience…" He paused but had to speak, though his voice shook. "My brother killed my father. Shooting accident. He was twelve."

Nell gasped. Mr. Smith's jaw dropped. He lifted his glass, tossed back the dram, and wiped his lips with his fingers. "I'm sorry for your loss, Henry. You're right. It's not worth the risk. I'll store it safely away."

"You never said, Henry. I, too, give you my deepest sympathy." She poured three more drams and refilled her father's glass.

"We shall drink to the future. Wish us well, Papa." She smacked her lips. "Aye, but that's a fine single malt. Fit for a king." She raised her glass and put on a thick brogue. Mary and Henry laughed.

"You're a true Scottish lassie, Nell," Mr. Smith said, his green eyes twinkling at her. "Listen, the train's my gift so's you won't be beholden to Verna. Make a clean breast of it."

"Oh no, Papa." Nell gave a wicked smile. "Let her be out of pocket. She'll feel superior. And you know how that pleases her."

CHAPTER FIFTY-THREE

She tammylt liayr nearyr's honnick mee shiu:
Long time, no see.

Manitowaning to Cheboygan
October, 1910

THE night before departing, Henry couldn't sleep. Nell had vacated the bedroom for them. She took the spare room; Mary wouldn't set foot in it.

Cheboygan. He'd hoped to have the boys come to Saskatchewan. Mary insisted he patch things up with Mum. So, he'd sent a telegram to Mrs. Miller, asking her to arrange with Pete for the family to come to The Ottawa. *What if Mum refuses to meet? Why wouldn't she after what I did? Least of all… the other business.* He could still feel the snow burning his face as her boots contacted his ribs.

Mr. Smith had sent everything from soup to nuts. Jim's lumber wagon and the back of the buckboard were loaded to the gunnels, leaving no room for Verna or the boys. Just as well. The tension in the house was intolerable; the women snapped openly at each other, and Nell had completely lost patience with

Lorne and Fred. *In that regard, it'll be nice to set sail. Can't believe I'm thinking that. What if Mum... what if Thomas...?*

* * *

They stood next to the wagon, looking anywhere but at each other. The boys twisted their feet in their mother's shadow. Henry kept his hands in his pockets. After her treatment of Mary, Nell, and Florence, Verna didn't deserve a fond farewell.

"Oh, for land's sake—" she said, clicking her tongue, "—get youse gone," she said to Jim, as if scaring off a stray dog. Turning to Henry, she extended her hand. Her eyes were coal black. Unreadable. "You're a fine young man. Mary's lucky."

"I'm the lucky one, Mrs. Smith." He lightly shook her limp hand. "Thank you for the hospitality, ma'am. I appreciate you putting me up." *And I'll be glad never to see your miserable face again.* He smirked at his silent, parting words.

Nell quietly said to the boys, "When people depart, it's customary to shake hands, Lorne. Fred. Kiss your little sister goodbye. You'll never see her again. She won't remember you, but you'll remember her."

They seemed rooted to the ground, tears spilling from their eyes. Henry's chest tightened. *Poor lads, stuck here with Verna.*

"Florence isn't—" she started to say.

Mr. Smith growled at her. She yanked the boys up the stairs, slamming the door.

The five-hour drive to Manitowaning was hot and uncomfortable. Jim had squeezed into the back and kept chattering on, but Henry only grunted or pretended not to hear above the clattering wheels. *Why'd he come along? Not as if the girls will miss him. Who's bringing the buckboard, then?* He pitied Mary and Nell, seated up front with their father. *Was he offering last-minute advice like Grandad?* Behind closed eyes, he saw the white cottage perched on the cliff. Nan and Grandad standing in the dusty road, smiling, waving goodbye. He rocked with the wagon, feeling Ann against his chest, sobbing. He heard Blackie's howls of longing in the creak of the wheels. He opened his eyes. The image disappeared. *This will be the last time the girls will see their father, and Florence, her grandfather. It's a sad day. Mr. Smith probably hates me. Like Tina. Like Mum.*

When they reached the dock, porters ferried the crates aboard, and Mr. Smith helped with their bags. He kept hold of a big leather suitcase. Henry recalled his parents' fierce arguments while packing. *If Mary wants a few more items, fine. Hope she brought her tea dress. We'll have a proper wedding with a dance, someday.*

"I'll help youse aboard with the luggage," Mr. Smith said, encircling Henry's shoulder.

They found seats on the promenade deck. With Florence between them, Nell and Mary held hands, their shoulders trembling. Mr. Smith was making a good show of hiding his feelings, chatting like they had all the time in the world. When the purser announced they were about to slip anchor, Mr. Smith stayed put. Nell touched his arm. Tears spilled from her eyes.

"Time to go, Papa," she said.

Mr. Smith patted the leather suitcase and removed his hat. "Not for me, it ain't. I paid my fare." He beamed at them, nodding and smiling.

Nell and Mary jumped to their feet, both speaking at once. "What? You don't mean… You're coming? How… what will Verna… leave our place… coming to Saskatchewan?"

"Yup." Mr. Smith nodded, tucking his thumbs in his suspenders. "I'm through with Verna. I arranged for Jim to sell up everything, give her half. He'll sell your land too, Henry. There'll be a commission, of course, knowing him, but it's worth it. I couldn't let you girls go West without me. Alright with you, Henry?"

Henry shook his hand warmly, hoping to communicate sincere joy. *We'll be a true family now. Mary and Nell won't pine for him.*

"Oh, Papa," Nell said. "That's wonderful. You'll come to

Chicago, too? See Mel? He's sixteen now—"

"Oh yes, please come. Let bygones be bygones. A fresh start, for all of us," Mary said, whirling Florence in her arms, almost dancing.

"Can't do that, I'm afraid." Mr. Smith said, his voice thick with emotion. "I'll leave youse in Owen Sound, go on to Fort William. I'll accompany the goods to Saskatoon."

* * *

As the stately side-wheeler *City of Alpena* came alongside the quay in Cheboygan, Henry imagined himself back aboard *Topinabee*. So much had changed in four years. Back then, he didn't even debark. Now, he'd just experienced the true luxuries of steamship travel; dining first-class, strolling the promenade under the stars, sleeping like babies rocking on gentle waves. Yet despite the enjoyment, he'd been unable to distance himself; sweat rolled down his sides as if he were below decks. While traversing Lake Huron, he'd pointed to the plume of smoke trailing behind a ship's funnel.

"You know what that pretty cloud represents, ladies?" He displayed his callused palms.

"Kinda spoils the beauty, doesn't it, Mary?" Nell said, shaking her head. "I've never once thought about the men working to power the ship."

"I love your big, strong hands, Henry," Mary said, wrapping her small fingers around them. "They make me feel safe."

As they descended the gangplank to the wooden dock, Henry's heart lifted to see Mrs. Miller and Pete, waving like mad. His grin actually hurt his cheeks while presenting Mary, Florence, and Nell.

"My family. From Manitoulin. We're headed West. My father-in-law meets us there. In Saskatchewan." His voice came out stilted. He struggled to form words.

Pete's old coveralls were worse for wear. His shoulders

seemed more stooped, and when he removed his hat, his head resembled a withered orange. Henry had forewarned the ladies about his scars. Nell had said she completely understood.

Mrs. Miller had foregone her work clothes for the occasion. She wore a fitted sateen dress striped in varying shades of blue and brown, high-laced boots, white gloves, and a brimmed hat with an enormous blue plume. Her curly grey hair framed her wide face, wrinkled and soft as a sun-dried apple. The vibrancy of her dress enhanced the colour of her eyes. Henry could at last believe she'd come from English nobility.

"So good to see you… both."

"Don't look so shocked, Henry," Mrs. Miller said. "We've grown a few whiskers, both Pete and yours truly, but then, so have you. Come here, lad." Her hug smelled of violets. A lump rose to his throat; he coughed and stepped back, stumbling against Mary. "Forgive the bear hug, but it does my heart good to see you, Henry," Mrs. Miller said. "And you've a family. How wonderful." Her eyes beamed at Mary.

"I'm delighted to meet you, too, Mrs. Miller," Mary said, smiling as she straightened Florence's dress, bunched against her arm. "Henry has told me so much about you."

"All good, I'm sure," she said, laughing. "I tend to have strong opinions, isn't that so, Henry? This little beauty is a delightful surprise." She gave Florence's fist a shake. "I'm Mrs. Miller, Florence. How do you do?"

Henry reckoned she'd see Florence wasn't his child, but wouldn't let on. He turned to Pete. "How you been, Pete? How're the girls? And my… the team? Buster and Slick; you were right, I missed them."

Pete's warm brown eyes met his as he shook his hand, a bit longer than necessary. "No worse'n some and better'n most, Henry. Times been tough these parts, but being a bachelor, I manage. You made it to Canada, after all, like you planned. Got married even." Pete fumbled in the pocket of his overalls and presented a fuzzy humbug to Florence with a questioning look at Mary.

"Oh dear, I'm sorry, sir, but she's too young for hard candy. Thank you, though."

Henry felt a rush of appreciation for Mary's gentle manner. Mrs. Miller produced a wrapped chocolate bar from her handbag.

"Gosh, Mrs. Miller. That *is* a treat," Mary said.

"My pleasure," she said, removing her glove to break off a piece and pop it into Florence's mouth. "I always carry a Hershey's in case of emergencies."

Florence's wide-eyed reaction as the chocolate oozed down her chin made everyone laugh. She put out her hand for more, saying, "Ma, ma, ma."

"Mustn't be a greedy goose, missy," Mary said. "She's hungry, Henry."

"Yes, we must go." He turned to Pete. "You're here with the team? Can't wait to see them again." He put his arm around Pete to walk with him. "Didn't find time to write many letters, unfortunately. Seems a lifetime of adventures in just four years. I'll tell you all about it at The Ottawa. You booked us our rooms, Mrs. Miller?"

"Of course, though I do wish you'd come to ours. Leon stayed home to mind the place. He never comes into town anymore; the wagon ride plays hell... heck with his lumbago. You can catch up with him tomorrow on your way to the farm."

Henry stopped, mid-stride. "Uh, no, ma'am." He shook his head. "I've no intention of going out there. None." He wanted to correct her, but politely. "I thought... sorry, but I asked for Mum to meet us with the boys and the little ones."

The cool breeze from the river blew around his shirt collar and under his hat. He felt a chill.

"You warm enough, love? We should've worn our coats." He crossed his arms over his chest. "I swore I'd never look that man in the eye again, Mrs. Miller."

"Well, you're in luck; he's in Boston, seeking a patent on that shingle planing contraption. Pete will bring you to Mullet Lake so's Mrs. Carin and Miss Smith can meet the family properly." She nodded and smiled.

"Just Mary, please, ma'am."

Nell stepped forward. "And I'm Nell. Henry says you play the piano beautifully, Mrs. Miller. I play also."

"Oh, I'd love to hear you. The arthritis makes it harder these days. I'm missing John's daily practice now he's gone."

Henry felt the world tilt. "Gone? What? What's happened to John?" His knees buckled. Mary caught him under the arm. *Oh, God, not John. He always was frail—*

"Oh, my stars, Henry," Mrs. Miller reached out to help Mary. "Don't fret, he's alive and well. Sorry for giving you a turn. All part of the news." She looped her arm in his. "Come, let's get you settled and have dinner. I've booked myself a room. There's a few things you must know before tomorrow. Pete wants to put up in the stable."

Henry returned Pete's crooked grin. "I've been sleeping in a stable for months, myself, Pete. Ah, the warm smell of the hay, the horses crunching their oats, a soft, straw mattress, fresh milk in the morning… who needs a hotel?"

"Gee whiz, Henry, I didn't know you liked it so well; I'd never have brought you into the house," Mary said, smacking his arm, and smiling at Mrs. Miller.

* * *

Seated in The Ottawa's comfortable dining room, with Mrs. Tucker fussing over them, Henry felt at home. Nell and Mary praised the fine dinner of chicken and dumplings, with apple pie and homemade ice cream for dessert. Mrs. Miller looked after the small talk, inquiring about Henry's time as a stoker, questioning Nell and Mary about Manitoulin Island and their reasons for going west.

"Saskatchewan, you say. Never heard of it. What gave you that notion, if I may be so bold…"

Henry ate quickly, tapping his foot under the table, anxious for Mrs. Miller's news. Tom's letter was smouldering in his breast pocket. Obviously, he'd left some things out.

After Nell and Mary had retired with Florence, Mrs. Tucker offered her office for privacy. Henry caught a look pass between her and Mrs. Miller. She poured them each a glass of brandy, leaving the bottle, before gently closing the glass French doors.

"A lot has transpired, Henry. You're in for some surprises. Some, I'm at liberty to share. The rest you must hear from your mother."

"Whatever you think best. It's bad, isn't it?"

"Depends how you look at it. After you left, Leon and I adopted John. We're fond of him… he seemed to be foundering over there. I taught him piano, and he helped with the garden. A hard worker, good with flowers. He thrived at school here in town. I took him to England to study art in a boarding school. He spends holidays with my family in London."

Henry clapped his hands together. "Why, that's wonderful. He's away from Thomas, and he'll get a good education. He had a gift for drawing." He felt genuine delight for John, but sadness for himself. "I'll likely never see him again, though."

He pictured John's big chestnut eyes, his shock of brown hair always falling into them, and his fine, small-boned hands that could render anything in pencil or ink. With feeling. Speed in the line. Depth in the shading. *Oh, my sweet brother. Thomas could've destroyed your spirit.* His nose tingled and tears pricked his eyes. *Thank you, mooinjer vegewere, for Mrs. Miller.* He exhaled. His hand shook as he brought the glass to his lips.

"Go on, Henry; you could do with a stiffener." She took a drink and set down her glass. "Next big change; your mother married Thomas." Her voice was deep as if she were planting the fact.

"I know. Tom wrote." He unfolded the letter, shaking his head. "I still can't believe it." He stood up, banging his shin on the coffee table. "Dammit."

"A woman alone with five children—"

Henry put up his hands. "Don't worry, Mrs. Miller. You don't have to explain. I've come to understand things more clearly since meeting Mary."

"Mary's a lovely young woman, I can tell. I'm pleased you aren't… angry. Thomas is, well, he—"

"Doesn't mean I've forgiven him. Never. He had this in mind all along, don't you see? He knew Da was dying when he sponsored us. He's been after Mother since… well, there are things I can't say, either." He twisted his hard knuckles together like knots of twine. Blood surged in his legs, roared in his ears. "I see him again, I'll wring his bloody neck."

"Good job he's not here then. You'll be in and out of the house and him none the wiser. Your mother's expecting you."

Her response startled him. "She knows?"

She refilled her glass and nosed the brandy. "Only seemed right."

He ran his hand through his hair. "And Edward? How's Edward?" He pictured Edward's stricken face after the shooting. *What's he like now? Can I forgive him, as Da wanted?*

"Edward still doesn't speak. Makes himself understood by gestures, when he engages at all. Very sad. I helped your mother consult a physician. There's nothing they can do; it's a choice on his part." Mrs. Miller took a final swig and pushed up on the sofa. Henry offered his arm. "My back's killing me. Not used to stays. What we women suffer!"

She squeezed Henry's hand. "That's enough for one night. Your mother must fill in the rest. I've shopping to do. Show the girls around in the morning, leave after lunch?"

Henry nodded, agreeing to whatever she said. His mind

reeled. Maybe the brandy had gone to his head. *Edward's still mute? I'll face everyone tomorrow? Mum. What can I say to her, after accusing her, abandoning her, against Nan's wishes? Has she forgiven me? Can I forgive her?*

Mrs. Miller fairly pushed him up the stairs. "Let's be for our beds. Everything will look better come morning."

Chapter Fifty-Four

Faeries, if I heed your calling,
if I take your out-stretched hands,
Will you lead me through the sunrise
to your wondrous golden lands?
"If your heart is as a child's heart,
you shall cross the sunrise bar,
And the ocean that is lighted by a star.
You shall see our lands of gladness—
hills all green and gold and grey,
and shall wander in the bluebell glens
beside the tossing spray!"

Manx Song & Maiden Song,
Mona Douglas, 1915

EUPHEMIA stood on the porch, arms across her chest, boots welded to the floor. From the second-storey window, Ann had seen the wagon approaching and raced downstairs, shouting, "Henry! He's home!" Hugh and Eliza abandoned their game of jacks on the parlour floor and followed her out. Tom leapt on his horse to meet the wagon. Edward remained indoors with Sophie. Euphemia couldn't blame him. She'd breathed a sigh of relief when Mrs. Miller had shared the telegram, glad to know Henry was still alive. But she was puzzled. *Why is he coming here before going off again, this time for good? What does he want? How am I supposed to feel?*

Pete's wagon rolled up. A tall, muscular young man, wearing fine clothes and a Derby hat jumped down. Henry? She'd have passed him on the street. Even more surprising, he was helping two women alight, one holding a little girl.

"Hello, Mum," he called, waving over Ann's shoulder. She'd vaulted into his arms, encircling his neck, kicking her feet like a five-year-old. Tom tossed the horse's reins on the hitching post and rushed over, embracing them both. They danced in a circle, then dropped arms but kept hold of each other's hands, twittering like birds on a wire. Sal sauntered up and licked Henry's outstretched hand. Henry bent down and wrapped his arms around her. When he introduced the women and child, they all smiled and shook hands.

Hugh and Eliza tumbled down the stairs and stood watching the spectacle, waiting to be noticed by the brother neither remembered. Henry hugged Hugh, exclaiming at his height, and lightly touched Eliza's chubby cheeks. He carried the toddler over to meet her. The little girl plumped down on the ground, dirtying her white dress.

From her perspective on the porch, the scene was a silent movie, in blazing fall colours, not black and white. Euphemia felt no rush of love. Her body was a block of ice, wrapped in straw. Clenching her jaw, she struggled for words of welcome. *Four years of worrying and wondering, and now I'm empty. I've cried all my tears. He's a stranger—*

Ann carried the child while Tom hauled him up the stairs and gave him a light shove. "It's grand he's come home," Tom said. "Isn't it, Mum? We've missed you, haven't we?"

Her arms were twenty-five-pound flour sacks, too heavy to lift. Henry's eyes sought hers. *William's eyes.* Crystal blue irises, rimmed by navy circles. His black hair brushed her cheek as she stood in his embrace. She'd never imagined him surpassing her in height. *Tall as his father.*

He turned and gestured for the women to approach. "I've come to present my family, Mum." His voice sounded distant as if he were speaking into a brisk wind. "Mary, my wife. Our daughter, Florence. Her sister, Nell. From Manitoulin Island. Ontario. Canada."

The sister-in-law put out her hand. "Pleased to make your acquaintance, Mrs. Carine."

Mary looked up under heavy eyebrows. "How do you do, ma'am? Henry's told me—"

Henry broke in. "We're on our way to the Canadian west, Mum, to homestead. More than fifteen hundred miles, not including a stop in Chicago. We came to say hello, and goodbye."

That was impolite. I taught him better. Nell's handshake was awkward, something's wrong with her hand. She has a lovely smile. Mary has pretty red hair and sparkling green eyes, but her fair skin's so freckled. She ought to avoid the sun. They're in plain goods, well-tailored. Which one's the seamstress, I wonder? Mary's delicate as a teacup. And a child… What on earth is he thinking?

She expelled the air locked in her chest. "It's my lot in life, it seems. Meetings and partings. Partings, mostly. Isn't that so, Henry?" He lowered his head.

"You'll be wanting tea, I shouldn't wonder." She heard herself employ the tone she'd developed for paying guests. "Sophie and Edward are fixing lunch. You remember Sophie, Henry? From The Ottawa? Mrs. Miller's likely explained I can't put youse up. I've taken in boarders."

She cleared her throat, straightened her shoulders, and smoothed the front of her dress. Opening the door, she motioned to Tom. "Show them through to the dining room. You'll be surprised to see tables in the parlour and the hall, Henry. You may have noticed the sign at the top of the road. I run a roadhouse. Customers might show up anytime expecting service."

"Oh please, Mum, let them stay," Ann said, as she carried the little girl across the threshold. "Florence, I've something to show you upstairs. Come, Eliza, let's show her the dollhouse." She smiled at Henry. "Didn't bring *Little Ones* along by chance? Ours left, remember?"

Henry shook his head. "Sadly, no. I found some, out Manitoulin way—"

"You ladies may follow Ann. There's a bathroom to refresh yourselves. I've just had it put in." Euphemia watched Florence take the stairs, one at a time, holding Ann's hand. She estimated her age at about two. Henry called her his daughter, but she knew that he'd been aboard ship when he left home. Tom had reluctantly shared Henry's letters, swearing he'd had no word in a year. They assumed he'd been lost in a storm. That must be when he went to Canada. *Florence isn't his child. Interesting.*

When lunch was ready, Ann set four more places at the dining room table. Tom brought a highchair for Florence and insisted Pete join them when he stayed in the kitchen.

"You're family, Pete. Hell, we'd never have made a go of this place without you."

The swinging kitchen door opened, and Henry rushed to his feet.

"Hello, Sophie. Good to see you," he said. She nodded and smiled at the tray of sandwiches.

"Glad you're safe and sound, Henry. Your mother feared—"

"The sandwiches look lovely, dear," Euphemia said. "Where's Edward?" She raised her voice. "Edward, bring the tea and greet your brother and his family." She noticed Mary flinch. "Sorry to startle you. Sometimes, I think my son is deaf."

She sighed as Edward pushed back the saloon doors. "There you are. Can't you at least say a word to Henry?" Her hand shook as she set down the tray. *It's a choice, the doctor said. Maybe seeing Henry will shock him out of it.* She watched to see if he'd accept Henry's extended hand. He walked past him and placed the teapot on the buffet, then perched on a stool next to the window. Sophie circulated, pouring out tea and lemonade.

Shaking her head, she caught Hugh and Eliza fidgeting. At seven and four, neither could easily reach the table. Eliza squirmed on a cushion that constantly fell to the floor. Euphemia tapped her spoon. "Behave for the company, you two. Excuse them please, ladies. The children usually eat in the kitchen."

"Oh, Mum, you haven't gone and banned them—"

"I've a business to run, Henry." Raising her teacup, she made eye contact with Mary. "Enlighten me, please, as to how you first met. When was it?"

Mary opened her mouth, but Nell jumped in. "Your son saved Mary's life. We were on a trip to Mackinac Island on the *Manitou*. He rescued her in the nick of time, about to be swept overboard. Maybe you heard of the storm? Last August? Lives were lost, ships went down in the Straits. We were lucky."

"Then Henry looked us up on Manitoulin. This June."

Euphemia smiled. "Good gracious, you're a hero, my son. Henry must've swept you off your feet, like that wave, Mary. A quick courtship." She tipped her head to indicate Mary's wedding ring. "Very pretty."

"Remember Grandad's saying about a short courting, Mum? It was love at first sight, on my part. I'm glad she felt the same." He lifted and kissed Mary's left hand.

"Nothing beats young love. Your father and I didn't take long to decide either," Euphemia said, heartened by Henry's gesture. "We did hear about that terrible storm. Praise be, you're all safe. Was Florence with you? I still have nightmares about our crossing. We were all sick, except Henry. Hugh nearly died of fever. Travelling with children on a ship is—"

"Which is why, once we reach Duluth, I'll never set foot aboard a ship again." Henry rattled the teacup in his saucer. "I've had one too many escapes for my liking."

"The faeries helped you, Henry. I'm sure," Ann said.

"I didn't sleep a wink during John's crossing with Mrs. Miller until I received word they'd arrived in Liverpool."

"Remember Liverpool, Henry?" Tom said, laughing. "That funny parrot? Jim? 'Good Jim, lovely Jim,'" he mimicked. "You set him free, eh, Edward? That was a lark! There's a photograph of us, with Da… where is it, Mum? I'd like to show—"

"I remember now," Ann said, her blue eyes lit with excitement. "Holy cow! I thought I'd dreamt it. There was a parrot flying loose and a man talking to it." She turned to Eliza. "A parrot is a colourful bird that can talk. Really."

"About the only good memory from that trip," Euphemia said. She wiped her mouth on her napkin and looked across the table at Henry. *He's sat in his old seat. Old habits die hard.*

"So now, explain this hare-brained scheme of yours, Henry," Euphemia said. "To go the other side of the continent, to the wild west. To farm? What do you know about farming?"

"No more foolish than crossing an ocean, I expect," Henry spoke into his teacup.

"That wasn't my idea. Your nan cooked up that scheme. With Thomas, as we discovered later to our cost. I warned William, but my words counted for naught." Euphemia felt her temper redden her cheeks. "I hope you women have a say."

"Oh, yes, indeed, Mrs. Carine," Mary said, nodding. "Nell and I suggested it, in fact. My father's meeting us in Saskatchewan. He homesteaded on Manitoulin with his brother. I've got the government pamphlet in my bag to show you. Ten dollars for one-hundred-sixty acres of wide-open prairie never tilled. It's called 'virgin soil.' Easy as pie—"

"Oh dear. You'll want to ask Mrs. Miller about that." Euphemia returned her gaze to Henry, who was twisting his napkin into a knot. "Thomas touted Michigan as the land of milk and honey, a cure-all for your father, a better life for us. Isn't that so, Henry? And we believed him."

Henry tossed down his napkin and pushed back his chair. "I'm not Thomas. May we speak outside, please?"

CHAPTER FIFTY-FIVE

Cair Vie! Fair Winds!

EUPHEMIA collected her tobacco from the kitchen as they exited through the back door. They sat side by side on the porch bench. Euphemia lit up and then handed the pouch to Henry.

"How do you find us then, eh? Much changed?" She picked a bit of tobacco from her tongue.

"Yes, to be honest, Mum." Henry took a deep pull on his cigarette. "Boarders? A roadhouse? You all crowded upstairs, Sophie sleeping in the parlour? I'm sorry you have to live this way."

"Well, I'm not." She fairly spat the words. "For the first time since I worked at the Sugarland, I'm earning my own money. I spend it as I please. No man to boss me."

"What's Thomas doing? Mrs. Miller said you'd explain. Is everything alright?"

"Thomas is a liar, as you know. He's also a bigamist. Ha!" She waited for him to close his open mouth. "You're as surprised as I was. Well, it came as a shock but has turned to my advantage. It's his shame, not mine. Now he's in my debt, and the property's in my name." She tapped her thumb against her chest. "So, you see, I'm doing well actually. Pete's taken over the fields; we share the profits. Tom, Ann, and Hugh help with cooking and washing up, Sophie does the housekeeping and minds Eliza. They've a tutor, twice a week. Everything runs like clockwork… except for Edward." She fiddled with her cigarette. "I've no idea what to do with him. But Thomas? He hasn't a leg to stand on."

Her triumph resonated, deep within; she heard it in her voice. "Unlike your Manx fellow, who spins around on three." She nudged Henry's shoulder.

He took her hand and squeezed. "Thomas is still here, though. Has his temperament changed?" He searched her eyes. "Didn't think so. Listen, come with us, Mum. As a widow, you could have your own homestead. Maybe Pete would join us, help me train a team. I'd love that. I imagine there's a school—"

"A foolish notion, Son." She blew smoke through her nose. "This property is mine, lock, stock, and barrel. I deserve it. Besides, I won't uproot the children again. Remember how Nan loved sitting in the cemetery, surrounded by the ancestors? Your father was the first Carine buried on foreign ground. He's here. I bought him a headstone; I must show you. I'll lie beside him someday." Her voice caught on the truth of her ultimate ambition.

"So, this really is goodbye then?" Henry lifted her chin. She turned her face away.

"I've said goodbye so many times. Nan, Grandad, two lost lambs that never made it into this world you didn't know about—" She stubbed her cigarette out on the floorboards, then bent to collect the butt. "Then William, then you… Edward and John, both gone or as good as… So."

"I… I also came to say… I'm sorry, Mum. I'm so sorry I hurt you and then ran off. Especially after promising Da on his deathbed to head the family. He gave me his ring… Grandad's… and I… I lost it." He dropped his head into his hands, sobbing.

She stood and gently lifted Henry by the arm. He slumped against her. She held him tight, patting his back, shushing him, like she did when he was a little boy. A lump rose to her throat, and her eyes tingled. Fumbling in her sleeve, she extracted the handkerchief tucked under her cuff. She wiped his face, letting her own tears flow, then sat them both down again.

"I've had a lot of time to think since you left, Henry." Her lip trembled. She wanted him to know the whole truth before leaving. "I blame myself. I relied on you too heavily, made you grow up too fast, and then, when you found out about me, Thomas, Edward… a step too far for anybody. Don't carry the blame, Henry. It's a fire that burns the one who holds it."

"I understand now, Mum. I do. Mary helped. I know you did your best."

"Not always. I made mistakes, I admit. Say, I just want to ask you something. What do intend to say to your… daughter, when she's older? Don't make the mistake I did. I felt I had no choice. That's all I want now; freedom to choose my own path. That's why I let John go, though it broke my heart. He'll be educated. At the orphanage, I couldn't think for myself. I learned nothing but how to work hard." She pressed her hands against her hollow stomach. "And to pray. I still pray." She smirked a little. "It helps."

"And sing, Mum. Do you sing anymore?" Henry took her by the shoulders in an embrace she couldn't escape, so she leaned in. His musky, warm tobacco scent was William's. She reached up and put her palm on the back of his head, smoothing the thick, black hair, realizing how startled he must've been to see hers cut in a bob, shot with grey. She would never see his hair turn white. Nor John's either.

"'Safe journey,' they say, in Manx? Never 'goodbye.' I like that."

They jumped at the slam of the privy door. Edward stood, stock-still, his grey eyes wide.

"What is it, Edward?" Euphemia said. "If you've something to tell Henry, best do it now. You'll not see him again."

Edward didn't budge, even at the sound of a wagon pulling up out front. Euphemia gripped Henry's arm and covered her lips with her hand.

"Oh, God. It's Thomas. Back, already? Shit. You'd best gather your family and go."

"No. I'll leave when I'm good and ready. I've a right to visit—"

Thomas lumbered toward the back door, shouting and waving a paper. "Got it, Pheme. My patent! I can start building the planes—say, what's Pete doing here?" He halted, removed his hat, and squinted into the sun. "Who's this, then? A new hand… Oh, Christ, no—"

"Not Christ, Thomas," Henry said. "It's me, Henry. Remember? Oh, maybe you forgot my name. I'm here visiting my family."

Henry's tone and wide-legged stance spelled trouble. Euphemia had to act, and quickly.

"Edward, go, round up Pete, tell him our guests are leaving." She turned to smile down at Thomas. "Good news about the patent. You must be pleased. Henry just brought his new family to meet me… us." She stood, straightened her skirt, and pulled down her sleeves. "You'll want to be off now, Henry. Mrs. Miller will have supper for youse this evening. Lunch guests are arriving any minute."

Through the screen door, she called, "Sophie, please clean my Brown Betty. I'm giving it to Mary and Henry as a wedding gift." She adopted a cajoling tone. "Henry's married, Thomas. She's a lovely girl with a sweet little red-haired daughter—"

"I couldn't care less. I told you to piss off four years ago and never come back. The upset you caused to your mother and... the others. Selfish bastard. Get the hell off my property, or I swear I'll—"

"Another of your lies, Thomas. Can't help yourself, can you?" Henry said, his voice seething with rage.

Mary opened the door. Henry motioned her back. "Never mind, love, I don't want you to meet this—baggage. Please, just stay inside, keep the children together. My uncle and I have business to discuss. Then we'll leave."

"Business?" Thomas roared. "Ah, so it's money you're after, is it? Figures. Don't you be giving him one thin dime, Pheme. I told you he'd be back, tail between his legs. You ruined everything, you little fucker."

"I... I... ruined—" Henry gasped for breath. "Fuck you for the liar you are!"

Thomas was mounting the steps, head lowered like a bull about to charge. Suddenly his body jerked backwards. He tumbled to the ground, splayed out, raising a cloud of dust. His hat rolled away. Edward stood over him, brandishing an axe. Euphemia screamed and stumbled down the steps. Edward seemed unaware of her presence.

"Leave Henry alone," Edward said, his voice even. He brought the axe closer to Thomas' face. "I know you're my father now. All the more reason to split your head open like a goddamn melon. I hate your fucking guts."

Euphemia put her hand on Edward's back. "It's all right now, love. I know you're trying to help. Henry's going, aren't you, Henry? He'll be safe."

Henry came down and stood beside her. Her eyes implored him to retreat before Edward did something foolish. He shook his head, hands on hips.

"No, Mum, I'll have my say. I've waited long enough." He spat on the ground beside Thomas' prone figure. "I didn't leave my family, asshole. I left you. You tricked us into coming here, then used us like unpaid servants. You never wanted to help Da, just yourself." He made a fist and pounded it into his hand.

Thomas rolled on his side, making to get up. "Pheme's all I ever wanted. She's my—"

Henry pushed him, sending him sprawling face-first. "Second wife. I know. Caught with your pants down, again, eh? Like when I was a kid? Listen, you, I'm not fifteen anymore. I've been a stoker and a stevedore and could knock your lights out, old man. If I hear you're mistreating any of my family… you watch your back. There's a man I know would slit your throat for a pint of beer."

Euphemia kicked Thomas' booted foot. "Get to the barn, Thomas, and stay there until they leave. I say who comes and goes around here. I don't belong to you. Move your arse. Now."

* * *

Euphemia sighed as the wagon pulled away. She held hands with Tom and Sophie on either side. *It's as if we're on the dock this time, waving to a ship setting sail. Another parting for all of us.* Ann hugged Florence close, sobbing into her hair until Mary gently said, "We must go, sweetheart. It's been lovely meeting you."

"Take the dollhouse for Florence, please, Henry. Faeries will move in at your new place. Is it far? Can I come visit?"

"It's impossible to transport right now. You'll bring it to us someday," Henry said, lifting her up. "You're a doll yourself, my sweetheart. That's what the photographer in Liverpool said, remember, Mum? He gave us some free prints so's he could keep your picture on display. It's probably still there next to Jim's cage, him sassing everyone. Parrots live a long time." He bent to kiss her head, and Euphemia saw the pain in his eyes, though his voice was bright. "You're growing up beautiful, clever, and strong. We'll meet again. I'll be sure to write often. I hope to get a camera to take pictures for you all. Of our farm."

Euphemia sensed Ann watching now from the upstairs window. Edward had dropped the axe and run off. Euphemia wondered if he'd just talked for the last time. She hoped not.

Maybe the spell is broken. But now he knows, things could be worse.

She squeezed Tom's icy hand. "Thank you for staying, pet. I know you'd like to… join them. I hope you won't regret it. I love teaching you to cook, I really do." She couldn't say more.

"I won't leave you, Mum. I'm a man now. It's my duty," Tom said.

Sophie clicked her tongue. "I'm sorry for you all. The family's broken up," she said. "A fine gift, Mrs. Carin, your precious teapot. I've never seen another one like it."

"I've been thinking of switching to coffee, any road," Euphemia said with a little laugh.

As the wagon wheels revolved in a cloud of dust, she saw Edward run up and leap into the back next to Mary, Nell, and Florence. Seated beside Pete, Henry obviously hadn't noticed. When Mary tapped his back, he swivelled. Pete pulled the reins, but Edward gestured to keep moving. He waved goodbye with his cap and raised his face to the upstairs window. Shielding her eyes from the sunlight, she couldn't see his expression. Henry called out to her. Euphemia waved.

"Let him go," she told herself aloud. "Stick together, my dears. *Cair vie.*"

Epilogue

Te aashagh fuinney raad to palçhey meinn:
It is easy to bake where there is plenty of meal.

NW Section 32, Township 48, Range 14 W2
Saskatchewan, Canada
September 25, 1936

"GET a move on, Henry," Edward shouted from the truck. "What's the hold-up? Everyone's getting restless. Time's a-wastin'. Gotta make a mile 'fore dark."

"Coming," Henry said, struggling to place the stone hammer without dropping it on his foot. He braced the chiselled groove against the door jamb. Just try and blow that closed now, you goddamn wind. Henceforth, the spirits could roam in and out of the house, free. Leave them to it. He reached into his pocket for his handkerchief. The arrowhead, his talisman, dropped to the floor. It had appeared at the toe of his boot twenty-two years ago, while he was ploughing a furrow through the matted grass. He'd stood under the hot sun in the midst of his first one-hundred-sixty-acre parcel. So happy. So proud. Just twenty-one, already a landowner, with a family to support. His dream come true.

Amongst the wealth of stones to clear, this shape had caught his eye. Not natural. He'd bent to collect it, squeezing the tip against the palm of his hand. It hurt. *How long has this been here? Fifty years, maybe more?* Every day afterward, walking behind the plough uprooting the prairie wool, points appeared, seeking the light. Sometimes the coulter broke them in two. Some were delicate, shaped with precision, made for flight at the end of an arrow and then to pierce… a bird, perhaps? Others were heavy and crude, not meant for an arrow but a spear. What animals had they killed he wondered. Bison? Giant bears? People had fashioned weapons to hunt on this very land where, by some miracle, he'd ended up. A Manxman. From so far away. His land. Was it, though?

He'd selected the best arrowheads for a collection, attaching them with wire to an old board. When the space was full he quit, though he could've started another. He hung it in the living room, crowned by the antlers of the first deer he'd hunted for food. He hated shooting, but Thomas had been right in that respect: "You don't hunt, you don't eat."

One day, he found a large, sculpted boulder, which he realized would have been strapped to a handle of wood or bone. He kept it by the bench outside where he'd sit and smoke of an evening. Hefting it in his hand, he'd felt a line extending between him and the maker, running along that groove. Someone had painstakingly chiselled solid rock for a hammer. Right here. He'd work this land as that one had fashioned the hard stone, to make something of it.

Now, years on, they were giving up. Tired, strength gone, hope extinguished in grass fires, flown off on grasshoppers' wings that devoured everything, even the paint on the house, swept out of doors in fine dust sifting through cracks in windows and doors. Mary's garden was a cemetery, the plant markers all askew, crosses marking dead plants. The vervain had not survived. He'd never sensed the faeries hereabouts, any road. He glanced at the highchair standing in the corner. A masterpiece. Too big to bring along. No child would ever sit there again. He'd bought a camera and taken photographs over the years. He couldn't take any more.

They could do no more. The elation of bumper crops in '14 and '15 had given way to depression and debt as they took on more land, he and Edward too, when he was old enough.

"Rain will follow the plough," they'd said. Liars. The idyllic images on the posters in the General Store? False. The deeper they tilled, the more soil drifted into the air like the Canada Geese flying in V's, headed south. *We never should have torn up the buffalo grass. We ought to have left this land to them as knew how to live here. We can't survive as they did for time out of mind. Sometimes I wish we'd never left Man. But then I'd never have met Mary.*

He coughed. The dust had gotten to him. He'd suffered pneumonia last winter. He and Edward both had paying jobs waiting. In the new Atlas Coal Mine. Edward would mine. Henry's planing skills meant he'd help build the tipple. He would work above ground. He worried about Edward, but they had no choice. *Da and Mum left everything behind on Man for our sake. We must do as much, for our children.*

He'd seen the advertisement in the paper, offering jobs in a place called Drumheller. Across the border in Alberta. Further west, almost 900 miles. Good wages. Modern safety measures. They said the winters were mild and the dry air was healthy. The company provided a white-washed cottage with a kitchen garden. *Mary will like that. First thing I'll do is paint the door red. She'll plant vervain...* He forced himself to smile. Giving up the two sections of land they'd proved up was not the hardest part. He could walk away with nothing to show for twenty-two years but more calluses on his hands, more aches and pains in his back. Selling the horses though, that nearly killed him.

Nan's voice echoed in his head, bouncing off the walls in

the empty house: "You boys will go down the mine over my dead body." *It is so, Nan. I'm sorry. But not our John, I promise. There's a high school in the town for him and Edward and Nell's girl, Susan. John will be educated, like one of his two namesakes.* Henry's nose tingled, not from dust. *Both are gone now.* Mr. Smith, who'd helped them get settled, then started his own harness-making business in town. *Died in his traces. That would've pleased him.* Sad as they were, they'd accepted it; he was old. Worse news had only just arrived from Mrs. Miller. John and her English relations had been killed in a motorcar accident in France. She and Euphemia were on their way to see him buried on Man. Mrs. Miller would stay in England. Leon had passed. She'd take over the family estate she'd abandoned long ago. She wrote to Henry that to her surprise, she wanted to die at home.

Meetings and partings. Mary was thrilled her daughter had become a schoolteacher, fulfilling her own dream. Henry wondered if she had regrets, though she denied it. Florence worked in Pontrillas; teaching jobs were hard to come by, especially now. They'd search when they got to Alberta. *Maybe she will join us next year.* He shivered. He hated those words, though they'd come back time and time again, with every hailstorm, every blighted crop. Next year. Things will be better then.

A gust of wind caught the door. The stone hammer wobbled. He leaned down to wedge it in place. Sunlight chased dust motes in the hollow kitchen. They would fly free, swirl, and dance undisturbed on the Saskatchewan prairie, forever. Where they were meant to be. *Slane lhui, mooinjer vegewere.* "Goodbye." He closed his eyes. And squeezed. Just for a moment.

ACKNOWLEDGEMENTS

A book cover bears an author's name, but many supportive people bring it from a dream to reality. Such has been true of the ten-year journey of *Time Enough*.

I am indebted to family, friends, professionals, colleagues, and the hundreds of books I have read. Foremost, I acknowledge my beloved Jeremy, my champion, astute critic, and partner in life, parenting, and love for half a century. A skilled artist, Jeremy Mayne's work graces the covers of both my novels with beauty and symbolism.

Thank you to Gail Anderson-Dargatz, my mentor throughout the development of this novel. Writers-in-residence who provided feedback and support include Ian Williams, Louise Halfe, and Richard Van Camp. Richard kicked me through the goalpost when I was about to give up. Eternal gratitude, Richard.

Editors Donna-Lee Wybert, *TextualMatters, Inc.*, and Peter Biello, *Burlington Writers' Workshop*, provided detailed critiques. Tom W. Parkin, the author of *A Land of Their Own*, introduced me to our shared Manitoulin ancestry and the history sparked my imagination. I greatly appreciate his support as a beta-reader, and that of my sister-in-law Laurel Deedrick-Mayne, award-winning author of *A Wake For The Dreamland*.

Thank you to authors Ali Bryan and Joan Fernandez for reviewing the advanced reader copy. My daughter, Jessica, and her husband, Tory, have given me their never-ending love and encouragement, as well as our two beautiful grandchildren.

Thank you to *Sunspot Literary Journal* for publishing the first three chapters of *Time Enough* in the Rigel Contest, 2022.

All this encouragement has sustained me. Friends and readers kept asking, "When is your next book coming out?" Thanks for waiting and believing. Always, a shout-out to my early teachers, Mrs. Kassian, and Mrs. Rita Wold, for nurturing my passion for writing. I had many good teachers, whose examples I tried to follow in my career as a teacher and principal.

My heartfelt thanks to Dr. Karen Croftcheck, publisher at *Oprelle Publications*, for believing in this book. She understood the depth of the immigrants' struggle to survive and the fragility of their hopes and dreams. *Time Enough* has been held behind my eyes like an after-image for decades. Karen brought it into the light. Thank you to the wonderful eagle-eyed staff at *Oprelle* for their fastidious dedication.

With only a smattering of family history details, I created imaginary characters and events tracing emigration from the Isle of Man to Michigan, the Isle of Colonsay to Manitoulin Island, and finally to Saskatchewan in the early 1900s. The last scene was my original inspiration. My grandmother recounted Grandpa's gesture of farewell to their homestead near Nipawin, Saskatchewan, in the 1930s. My grandparents respected First Nations people. As a child, I was fascinated by grandpa's collection of found arrowheads, passed down to me. I cried over his grief at leaving the land. Mom said he was never the same. I acknowledge the debt owed to the original inhabitants of the prairies before the fences, where they raised families for millennia. May our remembrance and a clearer understanding of the past foster awareness and bring us together.

Citations

"My prairie song-bird, An Indian love song," Drislane, Jack, 1909.

Courtesy the Frances G. Spencer Collection of American Popular Sheet Music, Arts and Special Collections Research Center, Baylor University. Waco, Texas.

https://tinyurl.com/y3jrp6zx.

"Waltz Me Around Again, Willie ('Round-'Round-'Round)," Cobb, Will D., lyrics; Shields, Ren, music, 1906.

Courtesy the Levy Sheet Music Collection, Box 150, Item 120. Johns Hopkins University Collection.

https://levysheetmusic.mse.jhu.edu/collection/150/120

"Daisy Bell," Dacre, Harry, 1892.

Courtesy the Levy Sheet Music Collection, Box 140, Item 090. Johns Hopkins University Collection. Archived from the original on 19 April 2014.

https://levysheetmusic.mse.jhu.edu/collection/140/090

"Fairies," *Manx Song & Maiden Song*, Douglas, Mona, William Morris Press Ltd., Manchester, England, 1915.

Used with kind permission of Manx National Heritage.

https://manxliterature.com/sort-by-genre/genre/manx-song-and-maiden-song/

Photo Credit: Lorraine Hjalte Photography

About the Author

LISE MAYNE writes from her home in Nanton, Alberta. Injustice and the search for home are themes of her work. *Time Enough* is her second historical novel. Her poetry appears in nine international literary journals, honoured with four awards. An excerpt of *Time Enough* was published by *Sunspot Literary Journal* in the Rigel Contest, 2022. A retired bilingual educator, Lise volunteers as a Rocky Mountain bluebird monitor on the Eastern Slopes. In her spare time, she does embroidery and plays the harp.

Website
https://lisemayne.ca

Instagram
https://www.instagram.com/maynelise_author

LinkedIn
https://www.linkedin.com/in/lise-mayne-lg-pomerleau-006130a4